BANEHUNTER

Also by Greg McLeod

Godhead

King of Dreams

GREG MCLEOD

BANEHUNTER

VERELDAN

ISBN 978-88-940221-2-4

For Bear.

Part I – Three Walls

1

Nightfall came early in the shadow of the high Tallamors, even three months past midwinter. This evening, full dark arrived with a fierce westerly chasing ragged clouds across the sky. Limned in pretty silver by a gibbous moon, they seemed to pause and linger in the light like fleeting promises of better things to come. But the wind drove them on relentlessly, out into the vaster darkness and back to their true colors: soot and ashes, harbingers of storm and ruin.

On all sides, the mountains rose stark and black, jagged silhouettes ripped out of the heavens by a god-child's willful hand. Now and then, stray moonbeams stole through the clouds, flitting over snow-laden flanks and icy peaks and backlighting sweeping plumes of powder flayed from the ridges and summits by the rising gale.

Down in Haster's Pass, only the occasional gust yet stirred the weather-beaten pines huddled along a flat expanse of snow, a field of dirty white crisscrossed by game trails and cut in two by a sharp, considered slash: Oldwall, straddling the pass at its highest point.

A set of human footprints tracked a straight line up the snowfield's southern half, ending at a pair of crumbling towers midway along the wall. Once, the towers had guarded a sturdy gate; now they flanked nothing but a few rotting timbers, half buried under an old drift begrimed with the thawed-out detritus of the winter's storms and fast dwindling in an early warm spell.

Done setting a circle of Wards around the western tower, Graeme Banehunter stood for a moment looking back the way he'd come, his face a stark relief of planes and angles carved from moonlight and shadows. With a disgruntled *caw!* a raven flew up and flapped away into the night. Graeme saw dark shapes detach themselves from the trees, two, three, five of them. Rooters, the first he'd seen in a couple of weeks. Not the worst the Bane had to offer but bad enough, and damnably hard to kill. A few yards out they halted, heads turning this way and that as they sought the scent of prey on the chill mountain air. Seeing them standing there, one might have easily taken them for tallish stumps, remnants perhaps of pines beheaded by wind or lightning.

But stumps didn't move about, nor did they communicate an intense sense of craving, a mindless hunger palpable even from two hundred yards away. No doubt they'd close in on the tower during the night, drawn by the proximity of living human flesh. Hopefully the Wards would keep them out. If not, they'd at least provide an advance warning, give Graeme time to clear out. Which was why he'd set them a good thirty yards out, even if it meant putting up twice as many. Still, not for the first time he wished there was a mage along to handle the Warding.

Fifteen years ago, when he'd started out a green recruit, there had still been a handful of real mages fit enough to go out ranging with

10

the hunters. Life had been easier then, and a lot less lonely. Now they were gone, victims of duty or time, and there was but a single one left: old Cuinnear, half blind and hampered by the shakes but still valiantly struggling to maintain Deepwall's Wards and keep safe all those who sheltered behind it. Real Wards, those, potent stuff, and nothing at all like Graeme's, who had only a woodsman's skills to work with, bolstered by a smidgen of Talent.

Nonetheless, if you planned to spend any amount of time in Baintry's wilderness it was something best learned early on, other-wise your chances of surviving were slim, and south of Deepwall nonexistent. Out here, at Oldwall and beyond, every Ward you set, even if perfectly made, was a gamble, a shot in the dark. You did your best and hoped it was enough; you prayed the things you'd come to hunt hadn't learned some new trick while you weren't look-ing; and, bedding down, you fervently wished this wouldn't turn out to be the night you woke to find them standing over you, about to rip the flesh from your bones and root out your very soul from wherever the gods in their infinite wisdom had seen fit to house it within your mortal form.

Would that we had a hundred Cuinnears, and younger ones at that, Graeme thought as he sought sleep in the tower's bare, third-floor chamber after a frugal meal of hard bread and dried meat.

What would happen once Cuinnear was gone didn't bear think-ing on. No one ever said it aloud, and no one needed to, but every-one had known from the start that, in the long haul, the Vales were doomed. Now they had run out of mages, and they'd run out of hunters willing to go ranging beyond Oldwall without true magic to keep them safe. None left save crazy Graeme. Crazy Graeme Death-

11

hunter, they called him, though never to his face. Crazy Graeme, who went out time and again to hunt his doom, and all he ever found lying in wait for him was the gods' own luck. Crazy Graeme who knew no fear.

How little they understand. Fool I may be, but never fearless. Forget to fear the thing you hunt, and it will kill you for a certainty. No, it's just that I've another, greater fear to balance it: the thought of spending the rest of my years standing on Deepwall and waiting for the Bane to come to me. That scares me more than anything I've ever come across in the wilds south of Oldwall. I need to take the fight to the enemy. It's what I've been taught to do. It's what I am.

Raising himself on an elbow, he tossed another piece of wood onto the small fire he'd lit for the sake of safety rather than warmth – if nothing else, the Rooters burned quite nicely. *You're turning into a right philosopher,* he told himself wryly. *Best put a lid on it and get some sleep, else you'll go stumbling into something nasty on the morrow.*

It was sometime after midnight when he awoke.

Passing from light sleep to full alertness in a heartbeat was one of the things that helped keep a man alive out here, which was why he'd refined the ability to an art. Motionless, his breathing steady, he opened his eyes and checked the room.

The fire had burned down, but the softly glowing embers shed all the light he needed. Nothing there. No Rooters. No rootlets worming their way in through the cracks between the stones. But something had woken him, and Oldwall was not a place where you discounted *any* disturbance, however slight. For long moments, he lay still, watching, listening, sensing. Then he felt it again: something brushing up against one of his Wards, ever so lightly.

It could have been an animal. It could have been the snow underneath the Wards, minimally shifting with the night's frost. Or the wind blowing something against them: a leaf, snow crystals, grit. Lots of possibilities. None of them likely. Nine times out of ten, disturbed Wards meant that the Bane was testing the boundaries of his safe zone. The problem was, he couldn't say for sure which of the thirty-odd Wards he'd set was being probed – until whatever was out there ran out of patience and gave the Ward a hard poke. Now he knew exactly where it was: up on the western half of the wall.

In a trice, he was up, scooping a double handful of twigs onto the embers. He blew on them until they burst into flame. Added a few larger pieces. Strung his bow and clipped the quiver to his belt. Felt another poke probing the Ward, stronger this time, almost hard enough to burst it wide open. Not good. If those were Rooters out there, they were damn strong ones. Gods give it wasn't something worse.

Holding the bow in his left hand, he held a torch from his dwindling supply into the flames until it caught fire. The light would alert whatever was out there to the fact that he'd noticed, and it also interfered with his night vision, but there was no way around it. Unless you got miraculously lucky with every single shot, shooting at Rooters in the dark with ordinary arrows was like trying to fell a tree with a pen knife. Taking a deep, calming breath, he stepped out onto the walkway and immediately stuck the torch into a sconce he'd affixed to the outer tower wall already years ago, high and to the right so his own shadow wouldn't get in the way.

13

Thirty yards out, three Rooters were crowding the walkway.

Not ten paces behind them there was a breach in the wall, a remnant of the Watch's last stand at Oldwall that had left a rubble-filled gap – and a way for the Rooters to reach the top of the wall. For the moment, they seemed to have given up attacking the Ward head-on. Instead, Graeme heard the scrape and grind of stressed stone as unseen roots wormed their way into joints and cracks. Give them enough time, they'd bring down a whole section of the wall and dislodge his Ward.

He lit a fire arrow, took careful aim, and loosed, just as two yards' worth of crenels toppled over and vanished into the night, landing in the snow at the foot of the wall with a series of dull thuds.

His shot hit the mark, but the fire didn't take. Probably a moist patch on the thing's skin, left over from yesterday's snowfall. He fired again. This time, the target burst into flame. For several moments it stood swaying, shrieking in a register so high it was nearly beyond Graeme's hearing, the dumb agony in its almost-but-not-quite-human eyes a sickening sight that still managed to get to him, even after all these years.

Then it fell over forwards, straight into the Ward, shattering it.

With the way clear, the other two pulled up roots and came for Graeme, their branch-like arms weaving and swaying with frenzied hunger. Given the light from the burning Rooter, Graeme chose an arrow with a bodkin head and went for a head shot. Aiming at the Rooter in the lead, he realized a fraction too late that, except for the eyes, this one's face was all thick, tough bark. He tried to adjust but missed, hitting it just below the eye, less than half an inch of the tip penetrating the ligneous skin. He got off one last shot, missed again.

14

Slow as they were, the Rooters were closing fast, leaving him barely enough time to discard the bow and draw his sword.

Fighting them at close quarters was a dangerous business. Deadly dangerous. They didn't even need to bring him down and bury their roots in him. One scratch was all it took. One scratch, and it was all over.

The first one was a bitch. Graeme barely managed to avoid its darting, whipping branches while he looked for a soft spot somewhere in the bark-like skin. Nothing doing. Transferring the sword to his left hand, he reached behind him, found the torch, and stuck it straight into the thing's rudimentary face. With a high-pitched screech, it fell back against its companion, setting it alight as well. Gods' own luck.

Breathing heavily, trembling with the aftershock of battle, Graeme watched them burn, until a gust of wind blowing the mixed stench of smoldering bark and roasting flesh in his face roused him, reminding him that it wasn't over yet. There were more Rooters out there, and gods knew what else. He set a new Ward in place of the old one before retreating into the tower. There would be no more sleep tonight, but standing watch outside would accomplish nothing the Wards couldn't do, and he needed to stay warm.

Early the next morning, Graeme set out for Deepwall.

He was out of supplies and out of human company, though he doubted he'd find any of the latter worth keeping, apart from old Cuinnear maybe. Undoing last night's Wards, he noted that a couple more Rooters, much less than he'd expected, had tried to break the circle of Wards down on the ground, and been foiled by it. They'd left before first light. What remained was a strip of bared earth around the warded space, churned and perforated by dozens of holes where they'd tried to reach him through the ground.

Rooting through thirty yards of rock-hard, frozen soil was hard work, and worming under the Wards was a damn sight harder still. Daylight had overtaken them before they'd gotten anywhere. A good thing too. The tower's walls wouldn't have held them off for very long. They could infiltrate and rend and tear most anything apart, stone included – as the half dozen gaps in Oldwall proved beyond a doubt. What they could do to human flesh…

Graeme refused to think about it. He'd seen it happen, and would forever wish he hadn't.

Worthwhile or no, after weeks of solitude he found himself looking forward to a bit of conversation with someone other than himself. Suddenly, the idea of haggling over a half-copper in the marketplace or exchanging comments on the weather with a stranger in a tavern seemed greatly preferable to the occasional soliloquies and sheer endless stretches of silence that defined his days alone. He knew well enough that the comfort he might take from being among other people again wasn't likely to outlast the day, but for now, the prospect spurred him on.

Down, down he went, from woodless heights to open stands of ancient, gnarled larches, winter-bare and still many weeks away from donning the tender green of spring. Last night's frost had hardened the snow sufficiently to bear his weight, and the walking was easy. He could have gone faster, could have flown down the mountain, but that would have meant courting disaster.

Most of the Bane's creatures hated the sun and avoided it at all costs, but some were not so squeamish. Blunder into one of those, and your day would definitely be ruined.

Some time later, the sun's first rays found him crossing a stretch of mixed forest, the white and grey trunks of birch and beech standing out against the dark greens of yew, fir, and juniper. With the sun came warmth, and soon the woods were adrip with melting snow. Gradually, as the hours passed, drops joined into trickles and rills became rivulets, until by midday he was walking alongside a blustery mountain stream frothing down its rocky bed as if impatient to reach the sea.

Long way to go, mate, he thought. *You'll be all grown up and a big, wide river by the time you get there.*

And you, he admonished himself, *pay attention! You won't be going anywhere for much longer, letting your mind wander like this. Another two hours to Deepwall, if all goes well. Once you're there, you can relax and be as stupid as you like. Until then, stay sharp.*

The sun was well into its downward arc by the time Graeme reached Deepwall. It was an impressive structure – if you discounted what the creatures it was supposed to keep out were capable of. Built on the Waist where Baintry was narrowest, the wall stretched nearly eighty miles from coast to coast, marching across valley floors and wending over hills and mountains. Where it ran through forest – which was most of the way – a strip fifty and more yards wide had been cleared on the southward side, with nothing taller than a blade of grass left standing. The countless thousands of trees felled to

17

make the clearing had gone into the wall, a double row of massive trunks sunk deep into the earth, the space between filled in with rocks and earth. The gatehouses, one in each of the Four Vales, were built from stone and could have graced any great fortress.

The whole thing had been thrown up in an amazingly short time when it became clear that Oldwall wasn't up to the job any longer and would have to be abandoned. His first three years in the watch, Graeme had ranged from Oldwall. Then they'd had to move back, giving up the pass and most of the high pastures. Since then, twelve years had passed and, for a wonder, Deepwall still held.

As soon as he stepped out into the open, Graeme was hailed from atop the wall.

'Hoy! Who goes there? Identify yourself!' It was fat Dicken Serl, not too bright and a stickler for the rules. Graeme didn't feel like shouting. He continued walking until he was thirty feet from the gate and Dicken raised his crossbow.

'Hold! Or I'll shoot!'

'Good to see you too, Dicken. So shoot already, or open the damned gate. I'm tired, I'm hungry, and I don't have the patience for your whole rigmarole.'

'Sorry, Graeme, but you know as well as I do there's rules need to be followed.' Dicken wasn't a bad sort, but on gate duty he could tempt a man to ill-considered violence. 'It's for everyone's safety, and I can't go making exceptions, not even for you.' He drew himself up to his full height, which was still half a head shorter than any other man on the wall. 'So. Do you swear it's you, Graeme Banehunter, and none other?'

Graeme sighed. 'It's me, Dicken. I swear it on your grandmother's blackened, turned-up toenails.'

'And do you further swear you're not a Bitten looking to gain entrance?'

'Merciful gods, Dicken, no. I've not been bitten. Not even by a flea. Now open up.'

'Not so fast. I'll need to hear the password from you.'

'Dicken.' Wearily, Graeme summoned what little patience he had left. 'We've been through this how many times? The password changes every week, remember? I've been gone for nearly a month. So how am I supposed to know what it is? Read your mind?'

Fat chance of finding anything at all in there.

'Right,' Dicken said, unruffled. 'You can come in, I guess. Captain wants to see you.'

*   *   *

'No, father, please. I can't.'

Passing by her father's study, Breanne quickened her steps when she heard her brother Arden's tearful voice. It was likely another of Asher Thorley's attempts to push his weakling son towards something resembling manhood. She didn't want to hear it, not again. Arden would come looking for her in any case, as soon as he'd escaped their father.

'You *will* go!' Asher grated. 'This time, I'm going to *make* you, and no amount of whining is going to get you out of it. I'll have you dragged out there by main force, if that's what it takes. You can make an effort and show some backbone, or you can disgrace yourself – I'm past caring how you leave. But you'll come back a man, or you'd best not come back at all. Now go, and for the gods' sake pull yourself together and at least try not to blubber in front of the servants.'

Breanne hurried on down the cold, stone-flagged hallway, wary of being dragged into their argument. Whatever her father's most recent plan for his son, Arden would manage to wriggle out of it on his own. So far, he always had. Needs be, he'd work himself up to one of his fits. Father usually gave in before Arden ended up twitching on the floor, eyes rolled up into his head and spittle running from his mouth, with whoever happened to be around looking on in pity, or embarrassment, or ill-concealed disgust.

She briefly considered taking herself off to some remote part of Thorhold Castle where Arden wouldn't easily find her but knew she didn't have the heart for it. She never did. Even at nearly eighteen, he was still the baby brother who'd only ever had her to care for him.

She'd barely shut the door to her rooms behind her when she heard his knock, unmistakable in that it managed to sound timid and urgent at once.

'Come,' she called, settling into a chair and bracing herself against his overwhelming neediness.

He was a picture of misery, his thin, pale face and dark eyes so full of hurt it pained her to look at him. With a strangled sob, he slumped at her feet, resting a tear-stained cheek against her knee.

'What?' she asked softly, suppressing a sigh and clasping her hands together tightly. She couldn't bring herself to touch him, not even to smooth down his tousled brown hair. His head against her leg was the limit of what she could bear.

It frightened her, that she should feel this way. She'd always been there for him, never holding back. And now? What was happening to her love for him? What was happening with *her*, to the person who lived inside her, the one she'd always thought she'd known so well? Of late, she felt more and more often as if she were seeing at a total stranger staring back at her from the mirror.

'What do you think?' His voice was muffled against her skirts. 'It's father. He's gone completely mad. Do you know what he's asking me to do this time? He wants me to go outside the wall. I'm supposed to go ranging with the Banehunter, all the way to Old-wall.'

Breanne was shocked: mad indeed, to send Arden into the Bane. Despite all the training he'd been made to suffer through, he was still more apt to harm himself with a sword or bow than hurt an enemy. But she kept those thoughts to herself.

'Perhaps it won't be as bad as you think,' she said instead. 'He's not called the Banehunter for nothing. They say there's none better than him. I'm sure he'll take good care of you, and bring you back safe and sound. You know – perhaps Father isn't all wrong, and it'll do you good to get out of here for once.'

'No!' Arden wailed. 'All he wants is I should die out there, and rid him once and for all of his useless embarrassment of a son.'

'Hush. You mustn't talk like that. You mustn't even think such things. I know it's hard for you to see, but Father does love you, in his own way. Do him the favor and go with Graeme, and maybe afterwards things will go easier between the two of you. I know it's

21

silly of him, but he needs something to make him proud of you, just the once. So give it to him, show him you can do it, and you'll have peace.'

'You think?' Arden sniffled.

'Yes,' she said, though she was anything but sure. 'I do.'

Little did she know how soon, how deeply and lastingly she'd come to regret these words. For now, she was simply relieved to see her brother stiffen with resolve as if he'd just discovered he had a backbone after all, or at least the semblance of one.

'All right,' he said, swiping a hand across his runny nose. 'If you think I should, I'll do it. Not for Father – but for you, I will.'

'It's yourself you should be doing this for, not me *or* Father. But I promise you my thoughts will be with you all the way, and I'll send a whole army of good wishes to watch over you.'

That seemed to satisfy him, and he left in a better mood than she'd seen him in for a long time. When he was gone, she remained sitting in her chair a while longer, slender, white fingers restlessly picking at the fringe of her shawl as she tried to convince herself that she'd done the right thing by saying what she had.

*   *   *

Hinges creaking, the massive gate swung open just far enough to let Graeme slip through. Orsen Dunne, captain of the Freewatch, was already waiting for him on the other side. Orsen didn't look happy. But then, he never did. Strong-featured, balding, his brow permanently set in a worried frown, he was the kind of man who was always on duty and never at ease.

'Graeme. Good to have you back.' There was no great love lost between the two men, not least because Dunne had been offered the job only after Graeme had turned it down more than once. But there was a measure of respect accorded one professional by another, and Dunne was wise enough to value Graeme for the risks he took in all their steads, and for the intelligence he brought back from his solitary forays. 'What news from the Bane? It's been uncommonly quiet here while you were gone. Too quiet.'

'It's the same out there,' Graeme said. 'There are Rooters out and about, but a lot less than you'd expect this time of year, with the pass open and the weather holding up as it is. And not a single Shifter. Leastwise none that I saw. It doesn't feel right. As if there's something nasty headed this way, nastier than usual.'

'Aye. My feeling exactly. But what? What could be worse than what we've already seen?' Instinctively, Dunne's gaze wandered south. There was nothing to see there, only the gate, closed and barred and no answers written on it.

Graeme shrugged. 'I suppose we'll find out soon enough. But I reckon it would make sense to run a double watch, put the men on full alert.'

'Already done,' the captain said. 'I've called in the reserves as well. But I still can't shake the feeling that we're missing something important. Any road – Lord Thorley asked to see you, once you're rested and presentable. Tomorrow will do. I suppose you'll be staying for a little while. Let me know when you're ready to go out again. Mayhap I'll accompany you a ways, have a look for myself.'

Graeme gave him a nod, glad to be away. Home for him was still a way off. Accustomed as he was to solitude and the silence of the mountains, nothing could persuade him to spend the night among

23

snoring, farting men in the Watch's barracks under the wall. Nor was he tempted by Stonebridge's taverns, at least not tonight.

Leaving behind the wall and the bustling town with its half-timbered, shingle-roofed houses, the low-hanging smoke from freshly stoked hearths and the smell of stables and middens mixing with that of the evening's cooking, he walked north past the turn-off to Thorhold Castle, sitting grim and commanding on a steep crag to his right, until a few miles on he reached Blackwood village, where he owned a small cottage inherited from his foster parents, twelve years dead of the ague come summer.

They'd been good people, and he'd forever owe them for taking him in, a ten-year-old boy come running over the mountains with nothing to his name but the shirt on his back, one of only two hundred and seventy-nine souls who'd made it over Haster's Pass alive. More had reached the other Vales, but, all told, the survivors from Marillin had still numbered less than a thousand.

With Marillin sinking ever deeper into uncertainty and confusion, Oldwall had fallen into the hands of the Barbary King's men. They were a fearsome lot, armed with axes, horn bows and javelins and wearing a wild assortment of chain, plate, boiled leather and bone under cloaks made from the pelts of wolf, lynx or bear. Some of the painted faces looking down on Graeme and the other fugitives were crowned with antlers or skulls. He heard a woman moan that the sea-monsters had overtaken them and were already up there on the wall awaiting them. But he'd seen the Bane firsthand, and so he knew that these were only men, however strange they might seem.

The Marillians' flight was brought up short outside of Oldwall, where they spent two weeks huddling through fearful days and sleepless nights while fast riders were dispatched to Colasar to fetch orders from the Barbary King. At first – so it became known later on – he was of a mind to have the fugitives chased back south, perhaps as an offering of sorts to whatever was coming out of Marillin. Maybe thus, it could be placated for a while, hopefully long enough for the king and his council of chiefs to come up with some kind of plan for Barbary's defense. But after further deliberation it was decided that they should be let in after all, under three conditions: first, that they swear fealty to the local lords of the Vales; second, that they actively assume the wall's defense; and third, that they never set foot on Barbary soil proper, on pain of death.

To make sure the latter condition was observed, over the next ten years another wall was raised across the Waist's northern end. Lastwall, the Valers called it, relieved on the one hand to finally be rid of their Barbarian overlords, bitter on the other to find themselves used as human shields against an unknown, terrifying enemy, locked between walls and stuck with a horde of hungry, destitute fugitives – nearly three hundred of them in Longvale alone.

Some Marillians and even a few Valers thought to find themselves a better life across the sea. Those who went west found a rocky coast where giant waves crashed against unscalable cliffs. And in the east, bands of Barbarian warriors were stationed in coastal towns and fishing villages to make sure that no one got away by ship or boat.

Graeme never looked back. On his fifteenth nameday, he joined the Freewatch, and a year later received his ranger's pin, wrought from silver in the shape of an ivy leaf. He never wore it. Out in the

25

wilderness, the shiny metal was a dead giveaway even on sunless days, and this side of the wall he simply couldn't be bothered. They all knew who and what he was, with or without it.

The house was as he'd left it, clean and tidy.

A fire in the hearth soon drove out the cold. Stepping out for more firewood, he saw a distant light burning in an upper-floor window on Balder's farm, lit by fair-skinned, flaxen-haired Glenna, already aware of his return.

Ten winters back, Glenna's husband Balder had fallen from his roof while clearing off the snow. It was a bad fall that left him a mindless, crippled husk who ate, drank, shat, pissed, and steadfastly refused to die. One evening a year after the accident, Glenna came by with a basket of vegetables from her kitchen garden. Almost inevitably, she and Graeme ended up in bed together. Since then, they'd given each other a measure of comfort. Affection had nothing to do with it, much less love, and there was never any pretence of either. And they'd only ever lain together in Graeme's house, neither of them able to countenance poor Balder lying in the next room and hearing whatever he might hear.

Graeme considered lighting a candle of his own, a sign for Glenna that she was welcome, but found he wasn't in the mood. As usual, he'd brought some part of the wilds back home with him from beyond the wall, and it would take at least the night to wear off and leave him fit for human company.

Later, sipping tea and drowsing by the fireside, he wondered for a fleeting moment what Asher Thorley might want from him but didn't worry the thought. It could be all sorts of things, and he'd find

26

out on the morrow in any case.

*   *   *

2

Breanne knew from bitter experience that pleading Arden's case with her father was useless. On the contrary, chances were she'd only make things worse. So she'd decided on a different approach this time. Standing outside the open door of her father's study, she steeled herself against a cold welcome, the only kind she'd get from him. The room was austere, the fireplace unlit, not even a tapestry hung to alleviate the dull grey of the bare stone walls. She knocked on the doorframe.

'What?' He was immersed in a document, with more of them in a pile at his elbow. When he didn't get an answer he looked up, his eyes dark like Arden's but hard and impenetrable where her brother's were wide open windows onto a vulnerable soul. 'Oh, it's you. What do you want?'

'I spoke to Arden.' Seeing his face darken, she hurried on. 'I told him he should go. He's agreed. He'll do it. I think – '

He cut her off. 'I don't need you to tell me what Arden has agreed to do. His consent isn't necessary in any case. He'll do as he's been told, whether he likes it or not. And I thought that you and I were agreed you'd stop your foolish meddling.'

Breanne could see he was furious. Gods, and she'd thought for once he'd be glad for what she had to tell him. But all she'd done was provoke his anger – again. Not that it was hard to do on the best of days. It was always there, ready to ignite, obvious even in his bearing.

Over the years, the strength of it had forced his body into hard, unyielding lines that constricted his angular frame like an ill-made suit of armor. And, she thought, it had warped his heart as well, robbing him of any warmth, grace, or mildness he might have once possessed. Still, somehow she had to make him understand.

'But I merely wanted to – '

'No!' He struck the desk with the flat of his hand. Not hard, but it made her jump all the same. 'Leave off. Arden is none of your business anymore. You've done enough damage with your misguided mothering of him. But I suppose such foolishness is only to be expected from a woman who hasn't birthed children of her own in a timely fashion.'

It was a low blow, and brutal, but he didn't seem to know or care. Fighting back tears, Breanne struggled for a response that would let her hold on to at least the tatters of her dignity. 'I only meant – '

'Which reminds me.' He talked right over her, as if she had no right to speak at all. 'I've managed to find you a husband.'

The shock of this completely unexpected turn left Breanne defenseless.

'Who is it?' she asked, though she was sure she didn't want to know. Even the marginally eligible candidates had been eliminated

30

already years ago. In that respect, as in so many others, she was definitely not the daughter of her father's dreams – not the buxom, nubile material out of which gainful alliances were forged. Slight and plain, she had neither the pretty face of a Carlin Pace nor the childbearing hips of an Aidith Joylon, both of them childhood companions who had long since been married off to the satisfaction of everyone involved.

She might have attracted suitors regardless, if not for the seizures she'd suffered ever since her first blood, debilitating bouts that brought on a sudden blindness and could last anywhere from minutes to days. To boot, they were often accompanied by strange visions, insights she was sometimes forced to speak aloud and in a voice that sounded nothing like her own. Her father never paid these utterances any heed, brushing them aside as the self-indulgent eccentricities of a hysterical girl. But it didn't change the fact that her affliction, once it became known, kept all of the Vales' marriageable young men at a safe distance. Her twenty-sixth nameday had come and gone, and no doubt she'd already passed from maiden to spinster in everyone else's books without so much as a hiccup, as if they'd always taken it for granted that she was destined to wither on the stem.

'Rothger Paxton,' her father said.

Breanne couldn't believe her ears. 'But he's old, and fat, and a brute,' she said, struggling for a measured tone. One did not scream at Asher Thorley, no matter how deep the hurt.

'Ah, but he's also the only one who will have you. And he's rich.'

'What? Are we suddenly destitute, that you have to sell your

31

daughter to a man who's known to make a sport of beating servants and tavern wenches bloody?' Breanne asked, the bitterness of the countless defeats she'd suffered by his hand threatening to spill over. I will *not* cry, she told herself.

'No.' As always, her father was blind to her inner turmoil. Other people's pain was nothing to him. Beneath his notice. 'But he's agreed to send an extra forty men to the wall, armed and paid for. That's Longvale's safety we're talking about. And as to his predilections: I'm sure he'd never lay hand to a woman highborn. Besides, after all the experience you've had with coddling your brother I trust you'll find a way to unman Rothger as well, and wean him off the worst of his habits. It's either that, or I'm sending you to the Sisters in Midvale. My patience with you is at an end.'

It was one insult too many. Suddenly Breanne was incensed.

'Very well. I'll join the Sisters, then. But I'll have you know that I won't be *sent* anywhere, not by you or by anyone else. I'm going, but I'm doing it of my own free will. And now, excuse me. I've got packing to see to.'

She'd never openly defied her father before. A part of her felt wildly elated at this act of daring even as another quailed at the storm of wrath that was sure to follow. But he seemed to have lost interest in her, his anger back on the leash, or in the kennel, or wherever it went when he wasn't making someone's life miserable.

'All in good time,' he said, his attention already returned to his work. 'The convent can wait. As you'll remember, we have guests tomorrow night. You'll do the honors as usual. You may go now.'

I shall be glad to leave this place, Breanne thought, once she was

32

over the worst of her anger. *And glad to let father and Arden settle things between them. I've let them use me as their go-between for far too long. I do want something I can call mine, even if it's just a few square feet and a bed in a nunnery. Let them see how they get along on their own. Who knows, but Arden might be better off without me. Father doesn't care either way. At the end of the day, I suppose one can only feel sorry for them.*

She wasn't sure which of the two she pitied more for being so thoroughly trapped by what they were: Arden a walking disappointment practically since the day he'd been born, and their father a joyless, embittered man, aged beyond his years by his constant struggle against a never-ending string of perceived injustices heaped on him by life, the gods, or some mysterious curse. It was all so senseless. Much of his anger had to do with things he didn't even want and couldn't have changed if he did. But simply not being able to have them gnawed at him like slow acid.

Like everyone in the Vales, since the advent of the Marillians he was no longer free to travel north of Lastwall. Back when he'd still been able to, he'd have counted going to Colasar and gracing the enemy with his presence as near treason, but now he chafed at being excluded from the Barbary King's court and council.

His marriage had been dictated by convenience, not by love, and, apart from siring Breanne and Arden on their mother, he'd never had much use for her. But when she dared to go and die on him in childbed he took it as a personal slight and to this day had not forgiven her the betrayal.

His children he saw as cruel japes of the gods. Instead of letting

Arden be as he was and making the best of what gifts he did have, he insisted his son should be a fearless warrior and leader of men, making both their lives pure misery in the pursuit of an unattainable goal.

Poor Arden. He loved books and the lute, preferred poetry to swordplay and music to the hunt. He did have a way with words, and a pleasant singing voice. In Breanne's opinion, with the right tutoring he would have made a fair bard, maybe even a very fine one. But in Asher Thorley's world, holy books were a pastime fit for women and faggots, and all others were the Dark One's work. And bards were but a small step up from common criminals.

During the last big fight with his son he'd smashed Arden's lute to splinters and doubled his fencing and archery lessons in the aftermath. Arden bore the extra weapons training in silence but cried over the lute for days.

Maybe it was time for him to be given a taste of the real world, however hard and dangerous it might be.

*   *   *

Most would have counted an invitation to sup at Thorhold a rare privilege. Graeme would have gladly foregone the honor. Lord Thorley liked few things better than to show off his famous huntsman. Both long-tables in the smoky, torch-lit hall were packed with a cull of Longvale's nobility and the officers and men of Thorley's House Guard. All were seated by rank, from the high table fronting the huge fireplace down to the great hall's doors where the common men-at-arms combated the chill draft with large amounts of ale.

Seated at the high table where everyone had a good view of him,

Graeme endured furtive, wide-eyed glances from blushing maidens, cold, appraising looks from their mothers that made him feel like a choice cut on the butcher's block, and hard stares from men who likely begrudged him his place and were secretly calculating whether they could best him in a fight.

He'd just finished giving Thorley an exhaustive account of the weeks he'd spent in the wilds and was trying to concentrate on his food when he felt a different sort of gaze resting on him. Looking up, he saw it was Breanne, Lord Asher's daughter. A wisp of a woman, plain-faced and mousy-haired, she had the diffident looks and bearing of a girl half her age. Which made the steady, open gaze she was studying him with all the more surprising – until he realized she wasn't really seeing him at all. Her large eyes – light hazel with shades of grey and green, he noticed for the first time – seemed to be focused on something much farther away.

He'd heard about her strange blind spells, and reckoned she was having one right there at table, though to him it looked as if she were seeing well enough – just not something anyone else could see. Still staring at or rather through him, she said something he couldn't hear over the general din and likely wasn't meant to. He had the distinct impression she was talking to no one in particular, perhaps not even to herself. Reaching for her cup without looking, she missed and overturned it. Red wine spilled across the table, and Graeme had a sudden, chilling notion that he was looking at a sign: the blood of someone soon to die. He shook it off; he was not one for superstitions.

An elderly, kind-eyed lady-in-waiting spotted the disturbance and hastened to Breanne's aid, helping her to rise and leading her away. Neither Lord Thorley nor anyone else seemed to pay the incident any heed – no one except her brother Arden, who'd made to rise until he saw the matron already arriving and now stood gazing after his sister with a forlorn and worried mien, his pale, slender hands twitching restlessly by his sides as if they wished to reach out and find something dependable to hold on to.

'Arden!' Asher struck the table sharply. 'Pay attention.'

Talk in the hall quickly subsided to a murmur, all eyes fixing on the high table. Asher turned to Graeme, who as always found the lord's gaze difficult to endure: dark, and made darker still by an implacable rage that seemed to perpetually fester just below the surface of the man's skin, to run through his veins like poison.

'Master Banehunter. I've been thinking. The Vales are in sore need of more men with your skills. And though I trust you have a good many years of service left in you, you're not getting any younger. It's past time you took on apprentices and bequeathed us a new generation of hunters worthy of the name. I've decided to give you my son to begin with. You'll take him out to Oldwall for a spell, show him the ropes and such. Later on, we'll see about others.'

Graeme was stunned. And outraged. Of all Longvale's young men, Arden Thorley was the least likely candidate for such a job. He thought he knew what Asher was doing: having failed to force his weakling son into the desired mold, he was now foisting the task off on Graeme. But he needed to tread carefully. Asher had a lightning-quick temper, and he'd been drinking steadily all evening. He was hard enough to deal with when sober. In his cups, he was unpredictable, could become downright dangerous.

36

'My lord,' Graeme said, struggling for composure. 'By your leave. There are hard and seasoned fighters in the Freewatch, men who've faced the Bane a hundred times and more. Mayhap a handful of them might be persuaded to range beyond Oldwall. But there's not a one of them I'd take with me, at least not gladly – for the simple reason that I wouldn't want their deaths on my conscience. A man has to be born to what I do, and none of them are. Least of all your son. No offense, my lord, but you're asking – '

'Enough!' Asher spat, a fat vein pulsing on his forehead like an angry worm. 'I *am* your lord, and I'm not asking. I'm giving you a simple, straightforward order. You'll do as you're told, or tender your resignation immediately.'

Damn the man! Graeme thought furiously. *He sees exactly where my weak spot lies, and doesn't hesitate to use it against me. The job is my life, and he knows it. Very well. I'll take the lad out – once, and just for a few days. A few Rooters up close and maybe a Shifter or two should be enough to put him off for good. He'll be more apt to slit his wrists than go out again, no matter what he's threatened with. But I'm not going to hang for it if anything happens to him.*

'You were allowed into the Vales on sufferance,' Thorley went on, dealing Grame another blow. 'Must I remind you of the oath you swore? And don't tell me you were only a boy of ten. An oath is an oath, and you should thank the gods that they let you live to speak it. You'll keep it to the letter, or be dismissed.'

Asher's words stirred up the worst of Graeme's memories.
No way would he ever forget that day twenty years ago, when the world as he'd known it until then had ended in blood and screams.

Raised on a farm in the Tallamors' southern foothills, he'd been a happy child, a nestling whose greatest worry was that, no matter how hard he tried to grow up faster than his older siblings and overtake or at least catch up with them, they always seemed to stay ahead. True, there were evenings when he lay in his bed in the loft above the kitchen, falling asleep to half-heard, worried whispers from below, the grown-ups mulling over a fresh piece of news from down south arrived with a tinker or a passing merchant train. Odd, disquieting rumors that got ever more unlikely as time went on.

A fearsome plague had broken out down south that turned people into flesh-eating plants. The king and his knights had gone mad and turned on their own people. Fish from the sea – some said giant grey eels – walked on land, devouring whatever got in their way. What little of this Graeme understood didn't sink in far enough to shake his limitless trust in his parents' ability to deal with anything that was wrong with the world. And so for him it remained a thing apart, like Grandma's fairy tales, a sleep-soaked bubble of firelight and murmuring voices that only sometimes burst open into dreams filled with vague, unfinished images and an unnamed, faceless threat.

The end, when it came, arrived with a swift violence that found them completely unprepared.

One day, a handful of shocked and babbling fugitives came hurrying past, seeking refuge in the mountains; the day after, the Bane arrived.

Graeme was in the lower field with his father, his two brothers Ivan and Jerrod, and his sister Adelle, helping with the haying. It was one of those sultry summer evenings when a storm was in the offing but no breath of wind yet stirred the air and everything was uncommonly quiet. Even the birds seemed too exhausted to do anything but huddle on a shaded branch and doze away the hours until the weather broke.

Suddenly there was a blur of movement by the forest's edge. Before any of them could get a good look at what it was, three indistinct, greyish figures came racing towards them. It seemed impossible, but Graeme was sure he saw them stretch or flow rather than run across the field. One moment, they were *over there,* and then, much too fast and somehow still not clearly formed, they were *here.* With them came a sense of weirdness, a strange lassitude that made Graeme feel as if he were asleep with his eyes open. All he really took in were wide, lipless mouths and inward-curving teeth like rows of wickedly sharp sickles. Numbly, he watched as gaping jaws unhinged on darkly pulsing maws.

A violent noise startled him from his stupor: his father shouting.
Pa, who hardly ever raised his voice. Pale-faced and sweating, eyes wide with disbelief and fear, he was brandishing his pitchfork in a valiant attempt to fend off the intruders.

'Run!' he yelled. 'Run for the house and find your mother and your grandma! And then head for the mountains and don't stop until you're the other side of Oldwall! Go, all of you!'

Ivan and Jerrod disobeyed, taking a stand beside their father. Adelle seemed of a mind to do as Pa had said, but then one of the things got her. She went down with a scream, her brothers rushing to her aid. Pa let out a weird sound, a kind of bellowing sob, and slapped Graeme hard across the face.

'Run, godsdammit!' he hollered. Pa didn't swear, and he'd never hit Graeme before – or anyone else, for that matter – and it was the shock of this more than anything else that finally set Graeme in motion. He ran. The last thing he saw was his sister Adelle lying on the ground, her face smeared with blood, the light already gone from her eyes. And still her sightless gaze seemed to follow him even as the rest of her was being mauled and ripped to shreds. Of all the horrific things he'd seen since then, this was the image that had etched itself deepest into his memory. It still managed to wake him in a cold sweat some nights.

But the worst of it, the true horror, was what remained hidden somewhere in the trees that day: an unseen, chilling presence that in Graeme's mind was the dark, malevolent force behind the things that had attacked and killed his family.

He never found his ma or his grandma – unless they were the reason why the big trough in the yard was running all red. So he kept going until he reached the other side just like Pa had said he should, though there was no way he could manage it without stopping. The Land of Barbary had always seemed so very far away in Grandma's fairytales. In truth, it was much, much farther.

With a start, he realized he'd been miles away when the current situation needed all his attention. Thorley was staring at him, expecting an answer. Graeme heaved an inward sigh. Foolish as the Lord Commander's request was, there was no way he could avoid it.

'As you say, my lord,' he said. 'So long as you're aware of the risk. It's a dangerous place out there.'

'You of all people shouldn't need to be told there's never any gain without risk.' Asher's expression had turned pinched and mean. 'Besides, I trust you'll bring him back in one piece. I'm holding you responsible for his safety. Are we understood?'

Graeme was a hair's breadth from quitting then. If he'd been wearing his ranger's pin, he'd have ripped it off and dropped it on Thorley's plate. But he wasn't, and the moment passed. What pulled him back from the brink was the look on Arden's face. The fear he saw there came as no surprise, but that wasn't all of it. The lad looked determined, and there was outright admiration in his gaze: a young pup wagging its tail, resolved to follow the old war-dog and prove it was worth a bone, no matter it was fit to piddle on the floor with dread. The sight stirred something in Graeme, a memory perhaps, though he didn't probe it any further.

'Understood, my lord. I plan on leaving again soon, and with the young lord coming along, I'll have preparations to make. If you'll excuse me...'

Thorley waved him off, in a more generous mood again now that he'd put the great Banehunter in his place and finally set his laggard son on a course of action, and all of it before an appreciative audience.

But Graeme wasn't free of the Thorleys yet. Arden caught up with him at the castle gate. He'd run, was out of breath, and Graeme saw the faint blue of veins pulsing under his delicate skin.

'Master Banehunter,' he panted. 'I just meant to say I'm sorry. For you having to take me along, I mean. I realize I'm nothing but a burden to you. But I promise I'll do everything you say and not get underfoot.'

Graeme merely nodded. Crossing the drawbridge, he called back over his shoulder, 'Meet me at the barracks in three days' time. First light. And dress warmly. It's still winter in the mountains, and a damned sight colder than you're used to down here.'

*   *   *

Suddenly Breanne could see again.

She was back in her rooms. And she was sobbing, though she had no idea why. She couldn't remember a thing since the moment she'd gone blind. Griselde was sitting across from her, holding both her hands.

'There, there, child,' the old woman said, her kindly round face settling into lines of commiseration. 'It's over now. Nothing but a bad dream.'

'What... what did I say?'

'Nothing. Nonsense. Absurdities. None of it worth repeating.' But Griselde looked shaken.

'Please tell me.'

'Best not, dear. It'll only upset you. And your father's forbidden it in any case. Come now, I'll have the maid bring some mulled wine, perhaps with a few drops of milk of the poppy. That'll calm you down and help you sleep, and tomorrow morning you'll be right as rain again.'

'Tell me,' Breanne said, surprised at the firmness in her voice. 'I want to know.'

Griselde fidgeted, sighed. 'Very well. But promise me you'll speak to no one else about it. Your father would throw me out if he knew I'd told you, and I've nowhere else to go. My brother's dead, and his son's a brute who'd let me starve on his doorstep before taking me in.'

I'll turn you out myself if you don't speak up, Breanne didn't say, disgusted with herself for even thinking it. Griselde was a good soul, and she'd been, if not a surrogate mother, then something like a distantly affectionate aunt for many years. 'I promise.'

Griselde heaved another sigh.

'You said...' she faltered. Breanne could see that the old woman was scared, and gave her hand an encouraging squeeze.

'You said that the Banesheart – that's what you called it – is gathering a new army, horrors the likes of which haven't been seen before. You said the three walls would fall and the creatures of darkness overrun Baintry, all the way to North Point. You spoke of fire and blood and many deaths, and you said that this would be only the beginning, unless...'

'Unless what?'

'Unless someone found the key and locked the door.'

'The key? What's that supposed to mean? And who? Who is supposed to go find it?'

'You said, Broken Steel and Sleeping Wood.'

'That was all? Broken Steel and Sleeping Wood? Nothing about who that's supposed to be, or where this key was to be found? Nothing about the door?' Breanne frowned. 'It's too little. Certainly not enough to make anyone listen.'

'Please,' Griselde implored her. She'd frightened the old woman. 'You promised. You know they wouldn't believe you in any case. In this, as in everything else, they follow your father's lead. They'd

43

give you nothing but scorn and mockery, say you'd taken leave of your senses for good this time.'

'And you? What do you think?'

Griselde stared into her lap, age-knotted fingers fumbling with one of her rings as she mulled over the question.

Wrinkles and liver spots, Breanne noted distractedly. *And her gout's gotten worse. When did she get so old?*

'I don't know what to think.'

The look Griselde gave her was uncommonly frank and a little unsettling, an old-person look freighted with the increasing distance of age and a life-time's worth of accepting bitter truths and hard realities. 'But I've heard the men murmuring about how the Bane has been unusually quiet this spring. They're saying there's something bad in the air, talking about a bad storm gathering in the south. And then there's the way you talk when you're having one of your spells... the words you use, and that strange voice that doesn't sound at all like yours. Who knows? Perhaps you do have the gift of true vision.'

'Gift?' Breanne gave a mirthless laugh that came out sounding more like a brittle sob. 'You call going blind and making a fool of myself babbling weird stuff that I can't even remember afterwards a *gift?* A gift from whom? The gods? Well, they can gladly have it back. I never asked for it, and I certainly don't want it.'

'Hush, child!' Giselde cast an anxious look around, making the sign of Elil over Breanne and, to be safe, over herself as well. 'You mustn't say such things. They might hear you, and decide to replace what they've given you with something they deem an ungrateful girl more deserving of. Something less pleasant. You know how they can be.'

'No, I don't. None of them has ever spoken to me, or done anything useful for me, as far as I can tell.'

'The ways of the gods are unfathomable,' Griselde said. 'They may not speak to you directly, but perhaps they're speaking through you. Granted, being chosen by the gods as their instrument is not a burden that sits lightly on anyone's shoulders. It's a great responsibility – one you mustn't shirk, no matter the cost.

'But what am I saying.' She reached out and patted Breanne's hand. 'Most likely it's nothing of the sort, just an unfortunate indisposition that may well pass as you get older.'

'Griselde. I *am* old. Look at me. I'm twenty-six, and already all the important parts of a woman's life have passed me by.'

'Oh, dear child.' Griselde chuckled. 'You've no idea what it means to be old. Thank the gods for that at least. You'll find out sooner than you like, as do we all. In the meantime, you've got a life to live, so off to bed with you. We've a long day of packing ahead of us tomorrow, if you're to have a hope of being gone before your father changes his mind.' She rose.

'Griselde?'

'Yes, dear?'

'Thank you. I know this isn't easy for you. You're a good friend, and I'm glad you're here.'

'Nowhere I'd rather be, child.' The old woman gave her a sweet and deeply honest smile. 'Nowhere at all.'

*   *   *

45

3

For once, Graeme made the trip to Haster's Pass on horseback, accompanied by Dunne and a dozen men of the Watch. They'd left Deepwall before first light, seeing as none of them except Graeme and Arden planned to spend the night at Oldwall, and the others would have a long ride back.

Arden had shown up at the appointed hour looking like he'd just gotten out of bed, shivering in his furs despite the fact that the morning wasn't all that cold for the time of year. Nerves, Graeme thought, and reckoned that, in Arden's place, he'd be feeling much the same. With a little luck the lad would never have to get used to this kind of thing.

It was a fine day, the sky cloudless and almost shockingly blue against the Tallamors' snowy peaks, the chill giving way and a first, premature hint of spring stealing into the air once the sun had risen over the mountains.

Orsen remained silent throughout most of the morning, but Graeme had a feeling there was more on the man's mind than the immediate danger of riding through territory infested by the Bane – though so far they'd seen nothing of it. It was close to noon and they

47

were nearing Oldwall when the captain kneed his mount alongside Graeme's and broached the subject he'd been ruminating on for the past few hours.

'Graeme.' Orsen kept his voice low. 'There's something we need to talk about. I've been thinking over this whole business of Thorley sending his son with you. I know you don't like it one bit, and I agree that Arden isn't the most likely choice for what he's got in mind. But other than that, I think Asher is right. We need young blood that's prepared to do what you do. If – gods forbid – anything should happen to you, we'd be blind to whatever goes on beyond Oldwall. You know as well as I do that sending out men who are neither willing nor experienced with this kind of thing means sending them to their death.' He held up a hand to forestall Graeme's protest. 'I'm not going to force you into anything. It's your choice. But I do have a likely candidate for you: young Wil. He's the big lad three rows back.'

Graeme turned in the saddle. 'The one who looks like he just got off his mother's teat?'

'Don't let his looks fool you,' Dunne said. 'He's sharp, he's eager, and he's more than handy with a bow and with that big axe of his. He's also fought outside the wall. Ran into a bunch of Rooters when he was riding patrol; chopped three of them to splinters. Seeing as you're already saddled with young Thorley, Wil might actually be a boon. Think it over, and let me know what you've decided before the rest of us head back.'

Graeme nodded.

Later, he fell back along the column until he was riding beside Wil.

'Captain says he thinks you'd make a decent ranger.'

'Sir.' The lad *was* big, probably had half a head and several stone on Graeme, who was no midget himself. Wil appeared shy and nervous, but he also impressed Graeme as someone able to take care of himself. Blond, blue-eyed, fair-skinned and beardless, he had a good chin that spoke of a strong will, and arms any blacksmith would have envied him. 'It's what I'd like most, if you could see your way to taking me on.'

'Graeme will do. I'm not an officer.' Graeme was hard put not to smile. The young man was desperately eager, and far too artless to think of hiding it. Graeme liked that. It reminded him of himself at that age. 'I hear you've already tangled with the Bane outside the Wall.'

'Rooters, sir – I mean, Graeme. Wasn't that many of them, but I can't say as I wasn't scared something fierce. But we got them all, and not a one got away.'

'It's good to be scared when you're dealing with the Bane,' Graeme said. 'And you need to stay that way if you're going to come with me. It's what keeps you alive out here.'

'So you'll take me?' Wil looked to be hovering between bitter dejection and fulsome happiness, all depending on the answer he got.

'Aye, I reckon we'll give it a try,' Graeme said. And there it was, the pleased grin, though the lad tried hard to keep a straight and earnest face. 'But it'll be hard work, mind. Young Lord Thorley will be spending some time at Oldwall, and I'll need you to help keep a discreet but watchful eye on him.'

No better way to keep Wil alert and vigilant than to entrust him with another's safety. And no need to point out that Graeme himself would be watching over both of them. 'So you're going to be looking out for two: yourself, and Arden. Think you'll be up to it?'

'I'll do my very best, sir – uh, Graeme. More than my best, though there's just the one of me. Which I think is a pity, if I may say so. I did try talking to some of the other men, but none of them are prepared to go south of Oldwall. Not for all the gold in the Vales, they said, and certainly not for the honor and glory.'

'Don't hold it against them. Over the years they've seen every ranger but one either come back as a Bitten or not at all.'

Every child in the Vales knew that a wound inflicted by a creature of the Bane was an immutable death sentence. Whether a man's skin was broken by the nails or teeth of a Bitten, whether he was punched full of holes by a Rooter or mauled beyond recognition by a Shifter, the result was always the same. Without fail, he'd fall ill with the Bane sickness within three days, at which time he'd turn into a Bitten himself, becoming a deadly danger to his fellow men, an inhuman stalker, mindless bloodlust on two legs. There was only one cure: a bolt between the eyes or a swift, clean cut to sever the head from the body.

Graeme had seen it applied to more than one of his fellow rangers, the ones who'd made it back to Deepwall in under three days. When the gate opened and a man stayed outside, everyone knew the score. Rather than die by his own hand, he was asking his comrades for the gift of a merciful death.

'The numbers don't add up into recommending the job,' Graeme went on. 'Going by the tally as it stands to date, your chances of surviving as long as I have are one in thirty-seven. I trust you're aware

50

of the fact.'

'Aye, I am. And I aim to better that rate by one.'

'So you say. And I'll do what I can to get you started. But sooner or later you'll be on your own out there, and then it's the gods' mercy and your own mettle that'll keep you going. Think it over. There's no shame in turning back from something that on second sight might look a size too big for you.'

Wil blushed. 'It doesn't, and I won't. Turn back, I mean. I've studied on this, and it's what I want – no, it's what I *have* to do.'

'Good. I'll see you at Oldwall, then.'

Graeme kneed his mount forward, leaving behind a young man sitting noticeably taller in the saddle and trying hard not to look proud. The lad wouldn't be feeling that way for long – not once he grasped the truth of what it meant to range in Bane country with only a comrade and a half instead of a whole company, and no Deepwall to fall back on. That was when he'd prove his worth. Or not.

The more immediate problem was keeping the three of them alive. After Dunne and the others had departed Oldwall for the safety of the Vales and the three of them deposited their stores and bedrolls in the western tower's third-floor room – the one with an escape route, a low, narrow door that let out onto the walkway atop the wall – Graeme took the lads outside and began teaching them Wards.

During the time he'd been gone, the snow had receded a good ways from the southern side of the wall, helped along by the dark stones reflecting the warmth of the strengthening sun. After checking to make sure that nothing untoward was occupying the snow-free stretch of ground, he plunged right into the first lesson.

51

'Warding is the most important thing you need to learn in order to survive out here,' he told them. 'Without Wards, you'll spend your nights fighting or on the run, and there's only so many nights you can keep that up before you give in to exhaustion and either make some stupid mistake or fall asleep. The one will get you killed as surely as the other.'

Graeme didn't add that those who merely died dealing with the Bane could count themselves lucky. Like everyone living behind Deepwall, the lads knew well enough what it meant to be bitten.

Pausing as he searched for the right words to present a concept that was at once complicated and simple, he noted that they were both paying attention. They looked focused, a bit anxious even, as if their lives depended on getting it right. Good – because that was exactly how it was.

'Putting up a Ward is something that happens mostly inside your head. Meaning, it's a way of doing things that takes some getting used to. Nonetheless, if properly done it does have an effect in the real world as well. So. We'll start with the simplest kind of Ward, one that will give you a warning but not keep anything out.

'Wil. Think of a bubble, the kind you can see floating on the water below a rapids or a fall, only make it the size of, say, a cart wheel. Fix the image firmly in your mind, and then focus on that piece of bare ground in front of you. Imagine placing the bubble there. You can close your eyes if it helps you concentrate. Now fill that bubble with a clear and strong command: tell it to burst and send you an alert when someone or something touches it. Got it?'

'I – I'm not sure,' Wil said hesitantly. 'How do I know it's working if I can't see it?'

'You don't have to see to find out. Go back inside the tower now, and don't look out. Arden and I are going to wait a bit, and then one of us will walk through your bubble. Give us a shout the moment you feel it happen. And don't be disappointed if it doesn't work the first time. It's not an easy thing to do.'

Graeme didn't add that not one in a hundred persons had that shred of Talent it took to do a passable Warding. No use putting the idea of failure into their heads right from the start. As was to be expected, Wil failed to notice anything. After both Graeme and Arden had walked over the spot more than once, Graeme called Wil out. The big lad looked utterly dejected.

'Don't worry,' Graeme said. 'No one's ever managed it on their first try. Patience will get you there. Arden, your turn. Same spot, same procedure.'

'Give him a moment to concentrate,' Graeme told Wil once Arden had set up his Ward and gone inside the tower. 'All right. Go.'

Wil walked over and stepped into Arden's bubble. The moment his foot touched the edge of the bare patch of earth, Arden called out from inside the tower. 'Wil! That was Wil.'

Graeme was stunned.

Of all the things he'd expected, this was the very last. 'Sure you weren't peeking?' he asked Arden when he'd rejoined them outside. The lad just shook his head, as surprised as Graeme was.

'Have you tried something like this before?'

Again Arden shook his head. 'Did I do good?' he asked hopefully, not quite prepared yet to accept that he might have actually gotten something right for a change.

'Good, aye,' Graeme said. 'That's one way of putting it. Performed a small miracle, would be another. I wasn't kidding when I said no one ever managed a Ward on their first try. And you just went and did it, and even knew to say it was Wil who'd disturbed it. Has Master Cuinnear by any chance ever mentioned the possibility of your having Talent?'

Arden nodded. 'He said he saw a strong Talent for music in me.'

'Nothing more? Perhaps he saw only the obvious, and neglected to look any further.'

'I wouldn't know,' Arden said, suddenly looking sheepish. 'But I do have something to confess: I didn't do it quite the way you said – setting up the Ward, I mean. Once I had the bubble fixed in my mind I filled it up with music, beautiful music I could hear even if I went inside the tower. Then I thought that, when one of you upset the Ward, the music should turn shrill and ugly, and that way I'd know when it happened.'

'Lad,' Graeme said, 'you can fill the damned bubble with whatever you like, as long as it works. Though I imagine having music in your head all night long might interfere with your sleep. But if it works for you, fine. What I'd very much like to know is how you could tell it was Wil who disturbed the Ward.'

Arden shrugged. 'I don't know. Maybe it was just a lucky guess.'

'Was it?'

'No, I suppose not. I just... I can't say how I did it.'

'All right. We'll get back to that later. Wil.' Wil, who'd been standing silently all through the exchange, was staring at Arden with something approaching admiration – and not a speck of envy or jealousy, bless his good and simple heart. 'Your turn. If you want to put something in your bubble like Arden did, go ahead. Actually, I'm going to let the two of you practice by yourselves for a while. I've still got things that need seeing to before dark.'

He was hoping that Wil – if he had what it took – would learn from Arden's example. And he liked the thought of Wil looking out for Arden, and Arden teaching Wil. It made for a balance of sorts. A balance that was needed out here – and everywhere else, for that matter.

Turning away, he caught an awkward moment when Arden said, 'Shall we?' and Wil answered, 'Yes, m'lord'.

'Please,' Arden said, 'it's Arden. 'I left "my lord" safely tucked away behind Deepwall when we rode out this morning. Out here we're all the same, or should be, don't you think?'

The lad continues to surprise me, Graeme thought as he walked towards the tower to see how they were doing for firewood. *Who knows but we might make a ranger of him yet. Though with the Talent he seems to have, perhaps it should be Cuinnear teaching him. Now that would be something to put fresh hope in everyone's hearts: a young mage to step into the old one's shoes. I'll have to tell Cuinnear about it as soon as we get back. He needs to take another look.*

Going out to set the night's Wards, he found the two of them still at it, and Wil looking a lot happier. It seemed he was slowly getting the knack of it as well. It also looked as if, for all they were so very different, the young men were fast becoming friends.

It gave Graeme's heart another little lurch upward, though he quickly forbade himself the thought of perhaps one day seeing them go out as a hunter-and-mage team like it had been in the old days. Too early to tell where and how far either one of them would be going. Still, he decided a bit of cautious optimism was permitted.

*   *   *

Breanne was packed and ready to depart.

The last thing left to do was sort through her mother's jewelry and decide what she'd take with her – not because she'd be wearing any of it where she was going but because she wanted something to remember her mother by. Moreover, she wanted a nest egg, something she could fall back on just in case. She wasn't at all sure she fancied spending the rest of her life in a nunnery, even if it was as a paying guest. And then there were those accursed visions. No telling what they might demand of her in the future, and whether she'd have the strength to resist them.

She'd just opened the strongbox and spread the jewelry out on the table when her father came striding into her rooms without knocking. He looked angry, but then he always did. He also looked as if he'd come with a purpose, no doubt because one of his toadies had noticed her fetching the box from the strongroom and run to rat her out to the lord of Thorhold in hopes of gaining favor.

'Just what exactly do you think you're doing?' he asked in an aggressive tone. He *was* angry.

But she was not going to let herself be intimidated. Not anymore. 'I'm looking through Mother's things to see if there's anything I want to take with me.'

'You'll not take anything that's not yours,' he snapped. 'And those jewels aren't. They're a family heirloom. A family you've re-

56

nounced through your stubborn insistence on joining the Sisters, and thus lost your claim to such things. Besides, where you're going you won't need any trinkets. I'm paying the Sisters enough for your lodging as it is. The jewels will serve much better for putting more men on the wall. Though perhaps I'll keep a few in case your brother at least manages to find himself a spouse.'

Something in Breanne snapped then, and for the first time in her life she didn't feel afraid of her father. Suddenly, she saw him with different eyes, found herself looking at him from a place of coldness and contempt. Her fear of him was gone, but so was the last shred of filial love she'd clung to until this moment.

'I'll remind you that it's you who's sending me off to join the Sisters,' she said levelly. 'And before you bring it up again: marrying a known abuser of women is not a viable alternative. I want something of my mother's, and I will have it. By right and custom these jewels are mine, to do with as I please.'

'Here,' Asher Thorley said, picking up an age-blackened silver circlet set with a single, dull-blue stone. He tossed it on the table before her and scooped the remaining jewels back into the box. 'You can have this. The rest stays in my safekeeping, whether you like it or not.'

'But she never wore this,' Breanne said, useless as she knew it was to argue any further. 'I wanted something to remember her by, a piece that was close to her heart – not one that's been moldering in a strongbox since before my great-great-grandmother's time.'

'Well, it's all you'll get. Now be off with you before I change my mind and let you have nothing at all.'

Breanne rose and picked up the circlet. Standing very straight, she looked her father directly in the eye. 'Farewell, Father. I might have said I'm sorry to leave you so very alone, but you already are, and have been for the longest time.'

Not waiting for an answer, she walked out on him, down the stairs and out to the waiting coach, feeling neither satisfaction nor regret. For now at least, she decided, she felt nothing at all, except relief that this part of her life was over.

The journey to Midvale was uneventful, if tedious.

As the crow flew, the distance between Thorhold and the convent was hardly more than a dozen miles – twelve miles of steep, rocky mountains and deep ravines, that was. The next passable road across was two thirds of the way to Lastwall, making for a trip of nearly a hundred miles.

Lost in thought, Breanne took little notice of the landscape drifting past, farms, hamlets, villages, a couple of towns, and every so often a keep or manor house. Only twice was she jolted out of her reverie: once when they passed Pace Castle, sitting on a man-made island in a bug-infested lake and now home to her childhood playmate Carlin – Carlin, who'd been bearing children at the rate of nearly one a year for... how long now? She must be working on number seven at least, Breanne thought, and wasn't sure she envied her. The second time, she found herself staring at a large keep up on a bluff to the left, a place so dreary and forbidding it made Thorhold seem almost quaint in comparison: Blackstone, seat of the infamous Rothger Paxton. She shuddered, glad she'd never have to see the place from any closer up.

Griselde, thrilled by the prospect of getting out and about, chatted away happily, no matter whether Breanne was listening or not. The coachman and the single man-at-arms Lord Thorley had spared them as a token escort remained largely uncommunicative throughout the trip, obviously bored with a task they deemed beneath their dignity and impatient to be done with it.

Breanne was in a strange, in-between state, neither sad nor happy, not missing what she'd left behind but not looking forward to what lay ahead either. Unlike Griselde, who actually seemed to savor the prospect of staying with the Sisters, she saw only a short moment of freedom that would last no longer than the journey, and then leave her in a place that was already beginning to feel like just another shade of prison.

So it was a pleasant surprise to find that Vereldal, seat of the Sisters of Verelda, the Mother, was very different from grim, grey Thorhold on its forbidding rock. Situated in the middle of the wide valley and surrounded by meadows, gardens and orchards, all of them still winter-bare, the convent was a two-story affair, a large square formed by four wings of equal length surrounding a secluded courtyard. The Mother's temple on the outer west wing presented an open, welcoming forecourt, its projecting roof supported by four massive wooden pillars wreathed in ivy. With its red-tiled roofs, light-ochre façade and windows framed in ornamental white, Vereldal looked inviting, tranquil, a place well suited for searching out the inner peace she so badly wanted to find.

The coach stopped in front of a weathered gate in the north wing. The coachman and the guard, less sullen now that the job looked to be over, unloaded the women's baggage and drove off with a hasty salute, leaving Breanne and Griselde stranded outside the gate with a pile of chests and bags. Cursing the louts, Griselde tried the small door set into the gate but found it locked, and no amount of knocking brought anyone to open it. Then Breanne spied a bell-pull and gave it a couple of energetic tugs. After a short wait, a plump young Sister with strawberry-blond hair and freckles came to let them in.

'Welcome,' she said. 'I'm Sister Helise. Please do come in, and not to worry about your baggage. I'll have someone fetch it straight away. The Reverend Mother is expecting you. This way, if you please.'

The passageway behind the gate led onto a garden that Breanne supposed would be a wonderful sight come spring and flowering. Even now it begged to be explored, but Sister Helise turned off into the surrounding cloisters, leading them around to the rear wing, up a flight of marble stairs, and to a door of polished oak already standing open.

'Our guests have arrived, Mother,' she announced with a knock on the doorframe and a demure curtsy.

The grey-haired woman who rose from behind an ornate desk that could have graced a royal palace was easily as rotund as Sister Helise, making Breanne think she'd perhaps finally manage to put on a few pounds in this place where everyone seemed so well fed.

'Lady Breanne, and mistress Griselde, welcome to Vereldal. I am Mother Edilda.' She had a warm smile, apple cheeks, and a sparkle in her eyes that warmed Breanne towards her immediately. 'And this is Roana, our Sister Confessor.'

The woman had been standing so perfectly still against the wall beside Edilda's desk that Breanne hadn't noticed her until now. The Confessor was tall, slender and dark-haired, a cool, serene beauty who was everything Breanne was not. Breanne disliked her instinctively, though she told herself she was being entirely unfair.

'Naturally,' Edilda went on, 'as a guest you're not required to attend confessions. But should you ever feel the need to unburden yourself, or simply want to discuss matters of the spirit, Roana will be there for you.'

Small chance of that *ever happening,* Breanne thought. Aloud she said, 'So I'm not expected to... join? As a Sister, I mean?'

'Oh, no, child. Not as long as your father is paying your upkeep. Should that ever change, you may still choose whether you want to stay with us as a lay or full Sister. And naturally you're always free to leave Vereldal, though I want you to know we'd be very happy should you some day decide to become one of us.

'But one thing at a time. As I was saying, you can turn to Roana here in all matters spiritual; and Helise, whom you've already met, will see to your material comforts. If there's anything you need that we can supply, just tell her and you shall have it. Now, I'm sure the journey has tired you, so I won't keep you any longer. Helise!'

The young Sister and immediately appeared at the door.

'Please show our guests to their rooms and see that they're as comfortable as we can make them.' Edilda turned back to Breanne. 'Welcome again, child, and may your stay in Vereldal be a happy and fruitful one.'

Through all of this Griselde had been standing beside Breanne, silent as a statue, her eyes shining with a reverent awe that made

Breanne wonder how long it would be before her companion asked to join the Sisters. Breanne knew Griselde was quite devout, but with the way she was looking at the Reverend Mother just now she feared the old woman might fall on her knees and ask to be accepted this very moment. Thankfully, she didn't.

They were given very nice rooms on the upper floor between the temple and the gate, and Breanne found it no hardship at all to settle into the quiet, steady rhythm of Vereldal, punctuated only by the three-hourly prayers attended by every Sister who wasn't busy outside the compound tending gardens or overseeing work on one of the twenty-odd farms owned by the convent.

Verelda, the Earth Goddess, was one of the old, elemental gods who to Breanne made a lot more sense than the new ones with their oftentimes fanatical devotees and dubious rituals. She'd never seen much use in praying, but for the sake of propriety she attended once a day, usually in the evenings. Griselde, on the other hand, went to all eight of them, from matins to compline, a fact Breanne welcomed for the time alone it gave her. Much as she liked Griselde, in such close quarters as they shared the old woman's incessant chatter was beginning to wear on her patience. She also took to spending time in the convent's well-stocked library, and she went for long walks in the countryside around Vereldal, something she'd always wanted to do but had never found the ease for in Thorhold with its oppressive atmosphere and rugged, pathless terrain.

Now, for the first time in many years – for the first time since her mother's death actually, come to think of it – she felt she could allow herself the luxury. Slowly, she managed to let go at least some of the anxiety that had been her constant companion for so long, relaxing to a point where she began to sleep through the nights and wake up mornings without a knot of worry already sitting hard in her chest. She felt delivered, like a very small animal that had somehow contrived to crawl out from under a big, crushing rock. It was an entirely new experience, one that for the nonce left her in the grip of sudden mood swings, one moment tentatively embracing something she assumed must be happiness and the next feeling an inexplicable urge to burst into tears.

Helise came visiting regularly, untiringly concerned with their wellbeing. She was a cheerful, outgoing person and soon struck up a friendship with Griselde. Breanne held back. She was far from ready to engage in anything more than cordially formal relations.

A week after their arrival in Vereldal, the Reverend Mother came by for a short visit. She found Breanne sitting at the table with the silver circlet laid out on a piece of cloth. Breanne had decided that, even if it hadn't been what she'd wanted, it was the only thing of her mother's she still possessed, and she'd honor it by giving it a thorough cleaning.

'Please don't bother,' Edilda said as Breanne made to rise. 'I didn't mean to disturb you, only to make sure you're well cared for. You're at work, I see. What have you got there, silver? I'm told the best way to get it clean is to boil it in saltwater for half an an hour. But you seem to have made quite a good job of it already.'

'It's just something of my mother's I managed to hold on to,' Breanne said. 'A rather ancient family heirloom, but the only thing my father would let me have.'

Edilda picked up the circlet, now shining as if newly wrought; only the blue stone remained as dull and unsightly as ever.

'A pretty piece for the period, if not too valuable. But then, it's not the material value that makes it precious to your heart, is it, dear? Well, I must be going. Too many things to do, and too few hours in the day to get them done. But I would like to have you over for supper one night. Perhaps the day after tomorrow would suit?'

'Thank you, Mother. Yes it would. It's not as if I have any other engagements,' Breanne said with a rueful smile.

'Ah, yes. One of the drawbacks of life in the convent. But I do trust you're coming to appreciate the advantages as well?'

'Oh, I most certainly am, Mother. Very much so.'

'Good. Then I'll see you day after tomorrow after vespers.' Edilda gave a wink. 'I'll be naughty and skip compline for once.' She turned to go but stopped at the door. 'Oh, look at me! I almost walked out with your mother's circlet still in my hands. How unmindful of me.'

Strange, Breanne thought when Edilda had left. *For a moment there, I could have sworn she looked... covetous. But it can't be. The circlet is neither valuable nor pretty, and the Sisters don't wear jewelry in any case. I'll have to keep an eye on my imagination, I think.*

The evening with Edilda was pleasant enough – at least it made for a welcome change in Breanne's uniform routine. Mercifully, Edilda's conversation stayed clear of religious topics, perhaps because she instinctively understood that such talk would merely serve to make Breanne uncomfortable. Surely she'd noticed that her guest visited the temple rather sparingly. She did invite her back for the following week, an invitation Breanne gladly accepted.

Helise was becoming an increasingly frequent presence in their rooms, always finding something or other that needed doing and getting held up time and again chatting with Griselde. It got to a point where Breanne began to wonder whether the woman had any other duties at all. It seemed strange that a full Sister should be spending so much of her time acting as a glorified maid to her and Griselde, who was perfectly capable of getting all the necessary things done without Helise's help. Then again, improbable as it seemed, maybe her father was paying the convent so lavishly they felt obligated to reciprocate in kind.

Roana came by twice, just to say hello and enquire after Breanne's well-being, she said. Her visits were short and perfunctory, and to Breanne's relief she never mentioned anything to do with confessions. Breanne was courteous but glad to see the back of her. Something about the woman's manner made her uneasy, as if Roana knew more about her than she let on.

Roana aside, life at Vereldal looked to be settling into an easy, comfortable groove, and Breanne was actually beginning to reconcile herself to the fate that had brought her here.

*   *   *

Graeme spent the first morning at Oldwall practicing Wards with Wil and Arden. The sun was out and they never strayed far from the tower, but he still kept an eye out for possible threats. The Bane had many forms, and not all of them were averse to daylight, nor were they always obvious.

65

After a frugal midday meal of bread and hard cheese, he let the lads practice some more while he went over to the edge of the woods and cut three lengths of wood that would serve them as staffs. It was time to acquaint Wil and Arden with some of the dangers that awaited them.

'You both know about the Rooters,' he began. 'Wil, you've already met them face to face, and Arden, you've probably seen them from the wall.'

Arden nodded, shivering; Graeme doubted it was from the cold.

'The one good thing about Rooters is, they're easy to see, at least when they're out in the open. It's when you're traveling in the woods that you have to keep an eye out for them, especially on an overcast day. That's when they're liable to be active even in the daytime. And believe me, they're bloody hard to spot in there among the trees. They have a knack for making themselves look so much like just another tree, you might walk right past one and not notice until it's too late. So stay sharp, and never trust anything you see out there. Which brings us to some of the sneakier stuff. Grab a staff, and we'll go find us a Lurker.'

He took them to a snow-free stretch of the old road that led down into what had once been Marillin, telling them to use their staffs to test every step of the ground in front of them.

'Stop,' he said when they'd reached a spot he'd chosen earlier. 'Look at the road. Tell me what you see.'

They stared at the gravelly surface, partly overgrown with grass and weeds that still looked dead and flat after having been buried for months under several feet of snow.

Wil shrugged. 'All I see is the road.'

'Arden?' Graeme asked.

Arden hesitated. 'Something's wrong... there.' He pointed with his staff. 'But I can't say what it is.'

'Look harder,' Graeme told them. 'Think flat and round, about four feet across.'

'Got it,' Wil said. 'I can make out the edge of it, though only just. What is it?'

'I'll show you,' Graeme said. Taking a cautious step forward, he set the heel of his staff down firmly in the middle of the spot in question. He'd barely touched it when a section of the road literally erupted, flying upward and wrapping itself tightly around the lower two feet of the staff in the blink of an eye.

'If that was my leg instead of the staff, I'd be in serious trouble now,' he said. 'Watch. It's not interested in wood, so it's going to let go in a moment.'

Shortly, the Lurker released its hold. Graeme pulled back the staff and showed it to the lads. The part that had been in the thing's grip was gouged and splintered as if scores of small, sharp teeth had dug into it. Meanwhile, the Lurker was making off with the slow, undulating motions of some weird, submarine creature.

'Aren't you going to kill it?' Arden asked, fear and disgust tugging at his face as he watched the Lurker crawl away.

'Only way to kill it is with this.' Graeme took a small clay ball with a protruding wick from his belt pouch. 'We call this an 'egg'. It contains Almorican Fire. Bloody dangerous stuff to be carrying around, and I'm not going to waste it on this one. It's a runt com- pared to some I've seen, and taking a blade to it would be useless. Cut it in half, and all you get is two of the things.' Carefully, he slipped the clay ball back into his pouch.

'So now you know why a ranger never goes anywhere without his staff, and why you're always going to use yours, even if it makes you feel like a blind man groping his way through the dark. Because oftentimes, with what we're facing out here, we *are* like blind men, and only utmost care and awareness are going to see us through.

'You need to watch for Lurkers everywhere, but mostly you'll find them along traveled routes, game trails for instance. They're attracted by the scent of living things. Walk somewhere more than once, and you can expect them to be hanging about there for weeks after. They can mimic their surroundings perfectly, and they come in different shapes.

'Be especially wary of vines, roots, and small to mid-sized boulders. The only places where you can walk safely are in or near flowing water. All the creatures of the Bane hate it and avoid it wherever they can.'

He decided to leave it at that for the moment and give the lads a breather. If he started in on the really bad stuff that was out there, he'd only have them running scared before they'd had half a chance to absorb what he'd shown them so far.

That evening while Wil was preparing supper, Graeme went out to set the Wards for the night. Arden asked if he could come along and watch.

'You can,' Graeme said. 'But only to watch. Don't get in my way, and no questions. If I make a mistake because I'm paying attention to you instead of what I'm doing, this might end up being our last night alive – at least alive in a way that won't make us wish we weren't.'

As soon as they stepped outside, Graeme was gripped by a feeling of unease. Arden seemed to feel it too, for he cast an apprehensive glance towards the woods.

'Rooters,' Graeme told him. 'They'll be moving in tonight for sure.'

In truth, it felt like more than Rooters, but he didn't say so. He set the Wards with extra care, a silent Arden following him around and watching his every move even though there was nothing to see – except maybe if you had a load of Talent, and who knew but perhaps the lad did.

If Graeme had learned anything useful in his time as a ranger it was to always trust his instincts, so when he was done setting the Wards he went back and checked them, twice. They were all that stood between a continued life as a human being and a fate too terrible to contemplate.

His unease persisting, he decided they'd keep a watch that night. Wil took the first shift. Graeme chose the middle one and left the last for Arden – that way, both boys would get a sufficiently long stretch of uninterrupted sleep.

It happened close to the end of Graeme's watch.

The lads were sleeping peacefully, the night outside so still you could have almost believed the world existed only inside the tower's walls. Suddenly Arden sat up, wide awake in less than a heartbeat and staring at the doorway leading to the stairs as if he expected the Dark One himself to appear there any moment. Following his gaze, Graeme reckoned the lad was seeing no more than the play of shadows cast by the firelight. But then, quieter than thought, a cloaked and hooded figure stepped into the tower room.

Graeme was on his feet in the blink of an eye, sword in hand, his sudden move rousing Wil from his dreams. The intruder didn't come closer. Graeme saw a pair of slender, white hands reach up and push back the hood, revealing a wealth of dark hair and a pale face with eyes that seemed to stare at him from the far side of a bridgeless chasm. A woman. A young woman, and surpassingly beautiful, even though her face was haggard and marked by faint patches of greenish fuzz, most pronounced around the corners of her mouth and eyes. The first signs of the Bane sickness. A Bitten.

By rights he should have killed her on the spot. But something held him in check – one of those feelings he'd learned to heed.

'Stay where you are,' he told the woman.

She nodded. 'Don't worry, I won't bite you. I haven't... changed.'

'Who are you? What do you want?' *And how the hell did you get here?* No woman would ever voluntarily set foot outside Deepwall, and no one would let her pass through one of the gates even if she tried.

She hesitated, as if she had to search for the right answer before she could give it. 'I am Wulfwyn of Archer's Rock, and I've come to seek help for my people. The Slayers are gathering in strength, and we are no longer safe.'

Graeme had never heard of a place called Archer's Rock, not in Longvale in any case. If it was in one of the other Vales, then that begged the question how the woman – Wulfwyn – had made it this far without going through the Change. Chances were high she'd

70

been bitten on her first day out, maybe her second, and three days were the longest it took for the Change to become complete. Not nearly enough time to travel through the wilderness between here and Westvale or Midvale, the ones closest to Longvale and to the only passable road leading south into the mountains. Before he could ask her about it, she raised an arm and pointed at Arden.

'You,' she said. 'You're the one I've come to find.' Then she turned on her heel and disappeared down the stairway as soundlessly as she'd come.

'Gods,' Wil said, still half asleep. 'What was that?'

Graeme let out a long breath. 'That,' he said, 'was a riddle that needs solving, and quickly. Perhaps Arden... Arden! Wake up, lad!'

Arden came to, his eyes slowly regaining focus. 'She has magic,' he said. 'Strong magic. It's what's keeping her from changing.' Then he lay back down, curled up, and went to sleep, and no amount of shaking could wake him.

There was no more sleep for Graeme that night. He went out to check the Wards and found them intact, undisturbed. Another riddle, and one with frightening implications.

Back in the tower, sitting by the fire with a heavy weight on his mind and a heavier one on his heart, he felt a growing certainty that this night had been pivotal, a moment when all their lives had taken a sharp and sudden turn towards a disastrous future, one whose exact nature was not yet clear but whose presence loomed as dark and threatening as any thunderhead he'd ever seen.

*   *   *

71

4

Breanne was rudely yanked from her budding sense of inner peace by another one of her episodes. She'd begun to hope that, in the shielded and comforting atmosphere of Vereldal, the spells would abate and leave her alone, but apparently it wasn't to be.

This time though, something was different.

She was trying to concentrate on a book over the chatter of Griselde and Helise, who were changing the sheets on the beds. It didn't help that whoever had copied the treatise on the history of Marillin had done so with a sloppy hand. And then, between one page and the next, she went blind as a bat, was caught in absolute darkness. Strangely, she wasn't afraid, just impatient to get it over with. It was out of her hands, and all she could do was wait for whatever was to come.

After a while, she noticed a strange light coming from somewhere above her head. She looked up but couldn't see its source. It seemed to follow the movements of her head, always staying just out of sight. She started walking. With every step she took the darkness receded, and slowly her surroundings were revealed. She was in a forest. Some ways ahead, she saw a mighty tree standing alone in the middle of a clearing, its trunk so wide you could have fitted a spacious room inside it.

Arden was there, leaning against the tree. He looked changed: older, more mature. Strong. And sad. He smiled at her, though the sadness in his eyes remained. Then he reached up and broke off a small, dead branch. Holding it like a lute – suddenly she realized it *was* a lute – he began to play the most wondrous music. Each time he plucked a string, a disembodied voice struck up a sweet and haunting melody, until eventually there was a choir of a hundred voices singing a hundred different tunes – and yet all of them together made a perfect, heartrending harmony.

Abruptly the scene changed. Instead of music, she heard thunder. She was in a landscape so desolate and wasted it made her want to cry for what had been done to it. A man was standing a few steps away with his back to her, looking towards a horizon that was black from end to end and top to bottom with a roiling wall of thunderheads.

The man turned around, and she saw it was the Banehunter. With his long, dark hair whipping in the wind and his cloak spread wide as if he were about to take wing, he looked like a hero out of the old songs: hard, grim, fearless. Stepping closer, he reached up and plucked something out of the air over her head. When he brought his hand down she saw he was holding a small, silver key.

Without transition she was back in Vereldal, her hands shaking uncontrollably, her book fallen to the floor. Griselde and Helise were by here side, looking concerned.

'Oh, thank the gods, she's back again,' Griselde said, looking into Breanne's eyes. 'You gave us a right scare, child, with all that talk of glowing heads and terrible storms.'

'I know,' Breanne said, shocked and elated. 'I can remember. Griselde, this is brilliant. I can remember! And I know who can help me now, don't you see? It's Graeme. He's the one who holds the key. I must talk to him. I have to go to Longvale immediately.'

'Easy now, dear.' Griselde laid a steadying hand on Breanne's shoulder. 'Graeme's at Oldwall with your brother, remember?'

'Maybe he's back by now. And if not, I'll just have to go out and find him.'

'Gods forefend!' Griselde looked truly shocked. Helise, Breanne noted, seemed more curious than taken aback by her rash announcement.

'You'll do nothing of the sort,' Griselde went on. 'To even think of going out into the Bane! I must say, you sound as if you've taken leave of your senses, child.'

'So I'll just wait until he gets back. They're not going to stay out there forever.'

'Oh dear! What to do with you?' Griselde said, throwing Helise a beseeching look.

'You're supping with the Reverend Mother tonight, aren't you?' Helise said to Breanne. 'Why don't you talk to her about all this? She's very knowledgeable on the topic of visions and such. I'm sure she'll be able to give you some sound advice.'

'Yes,' Breanne said, 'I'll do that. But I'm still going to Longvale.'

Griselde rolled her eyes heavenward but said nothing more.

That evening, Breanne decided to wear her circlet but couldn't find it anywhere. Neither Griselde nor Helise knew anything of its whereabouts, and there wasn't time for a thorough search, so she went without it. Surely she'd just mislaid it and it would turn up again sooner or later, probably in some stupid place where no one would ever think to look.

*   *   *

Graeme was faced with a hard decision.

He needed to take the lads back to Deepwall. They weren't safe anymore with the woman Wulfwyn out there, capable of walking through his Wards as if he'd never set any in the first place. On the other hand, finding her and learning her secrets was absolutely imperative for the safety of everyone in the Vales. In the end he decided he'd give himself a day to look for her. If he hadn't found her by evening, they'd head back to Longvale the next morning. With the boys out of harm's way he'd come back alone and continue looking, though Wulfwyn could be anywhere by then – and worse, she might have changed.

Arden had said she possessed magic. But even if that were true, how much longer would it give her? Once changed, she'd be useless to him, a mindless thing driven by nothing but hunger. And what would happen to her magic then? Would she lose it with the Change? Knowing there was a Bitten around was bad enough – but a Bitten with magic who went through Wards like a night breeze through an open window?

It didn't bear thinking on. He had to find her; there was no other way.

Leaving Arden and Wil with strict orders not to stray beyond the

Wards and to keep a sharp eye out for anything out of the ordinary, he set off in search of the mysterious woman, Wulfwyn the Bitten, Wulfwyn the Riddle. North of the wall, the snow cover was still continuous. There were the tracks left by the men and horses two days earlier. Thirty yards out it was only hoof prints, all of them pointed north, and not the ghost of a footprint that could have been made by a woman. So he headed south, quartering the valley floor and the slopes on both sides of the pass where they were accessible, advanc-ing ever deeper into Bane country.

An hour past noon, he had to admit defeat. He hadn't found a single trace of her passing, not in the snow nor out of it. It was time to turn back. If he went any farther he wouldn't reach Oldwall be-fore dark, and the lads would have to spend the night alone with Wards that couldn't be trusted anymore. He still hoped he might find Wulfwyn going back, that perhaps he'd missed her on his way out, unlikely as that was. But there was no sign of her, not hide nor hair.

He was still half an hour from Oldwall when he heard shouts in the distance. His heart lurching into double time in the space of half a beat, he quickened his pace, then broke into a run. Two hundred yards farther on he found Wil, looking utterly distraught.

'What in the good gods' name are you doing out here?' Graeme asked, breathing hard. 'And where is Arden?'

'That's just it. He's gone.' Wil was close to tears. 'I've been looking for him all afternoon. Gods! Where could he be? I – ' He faltered, his lower lip trembling.

'Wil,' Graeme said. 'Calm down. Tell it from the start. When did

77

Arden go missing?'

'It was noon. I was inside heating up last night's beans. When I hollered that the food was ready, he didn't answer. So I went down to fetch him, and he wasn't there. I've been trying to find him ever since.'

This is grim, Graeme thought. *This is exceedingly grim. Barely an hour of daylight left, and by now Arden could be just about anywhere.*

'Back to the tower,' he told Wil. 'I'll take it from here.'

'But sir, Graeme, I can – '

'No. Losing one of you is bad enough. I'm not going to risk you as well. Off with you. I'll be back in time to set fresh Wards, for all the good they'll do with that Bitten loose out here.'

'I think he's gone off with her,' Wil blurted. 'With that woman, Wulfwyn. He was sort of strange all morning, quiet like, not quite there. I heard him whisper her name a couple of times, like he was trying out the sound of it.'

'Where did they go, then?' Graeme was puzzled. 'Between us, we should have seen them – you going out and me coming back.'

'What if it's her magic? What if she can somehow make it so we can't see them?'

'I doubt it. But it's possible. Whatever. I want you back in the tower. I'll join you before nightfall.'

Graeme went over the terrain between the wall and the woods for the second time that day, but all he found were his own tracks from earlier in the day, and Wil's. Darkness forced him to abandon his search. He rejoined Wil in the tower and spent a sleepless night fretting over Arden, hoping against better knowledge that he'd still show up, or that they'd find him on the morrow, scared and chilled to the bones from a night outside but hale and unbitten.

For ten days they scoured the land south of Oldwall for any trace of Arden or the woman. Wil, once he'd gotten over the first shock of Arden's disappearance, pleaded so insistently to be included in the search that Graeme finally relented and took him along. He'd have preferred to know the lad safely back in the Vales but, truth be told, he was loathe to lose the two days it would have cost him if he'd escorted Wil back to Deepwall. As it was, Wil proved Dunne right: he was a boon rather than a hindrance. During the days and nights spent out in the wilderness, far from the relative safety of Oldwall, he bore up better than well, showed himself steady and levelheaded, a man Graeme was prepared to trust with his back.

For all that they penetrated farther south than Graeme was normally wont to do, they found nothing. Interestingly, there was no sign of the Bane either. It was as if all of them had moved down into the lowlands. Even the Lurkers, slow and mostly stationary creatures, seemed to have pulled up stakes and left. Some remained, but they were few and far between.

Graeme and Wil explored every tributary valley, every goat trail and footpath used by shepherds and woodsmen in the times before the Bane. They ranged through woods, scrambled over boulders, and examined dozens of crumbling cots and crude refuges built from undressed stone to shelter men and their beasts from the rough mountain clime. None of it brought them a single step closer to finding Arden.

Finally there was no more denying that what they were doing

was useless, a waste of time. Graeme had been dreading this moment, for it meant not just admitting that Arden was beyond rescue but also that he'd have to face Asher Thorley with the news that he'd lost his son. Though Graeme refused to dwell on the possible consequences, he knew they'd be dire.

'Only one thing left to do,' he told Wil, still clinging to the fragile hope that Arden in the meantime might have found his way back to the tower, or even to Deepwall. 'We'll take another look north of Oldwall. We're heading that way in any case.'

'We're going back, then?' Wil asked resignedly.

'No way around it,' Graeme said. 'I have to tell Lord Thorley about Arden.'

The look that Wil gave him said it all. The lad had no illusions about what awaited them in Longvale. Certainly not safety. Not anymore.

*   *   *

With patient questioning, Edilda got the whole history of Breanne's visions out of her. Then she launched into a rather long-winded account describing the fates of other people stricken with the same affliction. Most of them seemed to have ended badly. She wound up with observations on the nature of foretelling in general but offered none of the advice Helise had promised and Breanne had hoped for.

Breanne left the Reverend Mother's quarters feeling drained and overstrung, as if she'd spent the past two hours struggling with Edilda instead of having a quiet conversation. Edilda had spent all evening mining her for information, she realized, and given nothing in return.

I'm beginning to see there's another, quite different side to the woman, and I'm not sure I like it.

Back in her rooms, she was surprised to find Roana waiting for her, one hand resting comfortingly on Griselde's shoulder. The old woman, sitting hunched over at the table, looked decidedly out of sorts. The Confessor was her usual, cool self; only a slight tightness around the eyes betrayed the fact that she wasn't nearly as serene as she appeared.

'What's the matter?' Breanne asked, suddenly apprehensive.

'This,' Roana said, pulling Braenne's silver circlet from the folds of her habit and laying it on the table. 'This is the matter.'

'What... how...' Breanne was utterly confused.

'I'll explain while you change into these,' Roana said, indicating a pile of clothing on one of the chairs. Boots and leathers, a man's garb. 'You have to leave Vereldal immediately, and these are better suited for where you'll be going.'

'But – '

'Patience, child. I said I'd explain, and I will. But time presses. So start getting changed.'

Griselde, obviously in the know, gave Breanne a nod, so she did as Roana asked, still completely in the dark as to what this might be about.

'The circlet,' Roana said.

'Edilda, you must know, is fascinated with objects of power, and she's studied the histories extensively. So have I, seeing as I'm Vereldal's Confessor and it's my job to know what the Sisters – and the Reverend Mother – are up to, particularly the things they haven't seen fit to mention during confessions.

'Edilda believes – and I tend to agree – that your circlet is a powerful artifact, one of only three that have ever been known to exist in the world. The other two were lost ages ago, and never re-surfaced. It is believed they were made in times immemorial by the White, the Creator's First Children – and they are called Keys, with a capital K. Yes, I thought that would get yout attention.'

'Is that why you stole it?' Breanne asked.

'I didn't, at least not from you. Edilda had Helise take it, and I stole it back from Edilda. Helise's main task has always been to keep an eye on you, at first because Edilda likes to gather informa-tion on everyone, and then because she came across your circlet. The Reverend Mother is the kind of person whose preferred way of dealing with others is by manipulating them. She likes power, the more the better, and you presented her with a perfect opportunity.

'And she's found some very rational reasons to justify what she did. In her view she wasn't committing theft but taking into her cus-tody an invaluable object she deemed entirely unsafe in the hands of an ignorant girl. To be on the safe side, she presented the case to the Inner Circle, and they all agreed with her. Everyone except myself, though I didn't say so. I decided then and there it was wiser not to advocate my position but to take action instead.

'Unlike Edilda and the Circle, I am convinced that the Key has chosen you for a reason, and that you and it have a destiny to fulfill. I won't deny the danger of leaving it in your inexperienced hands. But it's a risk I'm willing to take. Because I know for an absolute certainty that in Edilda's hands it would quickly become a terrible weapon, one she'd end up using to further her own interests rather than for the common good.'

'What makes you think the circlet is one of these... Keys?'

'Two things. There's the stone: it's a very rare shade of blue, exactly the color described in Carric Three Suns' *The Secret History of Magic*. He also describes some of the symbols etched on the circlet.' Breanne had noticed the faint, convoluted lines but thought them no more than a somewhat half-hearted attempt at decoration. 'According to Three Suns, they are ancient runes used by the White, and only by them. And then there are your visions. I'd say they speak clearly enough where the Key is concerned.'

She fell silent, as if awaiting a response from Breanne.

'Gods,' Breanne said. 'That's a lot to take in all at once.'
She was done changing but not yet sure whether she was ready to go along with the rest of Roana's plan, whatever it was. She'd begun to doubt the purity of Edilda's motives already, but from there to what Roana had just told her still seemed like a very big leap.

'So what am I supposed to do? And what about Griselde?'

'She's agreed to stay here and keep up the pretense that you're sick in bed for as long as she can, buying you the time you'll need to get away safely. As to you: do what you intended. Find the Banehunter. Obviously, he's an important part of all this. Beyond that, I can't tell you what to do. Hopefully, your visions will continue to guide you. I'll pray they do. And now it's high time you left.

Five miles north of here, there's a lightning-split oak by the road. It marks the beginning of an old bridle path leading west. Follow it, and it will take you all the way to Longvale. It's a two-day ride, so you'll need to rest along the way. Make sure you lie up in a place that's well hidden. There's a palfrey waiting for you at – '

Suddenly the door flew open and Edilda strode into the room. She was in a cold fury, and nothing about her reminded of the benevolent, grandmotherly figure she'd presented to Breanne until recently. Something dark and ugly came swirling into the room with her. Had Breanne believed a Sister of the Mother's temple capable of such a thing, she would have said Edilda looked ready to kill.

*   *   *

Graeme and Wil were less than an hour away from Deepwall, and still no sign of Arden. Graeme was scanning the slopes to either side, as he'd been doing all morning, when Wil suddenly grabbed his arm.

'Look,' he said. 'Up ahead, the fallen tree by the side of the road.'

Searching with his eyes, Graeme found the tree, about a hundred yards down the road. There was someone sitting on it, hunched over and wrapped in a dark cloak. Wulfwyn, it looked like.

'All right,' he said grimly. 'Let's have us some answers.'

They were nearly there when the figure rose to meet them, drawing back the hood. Not Wulfwyn. Arden.

Relief started to well up in Graeme, but the next instant his heart plummeted. The green on Arden's face and hands was as yet only a very faint shimmer, but the signs were there, unmistakable.

'Graeme, Wil,' Arden said. 'I've been waiting for you. 'I'll walk with you as far as Deepwall. I have things to tell you, and I want to speak to my father.'

Wil was speechless. He looked sick. But not half as sick as

Graeme felt.

'Good gods, lad! How did you manage to get yourself...' Graeme faltered, shying away from using the word to Arden's face.

'Bitten?' Arden said. 'It was Wulfwyn. We had a long talk. After everything she told me, I asked her to do it. She didn't want to, but eventually she came round and saw that it was necessary.'

'You had her bite you on *purpose?* When there was no need and you could have gotten home safely?' Graeme couldn't believe what he was hearing. Neither could Wil, by the looks of him. A hammer-blow to the head couldn't have had a more devastating effect.

'But there *was* a need. A great need. Graeme, Wil, please. Listen to me. Wulfwyn told you she was from Archer's Rock. Well, Archer's Rock isn't in the Vales. It's in Marillin. There are people out there, Graeme. Living, breathing people who have survived unbitten for all these years. Wulfwyn told me. She was one of them, until she decided to sacrifice herself for a chance to save them. She came here looking for help. They're in trouble, Graeme. Bad trouble.'

'All right,' Graeme said. 'Say she's telling the truth. I can see how she might be. What's that got to do with you getting yourself bitten?'

'It was necessary. I do have magic. Talent. Lots of it. Wulfwyn helped me see it. And she showed me how to use it against the Change. I'm going with her, Graeme. I'm going to help her fight the Bane and save her people. And where I'm going I'd have been bitten sooner or later in any case. Better to have her do it and teach me how to deal with it.'

Graeme was at a loss for words. What Arden had done was staggeringly foolish – and incredibly brave. He had to admit he admired the lad, mad as it seemed. Graeme was no weakling, not by a far cry, but he'd never have found the courage to do what Arden had done.

'You did good,' Wil said, surprising all of them, even himself. 'I think you did good. If there are people out there, someone needs to help them. I wish I had the guts to do what you did, and go with you.'

'It's all right. Wil,' Arden told him. 'One of us is enough. You have a different task awaiting you, and it's important that you're where you need to be.' He reached out and laid a hand on Wil's shoulder. To his credit, Wil didn't flinch away. 'I'm glad we met. And perhaps we will again, before all this is over. Be well.'

'You too,' Wil said, his eyes moistening.

The lad has too big a heart for these heartless times, Graeme thought. *Gods give he doesn't end up with it broken into more pieces than he can fit back together.*

'Arden, lad,' he said aloud. 'There's no going back from what you've done, you realize that. And there's no place for you behind the wall anymore. They won't let you in. I wish it were different.'

'I know. I just want to see my father, and then I'll leave. I have to explain to him that none of this is your fault. That he can't hold you accountable. He can come out and talk to me.'

'I'm sure he will,' Graeme said, moved by Arden's concern, though he wasn't sure at all. There was no telling what Asher Thorley might do when he found out his son was Bitten.

When they reached Deepwall, Arden hung back a ways.
Graeme and Wil walked on to the gate. The men on the wall had seen them coming, and after a few moments the gate opened without

the usual fuss, fat Dicken Serl pushing back both wings as far as they would go. Asher Thorley was standing just inside the gate, waiting for them.

'Why isn't my son coming in?' he asked, squinting past them with a deepening frown.

'My lord,' Graeme said. 'There's no easy way to say this. I've failed you. Arden's been bitten. By a woman. He asked her to – '

Asher cut him off, waving him away. His face had gone completely blank, a chunk of pale stone devoid of all expression. For long moments, the lord of Longvale stood there staring out at his son, giving away nothing of what was going on inside him. Then he turned on his heel. 'Close the gate,' he ordered.

Dicken didn't move, just looked at Asher in disbelief.

'But, my lord,' Graeme said. 'At least talk to – '

'Quiet!' Asher shouted. 'And you, close that gate, godsdamnit! Or I'll throw your fat arse outside and you can join that thing out there.'

That was an easy decision for Dicken to make. Suddenly sweating, he heaved shut the gate and replaced the heavy bar.

Asher stormed up the steps to the walkway over the gate.

'Kill it!' he ordered the two men up top, pointing at Arden. His order was met by an embarrassed silence. Neither of them raised their weapons. With a weird utterance somewhere between a roar of anger and a tortured groan, Asher tore the crossbow from the nearest one's hands.

As if he'd suddenly been released from a spell, Graeme sprinted for the stairs.

Asher took his time, propping an elbow on a crenel and taking careful aim.

Graeme was going too fast for the steep, narrow stairs. He stumbled on the next to last step. It cost him only a heartbeat, but he knew it would make all the difference.

Asher loosed.

Graeme skidded to a stop, catching himself on the parapet. Thirty yards out, Arden stood very still, looking up at his father. Slowly, he spread his hands out to the sides. The gesture might have been meant to welcome another bolt, or to offer an embrace, or to ask for forgiveness – from this distance it was impossible to say.

Maybe all three, Graeme thought. *And maybe not. Maybe he's* offering *forgiveness.*

Arden remained like that for a moment; then he turned and walked away. Graeme breathed a sigh of relief. Asher had missed. He should thank all the gods that he had.

'You!' Asher turned on Graeme with a wealth of hate and fury that hit like a hot blast from hell. 'You killed my son!'

'No, my lord, I didn't. He chose this path himself.' Graeme didn't mention that Asher himself had just tried to kill Arden. The man was clearly out of his wits. Grief could do that.

'I trusted you,' Asher snarled. 'Give me your sword.'

'Begging your pardon, my lord, but I think not.'

'Give it to me, or I'll have you hanged on the spot.'

Reluctantly, Graeme unsheathed his sword and handed it to Asher, immediately stepping away from the man and gripping the hilt of his dagger. He wasn't about to go to his death like a lamb to slaughter. If Asher wanted him dead, he'd have to work for it.

But Asher had something different in mind.

Ramming the tip of Graeme's weapon deep into a gap between the stones, he leaned on the blade until it snapped with a brief, ringing crack, the death knell of a trusted friend. He tossed the pieces at Graeme's feet.

'You're dishonorably discharged from the Freewatch. You'll stay in the Vales. From this moment on, you're forbidden to come within a mile of the wall. Should I ever catch you trying to go back out there' – he pointed beyond the wall – 'you'll hang. Now get out of my sight.'

Graeme knew it was useless, but he had to try. Maybe Orsen at least would hear. The man was standing down in the forecourt with his mouth hanging open, dumb with shock.

'I'll do as you say, my lord. But you should know there are people out there, south of the mountains. People who've survived un-bitten. They're in dire straits. The Bane – '

'Hogwash!' Asher spat. 'One more word out of you and I'll have them measure you for the rope right here and now. Now away with you!'

Mustering what dignity he had left, Graeme bent to pick up the pieces of his sword.

The walk down the stairs was the longest of his life, longer even than the trek from Marillin so many years ago. Orsen looked like he wanted to say something as Graeme walked past him. Graeme shook his head. *Not now.* He did the same with Wil, who made to follow him. *Stay,* he mouthed. Asher hadn't thought to throw the lad in the same pot with Graeme yet, and maybe he wouldn't, if Wil just kept his head down for a while.

Then the wall lay behind him. He refused to think about what lay ahead. There'd be enough time for that later. More than enough time.

*   *   *

'You!' Edilda hissed, glaring at Roana.
'I always knew I couldn't fully trust you. But this – this is treason, pure and simple. Where is it?'

'You can't have it, Edilda.' The Confessor appeared as calm as ever. 'It has chosen the girl, not you, and for good reason.'

'We'll see about that.' Edilda said. She raised an arm, holding something in her hand and pointing it at Roana – a small snake carved from black stone, Breanne saw. Suddenly the Confessor seemed to be standing in the midst of a raging storm, a vicious wind whipping her hair around her face and flattening her robe against her body. It was eerie.

Two steps away, the air was perfectly still, the pages of Breanne's book on the table undisturbed. Breanne was stunned. She'd never had more than a vague notion concerning the workings of Talent, and no idea at all that there might be anyone except old Cuinnear left in the Vales who possessed it. Then why –

'Now give it up,' Edilda said sharply, 'or I'll have to hurt you.'

Roana shook her head. Her eyes narrowed against the wind, her lips pressed together, she seemed for once to have lost her calm. She looked shocked and angry.

'You had no idea, did you?' Edilda waggled the snake in Roana's face, gloating. 'Even with all your sneaking around and spying, you missed it completely. Well, now you know, for all the good it'll do you. So tell your little protégé there to hand over the circlet like a good girl. It doesn't belong in the hands of an inexperienced child, as you'd be the first to admit if you weren't such a nitpicking, righteous bore.'

'Don't give it to her,' Roana told Breanne, shouting to make herself heard above the raging wind, though she was the only one who could hear it.

'Very well,' Edilda said. 'If that's how you want it.' She raised her voice and called out 'Clericia! Luilda! Melisent! You can come in now.'

Three Sisters appeared in the doorway, all of them mature, seasoned women. They looked capable and resolute. The rest of Edilda's Inner Circle, Breanne guessed. Each of them held an object similar to Edilda's: a jade lizard, a garnet toad, a cairngorm mouse. With the three at her back, Edilda jabbed the snake at Roana.

The Confessor was hurled backwards as if she'd been struck by an avalanche, smacking into the wall so hard Breanne thought she heard bones crack. Roana remained upright, pressed against the wall and held there by whatever force the others were using against her. Hardly conscious, her head lolling and blood trickling from her nostrils, she still tried to speak but managed no more than an unintelligible murmur.

Edilda ignored her. The Reverend Mother's eyes were fixed on the circlet. Breanne had unthinkingly picked it up and was holding it protectively against her chest.

'I'll take that now, child.' Edilda reached out a hand. There was a coldness and greed in her eyes that frightened Breanne. At the same time it made her very angry. Come to think of it, she was even a bit annoyed with Roana. She was quite fed up with these women talking over her head as if she were a little girl, calling her 'child' and not giving a quarter copper about what she might want.

'No, you won't,' she said. With no thought to what she was doing, she raised the circlet and set it on her head.

Immediately there was a soft hum in her ears. She thought she glimpsed a blue light radiating from her brow, felt a tingling sensation start up in her temples that quickly spread out until it filled her whole body with a sense of calm and great strength.

'Go,' she told Edilda, her voice sounding suddenly large and commanding to her own ears. 'Leave.'

She had a feeling she must look different as well, for she saw a flicker of uncertainty in Edilda's eyes, perhaps even the beginnings of fear. But the woman wasn't ready to give up yet.

'Foolish child,' she hissed and reached out for Breanne with the power of the four artifacts. For a wonder, Breanne could see how it was done – not with her eyes, but with some other sense she hadn't even known she possessed. She saw filaments connecting the other three objects to Edilda's snake, feeding it power. And she saw dark lines of avarice, anger and violence emanating from the Mother Superior, interlacing with the objects' lines to form something like an ugly, twisting rope that spun out from Edilda's raised hand towards Breanne, meant to ensnare and bind her.

For two long heartbeats, she stood transfixed, staring dumbly as the horrifying thing came snaking towards her.

Then, with a sudden start, she realized the danger she was in, and that she needed to do something in a hurry. Without thinking, she grabbed the end of Edilda's rope, ripped it out of the her grasp, and cast it aside like some loathsome, slimy vermin.

It hit a window, blowing out the glass, mullion, and transom as if she'd lobbed a bolt of lightning at it.

Edilda and the three Sisters collapsed to the floor like puppets with their strings cut.

And Roana slid down the wall, leaving a thin trail of red where the back of her head had hit the wall. She was conscious but seemed to be having trouble getting her eyes to focus properly. Breanne had to kneel by her side and bend down low to hear what she was saying.

'Wrong,' Roana mumbled. 'Fix.'

Only two words, but Breanne understood perfectly.
Thoroughly shaken, she was already feeling horribly guilty about what she'd just done, though the shock of it was considerably dampened by the circlet's glorious power still coursing through her.

She glanced over to where Edilda and the others lay on the floor in crumpled heaps. They were alive, but just barely. Griselde was still sitting at the table, white as a sheet and clearly scared out of her wits. But she was unharmed, thank the gods.

Breanne had no better idea how to go about healing Roana than she'd had dealing with Edilda and her minions. All she could do was try, and hope she didn't make things worse than they already were. Roana's head seemed to have gotten the worst of it, so she cradled it in her hands and willed the Confessor to be all better.

Roana reared up, her eyes open wide, her body rigid as a plank.

Not knowing what else to do, Breanne held on. After a few moments, the Sister Confessor fell back with a sigh.

'Gods!' she groaned. 'I wouldn't want to have to go through that very often. But thank you all the same, child. I'm feeling much better. Now – '

'Stop calling me "child". I'm a grown woman.'

'You're right, Forgive me.' Roana sat up. Then, with a helping hand from Breanne, she struggled to her feet. 'Though what you did was foolish. And brave. And still wrong. But you couldn't be expected to know any better. Not then. Now you do, I trust: never, ever use the Key in anger. Do it too often, and it will lead you down a path from which there is no turning back. You don't want to go there, believe me. I've studied what records there are on the subject.'

'What do you know about it?'

'The Key is a force that in itself is neither good nor bad. It just is, and all it wants is to be used. But I suspect it was never meant to be used by mere humans, weak and fallible as we are. What makes it so dangerous is the fact that, if you use it with anything but the purest of intentions, it will lead you astray, and might easily swallow you whole, body, soul, and spirit. I urge you to keep that in mind. Use it sparingly, if at all. Now. Let's see to the others.'

Edilda and her minions were not in a good way.

But when Breanne made to heal them Roana held her back. 'No,' she said. 'They'll mend on their own eventually. It's probably going to take some time and involve a measure of pain, but they do need a reminder.'

'But what will they do with you when they wake up?' Breanne asked anxiously. 'Won't they want revenge?'

'I'm sure they will. But they won't get it. Their days of playing with borrowed magic are over. You've seen to that.'

'You mean I... damaged them somehow?' Breanne felt terrible. She'd never meant to hurt anyone. Or had she? Was that what Roana had been warning her about, not a moment ago?

'Let's say you took something away from them they're not likely to regain, at least not any time soon, and maybe never. They brought it upon themselves. They abused the power, and now they'll pay the price. Hopefully, the experience will remind them of their original purpose, which was to present an example of goodness to the world by leading a humble and selfless life in service of the Mother. And hopefully, they'll have lots of time to reflect on such matters. If I have my way, they'll wake up in the penitence cells. And if the full council supports me in this, they'll be spending quite some time there.'

'If they do support you, will you become the new Reverend Mother?' Griselde asked, startling them both. Apparently she was over the worst of it, enough to be thinking about the next step, in any case.

'That's not for me to say,' Roana answered. 'The Sisters choose a new Reverend Mother by vote. But it's possible.'

'Then I'd like to stay and join you, if I may. And offer any help I can give you. You've been very kind, and you've put yourself at great risk for Breanne and myself.'

'You're most welcome, if that's what you want.' Roana was quickly regaining her former poise. 'But now, we should see that

Breanne gets under way. Nothing has changed, really. Much depends on how many of the Sisters side with Edilda out of old habit, and how many see through to the truth. It's far from sure she's beaten, and Breanne still has a task to fulfill. The sooner she leaves, the better. And Breanne, dear – I think you can take off that circlet now. It really doesn't suit you all that well.'

'I have a question,' Breanne said, removing the ornament. 'How many of you have the Talent?'

'None of us do, at least not in significant amounts. But with artifacts such as these, a smidgen of Talent is all one needs to be able to use them. Besides, the snake, the lizard, the toad, and the mouse are all symbols of the Earth Goddess, so it's likely they're somehow attuned to us, her servants.'

'Where do you think they got them from?'

'I don't know. But Vereldal has an extensive store of relics and incunabula that's been collecting dust in the cellars for centuries. Perhaps that's where Edilda found them.' Roana sighed. 'Which means I'll have to go through the whole clutter and make sure there aren't more of them hidden away down there, just waiting to fall into the wrong hands. But that shouldn't concern you, child – forgive me, Breanne. You should be on your way now.'

Half an hour later, Breanne left Vereldal on the back of a shaggy brown palfrey. The farm boy who handed her the reins told her the horse was a mare who answered to the name 'Perseverance'.

She had a feeling she'd need lots of that in the days and weeks to come, so she decided to take her new mount's name as an omen and a reminder. In fact, she could use some right now. Because despite all her brave talk about going into the Bane after Graeme, already the prospect of traveling through the dividing mountains on her own scared her half to death.

*   *   *

With things moving on such a precipitate course, Helise was momentarily forgotten. She took advantage of the fact to write out a message on a small piece of parchment scraped so thin it was nearly translucent.

When she was done writing, she rolled up the message and slipped it into a tiny brass cylinder. Making her way to the rookery unobserved, she chose a bird, attached the cylinder to its leg, and let it fly.

The Reverend Mother wasn't the only one Helise had been spying for, and in this case she was even being paid a handsome sum for her troubles. She had no intention of spending the rest of her life in Vereldal.

Though she came from small beginnings, she'd always known she was made for bigger things.

*   *   *

5

Not even the breath of a breeze stirred the air around Haunt.

Under a ceiling of lowering cloud, the sea looked deep and hungry, the island sitting on its mirror-smooth waters like a black rock set on a sheet of dark glass.

In the uppermost chamber of the keep's main tower, the new master of Stormhold shut down his scrying device, perturbed. For a fleeting instant, he'd thought he'd found something there, a tiny flash of light far, far to the north, somewhere on the other side of the mountains. But it came and went so quickly, he wasn't even sure he'd seen anything at all. And still it left him with a vague, nagging sense of unease. He'd have to watch more regularly from now on, though chances were it had been no more than a fluke in the mechanism, or perhaps a speck of lint in his eye.

Extricating himself from the device, he rose, grunting with pain. To think he'd made it through Simbalan unscathed when a hundred thousand others had died – and now this. It was a damnably high price to pay, and not one he'd expected.

Simbalan...

One of the bloodiest battles the world had ever seen, and he in the middle of it – literally. He'd fought for one side and spied for the other, an extremely dangerous game. But by then he'd been a secret follower of Malamut for many years, and wholly convinced his master's incomparable might would lead to certain victory – Aelfinn Malamut, perhaps the greatest Adept of all times, as close to immortal as made no difference, and the first in ages to be chosen as the dark god Amut's Living Vessel.

Alas, he'd been mistaken, and forced to watch in horror as Malamut had been defeated and then captured. They didn't kill him, didn't dare for fear of loosing a cataclysm that might destroy half the continent. But the solution they came up with was a sentence worse than death.

His own betrayal went undiscovered all through the battle. His unsuspecting colleagues were competent at what they did, one had to give them that, but they were lesser minds compared to him. All but one: young Torgrim of Eldinga.

The others, Elwyn of Woodsbury, Orsen Burnthands and Gisbert the Good, all of them seasoned mages who should have seen through his deceit long before the youngling did, remained clueless almost to the very end. Until the young upstart from Aldara began casting doubt and accusations, poisoning the others' minds against him. He was left with no other choice but to flee, sneaking away like a thief in the middle of the night with not a shred of baggage but weighed down all the same by ignominy and failure. The youngling would pay for it one day.

No chance in hell he'd ever be forgotten.

He'd made his way to Castle Fellmere, Malamut's erstwhile haunt.

He'd always wanted to see the place, but it didn't deliver him the fulfillment he'd imagined it would. The dusty passages and empty, echoing halls held nothing save the bitter taste of defeat. And so he moved on – but not before he'd found an interesting piece of information. He came across it purely by chance, his roaming gaze catching on a book left lying on the desk in Malamut's study, a collection of myths and legends that at first glance seemed wholly innocuous. But, automatically reading a few lines, he immediately found the chapter the book was open to intriguing. It was an account of the life and death of Uthric Redhands, a lord and pirate who in ancient times had terrorized the southern coast of Baintry. A detail near the end of the story caught his attention, filling him with a sudden, nervous excitement and renewed energy. If what he suspected was true, then undoubtedly the god had decided to take a more decisive hand in the shaping of his destiny. Though he hardly dared examine the thought... was it not possible he'd perhaps been chosen to become the next Vessel?

A week later, he arrived in the port of Rannon, and already the day after found passage on a ship bound for Baintry.

He arrived on Haunt under cover of darkness, dropped off on the island's seaward side by a coastal trader's tender for an extra purse of gold. Exploring the ruins of Redhands' keep, Stormhold, he found his suspicions confirmed. It was a great and pivotal moment in his life, and in the Dark Side's fortunes. He'd discovered one of the fabled, mysterious portals said to lead to other worlds.

The first he'd heard about them had been during his time as a student with the Incantaria, the great collegium of mages in Orr. He'd been snooping around the forbidden part of the Incantaria's vast library when he came across Carric Three Suns' *The Secret History of Magic*.

In it, Three Suns had written: 'I shall now turn to the most secret matter of the Gates. Of these ancient and mysterious passageways, little is known by few. Owing to their great age, which reaches far back beyond all human remembrance, one can but speculate whether one should hold them to be wondrously advanced artifacts, left behind by incredibly powerful mages of a people so long gone from the face of this world as to have been forgotten even by legend, or whether they are some manner of natural phenomenon, come into existence when the Good Elil (praised be His name) breathed life into the eternal void and thus created the All.'

There was more, but that first, short paragraph had already sufficed to kindle a lifelong obsession in him. He wanted to find one of those Gates, and to have it all to himself. And now he had, and did.

When after meticulous preparations and with the utmost care he brought through the first entity from the other side, he found it sentient, intelligent – and infinitely dangerous. Darkling, it called itself, a fitting name for a being made of smoke and shadows, black as midnight and driven by a hunger voracious enough to rival the maws of hell. He struck a deal with it, and with others of its kind: he would provide them with unlimited amounts of the fare they craved, and they would help him conquer the world so he could lay it at the god's feet, pure and purged of anything touched by his eternal enemy's goodness and mercy. They brought him a host of dreadful creatures from the other side, but none of those were nearly as terrifying as the Darklings themselves. The lesser beasts were content to stuff themselves with human flesh; the Darklings dined on souls.

The pact was sealed in blood, and when fool King Oswin came knocking on Stormhold's door he was ready for him, ready to release the Others onto the mainland and wipe the kingdom of Marillin from the map of living memory.

All went well until his armies reached that blasted wall at Haster's Pass. There, their advance came to a standstill – and then three extremely unfortunate things happened, one after the other.

With everything south of the wall swept clean of living human beings, the Darklings were deprived of further sustenance, and he of his army's captains. Weakened and dissatisfied, they deserted him, returning to their own world by way of the Gate, though he tried everything in his power to block their retreat. He could have offered them the reserves he kept in Salt, but he needed those to fuel his magic. Without them, he'd be helpless. He had to let the Darklings go.

Then the damned Gate – already unreliable in that it seemed to open and close to the dictate of sudden, unpredictable fluctuations in the fabric of the All – shut down altogether, and remained impassable for almost fifteen years.

And lastly, he contracted the sickness. Though he'd found a way to keep it at bay, pain had been his constant companion ever since. But he'd let none of this discourage him. On the contrary: it had merely served to sharpen his purpose – and in any case, there was no walking away once you'd entered into Amut's service.

Now the Gate had opened again, and he was set to continue what he'd begun so many years ago. Finishing off Baintry was just the first step. A whole world was out there, waiting to be brought under the Dark God's rule, finally and forever.

*   *   *

Part II – Three Islands

6

For most of his adult life, Graeme had been a loner by choice.
Now he'd become an outcast, and that proved a different sort of solitude, one that was forced upon him and, though he wouldn't have
expected it, felt not a little wounding. Glenna dropped by, just the
once, to tell him she couldn't afford to be seen associating with a
man dishonored and despised, and that whatever they'd had was
over.

Wil came calling, his generous heart overflowing with sympathy
and support. Graeme sent him away, refusing his gift of friendship.
He told himself it was in the lad's own best interest, but it hurt all
the same.

Orsen Dunne appeared at his door late one night, and to him
Graeme talked, telling him the whole story of how Arden had been
bitten, and reiterating his plea to help the people who were caught
somewhere out there in the Bane, all on their own and faced with an
enemy that was apparently gathering its forces for a crushing assault. Dunne seemed to sympathize, and said he'd see what he could
do, but Graeme didn't get his hopes up. Getting help to those people
would require Dunne to go up against Asher Thorley, Lord Com-

mander of Longvale's Watch, and Graeme seriously doubted that Orsen would risk his position for such a questionable cause. And perhaps he'd be right not to. Perhaps mounting a rescue mission would only result in sending good men to their death, with nothing gained but a ruined reputation for the officer who'd ordered it.

There was never any question in Graeme's mind about what he had to do. But first, there were preparations to make. He needed a new sword, and he needed a fair supply of arrows. Neither presented a problem. He could purchase a sword without raising undue suspicion, and he'd make the arrows himself.

He also needed a rope, strong but light and supple. Buying it at a rope-maker's was out of the question. If word of it got back to Thorley, he'd immediately guess what Graeme wanted it for. He had to find another way.

Finding a map should be the easiest part; Cuinnear had an extensive collection.

The last item on his list was the most difficult to procure: eggs, Almorican Fire. They were stocked under the gatehouse, in a secure cellar behind an iron-banded door to which there was but one key – and that hung on the quartermaster's key ring and never left his person.

It took a while, but after some searching Graeme found a man who earned his livelihood climbing dizzying cliffs in the dividing mountains to collect rock martin's nests, a delicacy much sought after for the tables of the noble and the rich. The man used just the kind of rope Graeme wanted, and for the price of two new ones he was willing to sell it and forget the transaction had ever happened.

110

For the eggs, Graeme had no other choice but to turn to Orsen Dunne. It was a gamble, one that could see him dangling from the end of a rope if the captain decided his loyalties and future lay with Asher Thorley, mad or no. But Graeme was betting on Dunne's sense of decency, and he was prepared to play on it and on the guilty conscience the man probably had for not having taken a stand in the affair with Arden. He didn't have to.

Dunne listened to his request in silence.

'I knew you'd do this the moment Thorley told you you couldn't,' he said when Graeme was done. 'I don't have to tell you there will be no coming back this time. The men have orders to shoot you on sight if they see you anywhere near the wall – Thorley's orders, not mine. Some of them might turn a blind eye, but not if they see you on the wrong side of Deepwall. It's a crazy thing to do, going out there alone and for good, but I can't say I feel it's wrong. You have my blessing, for what it's worth. Give me a few days, and I'll get you what you're asking for.'

No word about the risk Dunne himself would be running, no mention that he might well end up on the rope next to Graeme's if things went awry. It raised the man a whole number of notches in Graeme's esteem.

'Thank you, captain. I won't forget this. If I see anything out there you should know about, I'll get word to you. Needs be, I'll tie a message to an arrow and shoot it over the wall. You know my mark: three black rings forward of the fletching.'

Three days later Dunne delivered, and Graeme was set to go. Then, on the evening of the night he intended to make his move, he received an unexpected visitor, and was forced to make a significant

111

change to his plans.

When he answered the insistent knock he found a shaggy, brown palfrey tethered to his apple tree and a woman in boots and leathers standing outside his door.

At first he took her for a stranger, dressed as she was, with wind-blown hair and cheeks reddened from the cold. And she'd changed in other ways as well, he saw. Gone was the girlish diffidence that had made him think of a fearful little mouse scurrying through Thor-hold's shadows. He felt as if he was looking at her for the first time, and found her bearing much more firm and self-assured than he'd remembered. He also noticed with something of a start that she was actually quite pleasing to the eye.

'My lady,' he said. 'This is a surprise.'

'Master Banehunter. May I come in? I've had quite enough of this freezing wind.'

Graeme stepped aside to let her in.

Yes, he thought as she brushed past him, bringing with her a smell of horse and leathers, and something subtler, a woman's scent. *This is no longer Breanne the Mouse. This is a woman with a purpose.*

He was strangely pleased for her – and immediately on his guard. She was Asher Thorley's daughter, after all.

She looked around the small but cozy room, saw his gear piled on the table in preparation for departure: the bulging pack, his weapons belt, the unstrung horn bow, his staff, the coiled rope. If she was here on an errand for her father, then he was already neck-deep in trouble.

'I see you're ready to leave,' she said. 'That's good. I'm coming with you.'

He would have laughed if she hadn't looked so serious and sounded as if she really meant it.

'My lady, if this is some kind of jest, then it's a cruel one. You know your lord father's forbidden me to even approach the wall. If he finds me – '

'No, I don't,' she interrupted him. 'I just got back from Midvale and came straight to your house. What has he done now?'

'It's not so much what he has done, but what your brother Arden...' he faltered, unsure how to go on. Gods! She had no idea what had happened, and now he of all persons was supposed to tell her? *Damn* fate and its ironic whims.

'Arden? What about him? What did he do?' She sounded worried now, and well she should be.

Graeme had no choice but to tell her the whole story, from the day he'd set out into the Bane with Arden and Wil to the moment when Arden turned his back on Deepwall and life as he'd known it until then, walking away into the wild, never to return.

She was in tears before he was halfway through. But they were quiet tears, the kind you'd expect from someone who'd been braced for bad news and had already passed through the first shock of it. Still, she looked devastated, and he wondered for a moment whether he should offer a comforting arm or a shoulder to cry on but decided against it. She was a highborn lady, and it was not his station. And, truth be told, he'd never been any good at this kind of thing.

'So it's true,' she said, swiping a sleeve across her face. 'I saw it, though I didn't understand what it meant at the time. You shouldn't blame yourself. And my father is a fool. Arden's finally found his purpose in life, and he's going where he needs to be. It must be so. I couldn't bear to believe otherwise.'

Gods give that you're right, Graeme thought. *Gods give he didn't throw away his life for nothing.*

She gave a last sniffle and blew her nose on a kerchief he offered her.

'And now I shall tell you exactly why you're going to take me with you,' she said, suddenly all business, and told him all about her visions: the Banesheart and the terrible threat it posed; Broken Steel and Sleeping Wood; Arden and the great tree; the Key.

When she'd finished, Graeme remained silent, not knowing what to say. He was half convinced there was truth to what she'd told him, not least because of the part with the broken sword. But it wasn't nearly enough to change his mind about taking her with him into the Bane.

'I'll be blunt, my lady,' he said. 'Even assuming your visions speak true, I don't see how risking your life out there is going to help. The Bane is no place for a woman. No place for anyone, for that matter. Your brother's fate is already on my head. I won't have your death on my hands as well. I'm sorry, but no.'

He could have added that she was practically asking him to place his head in the noose her father had waiting for him. Going over the wall alone was a risky thing, a fifty-fifty chance at best. If he had to haul her after him it would take a major miracle to keep them from getting caught.

But she wasn't prepared to give up.

'Very well,' she said. 'Since it's imperative I go with you, and since you obviously believe I'm not able to take care of myself, I'll show you different, just this once.'

She pulled a simple silver circlet with a dull blue stone from under her leather jerkin and set it on her brow. Watching in awed silence, Greame saw the stone flare into life and Breanne grow into a tall and fearsome goddess.

Then the floor suddenly disappeared from under his feet, and the world stood on its head.

*   *   *

For a moment, Breanne had to pause and look, filled with wonder. This time the change in what she saw – no, in *how* she saw – was much more dramatic. Everything around her suddenly seemed to consist not of solid matter but of glowing lines: the table, the chairs, the whole house were still recognizable as what they were, but only just.

The oldest lines she saw were of the earth itself, and she understood how the house had been placed upon them with aforethought and respect for what already existed. Next oldest were the remnant lines of growing wood and native stone, still preserved in the building materials. Then there were those laid down by masons and carpenters, confirmed and strengthened by the movements and actions of those who had lived here, ten-thousandfold repeated over countless generations.

And Graeme. He was still Graeme – tall, lithe, his unruly dark hair tied back with a strip of leather, his strong, angular face hardened by wind and weather, the grey eyes surprisingly deep – and he was also a blindingly bright blob of light trailing more lines, several of which were pointed in her direction. To her relief, they weren't threatening at all, nothing like Edilda's. His looked somehow... nice.

But she wasn't here to goggle.

She had to make him see the sense in taking her along. Forming a line of her own, she used it to reach out for him and ever so gently lifted him off his feet. Then, on a whim, she turned him upside down.

That should show him, she thought. *He actually looks quite funny hanging there with a face like someone just... turned him upside down.*

She called herself to order. It wasn't going to help her cause if he got the impression she was playing foolish tricks on him. Turning him right side up again, she set him down on the floor, letting go only when she was sure he had his feet back under him.

She would have loved to wear the circlet a bit longer. It felt so incredibly good. But she willed herself to take it off. It wasn't hers to use for her private amusement, and neither was she here to impress Graeme with a flashy show of borrowed grandeur. All she needed was for him to see reason and let her come into the Bane with him.

Seeing Graeme's face, she wasn't sure she'd done the right thing.

He didn't look overwhelmed by her show of power. Instead, he looked annoyed. Very annoyed.

116

'Bloody hell, woman,' he growled, reminding her of her father when he was angry with her. 'Do something like that again and I'll have you over my knee, highborn lady or not. Here I was thinking you appeared so much more mature than when I'd last seen you, and then you go and try to sway me with childish pranks. You don't handle a man like that and expect respect in return.'

'I'm so sorry,' Breanne said, and she was. 'I shouldn't have done that. But somehow I had to make you see – '

'All right,' he interrupted her. 'All right already. I *am* impressed. I can see that you've been entrusted with something very powerful, and I can see there must be a reason for it. Just have a care how and on whom you use it.'

'I will, I promise.'

'Fine. Then that's settled. But just so you know, you're going to have to carry your own pack. And it won't be light. A few days from now, when your shoulders are chafed and your legs and back are nothing but aches and pains, you'll curse me for letting you come along.'

Breanne felt a thrill of excitement. He was taking her with him! The very next instant, her heart dropped into her boots. Now that the prospect of going into the Bane had become real, she was suddenly terrified of what she'd find out there – or of what might find her.

'Now,' Graeme was saying. 'We need to be very clear about one thing: out there, it's me who gives the orders. And you'll follow them to the letter, or get us both killed. It's as simple as that. Are we agreed?'

'Yes, absolutely.' It would be all right. He would watch out for her. 'I'll do everything you say.'

'Good. Then let's find you a pack. I have a spare around here somewhere.'

'Graeme?'

'Yes, my lady.'

'Thank you.'

'Don't thank me yet. We're not even to the wall, much less over it. And the other side is where the real challenge begins.'

*   *   *

Graeme knew well enough how things worked on the wall.

Each of the men on night duty had a quarter-mile stretch to patrol, and they did it at a measured, unhurried pace. Walking the wall was about watching and listening, not running back and forth like a caged marten. When the man up top had walked by and Graeme reckoned he was halfway to the turning point, they made their move.

On the second throw, the loop he'd tied in the end of the rope caught on the tapered end of one of the massive, upright timbers the wall was built from. He gave it a tug. It held.

'I'll haul up the packs first,' he told Breanne in a whisper. 'Then I'll let the rope back down. Step into the loop and hold on tight. I'll pull you up.'

Reaching the top of the wall, he paused, listening. Nothing.

He swung over the parapet and hauled on the rope. Pulling up the packs turned out to be harder work then getting Breanne to the top. She was a light-weight, and when she was near the top he saw that instead of standing in the loop she'd slipped it around her shoulders and was leaning back, walking up the wall and taking some of the strain off his arms. Smart girl.

They made it to the ground on the other side just as Graeme heard the first, faint footfalls of the returning guard. It was then they hit a dangerous snag.

Graeme had doubled the rope for his own descent, laying it loosely around the top of a timber. But when he tried to pull it down it wouldn't budge, probably wedged tight in the cracks between the trunk and its neighbors. By now the guard was almost on a level with where they crouched in the shadows at the foot of the wall.

As soon as he saw the rope he'd sound the alarm, and Orsen would have no choice but to send out a mounted patrol. If that happened, Graeme and Breanne would be caught for a certainty.

The footsteps stopped.

Graeme briefly considered grabbing Breanne's hand and making a run for it but knew it would be no more than a hopeless gesture.

An eternity seemed to pass while they cowered in the shadows, waiting for the inevitable. Then a small light flared up, flickered for a moment, went out.

This is it, Graeme thought, swamped by a cold dread. *He's found the rope. Any moment now, he'll sound the alarm.*

But the man on the wall resumed his walk. No alarm, no braying horn betraying them into hands that would have shown them no mercy, at least not Graeme. Breanne might have gotten away with a slap on the wrist – though with the way Asher Thorley had been acting lately, not even that was a given.

Catching a whiff of pipe smoke, Graeme breathed a sigh of relief. Dunne would have had the man's hide for smoking on duty, but Graeme sent the fellow a heartfelt thanks.

119

Unfortunately, there was no way to free the rope, and no time to climb back up and work it out of the cracks. They could do without it, but it was a clear sign of their passing he'd have much preferred not to leave dangling where it was sure to be found come daylight.

'That was close, wasn't it?' Breanne whispered, her warm breath brushing his ear.

'It was. And we need to be gone from here when he comes back. Sooner or later someone's bound to notice the rope, and I want us to be as far away as possible when they do.'

As if the gods agreed, just then a bank of clouds obscured the moon, blanketing the open ground between the wall and the forest in darkness. Quiet as the softest of breezes rustling through the grass, they crossed the clearing and disappeared among the trees.

*   *   *

7

Orsen Dunne hadn't asked when Graeme planned to make his move. Truth be told, he didn't want to know. He was in too deep already. By chance he was away inspecting the western part of the wall when it happened, and so had no idea what awaited him back at the Longvale barracks. Had he known, he might have preferred not to return at all, and instead followed Graeme into the Bane.

He'd hardly set foot in his quarters when a man came to say that the Lord Commander had arrived and was asking to speak with the captain. A small knot of unease forming deep in his gut, he strapped on his weapons belt and went out to meet Asher Thorley.

He found Thorley in the forecourt, still ahorse, accompanied by a score of men from Thorhold's House Guard, two of them leading riderless horses. Fleetingly, he wondered where their riders were.

'Captain,' Thorley said. 'So good of you to come. It seems the Banehunter has gone missing. You wouldn't by any chance know something of his whereabouts, would you?'

'No, my lord,' Dunne said, the knot in his belly blooming to the size of a fist. 'I've been away for the past three days.'

'Very convenient, that, wouldn't you say?' Asher looked like something poisonous preparing to strike.

'I don't know what you mean to infer, my lord. I'm sure he simply got tired of sitting around in that little house of his and is traveling somewhere in the Vales.'

'Then pray take a look at this.' Thorley motioned to one of his men, who rode forward and tossed a coiled rope at Dunne's feet. It hit the dirt with a soft slap that to Dunne's ears carried a terrifying ring of finality.

'It was found hanging from the outside of the wall not half a mile from here,' Thorley went on. 'How do you suppose it got there? Any idea?'

'None at all, my lord. But I'll certainly do what I can to find out.'

'Don't bother,' Thorley said dismissively, then shouted, 'Raff! Warrin! Let's have Sergeant Raulin out here!'

Full-blown fear clutched at Dunne's bowels when the gatehouse door flew open and he saw Thorley's two missing men drag out the quartermaster. Raulin was barely conscious, hanging between them like a sack of meal, his bare, bloodied feet dragging in the dirt. They'd beaten him to a pulp, broken his nose and knocked out a few teeth. They'd also cut off two of his fingers and most of his toes. Dunne swallowed bile.

'Master Raulin has been kind enough to tell us about your recent requisition,' Thorley said. He seemed almost to be enjoying himself. 'The eggs. Would you care to tell us where they've gotten to?'

'I – I'm not sure, my lord. I'd have to go look in my – '

'Don't trouble yourself. I had your quarters searched while you

122

were away. They're not there. That's because you gave them to the Banehunter. And you helped him escape.'

'My lord – '

'Quiet! I'm not done yet. I've seen through *all* of your despicable schemes. I've had news from a trusted source in Midvale saying that my daughter left Vereldal five days ago. Her horse was found grazing near the Banehunter's house. The reasoning is simple enough. A halfwit could put it all together. He's abducted her and taken her with him into the Bane. That's the second child of mine he's about to murder, and you' – he pointed an accusing finger – 'are a part of it.'

'I know nothing of your daughter. And I'm sure it's too early still for such far-reaching conclusions – '

'Be still!' Thorley yelled, color rising to his face and spittle flying from his lips. 'I've heard enough of your filthy lies!' The next moment, he was eerily calm again, speaking in a deceptively even voice. 'The Banehunter got away because I was too lenient with him. I should have hanged the bloody traitor on the spot. Well, I'm not making that mistake twice. Conveniently, he's gone to the trouble of leaving us a rope for you. Fray.' He waved the man forward and pointed at Dunne. 'I want him hanged. Now.'

With the half dozen men of the Watch who'd been standing around the forecourt looking on in disbelief and mounting horror, Fray, captain of Thorley's House Guard, kneed his horse forward, drawing his sword as he did so. He was a big, ugly bruiser with an acne-scarred face and broken nose, a brutal ruffian like all of Thorley's men.

Sending a prayer to the gods to grant him an honorable death,

123

Dunne drew his own sword. No way was he going to let them hang him, not without a fight. Out of the corner of his eye, he saw two of his own men take a step forward.

They mustn't, he thought. *This isn't their quarrel.*

He was about to motion them back when several of Thorley's men rode between them, the horses blocking his view.

Then Fray began to badger him, riding up close and feinting left and right with his blade, a wicked grin on his nasty mug: a cat playing with a mouse, a bully mistaking hopeless odds for weakness. It was base. Dishonorable.

Suddenly Dunne had had enough. He lunged at Fray, and missed. A moment later, he felt a cold length of steel slide into his back, once, twice.

Why, the craven bastards! Twenty to one, and still they come from behind.

It was his last thought before the dusty ground came up to meet him in a rush and the sky swung around until all he saw was the sun, terribly, terribly bright, searing his eyes without mercy.

*　　　*　　　*

Wil stood frozen in shock.

'I said I wanted him hanged,' he heard Thorley chide Fray.

'Sorry, m'lord.' Fray looked anything but sorry. 'Guess we got a bit carried away there. But dead is dead, at the end of the day, if you don't mind my saying so. And we can still hang him from the wall if you like.'

'Do it,' Thorley said. 'He'll serve as an example for anyone who's not sure where he stands.'

He cast a meaningful glance at the men of the Watch. No one met his eye.

Wil had been one of the two who'd made to aid the captain. Now, feeling sicker than ever before in his life as he watched Thorley's brutes drag Dunne's body away like just another trophy of the hunt, he made a silent vow. He'd see justice done to Asher Thorley, and the captain's good name restored.

Well he knew that Asher Thorley was justice in Longvale. And well he knew that for a simple soldier like himself to fulfill such a vow the world would likely have to start turning backwards and the sun rise in the west. He didn't care. Somehow, he'd find a way.

But for now, there was worse to come.

'You!' Thorley pointed at the man standing closest. It was Dicken Serl. 'You'll be acting captain until further notice. I want a hundred men saddled up and ready to leave in half an hour. We're going to find my daughter.'

Dicken went white as a sheet, beads of sweat appearing on his brow as he stood staring at Thorley in utter shock. Then, visibly pulling himself together, he gave an awkward bow. 'Yes, m'lord. I'll see to it right away.'

What else can the poor bastard do? Wil thought. *He's likely already seeing himself dangling beside Dunne and wishing he'd never joined the Watch.* I'm *starting to wish I'd never joined. There's no honor in this anymore, none at all.*

With Thorley's men backing fat little Dicken, going through the barracks and stables with swords bared and not hesitating to use the flats of their blades on the legs or arms or backs of those they deem-

125

ed too slow, a hundred men were ready to leave almost within the time set by Thorley, though 'ready' was a hopeless exaggeration. They'd barely managed to get their gear together and their horses saddled when the gate swung open and Thorley, riding at the head of his House Guard, led them out into the Bane – and into something that in Wil's eyes was fast shaping up into becoming a full-blown disaster, and not just because they were leaving the wall dangerously undermanned.

Wil went with them, voluntarily, even though he'd just finished a turn of duty. He'd have felt like a craven traitor staying at home while his comrades rode out at the beck of a Lord Commander who was not only cruel and unjust but looked more and more to be at least half mad, and dangerous as a cut snake.

*   *   *

8

It was the longest and most nerve-wracking trip to Oldwall Graeme had ever made. In truth, it was pure madness. His original plan had been to go a short ways into the woods, set a circle of Wards, and wait until first light before going on. The damned rope had put paid to that.

Now, they had to go as far and fast as they could if they wanted to stay ahead of the search party that would come after them no later than tomorrow morning. Today, actually; it was past midnight. If their luck turned really ugly, Thorley would get wind of what was going on and send Fray after them. That bastard wouldn't even bother to drag them back inside the wall before he killed Graeme and did gods knew what to Breanne.

But traveling in the Bane in the dark was as sure a way to get them killed as if they'd sat down at the forest edge and waited for Fray to find them. The only reason he saw a chance to make it through at all was because things had been so quiet lately. Still, they had to get out of the trees as soon as possible. Every one of them could be a Rooter. Every vine or root could be a Lurker. And the Shifters were nigh on invisible in the dark – though he hadn't seen one of those in months, gods be thanked.

The road was a quarter mile to their right.

What would have been a short stroll in daytime was a sheer endless, nightmarish trek in the dark. He didn't tell Breanne any of this, just told her to stay right behind him and never stray from his footsteps. She obviously trusted he knew what he was doing, and it was enough if one of them was worried half witless. Staring into the blackness beneath the trees until his eyes began to tear, feeling his way step by careful step, every one of which could be his and Breanne's last, hoping against better knowledge that a fool's luck would steer him right yet expecting the Bane to attack any moment, he struck out for the road.

Finally, after what felt like hours, he saw it: an almost imperceptible lightening up ahead. Stepping out onto the gravelly surface, a band of lesser darkness caught between the forest's black and silent walls on either side, he breathed an audible sigh of relief.

'What?' Breanne said, keeping her voice down.

'Nothing. Just glad we made it out of Longvale. Are you good to go on? It's going to be a long walk.'

'I'm fine. I've been doing quite a bit of walking lately, which turns out to have been a good thing. And the pack's not all that heavy either.'

No, Graeme thought, *it isn't. Because I did some repacking before we departed, left as much of the heavy stuff as I could out of your pack and put it in mine.*

'Don't worry,' he told her. 'It'll get heavier by the mile. Packs have a way of doing that. They're nasty little things.'

128

She gave a soft laugh at that, the first he'd heard from her. It sounded nice.

Breanne struggled valiantly, but it still took them an hour longer than usual to reach Oldwall. The sun's early rays were peeking over the craggy peaks on the eastern side of the pass when they caught their first sight of the wall from afar, the gatehouse towers sitting in a swath of morning mist like a pair of sleeping giants.

Abruptly Graeme stopped.

A cloaked figure was standing at the eastern tower's parapet, sharply outlined against the high Tallamors' snow-covered flanks.

'Someone's up there,' he told Breanne. He'd taken her pack an hour ago, but even so she was near her limit, bathed in sweat and breathing heavily after the last, steep stretch of road.

'Is it Arden?' she panted, anxiously clutching his arm.

'Too far to tell. It could be, though. I suppose we'll find out soon enough. Whoever it is, they seem to be waiting for us.'

When next he looked, the figure was no longer on the tower. But as they crossed the last fifty yards to the wall it reappeared under the gate's empty arch, an arm raised in greeting.

'It's Wulfwyn,' he told Breanne. 'I wonder what she's doing here. Stay back a bit. She may have gone through the Change since last I saw her.'

'No, I haven't,' Wulfwyn called out. She seemed to have extraordinarily keen hearing. 'You're safe to come closer.'

Standing under Oldwall's crumbling gate surrounded by nothing but empty wilderness, Graeme dropped their packs and gear and made formal introductions, awkward as it felt under the circumstan-

129

ces. Wulfwyn looked the same as the last time they'd met, pale and dark-eyed, her exceptional beauty easily overriding the marks on her face, marks that were unchanged as far as he could tell. It appeared she *had* found a way to keep the Bane sickness in check.

'Wulfwyn of Archer's Rock,' he said. 'And this is Lady Breanne Thorley. She's come to find her brother Arden.'

'No,' Wulfwyn corrected him with unsettling certainty. 'She's come to find the Banesheart.'

'What – '

'Peace, Graeme,' Breanne said, laying a hand on his arm. 'She's right. I'd love to see Arden, but that's not why I'm here. Neither are you. We have a door to find, and a lock to turn, remember?'

'Where is Arden?' Graeme asked Wulfwyn. 'Is he here?'

'No. He's at Archer's Rock, trying to keep the Bane from over-running us. I've come to take you there. He wants to see you both. He says it's a necessary step on your journey to the Banesheart.'

*   *   *

As if Wulfwyn's words had invoked it, the blindness fell over Breanne like a thick, suffocating blanket, cutting her off from the light. Thankfully, she was already holding on to Graeme's arm. She gripped it tighter, glad to feel him beside her.

Then the vision came, and she heard herself speak in that eerie voice again, telling him and Wulfwyn what she saw.

'Three islands,' she said, the words seeming to come from some-where outside of her. 'One is succor, calm and removed. One is risk, storm-tossed and bare. And one is danger, darkness, and death. Three steps on the way, but not nearly the end of the journey.'

Moments later, she could see again. She felt weak, her knees threatening to buckle under her. Only Graeme's arm around her waist was keeping her upright.

'Come, sit,' he told her, leading her to a large rock a few steps from the gate. 'Rest for a moment. I'll make us some breakfast. And then you can sleep for a few hours. We won't be moving on until later.'

It was a risk, she knew. She tried to calculate what time it must be and how long a search party might take to reach them, but she was exhausted, her mind too muddled to figure it out. 'I'll rest while we eat. Then we can go on.'

'No,' Wulfwyn said. 'Sleep, both of you. Don't worry, I'll stand watch. I have very sharp eyes, and I'll see them when they come over the rise at the far end of the valley. It will give us an hour at least, more than we need. I know a trail they'll never find and couldn't follow if they did.'

Never in her wildest dreams had Breanne imagined she might one day trust a Bitten with her life. But she did. In truth, she couldn't think of anyone unbitten other than Graeme whom she trusted more than this beautiful, strange, selfless woman.

It seemed she'd just laid down her head when Graeme gently shook her awake.

'Time to go,' he told her. 'They're coming. It looks as if your father wants to catch us very badly. He's brought half of Longvale's garrison with him.'

She sat up with a groan, her shoulders crying out in protest. Her back was stiff as a board, and her legs felt as if they were swollen to twice their normal size. All of it hurt. At least she didn't have any blisters: the boots Roana had chosen for her were a perfect fit. Thank the gods for small favors. Still, she had no idea how she was supposed to get onto her feet, much less stay on them. But with a hand from Graeme she managed to stand, and found it wasn't quite as bad as she'd thought. He handed her a staff he'd cut for her. Her pleasure over the new walking aid was considerably dampened when he explained what it was really for. Still, she was glad to have it.

They set out almost immediately, Wulfwyn leading them south for a couple of miles, then turning east, heading for the mouth of a narrow ravine that was hardly more than a deep, narrow slash in a frighteningly steep mountainside. They entered a shadowed gorge, balancing along the rocky bank of a small stream frothing with snowmelt. Patches of tough mountain grass and a few stunted, weather-beaten trees clung to the near vertical slopes on either side; the rest was bare rock. For nearly half an hour they clambered over rocks and boulders until suddenly there was no way to go on.

They had arrived at the foot of a cliff. It wasn't all that high, perhaps twice the height of a tall man, but its face was smooth and unbroken, impossible to climb. A waterfall spilled from its lip, over-ly loud in the confined space and pricking her skin with droplets of icy spray. If Wulfwyn had wanted to lead them into a trap, she'd chosen the perfect place.

*   *   *

Graeme wasn't concerned.

He'd immediately spotted the tree leaning against the cliff, its age-

132

greyed trunk not much thicker than his arm, the old axe marks still visible where the branches had been cut off a hand's span from the trunk. It was larch, a wood that took forever to decay and had probably been standing there for a very long time, a device used by mountain dwellers since times immemorial. A primitive but serviceable ladder.

When they'd all reached the top of the cliff, he pulled the tree up after them, dragging it back from the lip so it wouldn't be visible from below. Wulfwyn had spoken the truth. No one would be able to follow them – not unless they figured out the trick with the tree and went back a good ways to find and cut a new one.

There was a trail now, a clayey, rocky groove worn out over generations by hundreds of feet, and progress became easier. An hour on, they came to another waterfall, this one at least two hundred feet high, the path zigzagging up the slope to their right and rejoining the stream at the top of the fall. It was steep and exposed, and a slip could easily lead to a fatal fall. But what worried him more was that, once they'd negotiated the climb, they'd be crossing into snow. If the trail farther up was anything like this, he didn't see how Breanne would be able to go on. She wasn't used to this kind of thing, was already pushing her limits as it was. And that wasn't taking into account that this time of year ice falls and avalanches could still put an abrupt and terminal stop to their journey even if everything else went well.

Somehow, they all made it up in one piece. At the top of the fall, Graeme saw with relief that the mountain leaned back, the gorge opening up into a wide, shallow valley. Up ahead, the snow-covered terrain rose gently towards a deeply notched ridge between two peaks, undoubtedly the pass they were headed for. Another hour, he reckoned, and they'd be walking downhill again. Then it would be high time to find some kind of shelter for the night.

They were in luck.

East of the pass and just below the snowline, they found a shepherd's cot. Inside, there was a pile of old hay, slightly damp but serviceable as a bed. And, for a wonder, a stack of firewood that was still good. Breanne spread her bedroll on the hay and was asleep in no time at all. Graeme lit a fire and cooked some beans with a few strips of jerky. When the food was ready, he managed to rouse Breanne and keep her awake long enough to get some of it into her. After he and Wulfwyn had eaten as well, they bedded down beside Breanne.

That night they didn't hold watch, though Graeme did set Wards. The creatures of the Bane seldom ventured this high up – and if against all odds one of them did, so be it. He'd just have to fight the damn thing and hope he wasn't too sleep-drugged to make a quick, clean kill of it.

He didn't wake Breanne until midmorning.

She looked like she could have slept through the rest of the day and the following night, and he wished he could have let her. But Wulfwyn said they needed to get going if they were to reach the next shelter before dark.

Once they were under way, he noted with relief that Breanne seemed to be doing much better, negotiating the narrow, winding trail with increasing confidence and surefootedness. It was surprising how quickly she was getting used to all this. A few more days of it, he reckoned, and she'd be fit as a mountain goat.

There were several more climbs but mostly it was downhill, following another nameless mountain stream that rustled and splashed its way down towards the lowlands. Far below, it flowed out into a wide valley, a river now, meandering through woods and open ground in large, lazy loops until it was lost from sight in the far, hazy distance.

It took them two more days to reach the lowlands, sleeping once in a shallow cave, and once in another cot. At a point about halfway down the last big ridge, Wulfwyn stopped at the top of a steep incline. From where they stood, they had a sweeping view of the valley below.

'From here on,' she said, 'we have to be very careful. The land you see down there is teeming with the Bane, and the closer we get to Archer's Rock, the worse it will be.'

Graeme nodded, strung his bow, and loosened the strings of his belt pouch so he could easily reach for an egg if the need should arise. Wulfwyn's warning turned out to be timely. Not ten steps farther on, a large Lurker had spread itself across the trail, twelve feet across and as good as invisible to someone who didn't know what he was looking for. They went around it, careful of others that might be hidden nearby, waiting for a man or a beast who, thinking to avoid the big one, would step right into one of the others instead.

There were more of them along the way, and Graeme saw dozens of Rooters standing in among the trees to either side of the trail. But the sun was still out, and none of them budged, though he had the eerie feeling that they shifted and turned when he wasn't look-ing. Increasingly worried they might run into a Shifter, he kept his bow at the ready, an arrow nocked. Thankfully, the trail stayed close to the stream, a last refuge if things got bad.

When they'd passed the last rapids Wulfwyn stopped again. 'The worst is over,' she told them. 'From here on, we travel by water.'

She had a boat hidden away in a thicket on the bank, a small, flat-bottomed river craft. Once on the water, they were glad to be off their feet for a change, drifting downriver at a leisurely pace with only the occasional stroke of an oar to keep them clear of the banks.

For the first time in weeks, Graeme allowed himself to relax, if only a little. But, the moment he gave his thoughts some rein, he was assailed by the sheer impossibility of what they were attempting. Breanne had her visions to go by, and apparently she was coming to believe in them more and more. He, however, felt increasingly like a blind man who had only the hand that was leading him to trust in. It was not a condition that sat well with his independent nature. And something else was bothering him, something he'd been trying to grasp ever since they'd begun their descent into Marillin. As yet, he had no idea what it might be.

'You look sad,' Breanne said. 'Is the place where you lived as a boy perhaps somewhere near here?'

He was surprised, not that she should know about his Marillian origins – most likely he'd been the subject of more than one conver-sation at Thorhold's high table – but by the uncanny precision with which she'd put her finger on what had been eluding him.

To his dismay, he found that he had no ready answer. In his mind's eye, he could see the meadow where his sister Adelle and Pa and his brothers had died, and he could recall the red-tinted water in the trough in the yard, but nothing else: not the house or its surroundings, nor where in Marillin it had stood. For some reason his inability to remember filled him with something close to panic, as if he'd just discovered that a vital part of himself had gone missing.

'I don't know,' he said. 'It's strange, but I can't seem to remember.'

'It's been twenty years,' Breanne said soothingly. 'And you were just a boy. Perhaps it was wrong of me to bring it up. Forgive me if I've touched on something painful.' She seemed genuinely concerned.

'No, it's all right. It'll probably come back to me sooner or later. I suppose there's just too much else on my mind right now.'

But it didn't come back, at least not then. The more he tried to remember, the more he felt as if he were staring into a dark, bottomless hole. He shook himself out of it. This was no time for brooding. But the question had lodged in his thoughts like a small splinter in the flesh that only calls itself back to mind when a wrong move causes it to flare with a short, sharp pain.

*   *   *

'Archer's Rock,' Wulfwyn said, rousing Breanne from her exhausted stupor. And there it was: a high crag rising from a long, looping bend in the river, presenting a sheer cliff riverward and surrounded by water on three sides. On the landward side it fell away in a steep, rocky slope that would make any enemy think twice whether att-

137

acking it was worth the trouble. As defensible positions went, it didn't get much better, she noted with the eye of someone raised in a castle.

But the Bane obviously didn't care about any of that. The sun was down, and just before they rounded the bend she caught a fleeting glimpse of a host of dark shapes moving among the ruins and widely spread trees at the foot of the slope. Even from this far away, she could feel their malignant intent focused on the top of the bluff and the humans sheltering behind a stockade that didn't look like it would hold for long once an enemy scaled the slope.

Then they were on the far side of the bend, Wulfwyn steering the boat into a small inlet and making fast beside a score of others, most of them considerably larger than their own. Breanne saw packs in some of them, as if they'd been readied for a journey.

There was a narrow strip of even ground at the foot of the cliff – but no way up, as far as Breanne could see. Wulfwyn tilted back her head and gave a piercing cry. Looking up, Breanne saw a boom swing out far overhead and then a large basket slowly descend towards them to the faint sound of a creaking winch.

When the basket reached the ground, Wulfwyn climbed in. 'Come,' she aid. 'It can easily take all three of us at once.'

Breanne wasn't sure she trusted the thing, but she didn't seem to have a choice.

At least the rope looked sturdy. Slowly, slowly they rose, the basket swaying slightly, the winch sounding louder now, tortured. Gripping the basket's rim with whitened knuckles and refusing to look down, she studied the far side of the river instead. She saw more dark shapes among the trees over there.

One of them, several shades lighter than the others, moved down to the bank. There was a sudden blur as it seemed to throw something resembling a thick, grey rope out over the water. The next moment it wasn't there anymore. Searching, she found it again on a small islet nearly a third of the way across the river.

The thing stood studying the remaining stretch of water as if it intended to cross it as well, but then it seemed to change its mind. It turned and jumped – or flowed, or cast itself – back to where it had started out.

'Damn,' Graeme breathed beside her. 'Damn, damn, damn.'

'Yes,' Wulfwyn said. 'They're getting stronger. Without the Wards, they'd be jumping over the wall, right into the compound.'

'What was that?' Breanne asked, shivering.

'A Shifter,' Graeme said. 'They're bad news.

'How many of them are here?' he asked Wulfwyn.

'Not many – not yet. We call them Grey Men. It's because of them we can't go out to gather and hunt anymore. If not for the river, they'd be starving us out. Though I'm sure that, by now, some of us would rather go hungry than see one more bite of fish in their bowls.'

It was getting dark by the time they reached the top, Breanne breathing a sigh of relief.

*   *   *

The two men working the winch locked down the mechanism and swung the boom around, bringing the basket to rest on solid ground again.

Behind them, a third man stood waiting. Not a young man,

Graeme saw. There was more grey than black in his hair and beard and his bare, muscular arms bore the scars of countless fights. His eyes were flat, his face impassive, as if putting on any expression at all was too much of a bother. A hard man, Graeme reckoned, made harder still by years of fighting to survive in the Bane. Too hard, maybe.

'Gamel,' Wulfwyn said, 'I bring you Breanne Thorley. She's the Treesinger's sister. And Graeme Banehunter, ranger from Long-vale.'

'Banehunter,' Gamel said with a sneer in his voice. 'Easy, when you have a wall to hide behind.'

'I've spent maybe six months of the past fifteen years behind that wall,' Graeme said evenly, 'and none of them hiding. The rest of the time I've been fighting the Bane, no different than you.'

'So you say.'

'So I say,' Graeme said, setting down his pack and staff. 'And if that's not good enough for you, we can settle the matter right here and now.' A fight was the last thing he wanted. But he had to protect Breanne, and he couldn't do it if he allowed men like Gamel to believe him weak.

'It's true,' Breanne offered. 'He's the only one who still ranges beyond Oldwall, all alone, and he's become something of a legend in the Vales.'

'A legend,' Gamel said. 'We don't need any more of those here. We already have your brother fast shaping up into one, and he's yet to live up to the promise.'

'Peace, Gamel,' Wulfwyn said. 'I've not risked my life and fetched people who can help us to have you treat them like this.

140

Show some respect, and save your anger for the Bane.'

Gamel gave a noncommittal grunt and stomped off towards a small gate in the stockade. 'Come, then,' he said over his shoulder, making it sound more like a threat than an invitation.

'Have patience with him,' Wulfwyn said in a low voice. 'These are evil times. Gamel is our chief, and the responsibility he bears for all of us weighs heavy on him. Come. Let's go find Arden.'

Graeme didn't budge. He still had questions for Wulfwyn. 'You said you had Wards.'

She nodded. 'We do.'

'And yet you can cross them as you please, even though you're a Bitten. I'd very much hoped they were better than mine.'

Wulfwyn gave him a small, tight smile. 'They are, Banehunter. They are. I doubt you'll find better Wards anywhere on Baintry. I made them, so you'll forgive me for leaving myself a loophole. And Arden – I've made one for him as well.'

It still didn't answer the question of how she'd been able to walk through his Wards as if they weren't even there, but he left that one for later.

The first thing that hit Graeme when he stepped through the gate was the smell, a mixture of wet loam, wood-smoke, fish, and un-washed bodies – and something else: the reek of fear, fear so old and ingrained it had become a part of these people, oozing from their pores along with their sweat.

He saw crude, wooden huts with bundled reeds for roofs, per-haps thirty of them. There were a few cook fires going, the men and women huddling around them swathed in hides and pelts, studying the newcomers with tired, desperate eyes. To his surprise, he saw children among them. It was amazing: even in the most dreadful of circumstances, nature would not be denied her offspring, whether there looked to be much of a future for them or not.

Following Gamel, Wulfwyn led them to the wall on the southern side of the compound, the side facing landward. Joining the chief on the walkway, they got their first good look at what was happening down below.

There were Rooters down there among the trees and the ruins of what had once been the original village – a lot of them. Three hundred at least, Graeme reckoned. The only other time he'd seen that many in one place had been when Oldwall fell.

The men on the wall were shooting fire arrows at them. A dozen or so had found their mark, and the area was lit by burning Rooters. Two trees had caught fire as well. It was all the light he needed to make out a small group of men gathered at the base of the slope. One of them stood alone, a few steps out to the front, his white shirt a glowing mark in the dark.

It was Arden. He was singing.

*   *   *

A wealth of emotions clutched at Breanne's heart when she caught sight of Arden – recognizing him instantly by his stance and the set of his shoulders – not the least of them worry and fear for his safety.

'What's he doing down there?' she asked Wulfwyn.

'He's singing to the Stricken. He says they listen. He says they're not finished changing.'

Breanne was shocked. 'You mean…' She fell silent. The idea

142

was too much to take in all at once.

'What?' Wulfwyn said.

'It's just... it's just that I never really thought about what happens to people once they're Bitten. I suppose I just assumed they die eventually. But what you just said...'

'Oh. Yes.' Wulfwyn looked grim, and sorrowful. 'What you call the Change is just the beginning. The next step is turning from Bitten to Stricken – or Rooters, as you call them. All those... things you see down there were once people. Arden says he can get them to remember. Though if I were one of them, remembering would be the last thing I'd wish for. But he says it's necessary.'

'How does he know all this?'

'He has magic. Talent. More than anyone I've ever met.'

All at once, Breanne sensed a strange pressure in the air, as if the weather had changed at the drop of a hat. Her ears popped. Time congealed. The world around her oozed to a halt, frozen in an oppressive silence that felt thick as curdled milk.

Then, with a sudden rush, a wave of fear unlike anything she'd ever experienced swept up the slope and came crashing over the wall. Leaving her breathless. Shivering as if all the blood in her veins had been replaced by ice water. Awash in a mindless panic. Drowning. Desperately, she tried to defend against it. And still it continued to rise, until her entire being seemed to have shrunken to a point of pure terror.

Vaguely, she noticed the men around her duck and shift anxiously, murmuring prayers and curses, all of them hard put not to run.

Down below, a Grey Man stepped from the trees, raising its eyeless head and seeming to stare straight at Breanne. Terrifying as the thing's gaze was, she knew instinctively that it wasn't the source of the mind-numbing dread that swirled around her like a cold breath from a crypt. For long moments, the terrifying sensation held them all its sway. Then it slowly receded, withdrawing down the slope, its force spent for the time being.

As if she'd been released from paralysis, Breanne suddenly found air for a deep, gasping breath. Beside her, Graeme raised his bow and sent arrows flying, one, two, three in seamless succession, drawing and releasing faster than the eye could follow. The Grey Man dodged the first one easily, shifting to the left in a quick blur. It managed to avoid the second one as well, again slipping left and straight into the path of the third. That one hit it square in the head – you could hardly call it a face when all it had was a mouth, wide open now, gleaming rows of teeth bared in a silent scream of rage. Squirming, it fell to the ground. A few more jerks, and it went still.

'Dagnabbit!' the man beside Graeme said.

He was old, well over sixty, she guessed. But he looked tough as old leather, and even in circumstances as dire as these there was an irrepressible, humorous twinkle in his deep-set eyes.

'That's a lovely bow you've got there. But, if you don't mind my saying so, you should teach yourself to do it in two. Three's a waste. Though I'll grant you it was along shot, and not the best light or angle either.'

'Two?' Graeme said, a look of disbelief on his face. 'You're joking. What if I miss with the second? It could get me killed.'

'Well, that's the trick now, isn't it? Not to miss with the second.'

'Don't let old Pers mess with your head,' another man said.

Young and plain-faced, he struck Breanne as a friendly, likeable person. 'He's the only one can do it on a good day, and he loves to let everybody know what a fine shot he is.'

'Good day, my arse, Finn,' Pers said. 'I could shoot off your pecker from two hundred yards, and do it so cleanly you wouldn't even miss it until you... oops! Begging your pardon, ladies.'

The fellow called Finn chuckled. Breanne hid a smile. She liked the old man.

'Pers,' Gamel growled. 'You're running at the mouth again, instead of shooting Stricken.'

'Right,' Pers said. 'Sorry, chief.'

Then a second wave hit, many times stronger than the first, and a huge, dark figure stepped out of the woods, a walking hole in the night, roiling with black smoke and shadows.

'Slayer!' someone hissed.

Breanne shuddered. Of a sudden the wall they were standing behind felt flimsy, no thicker than a sheet of parchment. Briefly, she had the weird sensation that the circlet was stirring under her shirt as if it wanted out, but then Gamel said they were leaving.

*   *   *

When the Slayer appeared, Graeme was instantly transported back to a sultry summer evening and a meadow replete with the smell of hay and the insistent chirping of crickets. Next, he was running, the dead, bloodied face of his sister Adelle freshly etched on his mind. And he felt again the creeping horror of the presence that had remained hidden somewhere in the trees that day.

Gripping the rough wood of the rampart so hard it drove splinters into his skin, he dragged himself back to the present. Though he had no name for it, he knew now what the thing down there was. He took an arrow from his quiver, nocked it to the string.

'Forget it,' Pers said. He'd been about to shoot at the Rooters, but now he lowered his bow. 'You can't kill it. You can't even scratch it. Arrows will go right through it, like water through a sieve.'

Graeme didn't doubt that Pers had the truth of it. He looked for another target. With the advent of the Slayer, Arden's song had grown louder, urgent, strained. Finally the men who were down there with him took hold of his arms and dragged him away, clambering back up the slope in headlong flight.

Slowly, deliberately, the Slayer came after them. Behind it, the Rooters started moving as well. Three more Shifters appeared out of the dark woods, ghastly shepherds to the mindless herd following the dark, nightmarish figure. And then a second Slayer materialized out of the night.

'Gods almighty,' Pers whispered. 'Two of them.'

'Sound the alarm!' Gamel barked. 'We're leaving.'

*   *   *

9

Wet and shivering, Breanne sat in the crowded boat beside Graeme. It was their third day on the river, and she felt just about ready to jump into the water and drown herself rather than go through a fourth. Their last meal had been a morsel of fish cooked over a driftwood fire on a lone sandbank in the middle of the river. That had been two days ago. They'd pulled up the boats and rested for less than two hours before Gamel, more anxious than ever, drove them on. He'd spent the whole time pacing up and down the fifty-yard stretch of gravel and rough, wet sand, watching the riverbanks for signs of the Bane.

Groaning, she stood, steadying herself with a hand on Graeme's shoulder. Her backside hurt abominably from three days of sitting on a hard rowing bench. And she'd give just about anything for the rain to stop. And for a safe place to land every so often. She could deal with the other hardships of this voyage, but having to relieve herself over the side of the boat with everybody who cared to watching was not something she'd ever get used to, not in a million years. It was incredibly embarrassing.

Graeme didn't look exactly happy either. But he was here with her, and that was already something to be glad for.

'Go,' he'd said when Finn on Gamel's word had blown three long, haunting blasts on a big aurochs horn that hung from a nail on the rampart. 'I'll meet you down at the boats.'

'I'll hold you to that,' she told him, shouldering her pack. 'Don't make me come back and get you.'

He laughed then, no matter that death was stalking them with a vengeance and the chances of getting everyone down to the boats in time seemed less than slim. As to that, she was in for a surprise.

At the winch she found things well organized and moving along in an orderly fashion, as if the people of Archer's Rock had practiced their getaway many a time and knew exactly what to do. The winchmen were packing women, children and old people into the basket, seven or eight at a time.

When it was full they let it down with dizzying speed, slowing and stopping it at the very last moment. They had a clever device for that, a lever that pressed a grooved and polished block of hardwood to the rope, catching it against another groove in the upright part of the boom. They'd dyed the last few yards of the rope an eye-catching red, and so had a mark that told them when to engage the lever and brake the descent before the basket slammed into the ground two hundred feet below. And winching it up went a lot faster when it was empty.

There were several more ropes dangling over the side. The men and even a few of the young women were going down them one at a time, passing the rope around their shoulders and under a leg and then rappelling down the cliff in leaps and bounds.

Faced with a choice between bad and worse, Breanne took the basket down. She was one of the last, and still Graeme hadn't shown up. Neither had Arden. Down below, most of the boats had already cast off and were crowded together near the mouth of the inlet, ready to push out onto the river.

Breanne waited to the very last.

She was starting to become seriously worried when, after a long pause fraught with sheer unbearable tension, the basket came whizzing down again. Seen from below, it seemed to be dropping from the sky in free fall and looked sure to crash into the ground in a welter of willow, rope and broken bodies. But it stopped just in time, mere inches from the ground, loaded way beyond capacity with those who had fought to the last to cover everyone else's retreat. Graeme was there, Arden, Gamel, Wulfwyn, Finn and old Pers, and Arden's four companions, all of them young men close to his own age. Four of the men who had stayed on the wall hadn't made it back. Another four lost to the Bane.

Moments later, the winchmen came sliding down the free-hanging ropes, pushing themselves off with their feet and descending in great, swinging arcs. All of them together made up the crew of the last and largest boat.

'Do we have any idea where we're going?' she asked Gamel once they were under way, leading of a convoy of twenty-odd boats that drifted silently down the night-dark river. Squinting into the darkness ahead, he adjusting their course with a gentle push on the rudder before answering.

'A bit of one, at least,' he said. 'Pers says he remembers hearing

149

something about a lake, maybe two hundred miles downriver. He also thinks there's an island where we'd be safe from the Bane. But that may be no more than an old man's memory playing tricks on him. It's been a long time since we've had contact with the rest of the world, and longer still since he heard these things. Or didn't.'

'Nothing wrong with my memory,' Pers grumbled, but even he didn't sound entirely convinced.

It was then Graeme remembered he'd brought a map.
Rummaging through his pack, he drew out a rolled-up piece of parchment. Pers struck a light and lit a lantern, shuttering the beam to a tiny thread. Looking over Graeme's shoulder, Breanne followed his finger until he'd found what he said must be Archer's Rock and the river, though neither was marked with a name, and maps in general were hardly exact or reliable. A good ways down the river, she saw a large blotch of blue.

'There is a lake,' Graeme said. 'Mirror Lake, it's called. It's big, if the map isn't lying. But I can't see an island anywhere.'

'Maybe they overlooked it,' Pers said hopefully, 'or forgot to draw it in.'

'Maybe,' Gamel said. 'And maybe we'll be having roast boar and a keg of ale for breakfast. But we'll look all the same, and hope for the best.'

'What if it's not there?' Breanne asked. 'Where do we go then?'

'To the sea,' Gamel said. 'That's where all rivers end up, isn't it? There's bound to be something there the Bane can't reach.'

He's grasping at straws, Breanne thought. *But then, that's all any of us can do. It's what the Bane has brought us to.*

150

Then she remembered something. Something important.

'It's going to be all right,' she told Gamel. 'I had a vision. Three islands, it said. Graeme and Wulfwyn both heard me speak it. And everything else I've foreseen so far has turned out true. We will find you your island, Gamel. A place of succor, calm and removed, the vision said.'

Gamel said nothing, but the look he gave her was thoughtful and might have even held a hint of awe. Arden gave her a smile that seemed to say, *Well done, sister. I knew it too, but they needed to hear it from you.* She gave a start. She was beginning to imagine things.

Someone shouted, jolting her out of her musings. Then panicked screams broke out somewhere behind them.

Gamel brought them about, Finn, Pers, and two of Arden's companions pulling hard on the oars. Graeme was up and had an arrow nocked before they were halfway into the turn. Griff, another of Arden's friends, grabbed a torch and bent down to light it from the lantern.

'Don't,' Graeme said. 'It'll only spoil our night vision.'

By the time they reached the rear end of the convoy it was all over.

They found the last two boats drifting close to the shore. They must have lost their bearings in the dark and strayed off course. Everyone in them was dead: fifteen people, five of them children. It was a horrific carnage. Breanne caught a glimpse and quickly turned away, her stomach trying to climb up her throat.

They fished a lone survivor out of the water, a woman who'd

lived because she'd been thrown overboard in the panic and confusion. She was shocked nearly senseless, grey in the face and shivering from a cold that had little or nothing to do with the water. Grey
Men, they learned from her when she was able to speak again.

The people in the boats had just noticed their mistake and turned
back towards the middle of the river when suddenly the Shifters
were there, an easy jump from the riverbank. She was pushed overboard and went under, swallowing water and nearly drowning. By
the time she found her bearings and resurfaced, the creatures were
already gone, their bloody work finished.

It was a staggering blow, and a terrible loss.
In a single night they'd lost nineteen out of less than a hundred. And
now, to complete their misery, they were faced with an impossible
choice: risk their lives to hastily bed the dead on land, leaving them
for wild beasts or the Bane to rip apart and devour, or dump them in
the river with the possible result of seeing their bodies again in the
morning, floating alongside the boats, bloated and fouling the water
they needed for drinking. The one was out of the question, the other
simply unthinkable.

It was Graeme who offered a solution, one that everyone accepted as the least of all evils. Drifting in a huddle in midstream, they
transferred all of the dead to a single boat. Graeme gave two of his
precious eggs to set it alight.

There was no ceremony, not even a hurried prayer. They had to
move on quickly, before they attracted more of the Bane. There was
no telling how far the Shifters would be willing to jump once the
smell of roasting flesh drove them to a feeding frenzy.

152

They had an extra boat now, a little more room. But Breanne didn't envy those who would spend the rest of the night sitting in the remainder of the hastily cleaned up mess until they had enough light in the morning to give the boat a thorough cleansing and wash away the last of the blood that had belonged to their dead companions.

*   *   *

The last half mile on the river was a nightmare.

It turned slow and sluggish, branching out into several arms that snaked through a maze of small islands, all of them thick with a forest of reeds growing taller than a man's head. If Shifters decided to attack them there, it would be unchecked havoc.

They could come from anywhere, slipping through the reeds and remaining unseen until the moment they jumped and appeared on the boats faster than anyone could react. Graeme and Pers kept arrows nocked anyway, sighting along half-drawn bows and wondering which part of a longish grey blur they should shoot at and hope to do any damage at all.

For a wonder, they didn't have to. Perhaps the ground was too wet for the Grey Men's liking, or maybe they'd lost the spoor, their senses confused by all the water. Whatever the reason, the convoy made it through without incident, until finally the reeds fell away to both sides and they reached the open waters of Mirror Lake.

Ahead of them the sun broke through the clouds for the first time in days, its rays casting a sparkling band of silver across the lake, and a weight lifted from all of their hearts, if only provisionally.

Mirror Lake was indeed a large body of water, large enough for the opposite shore to remain hidden in the distance – or maybe it was the haze that made it seem as if they were drifting out onto an ocean instead of inland waters surrounded and sheltered by forested hills.

Graeme unstrung his bow and took an oar. Arden's friends Raul, Tarr, and Hurn manned the others, and together they sent the boat flying, chasing the silver band across the water until the worst of the last few days' pent-up pressure was released and they settled down to a more sedate and sustainable pace. Gamel steered them south and east, hugging the shoreline but keeping a safe distance all the same. Graeme reckoned that everyone in the boats who wasn't rowing was peering ahead with anxious eyes, silently praying that Breanne's foretelling would prove true.

They passed by several lakeshore villages, all of them abandoned long ago, their only inhabitants ghosts and the Bane. There were watchtowers on some of the hills; deprived of human eyes, they were nothing but blind heaps of stone.

Twice Graeme saw noble lords' keeps sitting on steep-sided bluffs with strategic views over the lake. But they too were deserted, their gates standing open, their roofs and walls beginning to sag under the onslaught of time. Graeme reckoned their occupants might have held out for a while until they were either overrun by the Bane or gave in to the lure of an easier life on some island – provided there was one.

Late in the afternoon, with the lake's far end still hidden in the distance, they did find an island, though not the haven they were seeking.

It was a small thing, a grassy knoll with a stand of trees at one end and just enough space for everyone to find an even bit of ground to bed down on. After four days in the boats it seemed like a small piece of heaven. They found enough dry wood for a couple of fires, and even the fish they caught tasted better than usual.

Graeme had a dream that night, a tortuous struggle that led him nowhere, a balancing act on the edge of dark nothingness where the ground sank away beneath his feet with every step he took. Nothing happened, and yet he was utterly terrified. At the very end, just before he awoke, he caught a glimpse of an old man trudging along ahead. Although his gaunt frame was bowed under a double load of exhaustion and despair, there was also an air of stubbornness and indomitability about him, as if he were sustained by a nobility of the spirit that refused to surrender to anything short of death itself. Too tired to dwell on what the dream might mean, Graeme went back to sleep.

The next time he woke, it was to a clear sky that promised a warm and sunny day. Half an hour later they set out again, their spirits and confidence bolstered by a night spent on solid ground. In the bustle of departure, the last, tenuous threads tying Graeme to his dream came undone. Unnoticed, it drifted away to the place of all things forgotten.

Towards mid-afternoon of that day, they found what they were look-ing for, close to the lake's southern end. At first Graeme thought that the rocky, forested ridge rising steeply out of the water ahead must be a part of the mainland jutting out into the lake. But as they drew closer he saw a wide channel running around the back of it, maybe three hundred yards at its narrowest.

155

Gamel steered a long haul west. When they rounded the point they found a long, sandy beach and behind it a gentle green slope, just a little too high for them to see what lay beyond. A few boats were pulled up on the shore, similar to their own. None of them looked as if they'd been lying there for long. There was also a wooden jetty, weathered but intact.

A man was standing on it, arms crossed, hands hidden in the sleeves of a long, grey robe. Motionless, he watched them approach. If the robe was his and not borrowed or stolen, or salvaged off the corpse of a dead man, then this was a follower of Sulcen the Smith, one of the new gods – 'new' meaning a god who'd been around for something less than a thousand years.

Though Sulcen was said to be the maker of great and terrible weapons and most soldiers counted him their patron god, the Greys were a peaceful lot, the gentlest and most purely spiritual of all the various gods' adherents. Graeme hoped the man's presence was a good sign.

Just before they came into range of a long bowshot Gamel signaled the other boats to stay back. Moments later, their own boat's prow slid onto the sand.

'The lady and the Banehunter with me,' the chief said. 'The rest of you wait here. Spread out a bit, and keep an eye out for trouble. Just because there's only one of them doesn't mean there aren't others waiting where we can't see them.'

Graeme thought Gamel's cautious approach wise. He'd have done the same, though he'd also have sent a man or two to find out what lay beyond that gentle rise. He caught Pers's eye, indicating

156

the slope with a small jerk of his chin. Pers understood, and sauntered off in that direction.

They met the man in grey midway between their landing point and the jetty. The moment Graeme got a good look at his face and eyes, he knew that Gamel's mistrust had been prudent but needless. This was in truth a holy man, welcoming them with a smile that radiated simple, honest joy, and warmth, and an unassuming gentleness that could only stem from a deep love for all creatures suffering through life's manifold trials. Goodness was written in every line of his kind, elderly face.

'Welcome, my friends,' he said. 'I am Brother Ulric. There aren't words to say how much it means to see you safely arrived from whatever ordeals you've come through. The world of the living grows ever smaller, and every soul saved from the Bane is worthy of a joyous celebration. To see you here is to find new hope. Deer Island welcomes you. I daresay it's a trifle crowded with all those who have fled here since the Bane first appeared, but we'll find room for you all the same.'

'Thank you, Brother Ulric,' Breanne said. To Graeme, who was beginning to know her, she looked like she was fighting back tears. 'You're very kind. None of us dared dream of such a lovely welcome. This is Gamel, chief of the people of Archer's Rock. We are all in his debt for delivering us safely to your doorstep. I am Breanne Thorley, from the Vales, and this is Graeme Banehunter, also from the Vales.'

'The Vales,' Ulric said, clearly amazed. 'You've come a very long way, then. I can't begin to imagine how you made it so far through the Bane. But then, if the name Banehunter is anything to go by, I suppose you've chosen the right man for company and have been well protected.'

'I have,' Breanne said, glancing at Graeme with the hint of a blush. 'There's none better than him.'

Graeme was embarrassed, and at a complete loss for words.

Gamel saved him by clearing his throat. 'Begging your pardon, Brother. If it's all right with you, I'd like to let my people know they can come ashore now. They'll all be anxious to get their... to get off the boats.'

'Please,' Ulric said. 'By all means. We saw you coming from quite some way off, and the people of Deer Island have been busy these past two hours preparing a welcoming feast. As I said, every soul saved is worth a celebration. Come, I want to greet all your companions.'

As they walked with Ulric to meet the incoming boats, Graeme cast a sideways glance at Breanne. Her cheeks were still flushed – with joy and relief, he supposed – and she was smiling. She looked radiant when she smiled. Beautiful. There was no other way of putting it.

*　　　*　　　*

That night, Breanne slept in a bed for what felt like the first time in months, though when she thought back to the night she'd confronted Edilda, she realized it had been only eleven days since she'd left Vereldal.

During the welcoming feast, many Deer Islanders had come to offer the refugees from Archer's Rock a place under their roof for the time it would take the newcomers to set up on their own. There had been far more offers than refugees, and no one was left to sleep out in the open.

Ulric himself had taken in Graeme and Breanne, though his cottage on a small rise not far from the landing was barely large enough for one. He'd been adamant that Breanne should have his bed, spreading his blanket on the floor beside Graeme's.

It was still dark when she woke from a disquieting dream. A dream filled with blood and screams and fire and smoke – that was all she could remember. Unable to sleep any longer, she rose, tiptoeing past the sleepers on the floor and out onto the tiny porch. The first, faint shimmer of dawn was just stealing over the eastern horizon and the birds were beginning to stir when she heard the door open and Ulric came to sit beside her on the edge of the porch.

'I love early mornings,' he said, speaking softly so as not to wake Graeme. 'No other time feels so full of possibilities. It's as if the slate had been wiped clean over night and the world were stretching its arms, preparing to start everything anew.'

'That's a beautiful image,' Breanne said, and sighed. 'If only it were so.'

'It's not, is it? But we can still take some of that feeling with us into the day, let it ease our fears and help us face the trials ahead. Though I suspect the path you've chosen – or that has chosen you – is harder than some.'

'I don't know that I had much of a choice. But I suppose I'll see it through, wherever it leads.'

'So you're not staying.' He shook his head. 'No, I didn't think so. Where then will you go from here?'

'I'm not sure. South, in any case. Other than that, I'll follow my visions, and hope they don't lead me astray.'

'Visions.' Ulric went silent for a time.

'Not to pry,' he finally said, 'but provided you feel you can tell me about them, perhaps I could be of help.'

'I'd be grateful,' Breanne said, and found herself recounting everything that had led her to this place and this moment. At some point she made to pull the circlet from under her shirt and show it to Ulric. He stopped her with a gentle hand on her arm.

'No,' he said. 'I don't need to see it. I can feel felt its power, felt it approaching already hours before you arrived here. It's a great and dangerous thing, one that many would wish to possess. The longer it stays hidden, the better. As to your search for the Banesheart – I suppose we can agree that Deer Island must be the first of the three you saw in your vision.'

Breanne nodded. 'It is, I'm sure of it.'

'Good. Then I can tell you this much: if you follow the river Vitherel from where it leaves the lake again, you'll find that it soon turns east towards the coast. Five or six days should see you there. Another day heading south along the coast and there's an island, maybe two or three miles offshore.

'It's called Windward, and not without reason, seeing as it lies straight in the path of most every storm that comes out of the east. It's a barren, comfortless place, but there's still a good chance you'll find someone there, with the Bane having swept everyone it didn't kill off the mainland. I can't say for sure whether Windward is the place you're looking for, but it does seem a logical choice. Storm-tossed and bare. You'd be hard put to find an island that better fits the description.'

'Then that's where I'll go,' Breanne said, noticing how the sky was considerably lighter now and the birds were singing full tilt. 'Thank you, Brother Ulric. Just when I was beginning to feel I'd reached the end of my wits, you've given me hope and a fresh place to start from.'

'See?' Ulric said, and there was a twinkle in his eye. 'Early mornings are always a force to be reckoned with. And now, I daresay it's time for some breakfast.'

That day she talked to Arden, and found him much changed, closer to the Arden of her vision than to the one she'd seen off to the wall on a cold, dark morning nearly a month ago.

He'd kept his gentle nature, that deep, inner force that unerringly urged him to seek harmony and peace and that had made him seem weak in a society where brutal strength and a sure hand at killing were the true mark of a man.

No wonder he could never please Father, she thought. *He's made of altogether different stuff. And no wonder Father tried everything he could think of to break him: in some secret corner of his heart he must have always known that Arden was the better man.*

Other than that, Arden had grown into a man – or more than a man – someone who was filled with a purpose and with amazing courage, and who was sure enough of himself to admit to his doubts as well. There was a lot she had to learn about her little brother, she saw, and a lot she'd missed and would perhaps never understand now that he was moving away from her in giant leaps and bounds.

He and Wulfwyn looked to have become a pair, and she was glad for them both. Treading a path far beyond anything the rest of the world would ever be able to comprehend or even imagine, they were lifelines to each other, a source of strength without which neither of them would have made it beyond the first few precarious steps.

She'd hoped he would come with Graeme and herself, at least for part of the way, but it wasn't to be.

'The Bane is my remit,' he told her, 'the Stricken. When I sing to them, I can feel them straining to hear, and I know I can get them to listen. I almost had them back at Archer's Rock. If not for the Slayers, the beginning would have been made there. I will try again, try as often as it takes until they're ready to break free of their fetters and go forward. My task is to lead them to completion, and I'll see it through to the end. I must.'

Though she remembered herself saying much the same words to Ulric, she was far more worried for Arden than she'd ever been for herself. 'And if you succeed?' she asked, fearful of the answer. 'What then?'

'No wrongs will be righted,' he said, and there was both unbending resolve and heart-wrenching sadness in the look he gave her. 'No crimes undone, no restitution made. The world won't be a better place for it. But perhaps, for a time, it will be a little more... well.'

He left the next morning together with Wulfwyn and his young friends, Griff, Raul, Tarr and Hurn. She and Graeme accompanied them to the lake's southern end, with Ulric steering them to a landing place west of the Vitherel's outflow.

'Be well,' she told them, tears flowing freely. 'Be safe. I want to see all of you again once this is over.'

162

Graeme offered half of his precious eggs. Arden hesitated for a moment. Then he accepted. 'We've not come to wage war on the Stricken,' he said. 'But there are still the Shifters. With them there is no reasoning, no song that can reach them. For the Grey Men, the eggs will do.'

Graeme handed over the eggs and explained their use to the younglings. Then, with a last wave, Arden's party headed off into the woods and was soon lost from sight.

A few more days of rest, and it was their turn to leave.

She and Graeme weren't going alone, though. Pers had been by earlier to say he'd be coming with them. Graeme had refused him at first, but Pers simply wouldn't take no for an answer, said it was so much simpler if they all took the same boat instead him having to follow them in another. He'd hardly left when Finn showed up, announcing that, if Pers was going, so was he. Someone had to look out for the old rascal, he said.

They took the largest boat, the one they'd come in. Gamel had enlisted the help of some islanders and fitted it with a mast, a sail, and a retractable centerboard.

'Might help speed you along on the river,' he said, 'provided there's a favorable wind. And you'll need them for sure once you reach the sea.'

Ulric brought her a farewell present, a bag of soft, supple kidskin. 'For the Key,' he said. 'So it will rest less hard and cold against your skin.'

She thanked him, and wondered how he'd known. It *was* hard, and it never got warm, no matter it was nestled between her body

163

and two layers of clothing.

'I shall cherish my mornings from now on,' she told him, 'and think of you when I do.'

He gave her a wink and a smile, Gamel said, 'Farewell, m'lady' and squeezed her hand until she thought he would break it, and then they were off, cutting across the sun-sparkled waters with Pers and Finn pulling hard on the oars and Graeme at the tiller pointing them south towards the Vitherel, the sea, and a bleak, rocky island that would hopefully offer some sort of answer as to where they should go from there.

*　　*　　*

10

The trip down the Vitherel proved less of a hardship than the first part of the voyage from Archer's Rock. As if the gods had taken pity on them, there was always a sandbank or an islet to spend the night on, and, even more important to Breanne, a place where she could see to her bodily needs in privacy. It was her time of the month, and she wouldn't have hesitated to brave the riverbanks and the Bane if it hadn't been for those conveniently placed bits of dry land.

There was one frightening episode involving a long stretch of white water. The banks were too steep to portage the boat, which in any case would have meant fighting their way through rocky, forested terrain that was in all likelihood infested by the Bane. It left them no other choice but to take their chances on the rapids, and hope they'd somehow scrape through.

It was a breathless, nerve-wracking half hour, but with Pers expertly manning the rudder and Graeme and Finn each using an oar to push them away from the rocks, they did make it through in one piece. Drenched to the skin, they were eventually released onto calmer waters.

On the third day out, Breanne had another vision.

It began with a point of light in the dark, a pinprick that quickly resolved itself into a campfire as she drew close with a dreamer's uncanny speed. A man was sitting beside it. He was neither young nor old, though there was some grey in his black hair and beard, both of which could have used a cut or at the very least the acquaintance of a comb. He looked at her, his sharp gaze seeming to penetrate deep into hidden places. Then he gave her a wide smile, an endearingly mischievous grin she wasn't quite sure could be trusted, and offered her a place by the fire.

That was it. She returned to the here and now, puzzled by what she'd seen. Compared to her other visions, this one seemed so... commonplace. Not terribly significant. She was soon to find out it was anything but.

She never got around to telling Graeme about the vision.

The moment her sight was restored, she saw an obstacle ahead that none of them had reckoned with. They were nearing a town that sprawled over both sides of the river.

Like every other settlement they'd seen so far, it looked abandoned, well on its way to being reclaimed by the surrounding forest. But it wasn't the empty buildings that caused her chest to constrict with a sudden rush of fear, though as they drifted closer she saw dark, gnarled figures standing behind gaping doorways and shattered windows. Rooters, waiting in the shadows for darkness to arrive. It wouldn't be long now. The sun had already dipped behind the hills.

No, the cause of her fear stood right in the middle of a stone bridge that was looming in front of them, three long arches spanning the river: a Shifter, its grey, featureless head turned towards them, the wide, lipless slash of a mouth all it took to convey a sense of ravenous, slavering hunger.

Pers nocked an arrow, the butt of a second already clamped between the last two fingers and heel of his drawing hand, but the Shifter ducked down behind the parapet before he could loose.

Graeme steered them around and back in a wide half circle, Finn rowing hard as they turned against the current.

'Gold marks to fish guts the bugger is going to try and jump us the moment we're close enough to the bridge,' Pers said. 'What do we do now?'

'Two things,' Graeme said, bending down to strike a light. 'For one, we need to pass under that bridge with as much speed as we can manage. So we're going back a ways and taking a run-up. Pers, I want you at the tiller. Head straight for the middle arch. Finn and I will row.'

'But that'll take us right under the damned Grey Man,' Pers protested.

'Right.' Graeme lit the lantern. 'The closer you can steer to where it's hiding, the better.'

'You're the captain.' Pers said dubiously. 'So what's part two of your plan?'

'You'll see. Let's get moving. There's not all that much time left before it gets dark.'

About a hundred yards upstream, they turned again.
Then Graeme and Finn leaned into the oars until the water was frothing white around the bow.

Fifty yards from the bridge, Graeme shipped his oars. 'Keep her going,' he told Finn. He stood, planting his feet wide. Breanne saw he was holding an egg in his hand, the fuse already lit on the lantern's flame.

Twenty-five yards separated them from the bridge when the Shifter reappeared. Though it had no eyes, she knew it was measuring the distance. Two heartbeats, maybe three, and it would jump. Instinctively she drew back, her spine bumping painfully against the tip of the tiller arm.

'Easy there, lass,' Pers said, 'or you'll throw us off course.'

Graeme wound up for the throw. She knew that if he missed, they'd all be dead. Time seemed to slow down almost to a standstill.

The Shifter's outline was just beginning to blur into movement when Graeme's arm flashed forward. Momentarily she saw the egg suspended in mid-air, its fuse glowing brightly.

It struck the Shifter square in the chest, instantly engulfing it in flames. The thing stood tottering for a moment, its grey skin blistering and charring with frightening speed. Then it gave a horrible, high-pitched screech and fell over backwards. She lost sight of it as they passed into the cool, echoing shadows under the bridge, and then they were through, a column of black, oily smoke rising up behind them.

'Blast!' Finn said. 'I got a gob of that shite on my oar. It won't come off.'

'No, it won't,' Graeme said. 'It's Almorican Fire. Once it's stuck to something, all you can do is let it burn itself out. Count yourself lucky. Better a hole in your oar than a hole in your head. We're through, is all that matters.'

Breanne shuddered. She thought there had been an even chance

168

which way the Shifter would fall. It could just as easily have come crashing down on their heads, and... No. She didn't want to think about it.

'You all right, m'lady?' Pers asked. 'You look a bit green around the gills.'

'I'm fine,' she told him. And she was. She was alive and unhurt. A miracle, if you considered the hundreds of miles they'd already traveled through the Bane.

They reached the sea on the evening of the fifth day, just as Ulric had said. Unfortunately, there was nothing off the mainland that might have served as a refuge for the night, not even a large enough rock jutting out of the water.

The wind was up, and dark clouds on the eastern horizon presaged bad weather. Already the waves were alarmingly violent, smacking into their flat-bottomed river craft and drenching them in spray.

'Looks like there's a mother of a storm brewing out there,' Pers said. 'No way we can spend the night on the water.'

'No,' Graeme agreed. 'We'll have to take our chances on land, find a beach where we can pull up and weather it out.'

For half an hour they rowed along a shoreline that seemed to consist of nothing but sharp-edged rocks just waiting to tear their boat to splinters. The wind picked up, the waves growing steadily higher, until they were in imminent danger of getting swamped and capsizing.

It was already full dark when they rounded a point and found a deep, sheltered cove with what looked like a sandy beach. One glance told Breanne they weren't alone. Someone was already there,

169

had a fire going a ways back from the water.

'Blast!' Finn said. 'How could they possibly know we were coming?'

'How could *who* know we were coming?' Breanne asked, thoroughly confused.

'The Bane,' Finn said. 'Who else would it be?'

'I don't think so,' Graeme said. He sounded thoughtful. 'They don't use fire. They hate it. Whatever, we don't have a choice. We're going in. Pers, you might want to have an arrow ready, just in case.'

'And just what do you think I've got nocked to my string, laddie? A carrot?'

'All right then. Let's see what we've got here.'

With Finn giving a few more powerful pulls on the oars, Graeme steered them towards the shore until, with a lurch, the bottom of the boat ground up onto sand. Another, smaller craft was pulled up a few yards away. Drawing his sword, Graeme stepped onto the beach, Pers and Finn right behind him. Both of them had arrows nocked and their bows half drawn. Not knowing what else to do, Breanne climbed out of the boat and followed their dark silhouettes towards the flickering fire.

There was a man sitting beside it, she saw as she drew nearer, plodding through the deep, loose sand. There were streaks of silver in his unkempt beard and longish black hair, and he studied them with eyes that were sharp and penetrating. It was the same man she'd seen in her vision.

'About time,' he said. 'I expected you earlier.'

170

Graeme looked grim, prepared for violence.

'Who are you?' he asked, his voice hard. 'And what do you want from us?'

'I'm Torgrim of Eldinga. And I'm here because I thought it would make sense for us to meet.'

'How did you know we were coming?'

'Well now, that's an interesting question. In truth, I had no idea who was going to show up here. Let's just say I knew someone was coming, or rather some*thing*. Though things don't usually travel on their own. And as to the how: the object in question' – he gave each of them a searching look, his gaze coming to rest on Breanne – 'the one the young lady is carrying under her shirt, to be precise, is sort of hard to overlook for someone like me. I've felt it coming for days. That's why I interrupted my voyage and have been sitting here twiddling my thumbs for a day and a half.'

'What is that supposed that mean?' Breanne said. 'Someone like you?'

The man Torgrim was still looking at her with those unsettling eyes of his.

'Someone with a nose for Talent, you might say. Someone with a few tricks up his sleeve that might prove helpful to people headed south with a Key. But why don't you all put away those pointy implements and have a seat. With that storm brewing out there, none of us is going anywhere soon.'

'I think not,' Graeme said, his tone still no friendlier. 'How do we know we can trust you? You could be anyone, come here to lull us with lies and steal what's not yours. Which is not saying there is anything worth stealing.'

'Oh, but there is. And let me be blunt. If I wanted it, I'd take it from you, and there'd be nothing you could do about it, believe me.'

For a moment there, Breanne almost did believe him. Maybe it was the firelight's jumping shadows, or maybe just her imagination, but of a sudden Torgrim appeared large and threatening as if a dark, ruthless god were seated before them. Then he gave a sigh and seemed to shrink back to his normal size.

'But don't worry. I don't want it. I know my limits as well as the next man. Better, I daresay. Put power and power together, and things can get out of hand faster than you can say "Whoops! That's not what I intended."'

'How do we know you're who you say you are?' Finn butted in. 'If you're really one of them magickers, then why don't you go ahead and give us a little demonstration?'

'Hedge-wizards' tricks,' Pers snorted. 'What's that supposed to prove?'

'Nothing,' Torgrim said, sounding annoyed. 'And I don't do demonstrations. They're a needless waste of energy. But how about this: I'm trusting you people not to be complete, barking fools, even though I find you strolling through the Bane like you were on a feast-day outing. So perhaps you can find it within yourselves to return the favor and give me some credit.'

Although he'd just said he didn't do demonstrations, Breanne felt power gathering around him. 'Don't,' she said. 'It's not necessary.' She turned to Graeme. 'I saw him in a vision not two days ago. I think we were meant to meet.'

Graeme looked at her, raised an eyebrow, then slid his sword back into the sheath. 'Lady Breanne Thorley,' he told Torgrim, 'from the Vales. Pers and Finn from Archer's Rock. I'm Graeme Banehunter. I believe an explanation would be in order.'

Torgrim was just about to respond when suddenly the sand all around them erupted. In a trice, the whole beach came alive, and Breanne saw hundreds, no, thousands of small crabs scuttling towards the dark sea, tumbling and climbing over each other in their haste to reach the water.

'Sorry,' Torgrim said, grinning exactly like he'd done in Breanne's vision, his teeth shining white in the dark. 'The little buggers were just raring to go. Once I gave them a nudge, there was no more stopping them. Doesn't matter. One night ahead of schedule isn't going to hurt them. Where were we?'

'An explanation,' Graeme reminded him.

'An explanation. Right. But only if you sit. I can't stand it when people loom.'

*   *   *

Graeme still wasn't convinced.

But the thing with the crabs had him thinking. This Torgrim fellow might be more than a simple hedge wizard. So he'd give the man the benefit of the doubt and listen to what he had to say. And to be honest, the idea of having the help of someone versed in the Talent was more than tempting.

'Where to begin?' Torgrim mused. 'I assume you've heard of the Battle of Simbalan?'

Graeme shook his head. 'No. What about it?'

'It was in the autumn of the year of the two comets, which would make it, let me see… twenty-one years ago. It – '

'Less than a year before the Bane reached Oldwall,' Graeme interrupted. 'No wonder we know nothing about it. The Barbary King has kept the Vales cut off from the rest of the world since that time. Perhaps they had news of it in the east. If so, it never reached us in Longvale.'

'Well then.' Torgrim absently scratched his beard. 'It's a long story, and I'll save it for another time – except for a few facts that I think are relevant to the situation here on Baintry.

'We fought against the Dark Side on the high plains of Simbalan, against an army of sorcerers and their monstrous creations, the likes of which the world had never seen before and hopefully never will again. We – that was a coalition of the western kingdoms and the Empire, led by the mages of the Incantaria. I was one of them, and one of only five who survived to see the forces of darkness defeated.

'But one of us was a traitor who'd been secretly working for the other side for years. I'd caught on to him, was convinced he'd gone bad, but I hadn't yet managed to find definitive proof of his betrayal. He must have realized I was hard on his heels, for towards the end of the battle he simply disappeared, perhaps hoping he'd be counted among the twenty thousand dead littering the field that last day alone. And in fact the other three, Elwyn of Woodsbury, Orsen Burnthands and Gisbert the Good, believed it was so.

'I didn't, and went after him as soon as I could. I was able to track him to Fellmere, the Dark Side's stronghold in Tothmar, and from there to the port of Rannon. For weeks I hung about the place, trying to find out where he'd gone from there. It was no fun, I can tell you that much. Rannon is a cesspit of humanity, one that attracts every sort of lowlife under the sun: slavers, drunks, beggars, whores, sellswords, cutthroats, cardsharps, pickpockets – you name it, they've got it.

'Any road, I finally found a dockhand who thought he might have seen a man fitting the description embark on a ship bound for Enemathea, across the Southern Sea. So that's where I went next. But, as it turned out, the man I was looking for wasn't there. To make a long story short, I was eventually forced to give up the search and concern myself with other, more pressing matters.

'Ever since, I've kept an ear to the ground. Sooner or later, I knew, he was bound to do something that would cause some sort of ripples and put him back in my sights. Unfortunately, it wasn't until last year that I heard of the strange plague that had overrun Marillin, and then it still took me a while to realize that it might be connected to the traitor. As soon as the winter storms were over, I sailed to Cumbre on Eastvale's coast. Since no one was prepared to take me south, I bought a boat – and here I am.'

There was a moment's silence, the rest of them struggling with the implications of what Torgrim had just told them.

'So you're saying your traitor might have something to do with the Bane?' Graeme asked, though he had trouble grasping the idea of any man being so utterly steeped in madness and evil that he'd unleash a thing like the Bane.

'If it's really him, then yes.'

Torgrim looked troubled now, and Graeme thought he was beginning to see the real man behind the enigmatic air he'd greeted them with.

'It's possible. But whatever the cause, I reckon it's high time someone put an end to this thing. That's where I believe we can help each other out. Because I'm pretty sure you're not risking your lives to travel through the Bane with a Key in your baggage just for the fun of it. Please correct me if I'm wrong.'

'You're not,' Breanne said, surprising Graeme. 'We do have a Key, and we're looking to close some kind of door with it. At least that's what my visions have told me to do.'

'Dear, fumbling gods!' Torgrim smacked a palm against his forehead. 'A door! Of course. I should have seen it.'

'Seen what?' Graeme asked. 'You're speaking in riddles. Perhaps you'd care to enlighten us.'

'Sorry,' Torgrim said. 'It's just that it's so obvious, once you think of it that way. The door you're looking for. There's only one thing it can be: an extremely rare phenomenon called a Gate, something like an irregularity or a hole in the fabric of the All.

'You could say it's like a small piece of non-space and non-time intruding into space and time as we know them, creating a locus where two different worlds may touch, notwithstanding the fact that in reality they're infinitely far removed from one another. I know it sounds crazy, and honestly, I haven't begun to figure out how it works. But I do know of one other Gate, and that one I've seen, and been through it.'

'So you think the door we're looking for is such a... Gate,' Breanne said.

'It must be. From everything I've heard about the Bane, there's no other way such a plague could have come into existence. There's no living mage or sorcerer with the power to create its likes, and certainly not in so short a time, and most certainly not Keon the

Traitor – if he's the one behind this. His strength has always lain in manipulation rather than in creation.'

Graeme had noticed Breanne studying Torgrim intently all this time. Suddenly she did something as unexpected as it was dangerous. Tugging loose the strings of her jerkin and shirt, she fished out the bag containing the Key. Without a moment's hesitation she took the circlet out of the bag and offered it to Torgrim.

'You take it,' she said.

If Graeme had still harbored doubts about the man, they were laid to rest now.

'Put it away, lass,' Torgrim said. 'I'll forgive you for trying to tempt me because I know how badly you want reassurance. But you might as well be asking me to step over onto the Dark Side. Luckily for all of us, I have no desire at all to rule the world – and, whether I wanted it or not, that's what might very well happen if I joined my power to the Key's.'

'I'm sorry,' Breanne said. 'But you can see it had to be done. Now I know I can trust you.'

She didn't look sorry at all, Graeme thought. She looked… satisfied. And well she should be. She'd just put to the test the one man who could be an invaluable ally, and he'd passed with flying colors.

A short while later the storm struck.

They sheltered under the overturned boats, pulled far up onto the beach where they were out of reach of the waves if not of the cold wind. Graeme ended up lying beside Breanne, their bodies touching

177

from shoulder to thigh, the warmth of her comforting and at the same time highly unsettling. Given the circumstances, sleep was a long time finding him, so he tried to concentrate instead on the following day and what might await them on Windward, though without much success.

*   *   *

11

Breanne opened her eyes to a clear and sunny morning.

Only the moist sand and a dark line of debris and seaweed washed high up onto the beach reminded of last night's storm. Beyond it, the sunlight danced on pacified waves and the sky shone with a deep, freshly scrubbed blue.

With a twinge of guilt she saw that everyone else was already up and busy. Somehow they must have lifted and moved the boat without waking her. It now lay down by the water's edge, mast and sail rigged, ready to go. She saw no sign of Torgrim or his boat. Graeme wasn't there either. There was a cold wind blowing off the sea, and she felt no great desire to leave her warm nest of blankets. The sight of a small fire and the smell of feshly brewed kaf got her going all the same, with Finn and Pers falling over each other to offer her a seat and breakfast. She'd never known a maid back in Thorhold who was half as attentive, she thought with a smile. Though with these two in the house there had better not be anything breakable left lying around.

'Where's Graeme?' she asked. 'And Torgrim? Has he left already?'

'Graeme's gone a ways into the dunes,' Pers said. 'To make sure there's no nasties hiding out back there. Though seeing as it's broad daylight, I reckon he might have just wanted to take a... er, to have a moment to himself.'

'And Torgrim's gone on ahead,' Finn offered. 'Said he'd meet us on Windward, in a place called Colton's Bones. Not that I like the sound of it. Any rate, he's sure got himself a mighty fine little boat. Took off like a shot, though he didn't even look to be touching the tiller.'

'That's them mages for you,' Pers said darkly. 'Making things go their way and leaving us poor sods to sweat it as best we can.'

'He'll have his reasons.' It was Graeme, back from the dunes. 'But he seems to have left us with a nice northerly, so I reckon we'd best get going while we can still make some use of it.'

Around midday they caught their first sight of Windward.

As yet it was just a dark smear on the horizon, and even with a favorable wind it took them the rest of the day to get there. It was big, Breanne realized as they drew closer, much bigger than the storm-tossed rock she'd imagined. And it wasn't all that barren either. Though there wasn't a single tree, she saw green, grassy flanks dotted with grazing sheep, and small, stone houses sheltering behind bluffs or tucked into folds of the terrain where the wind was perhaps less likely to blow them away.

There was even a town and a harbor, safe in the lee of a tall cliff maybe three miles along the western shore. It was an unexpected sight after the the empty villages and ghost towns inside the Bane. She saw people on the docks, fishermen, dockhands and sailors

180

going about their work as if the Bane didn't exist and all was well with the world. There were even ships in the harbor, two of them. Though she knew nothing about ocean-going vessels, to her they looked sleek and fast, and smaller than she'd have thought they'd need to be to brave the open sea in a storm like last night's.

But, despite the appearance of normalcy prevailing on Windward, it felt as if there were something dark and heavy hanging over the island. It didn't strike her as a place where one should expect a cordial greeting, or smiles, or laughter.

Colton's Bones wasn't the name of the town, it turned out – that was called Old Harbor – but of a waterfront tavern that looked to Breanne as if it was a good place to get your purse stolen or your throat cut. They found Torgrim inside, deep in conversation with a dark-haired woman in her mid-thirties who looked tough as nails and, Breanne guessed, was able to hold her own against most any man.

She seemed to be doing pretty well with Torgrim, to judge by a round dozen empty tankards sitting on the table in front of them, but somehow Breanne had a feeling the woman had found her match in the mage: her cheeks were flushed, her light blue eyes looked slightly glassy, and when she saw them come in she set her mug down overly hard as if the tabletop had unexpectedly risen to meet it. Torgrim, on the other hand, looked fresh as a daisy.

'Ah, here they are,' he said. 'Mistress Goderun, allow me to present Lady Breanne Thorley and Graeme Banehunter of the Vales, and Pers and Finn from Archer's Rock. And this, my friends, is the honorable Captain Goderun Spray, mistress of the good ship *Goldspray*. Sit, all of you. The ale is drinkable, and word has it they're

181

serving lamb stew for dinner tonight.'

Six mugs down or no, the glance the captain threw Breanne was shrewd and alert. She was quite handsome in a weather-beaten way, and exceedingly well built, Breanne noted, feeling a small jolt of jealousy when she saw the look Goderun gave Graeme. It was unashamedly interested, the sort of look that didn't require any great skill at reading women to be understood for what it was – an open invitation. Breanne knew it well enough: in Thorhold she'd observed it many a time in the eyes of certain maids and serving girls of doubtful reputation. She was relieved to see that Graeme didn't seem to notice how he was being sized up.

He'd been quieter than usual these last few days, wrapped up in some private preoccupation she didn't feel entitled to intrude upon. Sitting there watching him, she was overcome by a vision of sorts – though it was different from the others in that, this time, she didn't go blind. Instead she saw ghostly images overlaying reality like wraiths strayed too far from Amut's realm of shades: the face of a young boy, undoubtedly Graeme's at that age, dirt-streaked, haunted, desperate; and another face, again a young boy, but definitely not Graeme. The two melted into one, then they parted and became distinct again before being replaced by a third face, that of an old man, etched with deep lines of exhaustion and worry that turned into a landscape of stark mountains and steep-sided gorges, a jumbled relief of cuts and rises as she imagined things would appear if seen through the eyes of a bird in flight.

Abruptly the images vanished, leaving her with a feeling of urgency she couldn't explain, and with a strong wish to tell Graeme what she'd seen. But now wasn't the time. With a start, she realized she'd already missed a good part of the conversation.

'… a village on Marillin's southern coast,' Torgrim was saying. 'From what she's told me, it could be the place we're looking for.' He gave Breanne a warning look and a slight shake of the head, which she interpreted as meaning it was better not to mention her visions.

'Aye,' Goderun said, with no sign of slurring her words. 'If you all are looking for trouble – and from what Master Torgrim says it would seem that you are – then Salt would be the place to go.' She pronounced the name as if it were a curse, making the sign of Elil as she said it.

'Though as to how you'd get there, or if you'd get there at all, that's another question. Not in a flimsy riverboat, that's for sure. South of here the coast turns ugly, a maze of shoals and reefs and nasty currents that can pull you and your ship under as easily as if you were sailing on nothing but a sodden piece of driftwood. And still farther south, beyond Point Blank… Suffice to say that nobody in their right mind would even think of going there.' She took a deep draught from her mug as if to wash away a bad taste.

'Apparently there's a ghost ship cruising those waters,' Torgrim explained when Goderun didn't elaborate further. 'The captain is said to be a demon, a creature of smoke and shadows that commands a crew of drowned men brought back from the Deep by the darkest of magicks. As Mistress Goderun tells it, ships that sail south past Point Blank tend not to return, and only one man ever survived to account for what supposedly goes on down there. He was found drifting on a northerly current, mad as you will, clinging to a broken

183

spar so tightly they had to pull it out of the water along with him. Try as they might, they couldn't prise his fingers away from the wood, and it seems that when he died a short time later he was still holding on to it.'

'True enough,' Goderun said. 'I happened to be on Windward when they buried him. Held on to the thing even in death, he did, which made for a mighty strange-looking grave. They had to dig it in the shape of a cross, so's they could fit him and his spar in the ground together.'

But Breanne wasn't interested in burials, strange as they might be. 'This Salt place,' she asked Goderun, 'is it an island?'

'I wouldn't know, dearie,' Goderun said, her tone dismissive. 'Seeing as I've never felt inclined to go there and get myself killed.'

'That's "my lady" to you, captain,' Breanne said firmly. She was done allowing people to ignore or belittle her, and especially not this swaggering maneater who thought she could behave however she pleased with Graeme. 'And I'm not asking out of idle curiosity. It's something I need to know.'

'Well, *my lady,*' Goderun said, leaning back in her chair with an insolent air. 'Curiosity or need, it makes no matter. I still don't have an answer for you.'

She let her eyes wander to Breanne's left, to where Graeme was sitting. Unable to stop herself, she followed Goderun's gaze, curious to see how he'd react to the woman's lascivious stare. Not at all, she noted with satisfaction. He seemed lost in thought, as if he hadn't been paying much attention to what was going on around him. When she looked back to Goderun, the insufferable woman gave her a slow wink. Beside her, Torgrim looked like he was trying hard not to smile. Pers was studying the ceiling, whistling tonelessly. Even the landlord, come with another round of drinks, looked amused. Mortified, Breanne felt color creep into her cheeks.

'Graeme,' she said quickly. 'Why don't we have a look at your map.'

'What?' He *had* been somewhere else. But not daydreaming – not by that troubled look he wasn't quite quick enough to hide.

'The map. We need to see if there's an island near this Salt place.'

'Right.' He dug the map from his pack and spread it out on the table, weighing the corners down with empty mugs. 'There,' he said after a moment's searching. 'There's Salt. And there is an island, right off the coast. It's called Haunt. But that still doesn't tell us whether it's the place we're looking for.'

'Well, now,' the landlord said, leaning forward and resting a meaty hand on the table. He was a bald, unhurried fellow whose enormous paunch betrayed a fondness for his own food and ale.

'Though I can't begin to imagine what you'd want with a place like that, I can tell you a story about Haunt that might make you think twice whether you really want to go there.'

He looked around to make sure he had everyone's attention.

A story-teller, Breanne thought. *Hopefully not the long-winded kind who talks mainly because he's in love with the sound of his own voice.*

'Please,' Torgrim said. 'We're all ears.'

'It's but an old tale, mind you,' the landlord commenced. 'My grandmum was from Salt, you see, and she used to tell it to me when

185

I was still a wee bairn: the story of Uthric Redhands, the last lord of Haunt. Now, you have to know that this was many, many years ago, in the dark times when King Josrin fought against the Barbarians and built the great wall to keep them out of Marillin...'

Where in his grandmum's time there were only tumbled stones and jagged ruins left, the landlord said, once a mighty fortress had crowned Haunt's black, guano-streaked cliffs, rising out of the dark water like a threatening fist: Stormhold, seat of Uthric Redhands, a lord by birth and a pirate by calling. Five hundred years ago he'd burned and plundered his way up and down the coast, not even sparing Salt, his own fiefdom.

But piracy was just the half of it, if legend was to be believed. By all accounts he'd been something far worse than just a simple robber, rapist and murderer. A follower of the Dark Side, Redhands was, a wielder of black and fearsome magicks who carried the fairest maidens off to his island lair and fed his dark obsessions on their virgin blood.

Only when King Josrin the Good ascended the throne of Marillin did Uthric's fortunes turn. Not three weeks after his coronation, Josrin arrived in strength, and in one fell day his fleet sent every last one of Uthric's red-sailed ships to the Deep, drowned with all hands.

But when the king set foot on Haunt Island, prepared to take the keep by storm and put an end to Uthric and his evil ways, he found the gates open and the villain and Stormhold's entire garrison dead, killed by some unspeakable horror the lord of Haunt had tried to raise as a last defense.

Deeply disturbed by what he'd seen that day, the king swore all

186

those present to life-long secrecy. Then he declared the island sealed and out of bounds, and that was the end of the story, as far as history was concerned.

But in Salt's collective memory some part of it lived on, a disquieting intimation of nameless danger that echoed in the cryptic mutterings of the very old, in warning tales of naughty children spirited away by Redhands' ghost and sometimes in leaden, sweat-soaked nightmares, stirring the Deep and sending disquieting ripples along the surface of otherwise becalmed waters.

It was a lengthy story the way the landlord told it, but not long-winded, at least not to Breanne. Towards the end, when he spoke of Uthric's death at the hands of a terrible demon the black-hearted villain had supposedly summoned as a last defense against Josrin's army, she felt a thrill of excitement. Could the thing Redhands had evoked have been a precursor of the Bane? Could Haunt be the place where it had all started?

She noticed Torgrim sitting up straight, his attention focused on the landlord as if he might draw more information out of the man by the intensity of his gaze alone. She remembered what he'd said about doors to other worlds, and suddenly she felt sure that Haunt was the third island of her vision.

*   *   *

Graeme was finding it hard to concentrate on the conversation – which was perhaps why he retained no clear memory of how Torgrim managed to convince Goderun that she should take them to Point Blank on her ship *Goldspray*.

Step by nearly imperceptible step, Breanne told him later, although she didn't seem all that clear about how Torgrim had done it either. As far as she was able to say, he hadn't begged or threatened but merely shined a very advantageous and enticing light on certain courses of action while making others appear fraught with danger and disgrace. She reckoned that, without actually manipulating Goderun in any appreciable way, he must have employed some sort of subtle magery to end up with all of them, the captain included, nodding in mute agreement and seeing things his way – which was entirely back to front, once you got a chance to think about it away from the charmed circle he'd somehow managed to draw around them at the table in *Colton's Bones*.

Though Goderun must have had some serious second thoughts as well, she proved to be a woman of her word and stuck by the bargain she'd made. And perhaps the two fat purses Torgrim produced from some hitherto hidden pockets of his cloak were also to blame for the fact that the captain went against what must have been her every seamanly instinct for survival.

But most of this passed Graeme by at the time, caught up as he was in his own private darkness, trapped in the clinging residue of a dream he'd had the night before after he'd finally managed to find his way into sleep back on the storm-tossed beach with the wind howling around the upturned boat and Breanne already fast asleep beside him.

In the dream he saw his sister Adelle again as she'd lain there with her face bloodied and the light gone out of her eyes, back when the horror had begun. But the Adelle he saw now wasn't where she was supposed to be, not on a meadow filled with cricket-song and the fragrance of hay and pine sap. Instead she lay on sheets of precious linen so badly stained with blood they appeared more red than white, her lifeless limbs sprawled over a big four-poster bed in a room that looked like it belonged in a rich man's home or a castle. Then Pa was yelling at him again, telling him to run, run, run – only it wasn't Pa, but an old man who seemed strangely familiar, though, try as he might, Graeme couldn't put a name to his face.

He awoke in a sweat, shaken to the core.

When the storm died down and the eastern horizon began to lighten he crawled out from under the boat and went to sit on a rock by the water, oblivious of the waves still breaking with enough force to run far up the shore and soak right through his boots. He spent the time until the others began to stir struggling to set things right, trying in his mind's eye to put Adelle back on the meadow, and to give Pa his own face again.

It didn't work. As if his memory had turned a page it wasn't prepared to flip back even for a quick glimpse, Adelle was now inextricably linked with those blood-stained sheets, and Pa refused to become Pa again. And everything else – Ivan, Jerrod, his mother and grandmother, the farm – all of it crumbled and faded as if it had never existed, and with it the very ground under his feet seemed to fall away, exposing a dark, yawning chasm that threatened to swallow him whole.

Breanne's hand on his, warm and soft and somehow comforting, brought him back to *Colton's Bones* and a steaming bowl of stew sitting on the table in front of him. She looked to be the only one paying him any attention, the others attacking their food and drink with a vengeance and laughing over some funny story Pers was telling.

'Graeme,' she said. 'You should eat. You must be starved.'

There was genuine concern in the look she gave him. That, and a soft pressure from her fingers before she withdrew her hand, suddenly made him want to be fully in the present again – and to hell with a past that had nothing to offer except uncertainty and pain. Belatedly registering the delicious smell rising from the stew, he found that he was ravenously hungry.

'Thank you, my lady,' he said, feeling awkward for not having more and better words to explain himself. She seemed to understand all the same.

'Graeme, please. It's Breanne. We've been through too much together to continue dragging along something that belongs in another place and time.' She lowered her voice so only he could hear. 'I only said what I did to Goderun earlier because she was... well, talking down to me.'

She paused, then seemed to make up her mind. 'There's something I should tell you, something I've seen. But you have to promise me you won't go wandering off again. I need you to be here with me.'

'I won't, I promise. Whatever it is, I'll try and face up to it like a man.' He managed a smile, and got one in return.

'All right. Just after we got here, I had a vision of sorts. I was looking at you, and then I saw other faces superimposed over yours. The first was you as a boy, I'm sure of it. It must have been around the time you lost... the time you were forced to flee to the Vales. There was a fresh cut under your left eye, right where you still have the scar.'

'Don't know how I got that,' Graeme said, though he saw a sudden flash of something bright and sharp, gone in an instant.

'The second was another boy, the same age as you, blond and a little chubby – '

'Tobin,' Graeme blurted, surprising even himself. 'Sorry,' he said. 'I've no idea where that just came from.'

'Don't be. I think what's been bothering you these past few days is something that wants to be remembered. Something that will out, or else keep you from the fullness of what you can be – perhaps even harm you in some way if it's not acknowledged.'

Like a rock dropped into the unseen depths of a murky pool, Breanne's words stirred up something dark and violent in Graeme, filling him with a sudden, inexplicable rage. He felt his fingers curl, as if, left to themselves, they would have liked nothing better than to clamp themselves around Breanne's throat and strangle her before she could utter more of her dangerous, corrosive lies.

At the same time, another part of him felt something entirely different for her: attraction, plain and simple, so strong it stirred his loins and set his heart stumbling for a few beats.

For an instant it was sheer madness. He felt torn down the middle, split in two, as if a dark twin had appeared from where it had been hiding behind the person he'd always thought of as himself. Forcefully, he wrenched himself away from both emotions and onto what he took for neutral ground – though the move cost him dearly and he knew right away it had gained him no more than a momentary semblance of relief.

Letting go the anger was by far the easier part. But the other was no option either, and had to go as well. She was a highborn lady, no matter what she said, and he a commoner, a loner and an outcast, a man her father would gladly kill if he could lay hands on him.

Enough, he told himself. *You promised her you'd take it like a man, so pull yourself together and act like one.*

But he remained shaken by the strength of what he'd just felt, appalled and frightened as much by what he'd recognized in himself as by what he'd lost.

'What?' Breanne gave him a searching look. She looked alarmed, as if she'd sensed something of what was going on inside him.

'Nothing. You said there were three faces.'

'Three, yes. The third was an old man, too old to be your father, I'd say. Could he have been your grandfather, perhaps?'

'I doubt it. I never knew him. He died before I was born. But tell me, what did he look like, this old man?'

Breanne closed her eyes as if to better recall the image. 'White hair, cut very short,' she said after a moment's thought. 'No beard. A large nose. And he looked kind, like a man noble of heart and spirit. Yes, a good man, I'd say.' She opened her eyes and looked at Graeme expectantly.

'This is passing strange,' he said. 'Twice I've dreamed of this man, and each time I thought I knew him. Even now I seem to have his name on the tip of my tongue. It just won't out.'

'Not yet, perhaps. But given time, I'm sure you'll remember. Be patient with yourself. And if there's anything I can do to help, and be it just to listen, I'll do it gladly, no need to even ask.'

'Thank you.' Graeme felt a sudden, overwhelming urge to take

192

her in his arms. Instead, he chose the only other course that presented itself, making light of the situation. 'You may come to regret the offer, once you get me started. I'm very good at rambling, though I usually indulge in it with only myself for an audience.'

To his surprise, she took his words seriously. 'Then it's high time you had someone else to talk to. I know how it is to keep too much of your own company and too little of anyone else's. It's not good for a person.'

They were set to sail for Point Blank the following morning, but at the last moment there was an unexpected delay. They were just finishing up an early breakfast when a dockhand came with a message from Goderun, begging their pardon for having forgotten to mention that she had a prior commitment, a quick run down the coast that would see her back in under a week.

'Darn!' Pers said, rubbing his sleeve over a grimy bull's eye pane to get a better view of the harbor. 'She's backing out on us.' He peered through the cleared spot. '*Goldspray's* gone, and so's the other ship. Now what?'

'I don't think we need to worry,' Torgrim said. 'I'm sure she'll be back and hold up her end of the bargain. But, as they say, you can't make a silk purse from a sow's ear. She is what she is, and no matter how much we pay her she'll never pass up an opportunity to make a quick killing.'

'Seeing as Windward doesn't seem to have much to offer except sheep and fish,' Graeme mused, 'I wonder what kind of cargo could be valuable enough to make her take off in such a hurry.'

'Someone else's,' Torgrim said drily.

Graeme wasn't surprised. He'd suspected as much. The others took a moment to grasp the import of Torgrim's words.

Breanne gave a small gasp. 'You mean, you bought us passage with a pirate?'

'Yup.' Torgrim grinned. 'But I wouldn't go calling her that to her face if I were you.'

'How could you? Who's to say she won't rob and murder us the moment we're out to sea?' She was clearly upset with him.

'She won't,' Torgrim said mildly. 'Mistress Spray is an honorable pirate.'

'Your word in the gods' ears.' Breanne didn't look much mollified. 'I'll have you know I'm not happy to find out you knew about this all along, and didn't see fit to tell us. How did you know, by the way?'

'Easy. She's got a very fast ship, and twice the crew she needs to sail it. Put that together with the fact that Windward has always been a haven for smugglers and the like, and the upshot practically jumps in your face. But trust me, we'll be safe with her.'

'I think he's right,' Graeme said, surprising himself by laying a comforting hand on Breanne's shoulder. 'I have a feeling Goderun is on the level as far as we're concerned.'

Breanne tilted her head to the side a fraction, an endearing hint of a move that brought her cheek closer to Graeme's hand and sent a small thrill through him. But the next moment she confused him entirely by turning to study him with a mistrustful look, as if he'd said something wrong. He let it go.

He'd been getting good at that lately, at letting things go, though he wasn't sure he wanted to make a habit of it. It felt too much like giving up, and that would never a part of him, no matter who or what he was, or wasn't.

Looking back, the days they spent waiting for the *Goldspray's* return seemed like a last reprieve to Graeme. Since they'd be staying long enough to warrant the move, they took rooms in an inn a few houses down and several grades up from *Colton's Bones*.

Breanne spent most of her time either having the maids haul endless pails of hot water and taking hours-long baths, or visiting a seamstress she'd found near the inn, armed with a purse she'd gotten from Torgrim – who seemed to have an interminable supply of the stuff – and determined to have at least one proper dress made by the time they left. Though what she needed a dress for where they were going, Graeme couldn't begin to imagine. He thought she looked just fine in her frayed shirt and scuffed leathers, a girl you could steal horses with.

Torgrim was gone for most of the time, roaming the island in search of gold, he said, which turned out to be nuggets of valuable information he claimed could be gleaned from local lore and old folks' tales.

Finn had taken a shine to one of *Colton's Bones'* kitchen maids and could be reliably found at all hours in one of three places: dicing in the common room, hanging about the kitchen, or having a good time in the girl's tiny room under the tavern's eaves. Pers struck up a friendship of sorts with one of the fishermen down on the wharf, where he kept himself busy angling their evening meals and gossiping with the locals.

Graeme went for long hikes, once or twice with Breanne but

mostly alone, and he found that exploring the island was a perfect antidote against brooding, that losing himself in the rhythm of walking and in new and unfamiliar sights was far healthier than falling back into a vicious circle of questions to which he had no answers in any case. Not yet, at least. If he was supposed to have them, he reckoned, they'd come to him in their own good time. Until then, he was done driving himself crazy.

Goderun did return, a day earlier than anticipated and ready to make good on their deal. Her left hand was wrapped in a bandage and she walked with a slight limp, but otherwise she seemed in high spirits. Whatever she'd been up to had obviously gone well.

The day after she arrived, they left for Point Blank on the morning tide, the *Goldspray's* sails swelled with a stiff northerly, her slender bow cutting through the waves as elegantly as the school of dolphins that shared her course for the first half hour of the journey.

It was a beautiful morning, and when Breanne came to join Graeme at the railing and share the majestic spectacle of the sea in silence it became perfect – or would have been, had they been headed for any other destination than the one they'd chosen. As it was, the sun, the wind and the waves, the slow roll of the ship, the tang of salt in the air and the cool droplets of spray on their skins seemed like a precious and perishable gift to Graeme, a last, excessive unfolding of nature's full beauty, behind which the unspeakable ugliness they were hunting lay hidden and waiting like something monstrous lurking in its lair.

*   *   *

Part III – Three Lives

12

Wil didn't usually dream, at least not that he remembered.

But, coming awake with a nervous start, he was sure he'd just had an extraordinary dream, one that had felt uncannily real, more real than waking life, in fact.

Lying in his bedroll under the stars of Marillin, he felt as if he'd just been given a taste of something much more vast and powerful than anything he'd ever known in normal life – though already he couldn't remember what it had been about. Something to do with slogging through a desert, he thought. And then even that was gone.

All around him, men tossed and stirred, sleeping restlessly or not at all. Soldiers, all of them, they were used to catching a round of sleep whenever there was a chance, and be it on the back of a horse. But three days into the Bane, farther than any of them had ever been before, they were more than simply scared. They were terrified. And hungry.

Forced to depart in a mad rush, not many of them had managed to grab more than a waterskin and a round or two of waybread, and most not even that. Not that they'd anticipated anything like this. Old habit had fixed Oldwall in their minds as an ultimate border, the limit of their remit, and none of them had thought different than that they'd turn around once they'd reached it and be back in the Vales by nightfall. But Thorley had other plans, and he wasn't asking anyone if they liked them.

Even so, if Wil had been in the Lord Commander's place he would have made camp at Oldwall and sent scouts and trackers south to pick up the fugitives' trail before a hundred-and-twenty-odd horses destroyed any chance of finding anything useful. In the meantime, he'd have ordered a squad back north to fetch a wagon-load or two of rations and supplies.

But Thorley pressed on as if he trusted that his fury and hate alone would lead them onto Graeme's and Breanne's trail. Perhaps in his maddened state he'd trusted in revenge to satisfy his hunger, but someone in his retinue had shown more sense. No man of the Watch had failed to notice that, unlike themselves, Thorley's House Guard had come prepared, their saddle bags filled to bursting, five of them leading pack horses piled high with gear, not the least of it two tents for themselves and a pavilion for his lordship. But if anyone had been so trusting as to think that Thorley's bunch would share, they were bitterly disappointed.

On the first night out, his empty stomach grumbling like everybody else's, Wil went to take the matter up with Dicken. Though he reckoned it was a waste of time, it was the only thing he could think of. Dicken was captain now, however laughable it seemed, and likely the only one who stood even the ghost of a chance of having a plea for food listened to.

He found Dicken alone, huddled in a blanket and nursing a pitiful fire with the few brittle sticks he'd been brave enough to go out and gather. He looked utterly miserable.

'Captain,' Wil said. 'Mind if I join you?'

'Don't call me that, Wil.' Dicken sounded close to tears. 'It's the cruelest joke anyone's ever thought to play on me, and everybody seems to believe I'm in on it. Right about now, I'm thinking I'd rather drop dead than listen to one more stupid jape.'

'All right then,' Wil said, settling down beside him. 'Dicken it is. I like it better than "Captain" anyway.' He could already see that sending Dicken to negotiate with Thorley wasn't an option.

'I know. The job just won't fit me.' Dicken managed a wan smile. 'It's like asking a wee bairn to step into in those big boots of yours and run a mile in them.'

Wil chuckled. 'The kid would have more luck if he used one of them as a boat. I reckon I've got the biggest size boots in all the Vales, and my feet aren't even done growing yet. Boots aside – I was thinking I'd go and talk to Thorley, see what can be done about rations. Just thought I'd check with you first, so as not to be stepping on anyone's toes.'

'Would you, really?' Dicken asked, eager as a neglected child – which wasn't far from the truth, Wil thought to himself.

'I will. But don't get your hopes up. I'm not sure our welfare counts for much with the Lord Commander. I'm not sure anything counts with him except getting his hands on Graeme and his daughter, no matter the cost. But I'll try. Well, then. Good talking to you, Dicken. And if I were you, I wouldn't take the men's japes amiss. We're all of us in the same leaky boat together, and they're just trying to make light of a bad situation. Not a one of them blames you,

203

that much is for sure. I'll let you know how it went with Thorley.'

'Thanks, Wil. You're a good sort. I wish we had someone like you for our Lord Commander. Then we'd have never gotten dragged into this in the first palace.'

'Shush, Dicken. Saying things like that can get us both strung up for treason. Just hang in there, now. Somehow or other we'll get through this.'

'Right,' Dicken said, not sounding as if he believed it.

Wil rose to leave. He had his own doubts concerning the outcome of this insane undertaking, but Dicken didn't need to hear about them.

He didn't make it in to see the Lord Commander.

Instead he ran into Fray sitting outside Thorley's pavilion with a bare blade across his knees. The tent was ridiculously large and fancy, something you'd have looked to find at a siege or a tournament. Out here it was completely misplaced, an unnecessary encumbrance and a slap in the face to a hundred men who were forced to sleep out in the open with nothing between themselves and the Bane but a handful of their comrades standing watch, and not a proper Ward in sight. Unless you trusted in the skills of Thorley's man Gage, a black-robed, shaven-headed bruiser who styled himself a priest of Amut and a practitioner of magic. To Wil, the man looked more like a two-bit hustler who sold miracle cures from the back of a donkey cart or fleeced easy marks with loaded dice in seedy taverns. But Thorley swore by him, his secret weapon against the Bane.

Fray spared Wil a contemptuous glance. 'What?'

'I'd like to speak with his lordship,' Wil said.

204

'You'd like, huh?' Fray sneered. 'Well, here's what *I'd* like, sweetling. I'd like you to turn around and walk away right smartly – unless you fancy a foot of steel shoved up your bung-hole, that is.'

Wil could see he'd not get anywhere with Fray. But he wasn't prepared to give up that easily. 'My lord!' he called out, taking a step back. 'Begging your pardon. A word, if you'd be so kind.'

Fray was up in a trice, looking ready to kill. Wil laid a hand on the head of his axe, giving back a level stare.

'Fucking weasel!' Fray hissed furiously, just as Thorley stepped through the entrance flap. He was wearing a nightshirt. A *nightshirt,* for the gods' sake! Who knew what else he'd brought along. Maybe he even had one of those portable commode things hidden away behind those gaudy walls of striped canvas.

'What is it?' Thorley asked impatiently.

'It's about the men, m'lord. They're hungry. With having to leave in such a hurry and not knowing they'd be gone for more than a day, no one thought to bring provisions.'

You *didn't think to bring them. It's* your *job to see that the men are fed.* You *took Orsen Dunne from us.*

'I say, that was certainly careless of them.' Thorley suppressed a yawn. 'A good soldier needs to be prepared for anything. Well, nothing for it. They'll just have to make do. They do know how to hunt, don't they? There you go. And they can gather what edible plants there are. Tell them that. And tell them not to come bothering me again with things they should be quite capable of reasoning out for themselves. Fray, see to it that there are no more disturbances.'

Are you going to leave us time to hunt? Wil wanted to ask. *Or do you expect game to line up beside the road for us so we can shoot at*

205

it while we're riding by in column? And are we supposed to hack tubers and such out of the snow and frozen ground, or is Gage going to perform some magic trick and make mushrooms and berries grow in April?

But Thorley was gone, and not coming back.

'You heard his lordship,' Fray snarled. 'Now git! And stay out of my sight, lest I forget myself.'

Wil left. He recognized a hopeless cause when it stared him in the face. At least it was clear now where everybody stood. Though he couldn't fathom why he of all persons should be charged with the burden, he suddenly felt the weight of a hundred men's fates settle onto his shoulders with indisputable finality.

Looks as if I don't have much of a choice, he thought. *Someone has to look out for them, else none of us will see Deepwall again.*

The next day, as they rode ever farther into the Bane, Wil moved up and down the column unobtrusively, seeking out the few sergeants Thorley had seen fit to bring along, Gael, Tait, and Quillan. They were all three seasoned fighters, men who were married to the Freewatch as much as to the wives they'd left back home. Men he trusted not to rat him out to Thorley, even should they not be prepared to go along with the plan that was beginning to take shape in his mind. Chances were, they'd see nothing in him but a green youngling reaching far beyond his station, and send him packing with a clout on the ear.

He needn't have worried. Quillan had led the sortie during which Wil had killed three Rooters, and Wil found to his surprise that his short stint with Graeme seemed to have already raised him in everyone's eyes to the status of a true ranger and something of a hero. It came as less of a surprise that all three of them were deeply troubled and well aware of Thorley's madness. They all listened to what Wil had to say, and agreed to a meeting that night in camp.

That day they lost two horses and a man to Lurkers. So far, it had seemed as if the Bane had moved south for good, but now they looked to be on the point of catching up with it.

*   *   *

13

Her sails swelled by a spanking northerly, *Goldspray* seemed to fly across the waves. The weather remained clear and sunny, too dazzlingly beautiful to spend even a minute in the tiny cabin Breanne could call hers by virtue of Goderun having bumped the second mate down to a hammock belowdecks, where Graeme and the others were lodged with the crew as well. She'd have shared with them, but there was barely enough space for one. A bunk, a chest that doubled as a table and a low chair bolted to the deck; that was it. At least Rhys, the second mate, had taken his exile with grace, even joking as to how such a fair lady's presence would ennoble his poor quarters for once and evermore. Quite mannerly for a pirate, Breanne thought, and slipped him one of Torgrim's golds.

But sometime during the night the wind turned, and when she came back on deck the following morning she found the sky grey with scudding clouds and *Goldspray* bucking in a heavy swell. Where there'd been the distant but comforting sight of land the day before, now she saw nothing but open sea.

'Bloody southerly,' Goderun informed her when she joined the

209

captain and Graeme on the aft deck. 'A long tack sou'east and then sou'west again should get us to Point Blank, but it'll cost us at least a day unless the wind changes again.'

It didn't, and Goderun became increasingly edgy as the day progressed, pacing the aft deck and barking orders to do with tightening lines and steering a degree this way or that. Breanne didn't know the first thing about sailing a ship, but to her it looked as if they were as close to the wind as they could possibly get, and the whole bustle was more about finding an outlet for Goderun's impatience than making them go any faster than they already were.

The captain wasn't the only one fretting. Down on the main deck, Torgrim paced as well, stopping every so often to cast a troubled glance southward as if he expected the mythical ghost ship with its dreadful crew to come sailing over the horizon at any moment. The only ones who didn't seem restless were Pers and Finn, sitting side by side on a heap of coiled ropes by the fo'c's'le, whittling away on something or other and exchanging friendly words with any sailor who happened to pass by.

On the spur of the moment she decided to go down and talk to Torgrim. Windward was still bothering her. He'd traveled here and there on the island, speaking with all sorts of people, and perhaps he'd heard something that could explain the disquieting impression she'd gotten there, a feeling as if there were some deeply buried secret no one was prepared to talk about or even acknowledge. When she asked him as much he nodded, looking even more troubled.

'Aye,' he said. 'You got that right. But be warned, it's not a nice story.'

'Tell me.'

'Well, then. You might have noticed there weren't a lot of people from the mainland on Windward.'

'Yes. I'd have expected many more refugees to have ended up there.'

'And it wasn't for lack of trying. There must have been thousands of desperate people crowding the mainland shore, and not nearly enough boats to take them across. The islanders had boats aplenty, and they could have gone and fetched hundreds to safety. Only they didn't, because apparently the majority of them reasoned there was barely enough food to go around on Windward as it was, and they feared that so many newcomers would inevitably cause famine and strife.

'To make matters worse, the weather was stormy for days on end, meaning the refugees were caught between the Bane and the sea, which must have been pretty rough at the time. They set out anyway, in boats that were hopelessly overcrowded and all too often manned by landlubbers who barely knew an oar from a pitchfork. Inevitably, a great many of them capsized and drowned.

'The islanders, on the other hand, were experienced seafarers. Admittedly it would have been a risk, but they could have gone out and saved lives – perhaps no longer hundreds but at least a few score. Some would have, but they were outnumbered and prevented from going, while the rest of them even went so far as to barricade the harbor mouth, leaving the handful of refugees who by some miracle made it across to drown in sight of dry land.

'A small number who knew the island managed to reach one of a few sandy coves, the only safe landings on Windward's western

211

shore aside from Old Harbor. Once they were there – and since they were few – their presence was perforce accepted. But to this day there's a rift as deep as the ocean separating islanders from islanders, and the refugees from everyone else.

'That's what you felt, and you'd probably still feel it if you visited Windward ten years from now, or twenty, or a hundred. This kind of thing tends to spoil a place and dog its people for a very long time.'

Breanne was shocked, hard put to believe that people could be so callous and murderously selfish. Torgrim had been right: better he shouldn't have told her. Seeing that his attention had wandered south again, she went to find Graeme, her one dependable point of reference in a world that was either incredibly cruel or utterly insane, or perhaps both.

How it came about she couldn't have said, since any sign of what was brewing seemed to have escaped her completely. But towards mid-afternoon Goderun, her mien suddenly loosening, slid down the companionway to the main deck and headed for her cabin. Moments later Breanne saw Finn get up and brush himself off. With a casual glance around he sauntered aft and followed Goderun below.

'Well, now,' Breanne said. She looked at Graeme, who merely raised an eyebrow. 'You don't seem surprised.'

'Not really,' Graeme said. 'Only that it didn't happen earlier. It's been in the making since the moment we set foot in *Colton's Bones.*'

'But… '

'But what?'

'Nothing. I just didn't expect Finn to be the kind of man she

212

fancied.' It was high time to choose a different subject. Before she could think of one, Graeme did it for her.

'There's something I've been wondering about,' he said. 'It's to do with your vision, the one about locking the door.'

She nodded.

'I suppose we're agreed on Broken Steel,' he went on. 'It makes sense. But Sleeping Wood? What does it mean?'

'I've no idea. For a while I thought it might be Arden, with his tree-singing and turning dead twigs into lutes. Now I'm not so sure anymore.'

'No. Your vision concerning Arden was separate and complete in itself, as far as I can tell. Sleeping Wood is you. It must be. I just can't figure out what it means.'

'Well,' she sighed, 'I suppose time will either tell, or it won't. As long as you and I are together, I don't really care whether I'm Sleeping Wood or Jumping Bean.' Realizing the import of what she'd just said, she felt herself blush.

There I go, shooting off my mouth again, she thought. *He'll think me awfully forward, worse than Goderun.*

To her surprise, Graeme turned and gave her a deep, beseeching look.

'Breanne,' he said, sounding terribly sober. 'I wish... I wish things were different and we could be more to each other than what we are, I honestly do. But you must know as well as I do that it can't be.'

For a wonder, the words didn't sting at all.

On the contrary: it was as if they'd released something in her, some-

213

thing that had been holding her back for as long as she could remember, and she realized that, up until now, she still hadn't left her
father and all he stood for behind. Now she did, and it gave her a
sense of freedom she'd have never thought possible.

'And why ever not?' she said, returning his gaze. 'Do you realize
where we are, and where we're going? Who's to tell us what we can
and cannot do? Who's to judge our actions but ourselves? I for one
would find myself terribly wanting if I forewent something I felt
was absolutely right, for fear of breaking with some stupid conven-
tion that makes as much sense in this place as... oh, I don't know –
as not spitting over the side because it might make the ocean over-
flow. Even if my father's sentiments counted for a whit out here, do
you honestly believe there's anything you can possibly do to fall further from his grace than you already have?'

'There is that,' Graeme said. He looked out to sea for a few
moments, and seemed to find an answer there. When he turned back
to her, it was with a gentle smile that almost managed to cancel out
the worry lines. 'You're absolutely right, my lady. I'm afraid this
man can be awfully stupid sometimes. Will you forgive me?'

'I will, this once, because I... Oh, all right! Because I'm very
fond of you, Graeme Blockhead, and I want to be with you for however much time we have left. There, now I've said it.'

For an answer, Graeme reached out a hand and gently touched
her cheek. Then he took her in his arms and kissed her, right in front
of half the crew and to a cacophony of whistles, catcalls and cheers.

When she finally came up for breath and looked to the main
deck, she saw Pers dancing a jig, arm in arm with one of the sailors.
Even Torgrim had interrupted his preoccupied wandering and was

214

standing there grinning from ear to ear. Seeing her look his way, he gave her a nod and a thumbs-up. Apparently, what had been building between her and Graeme ever since they'd left the Vales hadn't gone as unnoticed as she'd thought. No matter. She was done hiding things.

That night, her heart a-flutter with her own audacity, she took Graeme to her cabin.

Let them think what they like, she told herself, catching a knowing glance from Goderun. *The whole world can know, for all I care.*

But as the door closed behind her, all the little worries and fears she'd so far managed to suppress suddenly caught up with her, leaving her weak-kneed and trembling. What if she wasn't up to this? What if she disappointed Graeme, made a fool of herself? And what about the possible consequences?

To hell with the consequences, she thought. *We could all be dead an hour from now, or tomorrow, or the day after. It's our right, no, our duty, to make the most of the time we have left. Twenty-six years I've waited for this. Whatever may come, I will not be cheated out of my womanhood. I am* not *going to die a virgin.*

She'd gleaned what little she knew about the art of love-making years ago from whispered conversations among giggling, adolescent girls and from the songs of bards guesting at Thorhold, songs that tended to be either soppily romantic or shockingly lewd.

As it turned out, she needn't have worried. It hurt, of course, but that much she'd been prepared for. And the pain was balanced by the marvelous sense of fulfillment she felt. Still, Graeme noticed, and paused, a look of concern further softening the hard lines of his face.

'Does it hurt too much?' he asked.

'Only a little,' she lied. 'Please, don't stop now.'

The second time was better. Graeme possessed the experience she lacked, and he was a willing teacher. Gentle and considerate, he led her through the steps until she was ready to go forward on her own, filled with a sense of joyful wonder that sharing herself could be so natural, easy as breathing and immensely gratifying. The bunk was ridiculously small for two, but she wouldn't have exchanged it for a four-poster in a palace, not for anything in the world. Later, looking back, she thought that this night had been all she'd ever imagined it might be, and more. Much, much more.

*   *   *

It was late in the afternoon on their third day out from Deepwall. They'd left the Tallamors behind and were wending their way through the higher foothills when a broad, treeless rise just west of the road caught Wil's eye. There were three fingers of fresh green on its flanks, enough to give the horses good grazing; there was water, a lively little stream that had joined the road an hour back; and the place wasn't bad as defensible positions went, a point the Lord Commander had neglected to consider in choosing their two previous camps.

Any responsible officer would have counted himself lucky to find such a spot for the night. Thorley showed no sign he'd even seen it, and rode right on.

It was time, Wil decided. Time to make a stand and bring at least a small measure of sanity to this murderous enterprise.

Riding at the head of the column, he exchanged glances with Quillan, Gael, and Tait, indicating the hill with a small jerk of his chin. They nodded in agreement, a result of their meeting the night before. Another was that they'd spent all day working the column, having a few quiet words with the men and preparing them for this moment. No orders were issued, no signs given. The men in the lead simply stopped, half the column coming to a halt behind them while the other half began to spread out, moving off to the east and west.

Thorley and his guard rode on for another fifty yards, oblivious to what was happening behind them. Then Wil saw Fray look around, staring at the halted column and the men riding away to both sides as if he didn't quite trust his eyes. A moment later he was leaning over and whispering in Thorley's ear. Both of them wheeled around and came riding back at a canter. Thorley's face was dark with anger.

This is it, Wil thought. *Our moment of truth. If things go wrong, men are going to die here today.*

'What the devil's going on?' Thorley snarled. 'Are you men out of your wits?'

'Just following your orders, m'lord,' Wil said meekly. 'You said we should hunt for our food.'

'And since there was no chance to do it during the day,' Quillan took over, 'and there's no sense trying in the dark, we thought now would be a good time to see if we can rustle up some game.'

'Unless you say we should ride on, that is,' Tait joined in. 'Though I can't say as there won't be men falling out of their saddles on the morrow. Three days without food hasn't exactly done

217

them a lot of good.'

'I reckon we'll be seeing more of the Bane soon.' Gael turned his head to the side and spat on the ground. 'I'd sure hate to see the men having to fight against those ugly blighters on an empty stomach. No telling how that would go.'

For a moment Thorley sat there, fuming.

'All right,' he said. 'We'll make camp here. That hill over there looks like it will do. But in the future, you'll wait until you hear my orders. The next man who stops before I say so will be considered a deserter and treated accordingly. And you,' he gave Wil a hateful stare. 'Don't think for a moment I'm fooled by your innocent air. I'll be keeping an eye on you from now on. One wrong step, and you'll be the first to hang for insubordination.'

'Yes, m'lord,' Wil said, trying to look properly chastened.

Inwardly he exulted. They'd risked the first step, and it had worked. Thorley had given in and unwittingly set a precedence, not realizing that this was just the beginning of something larger. As the Lord Commander rode off to find himself the choicest spot up on the hill, Fray gave Wil a look that spelled bloody murder before giving his horse the spurs and trotting after his master.

That night the men of the Freewatch had their first proper meal in three days, venison and tubers. Not a feast exactly but enough to raise their spirits a notch or two, though the mood remained far from exuberant. Quillan posted a double watch, and Wil, his confidence in what little he'd learned from Graeme decidedly greater than in Gage's dubious arts, set Wards of his own around the camp. Even though the men had been told to bed down close together, it was still

218

a stretch for him, and a Ward every ten yards was the best he could manage. Better than nothing, he told himself, though he wished he could have done more. Some inner sense was warning him insistently that there was trouble in the offing. Judging by the air of tense readiness that took hold of the camp with the coming of darkness, the others seemed to feel it as well.

*   *   *

For two days now, they'd been beating against the wind.

It hadn't brought them appreciably closer to Point Blank. Graeme thought that if it hadn't been for Finn and his – apparently expert – ministrations, Goderun's fraying temper would have already snapped a while ago.

'It's as if someone doesn't want us to get there,' she told him, standing beside Rhys at the helm with her feet planted wide. 'Some nasty blighter who's in cahoots with the Wind God, or maybe it's Donal himself. Though with all the offerings I've made him and Urufin over the years, I reckon I could have bought a second ship by now. Ungrateful bastards.'

'It's the wind, isn't it?' Graeme said. 'It's always blowing straight off Point Blank, no matter where we are.'

'Damn right it is,' Goderun grumbled. 'And it's not bloody natural. If it goes on like this, we might never get there. Bleeding gods and their stupid games!'

Graeme didn't think the gods had anything to do with it, but the captain's words got him thinking. He went to join Torgrim, who'd been standing at the forward starboard railing and staring south for hours as if his feet had been bolted to the deck.

219

'What's with the wind?' Graeme asked. 'Goderun says it's un-natural, and I'm inclined to agree with her.'

'Not now,' was all he got for an answer.

'I already tried talking to him,' Pers called out from his seat by the fo'c's'le. 'I think he'd sooner have his butt-hairs plucked out one at a time than give a man a straight answer.'

Graeme was about to turn away when he felt a sudden, dramatic change in the atmosphere, a quickly mounting tension in the air that set his skin tingling and raised the hairs on his arms. The wind died down in the space of two heartbeats, leaving the sails hanging limp. Sparks like miniature lightning crackled in the rigging. Out of the corner of his eye he saw Breanne rush out onto the deck. She looked pale and frightened.

With a sudden start, Torgrim came to life. 'Captain, beware!' he shouted. 'Wind's moving astern! It's going to be a howler!'

Goderun must have grasped that this was no ordinary situation but something that went far beyond her seamanly ken. She shouted orders immediately, sending sailors scrambling up the rigging to reef the sails. Rhys spun the wheel to bring *Goldspray* about and set her before the wind. Luckily, she was still running with enough speed to follow the rudder smartly.

'Passengers below!' Goderun ordered. 'Now!'

Heading towards Breanne and the companionway, Graeme saw the sky astern darken with unnatural speed. He heard a rising hum, as if a gigantic swarm of hornets were fast approaching the ship. Putting an arm around Breanne, he accompanied her inside.

He'd barely closed the companionway hatch behind them when the storm hit. The ship seemed to duck and kneel for a moment, then

220

she rose and took up speed as if shot from a sling.

Suddenly the hatch banged open and Torgrim staggered in, already soaked to the skin. 'We need to talk,' he said.

'The wind's blowing the right way now,' Torgrim said, once they'd all found a place to sit in Breanne's cramped cabin. 'But that's just about all the good news there is.'

'Why, what's wrong?' Breanne asked.

'First of all,' Torgrim said, 'he now knows it's me coming after him – Keon, that is. I think we can now safely say that it's he who's behind this whole sorry mess. I reckon he knows about the Key as well, and he's bound to believe that I'm the one who has it. Which must scare him mightily, because he's been trying to hold us up with everything he's got.

'I would have much preferred to leave him in the dark, but that would have left us sailing these waters for all eternity. I had to do something, and that meant showing myself to him, no way around it.

'Unfortunately, the tricky bastard pulled one over on me. I won't go into the details, but think of what just happened between Keon and myself as a game of pull and push. He pushed, I pushed back, and when the pressure was greatest, instead of just letting go the bugger turned around and pulled. I barely avoided falling on my face, otherwise we'd all be slowly drifting towards the bottom of the sea right about now. But we're still in a shitload of trouble – begging your pardon, my lady.'

'Why?' Graeme asked. 'What's the problem? We're finally headed where we want to go, aren't we?'

'The problem is still Keon. He's changed his tactics. I've a feel-

221

ing that now he's trying to drive us towards the coast until we hit the shore or a reef and get smashed to smithereens. He's using sorcery, which means he can keep this storm going for however long it takes, providing he's got enough sacrifices lined up. I, on the other hand, am pretty much spent, and it's going to take me a while to regain my strength. So it all comes down to how much time we have left before we run aground.'

'The Key,' Breanne said. 'You can use that in the meantime.'

'No.' Torgrim shook his head. 'Out of the question.'

'Then I'll use it.'

'No again. He doesn't know about you, and he mustn't. You're our ace in the hole. The only one we have left, unless I have a divine inspiration and come up with something else. I'm working on it, at any rate. For now, I'm going to go see the captain and ask her to take it as slowly as possible, seeing as we're not in such a screaming hurry anymore.'

'I'm scared,' Breanne said when Torgrim had left. 'I set out thinking we were up against the Bane, which was bad enough. But this… ' She shuddered. 'Sacrifices?'

'We're still going after the Bane,' Graeme said. 'And this Keon seems to be at the heart of it.'

'Banesheart,' Breanne said, her eyes going wide.

'Right,' Graeme said, gently brushing a stray lock from her face while he searched for words that might comfort her, and himself. They weren't easy to find.

*   *   *

14

Wil's Wards remained undisturbed that night.

But in the morning one of the men who'd stood second watch was found dead a short ways outside the ring of Wards, his throat ripped out with animal force. The first Wil heard about it was when Quillan came to fetch him.

'I'd like you to come take a look,' the grizzled sergeant said, his weathered face set in grim lines. 'Something about it doesn't feel right.'

When they got to the site they found the Lord Commander there. He'd brought Fray and Gage with him.

'How do you explain this?' Thorley asked Gage. 'You claimed nothing could get through your Wards.'

'And so it is, my lord. Providing it's coming from the outside. The Wards are designed to keep the Bane out, not people in. This man must have left his post and strayed from safety. Much to his own detriment, I'd say.'

Coldhearted bastard, Wil thought.

'Where did you set the Wards?' Thorley asked.

'There.' Gage gestured vaguely. 'Clearly the man overstepped them by several feet, where even an inch can mean the difference between life and death.'

'Very well.' Thorley appeared almost normal today, but that could change at the drop of a pin, Wil knew. 'Quillan, I want the men strictly advised to stay inside the Wards. I'll not lose more of them through foolish negligence. And see that this one is put in the ground soonest. I don't want him fouling up the place. We'll be staying here for a time. Report to me once you've cleared away this mess.'

When Thorley had left with his henchman and his magicker in tow, Wil bent down to take a closer look at the dead man. It wasn't a pretty sight, much less on an empty stomach.

'See those round gouges at the edges of the wound?' Quillan asked.

'Yes,' Wil said. 'They look like claw marks. The size might fit a bear, except there's five of them, four on one side and a single one on the other.'

'Like four fingers and a thumb. A Rooter, maybe?'

'I doubt it. Could have been a Shifter, though. But either way I'd be looking for a lot more damage. Actually, I wouldn't expect to see this guy lying here at all unless they'd really taken him apart.'

'My thought exactly,' Quillan said. 'If it was the Bane he'd have gotten up and walked away by now, another Bitten to swell their ranks. So where does that leave us?'

'I don't know. You don't think...' Wil looked back towards the camp.

'I don't think anything at this point,' Quillan grated. 'But we

224

need to keep our eyes open. In all directions.'

Quillan returned from reporting to Thorley with news that the Lord Commander had belatedly decided to dispatch scouts and trackers to search for signs of Graeme and Breanne's passing. Wil reckoned it was a useless undertaking at this point, a dangerous folly that put men's lives at needless risk. But their situation was far too precarious to consider open rebellion. Inevitably, it would set the Watch against Thorley's Guard, and likely see their numbers decimated by half, once it was all over and time came to count the bodies.

A company of ten was sent west with Tait in command, another headed east under Gael. Wil would have gone with either of them, but Quillan had received specific orders from Thorley to hold him in camp.

He's keeping his enemies close, Wil thought. *Probably wise of him, seeing whom he's chosen as friends.*

At least Gael and Tait each had a man with rudimentary skills at Warding, for all the good it would do them if the Bane chose to attack: a moment's warning was all they'd have, time enough perhaps to take their own lives and spare themselves the fate of becoming Bitten.

Since it looked as if they'd be staying in place for some time, Wil suggested to Quillan they keep the men busy by having them build a line of defense that was somewhat more tangible than iffy Wards. Wil toiled with the rest of them, and a week of hauling rocks and logs and the remains of a collapsed farm they'd found nearby saw their camp surrounded by a chest-high wall. It would accomplish exactly nothing against Rooters and Shifters, but it gave them a sense of security all the same. They dug latrines at one end of the encampment, and a clay-lined pit filled with a reserve of water at the other.

And though they had to range ever farther to find game, the hunting was good, allowing them to smoke part of the meat and put aside a store of food.

None of it brought any real relief. Towards the end of the week the weather changed from sunny to miserable, and instead of working on the wall they built pine-bough shelters against the constant drizzle. The higher hills were soon wreathed in a cold mist that gradually thickened and dropped until the barrow they were sitting on became an island in a sea of impenetrable grey. The ground inside the camp turned muddy, lighting a fire became a near impossible chore, and wet leathers and rusting gear did nothing to improve the mood. Nor did the deaths of two more sentries, both of them killed in the same manner as the first, with still no clue as to how it had happened.

Eight days after they'd departed, Gael and two of his men came riding back to camp. Wil had just decided to finally sit down and mend his jerkin where two of the scaled platelets had busted their rivets and come loose when he heard the shouts. Together with Quillan and at least two score men of the Watch he rushed to the gate of their provisional wall to welcome them back.

The returning men were still some forty yards away when Thorley showed up with Gage, Fray, and his entire Guard. At least half of them carried crossbows spanned and loaded.

'Halt!' Fray ordered Gael. 'Stay where you are and report to the Lord Commander.'

Gael and his two companions, looking beaten down and utterly exhausted after gods knew what terrible things they'd gone through during the past seven days, reined in with looks of disbelief.

And Wil's heart nearly stood still with the shock of realization. He knew with uncanny certainty what was coming. So did Quillan, by the looks of him.

Wil took a step forward.

'My lord,' he said. 'You don't want to harm those men. There's nothing to say they're Bitten, and they've risked their lives for you, lost seven of their comrades in doing so. You owe them better than a bolt between the eyes, my lord.'

Thorley didn't even turn around. 'Shoot him,' he told Fray.

*　　　*　　　*

Wulfwyn was worried sick.

She saw the sense in what Arden was doing, saw the necessity and the rightness of it. But the risks he was willing to take were enormous.

They'd traveled only a few hours from the spot where Breanne and Graeme had dropped them off at the southern shore of Mirror Lake when Arden stopped, declaring they'd stay where they were and rest for the remainder of the day.

'We'll go on once it's dark,' he said. 'The Stricken won't follow us in daylight.'

Wulfwyn was shocked by the boldness of it, and surprised to see that Arden's four young friends didn't seem at all perturbed by the prospect of wandering through the forest at night when the Bane was at its most active. Their friendship for him bordering on worship, they trusted him almost blindly. Which was all good and well as far as it went but not the kind of premise that would keep them safe and alive for long. And keeping Arden alive had become the hub of her existence.

She loved him dearly, this strange, courageous youth. He and she were two of a kind – the only two unchanged Bitten in the whole world – which made the idea of losing him all the more unthinkable. She shared his purpose and his devotion, but not to the point of throwing everything else overboard.

'Arden,' she pleaded, 'be reasonable. I can't keep us Warded while we're on the move. There has to be another way.'

'There isn't,' he said and gave her one of his heart-wrenchingly sad smiles. 'And your Wards would only get in the way in any case. I can't reach the Stricken through them. But the Song will keep us safe, I promise.'

'Will you sing all through the night, then?' she asked.

'It's what I aim to do. I think I can.'

'All right.' She gave in with a sigh. 'But the moment you feel you can't go on, you let me know – and with time to spare so I can set my Wards. Promise me that.'

'I promise,' Arden said. 'Believe me, I'd do nothing to endanger you, my love – and you, my friends. I count myself immeasurably blessed to have you all with me.'

For the moment Wulfwyn couldn't think of any other argument. But she decided she'd at least Ward them during the daytime while they were resting, even if it didn't seem strictly necessary. The crea-

228

tures of the Bane were unpredictable, and she wasn't prepared to believe they wouldn't suddenly change their ways and risk the light of day to eliminate a threat as dire as Arden.

Whether by chance or design Arden had stopped in a sun-drenched clearing, where they slept away the afternoon bedded on sweet-smelling grass and warmed by the sun, lulled by birdsong and the buzz of insects busy harvesting sweet nectar from spring's first wild blossoms.

Near sunset they bestirred themselves and ate a frugal meal – dinner? Lunch? Breakfast? – and with the onset of darkness struck off again, Arden humming his strange song that reminded Wulfwyn of foresty things: wind in the treetops, the patter of rain on leaves, branches creaking in a storm or cracking in a severe frost, the burble of brooks and the rustle of large and small animals passing through the underbrush. The calls of birds and other beasts were in there as well, as was the stillness of those rare moments when the whole forest appeared to be sleeping and nothing seemed to move save the sun or the moon following their eternal courses across the sky.

At first it was pitch-black under the forest canopy.
But gradually their eyes adjusted to the darkness, and Wulfwyn saw that they weren't alone.

Here and there among the trees, dark shapes appeared: gnarled, twisted silhouettes approaching from all sides to move in parallel with Arden's course. Their numbers grew steadily as the night progressed, until she reckoned there were at least two score of them rustling through the trees on either side. None of the Stricken made a threatening move, and she was beginning to feel a wee bit reassured when suddenly the trees ahead thinned out and gave way onto a large clearing.

Only when Arden stopped in the middle of the clearing did she realize how far off she'd been with her count. Hundreds of Stricken streamed out into the open, gathering around the edges of the clearing. It seemed as if half the forest had pulled up roots to follow them. Arden was still singing, but in the feeble predawn light she saw that he was exhausted.

Readying to cast her Wards, she gave the lads a soft warning. They immediately spread out in a loose diamond formation, bows ready and arrows nocked.

Somewhere to the right a bird flew up with a loud screech.
Griff, guarding that side, shifted his aim to where the sound had come from – which was why he wasn't prepared for the Shifter that came flying out of the forest in a grey, elongated blur aimed straight for Arden.

Hurn on the left couldn't shoot for fear of hitting Arden. Raul and Tarr each loosed two arrows but missed. By the time Griff had turned and found his target it was too late.

Screaming in helpless agony, Wulfwyn threw herself at the Shifter that was already busy reducing Arden to a bloody waste of torn flesh and broken bones. Then something hit her with a force that seemed to take her head off her shoulders, and she knew nothing more.

*   *   *

Before anyone could react, Fray turned around, aimed and loosed.

Stunned, Wil watched the bolt wobble as it left the track and crept through the air towards him at the pace of a snail. He thought he should move aside, was about to do so when something hit him in the chest with the force of a sledgehammer.

Next he knew, he was lying on his back, the shocked, pale faces of his comrades hovering somewhere in the air above him. He tried to breathe but couldn't. Then Quillan was kneeling over him, holding his hand and telling him to 'Hang in there, it'll come out all right, just stay with me'. There were tears in Quillan's eyes, Wil saw, touched that someone should care so much for him. He wanted to tell Quillan that it didn't hurt but found he couldn't do that either. His vision began to fade, and he realized with a pang of regret that his heart had stopped beating.

The last thing to reach him was the Lord Commander's voice. Thorley was cursing. It appeared that Gael and the other two had seen their chance and galloped away, and not one of the bolts Thorley's men sent after them found its mark.

All right, then, Wil thought. *So all of this was good for something.*

Smiling, he died.

*   *   *

Standing at the edge of the clearing, Wulfwyn had the strangest sensation. Briefly, the view she was seeing seemed to flicker and the ground to shift beneath her feet as if the world had just taken a small step sideways. Eerie and disquieting as it felt, it was over in a heartbeat, and in any case she had no time to dwell on it.

231

Out in the middle of the clearing Arden was still singing, though in the feeble predawn light she saw that he was exhausted. Readying to cast her Wards, she gave the lads a soft warning. They immediately spread out in a loose diamond formation, bows ready and arrows nocked.

Somewhere to the right a bird flew up with a loud screech. Griff, guarding that side, didn't let it distract him, which was why he was prepared for the Shifter that came flying out of the forest in a grey, elongated blur aimed straight at Arden.

Hurn on the left couldn't shoot for fear of hitting Arden, and Raul and Tarr were a fraction too slow on the draw. But for a wonder, Griff's second and third arrow both found their mark. Not three yards from Arden the Shifter dropped out of the air, dead before it hit the ground.

Frantic with aftershock, Wulfwyn set Wards in record time. As soon as she was done, she collapsed, racked by uncontrollable sobs. A moment later, blinded by tears, she felt Arden's arms around her.

'I'm so sorry, love,' he said. 'You were right to worry. I promise we'll work out something better before we do this again.'

'I'm not budging an inch from here until we do,' she sniffled, and meant it.

Nothing was worth losing Arden, she was more certain of that than ever before.

*   *   *

15

Running before the storm under her bowsprit jib, *Goldspray* reared and plunged through the heavy swell. The time still remaining before she ran afoul of Point Blank's dreaded reefs was fast dwindling down to nothing, no matter she was trailing a sea anchor to slow her down.

Faced with the growing certainty that their quest was about to end in a welter of crashing waves and cutting rock, of splintered wood and mangled bodies, Breanne was ever more tempted to make use of the Key, notwithstanding Torgrim's advice against it.

It was calling to her, loud and clear, and resisting it was becoming harder by the hour. Luckily, she had something to distract her from its insistent summons. She, Goderun, Torgrim and Graeme were gathered in the captain's cabin, desperately trying to think of a way to escape Keon's and the storm's deadly grip.

They'd begun by telling Goderun about Keon, revealing as much about their mission as they dared. Breanne had expected the captain to explode in fury and threaten to cast them all overboard or throw them in the deepest hold, or do whatever else they did on ships with people who'd annoyed them. Instead Goderun seemed to focus all her anger on Keon, and apart from her colorful use of language she remained quite cold and practical about it.

'We have to find some way to get you there,' she said emphatically, sitting behind her captain's desk with the air if not the vocabulary of an embattled queen. 'I want to see you kick the whole damned Bane so far up that bleeding fiend's arsehole he chokes on it. Sorry, my lady.'

'Don't be,' Breanne said. 'I share your sentiments entirely.'

It got her an appreciative smile, and she thought that finally the ice between them had begun to break.

'We might try taking the longboat,' Torgrim reasoned. Unfortunately, he'd explained, he still wasn't back to fighting strength. 'Perhaps if we leave *Goldspray,* the storm will move away with us.'

Goderun snorted. 'You might as well jump overboard, get it over with quickly, and save me the price of a boat. Chancing the reefs in this weather is suicide, plain and simple. No, much as it may pain you, there's no way to put you ashore at Point Blank or anywhere near it. But that's not nearly the end of our problems. I've tried turning north, and guess what happened.'

'I noticed the wind shift to a northerly a while back,' Torgrim said.

'Exactly. Your bloody knob of a traitor doesn't want us getting out of this alive, it would seem. So we're left with two choices: we can beat against the storm and perhaps buy ourselves a few hours before we're blown aground anyway; or we can try going south and see what happens. Mayhap we'll get lucky and the black-magicking turd thinks he's got the south covered with that bloody ghost ship of his. And maybe we'll get even luckier and not run into it.'

234

'You'd risk that?' Breanne asked. 'Risk *Goldspray,* your crew, your life, for a cause that isn't even yours?'

'It is now,' Goderun said grimly. 'Someone threatens me and my ship, thinking they can push me around however it suits them, they're in for a nasty surprise.'

A short time later, all of them braving the storm with Rhys and the helmsman on the quarterdeck while the sailors on watch scrambled to set more canvas, *Goldspray's* bow veered to the south.

*　　　*　　　*

Disengaging from his scrying device, the master of Stormhold gingerly stretched stiff joints and muscles, grunting with pain but satisfied he had his enemies where he wanted them. About time, too. Getting them there had eaten a sizeable hole into the reserves he kept on Haunt. He'd have to order more brought over from the mainland soonest. It was a dependency he deeply disliked – but such were the exigencies of sorcery.

More than twenty years ago, when he'd set himself on this course, it had been clear to him from the outset that only the unreserved use of dark magic would enable him to accomplish his task. In any case it suited his temperament much better, and renouncing magery in its favor had been no hardship at all. On the contrary: it would have been an entirely liberating experience, if not for the annoying fact that one always had to keep sacrifices to hand. He hated having the stinking beggars anywhere near. Even Stormhold's deepest dungeons were still too close for his liking, so he kept most of them in Salt.

Back then, knowing he would need them, right after the bridgehead had been secured he ordered the rest of Salt's population spared and declared Salt and the surrounding countryside out of bounds to the Bane.

He also tasked the Darklings with bringing him the contents of Marillin's every jail, dungeon, oubliette, gibbet, and pillory, and to deliver them unharmed. He took what the Darklings brought – namely the worst dregs of humanity – and put this hitherto underrated human potential to good use, forming three companies out of them: sixty men to oversee his prison camp in Salt; a hundred, most of them former smugglers and pirates, to man the three ships Oswin had been good enough to leave him with; and the rest, thirty-odd mean, reckless bruisers, as Stormhold's garrison and his personal guard. One candidate had turned out to be of particular interest, and that one he'd entrusted with a special task a few years back, though to date he'd had no news of how the man was faring.

He'd solved the problem of keeping them all in line as well. It required some hard concessions, but he convinced the Darkling Oorik, the only one who didn't seem to share the rest of the Bane's aversion to water, to captain one of the ships and keep an eye on the others, a venture that paid off nicely. Stalking the southern shipping routes, they captured coin aplenty to pay the companies with – though gods knew what the morons thought they'd ever buy with it – enough soul food for Oorik to keep it fed and interested, and leftovers that went to replenish the reserves in Salt. Not that they were needed. With the companies raping every beddable woman and girl a hundred times over, the poxy rabble were multiplying like rats. There'd even been a rumor that a nag of nearly sixty had given birth to twins. Fine by him. He didn't care how it was done, as long as

236

they kept them coming.

Everything had been running smoothly until blasted Torgrim had shown up again. He should have suspected something of the sort when he caught the first whiff of a formidable source of power approaching from the north. But for the longest time he'd merely wondered which fool thought he could come anywhere near Haunt with something like that and hope to keep it. He was so bent on bringing whatever it was into his possession that he didn't pay enough attention to the question of who might be carrying it south, and why. And in all fairness, there'd been no sign that anyone of serious format was involved. Not until the previous day, when of a sudden he'd found himself battling for control over the wind and seen with a shock who his adversary was.

It had been a close call. Torgrim was by far the strongest mage he'd ever encountered, and for a while there he'd had a feeling that the Sky God himself was lending the enemy a hand. But sorcery, if properly sustained by human sacrifice, always ended up having the longer wind and could ride out even the meddling of a god, at least of a minor one like Donal.

He'd been positioning his land forces and was almost ready to turn the wind himself when Torgrim interfered. Right from the start he'd intended to herd the treasure south, and would have never allowed it to be lost in a shipwreck. He wanted the Key – for by now he was sure it could be nothing else – wanted it as badly as he'd ever wanted anything. With it, he could fulfill his pledge to the Dark God in one fell swoop, and to hell with more years of fumbling about with something as slow and unwieldy as the Bane.

But now he was of two minds. Quite frankly, he was scared. The Key was one thing; Torgrim *and* the Key were a different proposition altogether. And there could be only one reason for Torgrim's presence. He hadn't forgotten, and was coming for Keon.

Ignoring the pain, he paced the flagstones for over an hour, studying his dilemma from every possible angle until he found what looked like the perfect solution. With a groan he shoehorned himself into the scrying device for the second time that day and sent a message to Oorik. Then he mustered his forces and set about preparing a most cunning trap.

*   *   *

With Breanne by his side, Graeme stood at *Goldspray's* starboard railing, watching the coast draw nearer with frightening speed. Already they were close enough to make out Point Blank's outermost reefs, a boiling inferno of breakers and spray and sharp, gleaming rocks that emerged from the troughs like rows of black, decaying teeth, ready to rip, crush, and grind the proud ship to splinters. What they'd do to a body swimming in the water he dared not imagine.

Gripping Breanne's hand tighter, he felt her squeeze his in return. No matter what happened, he was not going to let her go. Never. He'd fight to his last breath to save her, get her to shore somehow, no matter it looked like nothing could possibly survive those shoals.

Then they were there, close enough to touch, it seemed. Graeme saw barnacles clinging to the rocks like alien passengers to a sunken vessel. The surf was suddenly deafening, hissing and roaring over the reefs and slamming *Goldspray's* groaning hull, spray drenching

238

the steeply canted deck and nearly blinding them as they clung to the railing and stared transfixed at what was probably the last thing they'd see as warm, living bodies. Just before the ship ran aground, they turned their heads as one and shared a last, intimate look, blinking against the salt water stinging their eyes. Breanne shouted something he couldn't hear but had no trouble reading from her lips.

I love you, he answered in kind.

Goldspray scraped by Point Blank with a hair's breadth to spare. Immediately after, they sailed into calmer waters, the wind abating to a moderate breeze. It was eerie: behind them, the storm, a dark, threatening front obscuring everything north and east of the point; and before them a pacified sea and a sun-drenched shoreline that fell away sharply to the west. Once they were past the reefs, Graeme remembered to breathe again, as did everyone else. Only Goderun seemed unimpressed, as if she did this kind of thing every other day.

Seriously angered by their unseen enemy's underhanded manipulations, she'd turned stubborn, deciding to sail all the way down the coast and drop them off as close to their destination as was feasible without attracting undue attention, thus saving them a long slog overland.

It wasn't to be.

Not half an hour after they'd left the storm behind, a ship appeared on the southern horizon, heading their way. Studying it through her spyglass, Goderun cursed.

'Black sails,' she said. 'Black hull. Three guesses who that is.'

'I think it's time you let us have your longboat,' Torgrim said, standing at the railing and seeming to see as much or more than the captain even without the aid of a glass.

'Bollocks!' Goderun said. 'That's a bloody cog. I can outrun her with both hands tied behind my back.'

'No, you can't,' Torgrim said, looking grim. 'Not with what's riding on that ship. And not with Keon pulling the strings. You've seen what he's capable of. And even if we did outrun her, we'd have her hounding us all the way south, with no way of putting us safely ashore. This may be our last and only chance. We have to go now. And you need to get out of here as soon as we've cast off.'

'Aye, all right then. But I'll take you in a ways still, else that blacksailed blighter will be here while you're still pulling for land.'

Cog or no, the black ship moved faster than should have been possible, its squat, lumbering hull bulling its way through the waves as it relentlessly bore down on them like a hungry beast risen from the ocean's profoundest depths to scour the seas for living bounty.

It was a race, and they won it with scant moments to spare. They'd just beached the boat when the black ship sailed by a long stone's throw away, so close Graeme could hear the swish of her bow wave and the wind in her rigging. A huge, man-shaped clot of roiling shadows stood on her starboard quarterdeck, sweeping the shore with a crushing wave of terror that subsided only when the ship turned and headed seawards again to take up the chase after *Goldspray*. Graeme didn't envy Goderun her chances with a Slayer on her tail.

'Looks as if they want to make sure we don't get any more help from Goderun,' he said.

'Aye,' Torgrim said. 'For a while now, I've had a feeling they've

240

been herding us like sheep towards the shearing. I'm surprised Keon didn't sic his dog on us right here and now. He must be very confident we'll come trotting along like good little bah-bahs. Which is exactly what we'll do for the time being.'

'Gods, how I wish there was some sort of bespelled arrow to kill Slayers with,' Pers said. 'The blighter was right there, not thirty yards away. A kid with a bent stick and a piece of string could have hit him.'

'Interesting notion,' Torgrim said. 'Let me give it some thought. In the meantime, I suggest we get moving. There's at least another two hours of daylight left, and we've got a lot of ground to cover.'

*   *   *

Wil didn't usually dream, at least not that he remembered.
Not sure he was dreaming now. He'd gone to sleep thinking they needed to do something about the problem with provisions. They'd all sleep a lot better with some food in their stomachs. This dream, if that was what it was, did seem powerfully real, though, more real than waking life, in fact.

He was walking over a high plain, and seemed to have been doing so already for quite some time. Hours maybe, or days, or weeks. There was a thinness to the air and a blueness to the plain's far edge that told him he was somewhere very high up – closer to the sky than to the lowlands, he thought. It was a barren, desert-like place, nothing but sharp-edged rocks and very fine sand that squeaked under his boots like snow did when the weather was very cold. The air was dry as bones, and his every step raised a puff of ochre dust. His clothes were covered with it, and when he wiped his sweating brow

241

it left a smear of pale clay on his sleeve.

Time passed, how much or how little he couldn't say, until finally he saw something other than sand and rock. Some ways ahead,
four dark, upright shapes hung in the air, wavering and rippling in
the heat like madmen dancing. At first he thought they might be
standing stones. Drawing closer, he saw that they were human figures, though he still couldn't tell whether they were living people or
statues carved from stone. People or statues – standing motionless
and silent on the plain's very edge, they seemed to be watching him
intently.

When he reached them it became clear that they were indeed people,
and alive: two men and two women. One of the men was in his
middle years and easily as big as Wil himself, the other was a handsome, slender youth. Of the women, one was old, a white-haired
crone. The second was much younger, and her hair was fiery red.
They looked like ordinary people, but there was something about
them that put him on his guard – scared him, actually, though he
couldn't have said why.

They didn't speak, just stood there unmoving, inspecting him
with unreadable expressions. His level of fear rose as he considered
the possibility that he might have inadvertently stumbled into the
realm of the dead – or worse, that he'd been actively summoned
there. Such things were said to happen, though rarely, and from
what he'd heard the experience seldom turned out to be beneficial
for the people concerned. The ones who returned from such a trip
were changed forever. Some never made it back at all, though their
bodies lived on, mindless, soulless husks that could last for years

before they gave out and died.

'Who are you?' he asked, summoning up all his courage. 'What have I done that you've brought me here?'

To his surprise, one of the four chuckled. The older man. His voice was deep and somehow... fluid. 'Mortals! Always with the questions. Well, then, let's see. What do we have on you? You were born, for one. With a just bit of ill-will, that could be considered a pretty bad mistake all by itself.'

'Urufin, leave off,' the red-haired women said.

Urufin? Suddenly Wil knew whom he was dealing with. No mortal man bore that name. These four must be gods, and old ones at that. Urufin was the name of the Water God. Which meant the red-haired one must be Moricanna, the Fire Goddess; the crone was Verelda, goddess of the Earth; and the youngling was Donal, the Wind God. This was worse than Wil had thought. Much worse.

It's not real, he reminded himself. *You're dead.*

Somehow he had trouble believing that. Just to be on the safe side he knelt, his forehead touching the ground.

'See? You're frightening the lad.' Moricanna said. 'And you, Wil, you shouldn't be cowering there in the dust like some over-zealous priestling. I detest groveling. Even the gods find it trying. Come, get up. It's very awkward talking to you like this.'

Still half expecting a thunderbolt to strike him dead at any moment, Wil got to his feet, astonished and confused by what Moricanna had just said about the gods.

'Begging your pardon if I'm being stupid, m'lady,' he said. 'All my life I've been taught different – but that just sounded like you don't consider yourselves to be true gods.'

'Now there's a tricky question,' Verelda answered in Moricanna's stead. 'Let's just say we prefer to see ourselves as representing principles, rather than as gods. And we'd be a lot happier if people would be content to honor those principles instead of paying us court in hopes of wheedling favors out of us. Which, I can assure you, they won't. Dealing in favors is not our remit. Upholding the principles is. Here, let me show you something.'

Wil never got to see what it was, because suddenly he was somewhere else – back in camp among hungry soldiers, perhaps, though he wasn't even sure of that anymore – his memory of where he'd just been wiped out as if it had never happened. For a fraction of an instant he clung to a wisp of an impression, something about having made a deal with some very strange and scary people. Then even that was erased, displaced by the sobering realization that he was dead.

Curious what the afterlife would look like, he opened his eyes.

The first thing he saw was Quillan's face hovering over him, filled with a mixture of worry and wonder.

'What are *you* doing here?' Wil asked groggily. 'Did they kill you too?'

Another face joined Quillan's: Gael, grinning like a loon.

'And you.' Wil said, trying not to mumble. 'I thought you got away. It's going to get mighty crowded over here if somebody doesn't stop Thorley soon.'

'Lad,' Quillan said, suddenly wearing the same idiot smile as Gael. 'Much as I hate to disappoint you, you're not in the hallowed halls yet. You're still with us, though for a while there I'd have sworn you were a goner.'

'You mean, I didn't die?'

'Oh, you died all right. Leastwise you weren't breathing and you're heart was stopped for near on half an hour. Actually we'd already carried you off down off the hill and were looking for stones to build you a nice, cozy cairn with. And then suddenly you coughed and spit and started breathing again. Scared me and Buck nearly shitless, you did.'

Buck, who had the teeth to go with his name, stuck his head in the picture and gave Wil a friendly wave. It seemed like everybody was grinning today.

'So how come I didn't stay dead?'

'Because you're a sloppy little bugger, is why,' Quillan said. 'Those loose platelets on your jerkin were what saved you.'

'I was about to fix those,' Wil said. 'But then Gael showed up.'

'You can thank the gods you didn't. Hanging down over the one below like they were, they made for a spot about four inches square that was covered by three layers of steel. And Fray did you the favor of hitting exactly that spot. Still made a hole in your hide, but not so deep as to... as to kill you, I almost said. I reckon it was the shock of the impact that stopped your heart for a while.'

'So where are we?'

'Safe, for now. Thinking it wasn't such a good idea to take you back into camp, we decided to get you set up somewhere out of the way. And lo and behold, whom should we run into but Gael, Yardley and Dice. You'll be staying with them until we figure something out.'

'Fray's time is up,' Wil said, not liking how hard and implacable he sounded. But there were things a man just couldn't tiptoe around, and this was one of them. 'He has to go. And so does Thorley.'

'I thought you'd say something like that. And I suppose you're right. It's the only way to put and end to this madness. But first you need to get back on your feet.'

'I'm fine,' Wil said. But when he tried to prove it by sitting up, he nearly fainted from the pain. And it wasn't just pain, either. There was something else wrong with him, though he couldn't put his finger on it. Like he'd lost something. Like a part of him had gone missing, leaving him... not quite how he'd used to be, was the closest he could get.

'Right,' Quillan said. 'Tell me that again in a couple of days and maybe I'll believe you. Now. Me and Buck need to get back to camp. But we'll keep in touch. And Gael, see that this young fool holds still for a while.' He chuckled. 'Like it or not, we might still need him.'

'Did you find any sign of Graeme and Breanne?' Wil asked Gael when Quillan and Buck had left.

'Not that I'd have told Thorley,' Gael said. 'But I think we found that Archer's Rock place you said they'd been talking about. Though I'd rather we hadn't, and the rest of the lads were still with us.'

'Tell me what happened.' Wil knew it was better to talk about these things than to keep them bottled up inside where they could poison a man's mind and drive him to desperate ends.

'As I said, we found Archer's Rock.' Gael paused, rubbing broad, calloused hands on his thighs as if he might wipe out the

246

things he'd seen. 'But we saw it only from afar. There were Rooters everywhere, and Shifters too, and we had to get out of there while it was light. On the way back, Smiler ran into a Lurker. One of those vine things. It got him round the neck, hauled him up into the treetops before the rest of us knew what was happening. Damn thing chose a mother of a tree that was impossible to climb and would've taken us hours to chop down.

'That night, Jace got the runs. He went just a few steps outside the Wards, but that was all it took. When he didn't come back or answer our calls we lit a couple of torches and went looking. Found him squirming under a Rooter, so full of holes you could have used him for a sieve. He was dead by the time we got the thing off of him. Corbin got bitten during the fight. Just a scratch on his hand, but you know how it is. He took off during the night, just disappeared while no one was looking. Shifters did for the others. I'll skip the details, if you don't mind.' He fell silent.

'I'm sorry, Gael,' Wil said. 'It should never have happened. And if I have anything to say about it, it won't happen again.'

Three days later, Wil was ready to step up again.

His whole left side hurt like hell, but he couldn't hold still any longer, plagued by the ominous feeling that time was running out on them and they had better move soon or it would be too late. That afternoon Quillan showed up with news.

'Last night,' he said, 'Dicken up and went to tell Thorley he was resigning from his post. When Thorley forbade it Dicken said too bad, but it was already done and dusted. For a wonder, he got lucky. Thorley told him he was too craven and worthless to waste a good rope on, and had Fray send him off with a kick in the arse.'

'That was brave of Dicken,' Wil said.

'Aye,' Gael agreed. 'Bravest thing the little man's ever done.'

'There's more,' Quillan said, looking like someone with a secret to tell. 'When they heard what Dicken had done, some of the men came to me saying they wanted a new captain, and not one appointed by Thorley. So, on the sly, we got word around and had us a little vote.' He paused, obviously savoring the moment.

'I suppose congratulations are in order,' Wil said.

'Not for me, they're not,' Quillan said. 'And thank the gods for that. It's you. The vote was unanimous. The job is yours.'

'But I don't want it,' Wil said, stunned.

'That's one of the reasons they chose you. It's one lesson they've learned the hard way: give power to a man who wants it, and he'll soon believe it was his to begin with. He'll use it for himself instead of the common good, and he won't give it up without things getting ugly. It's the hard-earned wisdom of simple men, but I'll take it over the clever arguments of the learned and the mighty any time. But what's more important, they trust you to find a way out of this mess and lead them back home.'

Wil sighed. 'All right, then. Maybe it's for the best. Because once we lay hands on Thorley we'll be branded mutineers and traitors, and they'll hang the lot of us as soon as we set foot in the Vales. But if the men can say they were just following orders, they should get off a lot easier.'

'Captain takes the fall.' Quillan shook his head. 'We'll see about that. It's not what we chose you for.'

'Time for that later,' Wil said. 'I've been thinking about how best to go through with this. Here's what I reckon we should do.'

He explained his plan. Quillan and Gael had a few suggestions, but even after they'd ironed out the kinks it still sounded mad – just a little less mad than doing nothing and letting Thorley lead them on into certain disaster.

Towards evening Wil, Gael, Yardley and Dice slipped into camp with the returning hunters. There was a heart-stopping moment when one of the men guarding the gate gave Wil a salute. Luckily, none of Thorley's men were around to notice the slip.

Shortly after, Quillan held a weapons inspection. It was only logical to do it on the piece of open ground between the Watch's and Thorley's sections of the camp. Trey the armorer set up shop there as well, ready to fix what was broken. Thorley's men, gathered around their own fire, spared the proceedings a few curious glances and then chose to ignore them – otherwise they might have noticed that a surprising number of crossbows seemed to need fixing.

Half the Watch must have been milling about when suddenly order emerged from the clutter and it wasn't a weapons inspection anymore but a double row of men facing Thorley's camp with cross-bows spanned and loaded, effectively trapping him and his House Guard against the southern arc of the wall.

Fray rose from his seat by the fire. 'The bloody fuck do you jackasses think you're doing?' he said, a scowl on his ugly mug. 'Been eating the wrong kind of mushrooms, have you? Well, go jerk off somewhere else. You're spoiling the view.'

Seeing the look on Fray's face when Wil stepped forward from the ranks was almost worth the pain of being shot at. For once, the great bruiser was at a loss for words. White as a sheet, he looked like a man visited by a ghost.

'Get Thorley out here,' Wil told him. 'On the double.'

Fray seemed of a mind to give lip, but then, still speechless, he turned and slipped into Thorley's pavilion.

The horses are unusually restive tonight, Wil noted. *I should...*

Then Thorley came out with Gage on his heels, and he never finished the thought.

'You again,' Thorley said when he saw Wil. 'I thought we'd gotten rid of you. So it's open mutiny now, is it? You'll – '

'Call it mutiny, if you like.' Wil was in no mood to listen to Thorley. 'I call it sanity. You may be past telling the difference, but you should have no problem understanding our terms. You'll hand over Fray to us, to be judged for his crimes. He'll have fair treatment, fairer than what you saw fit to give Dunne. The rest of your Guard will join the Freewatch, provided they swear the oaths. And you will resign as Lord Commander, your fate to be decided once we're back in the Vales.'

'You'll hang for this,' Thorley said, talking past Wil to the men of the Watch. 'Each and every one of you. There will be no mercy for traitors. But step away now from that misguided fool who's leading you all into disaster, and perhaps you'll receive a more lenient sentence.'

'No.' It was Quillan who spoke up. 'It's you who's misguided and is leading us to our deaths, not the captain. We've had enough of you. Give over, or I'll – '

Suddenly there was shouting down by the gate. Moments later, the big war horn sounded three mournful blasts, the sign that they were under attack.

'Nobody moves,' Wil said, and went to see for himself.

So it wasn't Thorley had me worried all this time but this, he thought, looking out on the dark shapes pouring from the woods and massing at the foot of the hill. Rooters, hundreds of them. And there were Shifters as well, six or seven at least by a quick count.

They couldn't have picked a worse moment. It's almost as if they knew to attack now. Damn it, and we were so close to putting a leash on Thorley and his thugs. Now what?

It was exactly the question Thorley asked when Wil returned. 'Now what, captain?' he said with a sardonic smile. 'Bit of a predicament, isn't it?'

'Not for me,' Wil said. 'The choice is yours to make: you can either swear by all you hold sacred that you and your men will surrender once this is over, in which case I'll let you fight with us. Or I can order them to shoot the lot of you on the spot and have done with the problem you pose. What's it to be? Answer me quick, before I decide for you.'

Gage whispered something in Thorley's ear. Thorley listened for a moment, then he shook his head.

'Very well,' he told Wil. 'I swear that my men and I will surrender to you after the battle. Satisfied?'

Wil nodded. Gael beside him looked as if he wanted to say something more, but then the shouts from the wall turned more urgent, and Wil sent everyone off to their stations.

Look at us, he thought. *We're like a handful of pebbles cast into the air. How many of us will fall where we can be found again, and*

251

how many will be lost forever?

Back at the gate, a gruesome sight awaited him.

While he'd been gone, one of the Shifters had jumped close and thrown something over the wall. It was human head, and though its features were a mess of cuts and bruises, Wil recognized them promptly: Tait, back from scouting the west but not in the way they'd all hoped for.

Gripped by a cold fury that seemed to rise like hoarfrost from the very bottom of his soul, Wil turned away and began issuing orders.

'Quillan, we need runners to light fire arrows and pass them around. No time to fill the braziers. Gael, the men to the north need to spread out more evenly. They've left gaps between them. And there's no sense having all our best archers massed at the gate. The enemy is coming from all sides, so place them accordingly.'

There was a short respite while they watched the mass of hideous creatures below begin to move up the hill. As the first of them came into range, a volley of fire arrows arced through the darkening sky. They looked harmless as fireflies, until some of them found their marks and the first Rooters burst into flames.

*   *   *

16

Goderun had dropped them off within sight of an abandoned fishing village. According to Graeme's map, there was a town a few miles inland, and a road leading south from there. The town was deserted but not empty. Graeme saw Rooters sheltering in the dark interiors of derelict buildings, and Lurkers infested every street and alley save the main thoroughfare.

As towns went, the place wasn't large. Walking through it with the Bane massed around them, it seemed to go on for miles. Pers and Finn had arrows nocked to half-drawn bows and kept turning this way and that as they tried to keep their small party covered. Graeme doubted they'd get off more than one shot, should worst come to worst: every door they passed stood open, and not a house that wasn't teeming with dark, gnarled shapes. He had his sword in hand, for all the good it would do against such overwhelming numbers. Breanne looked sickly pale, like she was about to lose her breakfast, but she was bearing up. Torgrim's mien was grim. Graeme sincerely hoped the mage had a few powerful tricks up his sleeve, else their chances of getting through this alive were slim going on none. And so they progressed, moving with what seemed like excruciating slowness, eyes constantly roaming, searching house after house, doorway after doorway, window after window.

Surprisingly, the Bane let them pass without attacking.

Twice, Graeme noticed movement on the rooftops: grey, blurry shapes that could only be Shifters. But they appeared more intent on staying hidden than causing the humans down on the road any grief.

They're watching, he thought, *making sure we go where we're supposed to. Torgrim was right when he said we were being herded.*

And then, after what felt like hours, time suddenly quickened again and they were walking past the last houses, relief written large on everyone's faces. Leaving town, they discussed whether they should take the road or try to shake off the watchers by heading cross-country.

'Might as well stick to the road for now,' Torgrim said. 'Sooner or later we'll want to slip away, but it can wait. I suspect by now Keon has found some way to keep track of the Key, but it's not nearly the same as having eyes on us. So we'll want to choose our moment with care, and make the most of it.'

That moment came four days later.

With the map saying they were only a little over two days away from Salt, Graeme reckoned it was time for them to become less conspicuous. Torgrim agreed. That night, as the nights before, they camped by the side of the road. When Torgrim set the Wards – real mage's Wards, these, something Graeme hadn't seen in a very long time – he explained that he was allowing for a small gap, a bolthole through which they could quietly disappear while leaving the Wards in place, hopefully fooling the watchers into believing they were still there.

'The Wards will decay eventually,' he said. 'But by then we should be halfway to Salt.'

'You aim to travel at night from now on?' Graeme asked, not liking the idea one bit.

'Only tonight,' Torgrim said. 'We have to put some distance between them and us right away, else we needn't even bother. Although it'll be a drain, I can and will look a ways ahead while we travel, keep us from running into nasty surprises.'

'I'm holding you to that,' Pers threatened. 'If one of them Lurkers gets hold of my nuts, you'll be welcome to give me yours as a replacement.'

'Don't worry,' Finn reassured Torgrim with a grin. 'No Lurker's going to touch the stringy old bastard. They'd only break their teeth on him if they did.'

'Better old and stringy than the loud-mouthed young fool who gets eaten first,' Pers said.

'That's enough talk about getting eaten, boys,' Breanne said. She sounded like a strict aunt, but Graeme would have bet she was smiling.

They settled down around a small fire, biding their time, going through their normal evening routine so as not to arouse the suspicion of those who were watching. Torgrim, sitting there cradling his staff and stroking it absently, seemed lost in thought.

'You sure you're not getting a little too attached to that thing?' Pers asked jokingly.

'What? No,' Torgrim said. 'But a man needs to look after his tools and his weapons.'

Graeme wholeheartedly agreed with the principle, though he had no idea how stroking a staff was supposed to make it any better or stronger. Whatever. Mages were mages – a species apart, it sometimes seemed – and good luck to the man who thought he could figure them out.

Sitting by the fire with nothing to do but wait, he drifted off for a spell, and dreamed.

He was somewhere in the mountains. The old man was there, and another boy – Tobin, yes, that was his name. He and Tobin were best friends, he knew, no matter they were very different, though he couldn't recall the reason why. They were walking behind the old man along a graveled road that curled ever upward with a dreamway's indifference to ordinary logic, going from road to mountain trail to goat track to steep, wayless slope, its final mutation an unscalable cliff. They turned around and tried another path, but it was a dead end as well.

Then the old man was gone, and it was just the two of them. Tobin pointed to a spot behind Graeme and said 'That's the way out.'

'All right, then,' Graeme said. 'Let's try it.'

'You go,' Tobin said. 'I can't. I never had a sister.'

It made a strange sort of sense, so Graeme went. But he'd taken only a few steps when he remembered that he'd forgotten something immensely important, though he couldn't recall what it was. He turned to ask Tobin if he knew, but Tobin wasn't there anymore.

Suddenly wary of what might happen if he dreamed on, Graeme struggled awake, feeling out of sorts and more confused than ever.

He reckoned it was close to midnight when they stole away, slipping into the pitch-dark forest with nothing but the stars above to guide them.

Following his woodsman's instincts more than his eyes, he found them a trail leading west, partly reclaimed by the woods but still passable. They'd been walking for less than an hour when Finn called out softly from behind.

'What is it?' Graeme asked.

'It's Breanne. She just stopped all of a sudden, and she's not re- sponding. I think she might be having one of them visions.'

Turning back, Graeme found her standing still as a statue, her face a pale oval in the feeble light of a sickle moon just rising over the treetops, her eyes unfathomable wells of darkness. He was won- dering what he should do when she spoke, the voice definitely not hers but brittle and rheumy like that of a very old woman.

'Three lives and three,' she said. 'Three we can spare, and three we can not. One is the cost of survival. One is the price for freedom. And one is the charge for mending what's been broken.'

She remained still for a moment longer. Then she stirred and looked around. 'Graeme?'

'I'm here.' He took her in his arms, feeling her shoulders shake with a silent sob. 'It's all right. I'm here. Tell me what you saw.'

'A battle,' she said, swallowing hard. 'A battle between men and monsters. There was a young man. He was big, a head taller than the others, and he looked very strong. I saw him standing on top of a wall, swinging a great axe. And then he fell, and I knew he was dead. It felt as if I'd lost someone dear, though I'd never seen him before.'

'Light, curly hair? Fair-skinned, beardless?' Graeme asked.

'Yes. Do you know him?'

'Wil.' It was crushing news. Wil, whom he'd taken to almost as a father would to a son. Wil, in whom he'd placed so much hope for the future.

'I'm sorry,' Breanne said. 'He means a lot to you, doesn't he?'

Graeme nodded, swallowing a lump in his throat. Then something occurred to him. 'You said three would be spared. Maybe what you saw hasn't happened yet. Maybe it won't. Maybe whoever was speaking through you can change things so Wil doesn't have to die.' He knew he was grasping at straws but couldn't have cared less.

'Maybe.' Breanne sounded bleak. 'I don't know.'

Torgrim, who'd remained silent so far, spoke up. 'That's the thing with visions, my friends. Sometimes they give you useful hints, and sometimes they sow nothing but confusion. I'd counsel you to put this one aside. No use fretting over something you'll not figure out until it's actually happened – if it happens at all. And we should get going. Neither time nor the Bane are going to wait while we try and sort this out.'

When dawn came they rested, but only for a few hours.

Graeme felt restless, on edge, and so did the others, as if tarrying too long might tip some great, imponderable scales and set the world on an even darker course, one where the possibility of redemption was no longer foreseen.

Stringing together a series of forest tracks and game trails, Graeme led them south. The land gradually changed from flat to hilly, and noon found them following a winding path through a maze of rocky knolls and steep-sided ravines.

A deep, persistent unease drove him to pick up the pace, a disquieting feeling as if something sharp and deadly were aimed at the spot between his shoulder blades. He felt an increasing need to check their back-trail. Looking behind, he found Torgrim doing he same.

Then the trail led them onto the highest rise yet, and to the edge of a chasm whose near side looked barely negotiable – though the question of whether they could get down it in one piece was mute, seeing as the other side was a sheer, vertical wall of rock.

There had once been a makeshift bridge here, the massive trunks of two felled trees laid side by side across the gap. One of them had slipped, its far end now resting on a ledge ten feet below the rim. The other one was still in place but looked dangerously rotten.

'I'll see if I can find a better place to get across,' he told the others.

'No time,' Torgrim said. He was facing the way they'd come, and when Graeme turned to look he saw a dozen Rooters coming towards them, fanned out in a half-circle to cut off any route of escape this side of the chasm. But they were only the vanguard. Behind them, a tall figure wreathed in shadow appeared, preceded by a wave of gut-freezing fear. A Slayer.

Its impossibly dark substance untouched by the moon's light, it approached like a black hole growing out of the night, a walking, vertiginous shaft that, if it bottomed out at all, did so in faraway, alien realms.

'Go!' Torgrim said. 'Get over there fast as you can, and then run! I'll catch up with you.'

But Graeme wasn't about to leave Torgrim to face the enemy alone. He looked to Pers, motioning him to go on with Breanne and Finn.

*　　*　　*

Too paralyzed with fear to think straight, Breanne allowed herself to be led over the uncertain bridge by Pers and Finn. Halfway across, she made the mistake of looking down. She saw no bottom, only ever deepening shadows that seemed to reach up and tug at her until she was sure she would fall. She was saved by Pers and Finn gripping her arms and holding her on course. Twice the log slipped, settling an inch or two, but it didn't fall.

Once she was on the other side and out of the Slayer's immediate reach, her muddled senses began to clear. She was still terrified, but the fear she felt now was real: Graeme was still over there, and so was Torgrim.

She saw the Rooters massed around Graeme, his sword darting this way and that, flashing like steel become lightning. But they were many, and he was alone.

Torgrim was beset by the Slayer, desperately fending off writhing tentacles that sprang from the shadow-being's indistinct form like black adder's tongues or sinuous whipcords, seeking to grip and ensnare him. They were lines, she knew, but dark and alien, not like any she'd ever seen before. Compared to these, the rope Edilda had made out of hatred and avarice seemed like a harmless little streamer cast by a naughty child.

The mage was using his staff as a weapon, whirling and striking with eye-twisting speed. Each time he hit a line, there was a sharp crack and a small shower of sparks. The Slayer seemed to cringe under the blows, as if they were actually causing it pain or at least some serious discomfort. But, pain or no, it kept on coming, forcing Torgrim ever closer to the edge of the abyss.

Graeme was still standing. Two Rooters were down. Another one fell. The rest of them continued to push him towards the chasm. Standing rooted to the spot, Breanne could only watch in helpless horror.

'Go!' Torgrim shouted again. 'There's nothing you can do here!'

Step by step, left with no other choice, Graeme retreated until he was teetering on the very edge. For a wonder, his searching foot found the bridge. A few precarious steps backwards took him out of range of the Rooters. They didn't follow, as if they'd achieved what they'd intended.

Slowly, shakily, he began to turn, dry moss and crumbling wood falling away under his feet. Hardly daring to breathe, Breanne silently urged him on.

Torgrim, on the other hand, had nowhere left to go.
Another step backwards, and he'd fall to his death. Suddenly he ducked and rolled under the Slayer's whipping tentacles. Coming up in a crouch, he whirled his staff around in a sweeping arc, catching the Slayer's legs. There was a blinding flash of light and an ear-splitting crash.

Briefly, the Slayer stood swaying on the lip of the gorge. Then it toppled over forwards and fell. Before Breanne could breathe a sigh of relief, a snaking black tentacle reached out and wrapped itself around the bridge.

With a crunch and a grind, the log was wrenched free of its precarious support. Graeme, three steps away from saving himself, lost his balance.

Falling, he cast her a last, heart-wrenching look of loss, regret, and surrender. Then he was gone.

Breanne didn't realize she was screaming until Pers hugged her tight, murmuring calming nonsense in her ear.

The next instant, a horrendous realization hit her with such crushing finality, she tore herself loose from Pers' arms and would have thrown herself into the deep if Finn hadn't caught her.

She could have saved Graeme, she saw, now that it was too late.

*   *   *

The first wave of Rooters reached the wall.

Quillan saw Wil set aside his bow. The next moment he was standing atop the wall, feet planted wide, laying about with his great axe and sending heads and limbs and pieces of moss and bark flying every which way.

That's what a true hero looks like, Quillan thought proudly. *We chose well when we made this lad – no, this man – our captain.*

He was about to join Wil on the wall when he felt a prickling on the back of his neck, as if some unnamed danger threatened from behind. Turning, he saw Gage gripping Thorley by the throat. Thorley was on his knees, eyes bulging in terror, hands scrabbling uselessly at Gage's wrist. The black priest was wearing some kind of glove harnessed to his left arm, the fingers ending in sharp steel claws that were dug deep into Thorley's flesh. Gage's other arm was outstretched, his splayed fingers pointing at Wil's undefended back.

262

Frantic, Quillan nocked an arrow and drew.

With a vicious jerk, Gage ripped out Thorley's throat. A lump of darkness formed around his outstretched right hand.

Beseeching the gods for a steady hand, Quillan found his aim and loosed.

Gage swept Quillan's arrow aside with an almost offhand gesture. Then he sent the black lump streaking at Wil. The wall under Wil exploded in a storm of flying rocks, throwing him forward, right into the enemy's midst.

Yelling, 'Man down!' Quillan climbed through the gap Gage's missile had ripped. Several men followed him. Together, they managed to hack their way through to where Wil lay on the ground, bleeding from an ugly wound on the side of his head. While the others fended off the Rooters pushing in from all sides, Quillan rolled Wil onto his back, grabbed him under the arms and dragged him back behind the wall where men stood ready to shore up the gap with pieces of timber.

Easing Wil to the ground, Quillan felt for a pulse.
Nothing. Not a twitch, not a flutter. Shaking with sorrow and rage, he stood and looked around, searching for Gage. The accursed priest was nowhere in sight.

Then Quillan heard another explosion, somewhere behind Thorley's and the Guard's tents. He grabbed a crossbow from one of the men and sprinted towards the tents. Rounding Thorley's pavilion, he nearly fell over one of the Guard lying there with his throat ripped out.

There was another gap in the wall, three dead soldiers half buried in the rubble. He caught a fleeting glimpse of Gage rushing out through the breach and disappearing to the left. Loosed a shot. Missed. Casting aside the now useless bow, Quillan ran for the nearest part of the wall and clambered onto the crown, thinking to cut Gage off.

And there the bastard was, right beneath him.

With an angry roar, Quillan hacked at the traitorous fiend, the tip of his sword raking the man's cheek and taking off half of an ear. Gage stumbled and fell but was back on his feet in an instant. Retreating a few steps, he glowered murder at Quillan, who was about to jump down and finish what he'd started. In a flash, the priest raised a hand and sent a bolt into the wall where the sergeant was standing.

The stones under Quillan's feet disintegrated in a shower of splinters and dust as a mighty fist flung him backwards, landing him hard on his back and driving every last bit of air from his lungs.

It was some moments before he could move again. He hurt all over, but luckily nothing seemed broken. Retching and coughing, he levered himself up with the help of his sword.

He found Gage lying spread-eagled outside the wall.

There was a look of surprise on the man's ugly face, and a huge carpenter's spike driven through the middle of his forehead. It must have been embedded in one of the logs they'd fetched from the ruined farm, and Gage had inadvertently shot himself in the head with it when he'd blasted the wall in his attempt to kill Quillan.

A freak accident or the gods' punishment, Quillan didn't care.

His thirst for retribution slaked but his heart none the lighter for it, he took command and rounded up a few men to repair the damage Gage had wrought. Though it was hardly more than a defiant gesture, he had them patch the gaps in the wall as best they could, knowing full well that the true breach of their defenses, the one Wil's death had left, was impossible to mend, and that it would likely spell the end for all of them.

*   *   *

As the Slayer stood swaying on the lip of the gorge, Breanne had the strangest impression of the world slipping sideways for a heartbeat, a short, dizzying lurch that made her knees buckle and left her momentarily disoriented. The feeling passed as quickly as it had come, and in any case she was too busy to pay it further heed.

The Slayer toppled over forwards and fell. Before she could breathe a sigh of relief, a snaking black tentacle reached out and wrapped itself around the bridge.

With a crunch and a grind, the log was wrenched free of its precarious support. Graeme, three steps away from saving himself, lost his balance.

Breanne was prepared.

Strangely, the Key hadn't stirred all this time, but she'd remembered it all the same. With seconds to spare, she donned it just as Graeme's and Torgrim's position went from bad to untenable. Using the Key's power, she reached out and plucked Graeme from the log a moment before it fell away from under his feet. Setting him down on firm ground, she reached out a second time.

The Slayer still hadn't given up. It had fastened another tentacle around Torgrim's leg. The mage was whacking away at it with his staff, but whatever he'd done to the wood earlier seemed to have been used up, and he was inexorably being dragged towards the precipice.

When her line met the Slayer's, she felt a tremendous shock, as if she'd touched a bolt of dark lightning. Swamped by an overpowering wave of revulsion and nausea, she nearly let go.

But she saw in an instant that the Slayer was weakened, that for now at least, she was the stronger. Swallowing bile and fear, she rallied. Ignoring the horror of having to touch the thing, she severed the Slayer's dark line. Losing its last hold, the abominable creature fell away into the deep and was gone. For now. Somehow she doubted it could be killed that easily.

She brought Torgrim across, though he didn't look happy about it. She didn't much care. The power flowing through her like a perfect storm was vast, unstoppable, intoxicating, like impregnable armor through which nothing could reach her, while she could reach out as she pleased, could touch anything in the world and make it do whatever she wanted. Lines and nodes of all kinds were whirling around her, offering themselves to her, ready to respond and bend to her will.

Of a sudden something caught at her, slowing her down and pulling her out of the dizzying rush. Graeme. He was shouting at her. So was Torgrim. They looked worried. Frightened. Though she could hardly hear them over the power roaring in her ears, she understood with abrupt and frightening clarity what they wanted, and how close she was to losing herself. She had to get out.

Only now, the Key was suddenly working against her. It wanted to stay where it was. She had to strain just to lift her hands to her head. And then she couldn't seem to grasp the silver band, her fumbling fingers finding nothing but skin and hair. But she fought on, finally getting a hold of the circlet.

She tore it off and threw it on the ground. Then she bent over and vomited until she thought the next thing to come up would be the very bottom of her soul.

When it was over, she looked up. The others were watching her. They all appeared shaken. Graeme attempted a smile. Pers and Finn looked frightened and awed. Torgrim's mien was as grim as she'd ever seen it.

'There was no other way,' she told him.

'I know,' he said. 'But the consequences may well prove exceedingly dire.' He let out a long, sighing breath. 'Ah, well. No helping it now. We're alive, we still have a job to do, and we'd best get to it before Keon figures out what happened and sends us another of his charming welcoming committees.'

*   *   *

17

The master of Stormhold was unsettled.

His attempt to eliminate Torgrim had failed. Worse, a Darkling had been struck down, easily defeated by a ten-foot-tall goddess bathed in blue light, an apparition as terrifying and grim as the Reaper himself. He knew she was merely a woman, knew it was the Key that made her such a frightening specter, but it was alarming all the same. The woman had power of her own, and not too little of it, else she'd not be nearly as strong as she was, Key or no.

At least it and his enemies were still heading in the right direction, though he wasn't sure anymore whether he wanted to be there when they arrived. He'd changed his plans accordingly, adding another, even deadlier element to the trap he'd prepared and moving his base of operations out of the immediate danger zone. He left a small contingent of guards in Salt and another at Stormhold, enough so it wouldn't look too much like a setup but not so many as to create an obstacle the bearer of the Key couldn't overcome.

For the trap, he persuaded the Darklings to bring something through the Gate that even they weren't comfortable with, a being of some size but no certain shape, its outward appearance a constant flux of changing forms determined only by its uncanny ability to reflect the deepest fears of those who beheld it.

Once, when he'd looked through the Gate into the Darklings' dry, dusty hell of a world, he'd seen such a monster in the distance, crouched atop a huge, wandering dune like the essence of all nightmares congealed into a giant lump of menacing darkness. The Darklings had an unpronounceable name for its kind that sounded like a stuttering scream. He called it a Hellhound. It was a pure, unfettered force of destruction, something even the bearer of the Key would find hard to survive.

As a precaution, he had the essentials of his trade moved to the ship *Nightshade.* His scrying device was set up in the stateroom, and the hold was crammed with more than a hundred sacrifices, fuel that should last him until the current problems were resolved.

There were provisions for several weeks, and a cache of weapons and gold still on board from *Nightshade's* most recent haul. *Nightstalker* was ready to sail as well, and Oorik with *Nightmare* was expected within the hour, back from sinking that meddlesome pirate from Windward. He should have sent a couple of ships to smoke out that rat hole already years ago.

Whatever. As soon as *Nightmare* was reprovisioned, they'd cast off and follow the events that were about to unfold on Haunt from a safe distance. Once the trap was sprung and his enemies destroyed, all that remained would be to stroll in and pluck the Key out of the rubble. Then nothing and no one would be able to stop him from completing his and the Dark One's work.

*   *   *

Arden's song had taken hold in a way Wulfwyn hadn't dared hope for. By now the Stricken following them must have surely numbered over a thousand. They'd taken up the song, made it their own and given it a new depth and urgency. She could hear it, if faintly: hundreds of voices, each singing its own variation – and yet all of them were in harmony, a heartbreaking coincidence of grief, and courage, and trust in the Treesinger's offer of freedom and salvation. Hearing it made her want to cry, and even paying it no mind wasn't proof against sudden and unexpected tears.

The song and its message, taken up and passed on from Stricken to Stricken, seemed to be spreading even to those who were still far, far away. They were coming, Arden said, thousands upon thousands of them, and that it was time to start planting.

She found out what exactly he meant by that the following night. She'd discovered a way to Ward them even while they were traveling, and to do it without blocking Arden's song. It wasn't as good as fixed Wards, but she could drop the shield she was carrying and bring it up to full strength in no time at all.

There was a drawback, though: the effort of sustaining it night after night was draining her, slowly but surely. What reserves she'd had were gone, used up, and it had begun feeding on her substance. Just this morning, Arden had remarked on how thin she looked, and insisted she eat more. In truth she was already eating twice what she normally did, three times even. It was just never enough, her body seeming to burn through whatever she gave it like a wildfire out of control.

That night they reached the edge of a wide stretch of open land, and

271

Arden said this was a good place for a Planting. Maintaining the shield, she settled down to watch, curious what would happen.

Nothing at first, it turned out – at least nothing she was aware of. But after a while she noticed that the song was subtly changing: slowing, calming, deepening. And then she heard other sounds as well: the soft spill of earth being displaced, the grinding of gravel and stone as roots sought their way downward, the small cracks and groans of branches spreading and growing, the rustle of leaves unfolding.

All through the night Arden's song never faltered, nor did that of his charges, and when the eastern horizon grew light and the sun made to take up its journey, Wulfwyn saw that what had happened that night had indeed been a Planting. Where before they'd been on the edge of a forest, they were now in the midst of one, grown overnight by at least a thousand new trees.

Looking around, she saw that most of them still carried some sign of their former existence. Many of the skyward-raised limbs still resembled arms more than branches, and there were gaps in the bark, as yet not quite closed, revealing glimpses of old lives irredeemably lost but finally giving way to something new: here a rib cage, there a thigh bone, and over there a face cast in shadow and completely covered in green but with eyes that looked back at her and seemed still to retain a last, fading spark of humanity.

What was definitely gone was the alien hunger that had driven these poor creatures for so long. Instead, she sensed something like a susurrus of relief pass through the Planting, and she imagined that if these strange, tragic beings felt anything that she with her human heart and mind might still be capable of understanding, it would be surrender, and conciliation and, hopefully, peace.

*   *   *

Here, let me show you something,' Verelda said.

Huh? Wil thought, remembering his long slog across the desert-like plain. *This place again? Looks like the gods aren't done with me yet.*

As if no time at all had elapsed since his last visit, Verelda waved a hand, and a hole opened up in the air in front of him. It was a window onto a distant place, giving him a bird's-eye view of a landscape so ravaged he didn't immediately recognize it for what it was. As his mind slowly began to make sense of what he saw, the jumble resolved itself into a flat stretch of land of indefinite size, a desolate plain where someone looked to have scattered tons of rusted metal about in huge, twisted heaps. Broken glass lay everywhere, more of it in this one place alone than existed in all of Baintry, he reckoned.

The ground seemed to consist mainly of a grey, compacted substance shot through with bars of iron. Large tracts of it had been ripped up and lay about in shattered, jagged chunks, some of them big as houses. Where there was earth, it was bare, sterile, blackened by fire and pocked with craters. The depressions were filled with brightly colored liquids, lurid pools of oily iridescence that might have looked pretty if they hadn't been so obviously unnatural.

Poisoned, Wil thought. *Dead.*

Rimmed around with a sickly-yellow froth, the holes reminded him of dying men's mouths, gaping wide to release a last foul, disease-ridden breath into the world of the living.

Only there wasn't anything alive down there, not a blade of grass

273

sprouting from the dead soil, not a vole or a rat scurrying from shadow to murky shadow, not a bird traversing the fecal brown haze that passed for a sky. The only thing moving was a sheet of rusted metal lazily flapping in the noxious breeze. Wil could hear the faint sound of it banging against the steel construct it had partly come loose from.

'That,' Verelda said, closing the window with another wave, 'is what happens when the principles are neglected, when people cease to respect and honor the foundations of life. And it's also why we've called you here. What is being done to Baintry – and what will be done to the rest of Vereld, if it isn't stopped – is being expedited by a different means and in a different manner than what you just saw, but the end result will be very nearly the same.'

'What she's trying to say,' Donal said, peering at Wil with a mixture of curiosity and commiseration, 'is that we want your help, provided you're willing to give it. Though I'll tell you straight away it's a terrible deal. Totally one-sided, with nothing in it for you that you could possibly want.'

'You're stirring up dust, flyboy,' Urufin rumbled. 'Save your wind, if you don't have anything helpful to say.'

'And there's nothing you can do?' Wil asked, ignoring them both.

'Not without you,' Verelda said.

'What about Elil? Doesn't he care what's happening?'

'He's the Creator,' Verelda said, 'not the administrator of what he's wrought. He doesn't interfere in the day-to-day workings. Sadly, I'd say for once.'

'What is it you want from me, then?' Wil asked, not at all sure he wanted to hear the answer.

'Your help in stopping the Bane,' Moricanna said. 'Three are already out there doing what they can, but it won't be enough. Because, as things stand, all three are going to die before they can finish what they've begun.'

Wil was shocked. 'Arden. Graeme. And Breanne.'

Moricanna nodded.

'I'll go and help them, then,' Wil said. 'I'll protect them, keep them safe. No need to even ask.'

'Alas, it's not that simple.' Verelda looked troubled. 'You can't reach them in time, and you couldn't save them if you did. No, what we're asking of you is a much harder thing, a sacrifice so great no man should have to contemplate it. But it's all that's left. Though you should know that if you refuse, we'll understand, and not count you a lesser man for it.'

'Stop tiptoeing around the issue, grandmum,' Donal nagged. 'Give him the straight and nasty before we all put down roots here.'

'Peace, Donal,' Moricanna said. 'Show some respect.' She sighed. 'All right. I'll say it. Wil. You understand balance.'

Wil nodded, still not sure where all this was headed.

'Well, if we're to save your friends – and the world – there has to be a balance. A life for a death. A death for a life. Normally it works out one-on-one, which is how it's supposed to be. You're given a life, and you're given a death. One of each, no less and no more.'

Suddenly Wil understood. And then immediately forgot all about it as the sound of voices reached him from somewhere close by.

275

'It's been three days now. If he was coming back, I reckon he'd have done so by now.'

What? Who... Oh.

'Aye. But look at him, will you? Fresh as a daisy, and not a whiff of him going bad. You ask me, there's gods taking a hand in this. And who can say but they don't still have plans for him.'

Pox on the gods, if this is their doing.

'Ah, but you know how gods can be. Fickle as the weather in April, no sense of time, and the memory span of mayflies – unless it's about holding a grudge. We might die of old age while we sit around here hoping they'll remember him any time soon.'

Forget the gods. Just give me a moment.

Quillan sighed. 'There's that. But what if we bury him and leave, and then he wakes up?'

No! Please. Anything but that.

'Well, we can't just leave him lying around for the wolves and bears to find, can we?' Gael said.

Right. Bad idea. You should take me with you if you can't stay here.

'We should take him with us,' Quillan said. 'Damn, but I wish that stupid old heart of his would start beating again like it did last time.' As he spoke, he let his clenched hand fall onto Wil's chest, once, twice, three times.

Thump!

That was my heart. Leastwise I think it was.

Next, there was a longish pause, as if the stupid old thing had forgotten what it was supposed to do. Then it seemed to bethink itself, and beat again, and again, and again, until it was thumping away as if it had never stood still.

'I'm hungry,' Wil said, opening his eyes.

If Wil had been something of a hero before, he now became a living legend. Quillan and Gael had put him up in Thorley's tent, and over the next two days most of the men who had survived the attack of the Rooters came by to pay him their respect. Many of them shyly touched him on the hand, arm, or leg, and when he asked Quillan about it the sergeant said it was for good luck.

'They think you're charmed, and they believe if they touch you some of it will rub off on them. Should I tell them to stop?'

'Please,' Wil said. 'I'm a man like the rest of you, not some sort of holy relic.'

In truth he felt more like a babe just beginning a new life. The muted light coming through the red-and-yellow-striped canvas and a from couple of braziers meant to keep him from catching a cold while he was recovering made the tent a warm, cozy place. It felt a bit like lying inside a womb. Pampered, cherished, safe.

'Well, just so you know, there's been talk of making you Lord Commander.'

'Absolutely not.' Wil was appalled. 'I've agreed to captain, and I'll stick to that. But Lord Commander is a noble's office. What do you think they'd say in the Vales if we came riding back and told them the position was already filled, and by a common soldier to boot?'

'Oh, I think they'd make a hell of a fuss. But some of them might also see what they owe you for bringing most of the Watch back alive. And you'd have the men behind you, if you wanted to make a point.'

'No. I'm not going to set Valer against Valer. As it is, we were lucky how things went with Thorley. Charmed or no, we shouldn't push our luck. And the Rooters. It's a wonder we're still alive at all. How many did we lose? And how did you get rid of the Bane? There must have been hundreds of them.'

'We didn't. They just suddenly froze and stood there, still as fence posts. Like they were listening for something. And then all of them up and left, else I wouldn't be sitting here talking to you. As to losses, we're down another eight, and three of those were killed by Gage, as were two of the Guard. I'm figuring Gage was somehow in cahoots with the Bane – at least that's where he was headed when things got too hot for him in camp. As for the rest of us, we owe our lives to the Rooters departing. Strange thing, that.'

'Any theories on why they left?'

'None that you'd want to hear about.'

'Meaning, I somehow performed a miracle while I was dead, and that's why they all ran away?'

'Something like that.'

'Quillan, this can't go on. You need to do something about it, bring the men to their senses. Put them through drills until they drop from exhaustion, or have them tear down the wall and build it up again. I don't care what, as long as it serves to get their feet back on the ground. Work them to the nub, if you have to. And tell them I ordered it. I'd rather they hated me than… than this.'

'Fat chance of that. But I'll see what I can do. Though I'd prefer it if the wall stayed up for the time being. The Rooters may be gone, but Fray and what's left of the Guard are out there somewhere. They snuck off when the Rooters started leaving. They're probably half-way to Deepwall by now, but better safe than sorry.'

'Right,' Wil said. The pain in his head was beginning to worsen again, his thinking becoming increasingly muddled. 'Just keep everyone busy for a few more days, and then we'll head on home.'

'Sounds like a plan,' Quillan said, and grinned.

Wil thought so too. A moment later he drifted off to sleep.

*   *   *

It was during the third Planting that things went terribly wrong.

The night was already far advanced, the Stricken's roots firmly embedded in the soil, the song losing its urgency and quieting down. Exhausted, Wulfwyn was looking forward to fixing the Wards, dropping in her tracks, and then sleeping all through the coming day, when suddenly a wave of terror swept through the Planting, a crippling deluge of mindless dread that broke up the song in a heartbeat, turning it into a cacophony of scattered and faltering voices between one note and the next.

'Slayer!' she hissed, bringing the Wards to full strength around Arden, the lads, and herself. Arden grabbed her hand and pressed it, hard, but didn't stop singing. She knew what he wanted: she'd left no gap for the song to pass through, and he couldn't reach the Stricken anymore. For once, she refused him, even reinforcing the Wards until they felt impervious to her as a wall of steel plate, although in truth they were no more than a futile gesture.

She knew well enough that no Wards she could make were strong enough to stop a Slayer. With luck, they'd slow it down for a bit. Long enough perhaps for them to end their own lives and so at

279

least deny it their souls.

The lads knew not to waste arrows on the thing, but they had Graeme's eggs out, and Raul was kneeling on the ground, lighting the lantern. She doubted even the eggs were capable of harming a Slayer. As Graeme had explained it, the stuff inside the eggs did its ghastly work by clinging to whatever it struck until it had burned itself out. But it would find no purchase on a being made of shadows and smoke.

And here it came, a man-shaped blotch of deeper darkness in the already dark night, black tentacles whipping out to rip Stricken from the earth and send them crashing into their neighbors, reducing root, branch and bone to splinters of screaming agony.

Tarr threw an egg that fell short.

Griff's aim was better. Briefly the Slayer was engulfed in red, oily flame. But, as Wulfwyn had feared, it just kept on coming, unharmed, and the only ones burning were a few hapless Stricken.

Then Arden did something with the song, changing it, calling up a breath-taking amount of power from some hidden reserves she'd never suspected he possessed. She could see how it hurt him to go against his every instinct and use a gift meant for healing and peace as a weapon. But he did, and turned it against the Slayer.

Suddenly the dread thing looked to be standing in a raging headwind, stopped dead in its tracks with its whip-like protuberances thrashing uselessly about in a gale so strong she could see shreds of it being ripped away and hurtling off into the night. But, incredible as it seemed in the face of the force Arden had unleashed, the Slayer rallied. Slowly, it began to move forward again.

A look at Arden told her he was way past his limits. He was deathly pale, sweating and shivering, and she reckoned there were mere moments to spare before he'd falter and whatever he was doing would come crashing down around them.

With no time to think what she was doing, much less to consider the consequences, Wulfwyn snatched up the Wards and gathered them to her. Took them into herself, turning her body into a living Ward. Her whole being trembling under the onslaught of far more power than she could hold on to for long, she stepped in front of Arden, blocking his line of sight on the Slayer.

'Stop,' she told him. 'You're killing yourself.'

She willed him to look at her, and he did, his eyes slowly finding a saner focus in hers.

'I love you,' she said.

Then she turned and, running, threw herself at the Slayer, flesh, soul, Wards and all. The last thing she heard was a heartbroken wail from Arden, filled with shock and grief so boundless it almost made her turn back.

*   *   *

18

It seemed to good to be true, and in a way it was.

There were people down there, living people, not Bitten, as far as Graeme could tell from the top of the hill they were using as cover and observation post. At first glance, the peasants below appeared to be going about their everyday business without a care in the world, working in fields and meadows, orchards and gardens as if the Bane had never happened.

But that tableau held only until one noticed how thin and starved they looked and how slowly they moved, hardly seeming to take note of each other as if each of them toiled in his own private haze of exhaustion, despondency and fear.

And Graeme had seen the signs at the edge of the forest, ugly, bleeding wounds carved into trunks every fifty yards or so. Torgrim said they were runes of forbidding – Blood Wards, he called them – and reckoned they'd been put there to warn off the creatures of the Bane. It was a reserve of sorts, half a county turned into a prison camp, and the people they were looking at were its inmates. Torgrim hazarded a guess as to its purpose, one that made Breanne visibly shudder and Graeme stiffen with anger and revulsion.

If you watched long enough you could see the odd guard passing by, mean-looking brutes on horseback wearing chainmail and armed to the teeth. They carried whips, using them freely on whoever was unlucky enough to come within their reach.

'There's bound to be more of the bastards in Salt,' Graeme said. They could see the village in the distance, and behind it the sea and a dark, forbidding rock that had to be Haunt. 'I think it's best if Pers, Finn, and I go in under cover of darkness. We'll see how many there are, and then decide how best to deal with them.'

'Aye,' Torgrim said. 'I'd go with you, but Breanne can't stay here alone.'

'I could come along,' Breanne said, and Graeme knew she'd do it and not miss a beat.

'No. With the Key, you'd likely bring everything Keon has waiting down on us, and without it you'd be needlessly putting yourself in danger. Besides, it's going to be dirty work, something you don't want to have a hand in, trust me.'

'All right.' She still seemed disappointed. 'But promise me you'll be careful. I want all three of you back here alive and hale.'

'Don't you worry now, lass,' Pers said with a wink. 'Me and Finn'll bring him back to you in good working order.'

There appeared to be a curfew in place, for at sunset they saw everyone hasten back to their houses, mud-walled, thatch-roofed shacks ducked low to the ground as if they shared their inhabitant's sense of oppression. In the space of a quarter-hour not a soul was left outside. Graeme noticed one of the guards heading off towards the village at a slow trot, and decided it was an opportunity too good to pass up.

'We'll go now,' he told Finn and Pers, 'and follow that guard. If we're lucky, he'll lead us straight to their lair.'

'Whatever you say, captain.' Pers gave a humorless grin. 'The sooner we start tidying this place up, the better. I'd swear I can smell the stink of those bastards even from up here.'

Sticking to the hedgerows, they followed the guard to Salt. It was dark by the time they reached the edge of the village. The streets were deserted, and no lights burned in any of the houses. The sole sign of life was the clip-clop of the horse's hooves on the cobbles of the main thoroughfare leading down to the harbor. Halfway down, the guard rode around to the back of a large building, the only one with lights burning inside. By the faded sign faintly creaking in a breeze off the sea, it had once been an inn called the *Full Hold*.

Slipping into the mouth of a dark alley across from the inn, they heard shouts and rough laughter from within, and Graeme reckoned they'd found their rats' nest in one. Two men were sitting on the wooden porch out front, ugly bruisers both of them, balanced on tilted-back chairs and drinking from large earthenware mugs.

'You two stay here,' he whispered to Pers. 'I'm going round the back, see if I can get a look inside.'

Pers nodded, and Graeme was just about to head out when he saw movement across the street. A dark, furtive figure was flitting from doorway to doorway, someone doing their best to stay out of the light. The men outside the inn obviously weren't all that drunk yet, for one of them noticed the skulker.

'Hoy!' he called out, the legs of his chair hitting the deck with a bang as he stood up. 'Who's the fucker thinks he can break curfew? Show yourself, you sneaking piece of shit, or I'll come and root you

285

out with my pig-sticker!'

His companion gave an ugly laugh.

Graeme melted back into the shadows.

Suddenly the skulker broke cover and came scampering across the street, headed straight for where they were hiding.

A moment later Graeme had him in a chokehold – only it wasn't a he. It was a young woman, he saw in the faint light falling from the inn's windows and open door. When he loosened his hold she immediately began to struggle.

'Quiet,' he hissed in her ear. 'We're friends, and we mean you no harm.'

She quieted, though he could feel her trembling like a cornered deer.

'Oh, sweetheart,' the guard called out in a nasty-sweet singsong, coming across the street, light glinting off a naked blade. 'I saw you. I'm coming for you. Hike up your skirts, bend over like a good girl, and I might let you off easy this once.'

Graeme let go of the girl and drew his knife. 'One of you will have to shoot the other one,' he breathed.

'Already got him lined up,' Pers whispered.

As the first man stepped into the alley Graeme grabbed him, whirled him around and pushed him face first into the wall. He didn't hesitate. A clean thrust to the heart, and the enemy was one down. He regretted having to kill a man, but in the circumstances there was no other choice, and this one had probably deserved it several times over. He saw that Pers had taken out the one on the porch with a well-placed shot.

'Go home,' he told the frightened girl. She threw him a look from large, unbelieving eyes, as if she doubted that any of this could really be happening. Then she was gone, vanished into the shadows.

'No helping it now,' he told Finn and Pers. 'We have to finish it, or they'll be all over the place as soon as the next one comes out and stumbles over his dead mate. I'll take the back. See if you can shoot through the windows and take a couple of them out before you go in. We still don't know how many there are.'

'Right,' Finn said. 'Meet you halfways.'

All told, there were a dozen men inside the building.

Long odds, except most of the guards were getting on in years, aging men who for two decades had done nothing much except sit around and drink when they weren't busy beating and raping and generally harassing a bunch of cowed and half-starved people who were in no position to put up any resistance whatsoever.

They were still mean bastards and killing them was hard work, but in the end they were no match for men who'd been fighting the Bane every day of their lives for as long as they could remember.

Coming in from the back, Graeme managed to shoot two of them before his moment of surprise was used up. Then it was swords, knives, chair legs, flying mugs and whatever else came to hand in the confusion of drunken, shouting men stumbling about between overturned tables and shattered stoneware, slipping and sliding in puddles of ale and blood while Graeme's blade found them one after the other.

Pers and Finn did their part with admirable dedication, both of them using hatchet and dagger, their preferred weapons for fighting

Rooters up close. Weapons that weren't half bad against human trash either, Pers noted later, when it was all over and done. Unlike Graeme, he didn't seem to have any problem with killing these men. A bottom-feeding disgrace to all mankind, he called them.

A surprise awaited them when they stepped back outside.

The girl from the alley was standing at the foot of the three steps leading up to the inn's porch. Behind her, a small crowd had gathered, a sad collection of ragged, careworn ghosts who looked as if a middling breeze might blow them away. None of them stirred. They simply stood there, silent, staring, their expressions as unbelieving as the girl's had been when Graeme released her and sent her home.

It was by far the weirdest situation he'd ever found himself in, and he had no idea at all what to do. What in the gods' name were you supposed to say on an occasion like this? 'Hello, I'm Graeme Banehunter, and I've come to free you?' Or perhaps 'Just hang on for a moment while I finish saving the world, and then we can talk?' Completely ridiculous. It would have been a good moment for Pers to say something, but for once even he seemed to have run out of words.

The crowd was still growing, more people coming out of the shadows, timid and quiet as mice. Then there was a disturbance at the back, the throng parting to make way for a very old man, white-haired, stooped, and braced on a staff. He stepped up to the porch, looking as if he meant to say something. Instead he gasped, his eyes going wide as he stared at Graeme in something like dawning recognition, then in disbelief, and finally in wonder.

Slowly and painfully, he lowered himself onto a knee.

288

'My lord,' he said. 'You've returned.'

Right this moment, Graeme would have given just about anything for the ability to simply up and disappear. This was definitely going too far. Way, way too far. He wondered whether the terrible things these people had been through might have driven them a little mad. May-be even more than just a little.

Quickly, before the situation went completely awry, he stepped down and gently helped the old man to his feet.

'I'm no lord,' he said. 'Just a man who never had the wits to stay out of the Bane. Which pretty much sums up the reason I'm here.'

'But, my lord,' the old man said, peering up at Graeme with eyes that belied the frailness of his body. 'Don't you remember me?'

'How could I... ' Graeme started to say, but something about the old man's face gave him pause. Was it the shape of the nose? The chin? The line of his brow? No. It was the eyes, he real-ized, dark blue and at once kind and sharp.

'Oakes,' he said, suddenly feeling lightheaded and fearfully short of breath. 'Corbin Oakes.'

'Yes, my lord.' The old man gave him a smile of such pure joy it seemed to make the night less dark. 'I was your late father's Master of Horse. It's a wonder how much you resemble him. Two peas in a pod would not be doing it justice, if you'll forgive the comparison.'

An old woman came forward and gave an awkward curtsy. 'It's true what he says, m'lord. I was there when the ships came in, and I saw your lord father with my own eyes. Twins, you could have been, if you'd been stood side by side.'

'I saw him too,' another ancient said. 'And I, and I,' others

289

chimed in.

More and more people took a knee then, looking awed, almost reverent, as if they'd just caught a glimpse of what might lie on the other side of the hell they'd been trapped in for so long.

Though he couldn't have said where it came from, Graeme felt a sudden, great affection for them. He would have embraced them with words, had he had any. More, he would have gone and taken every single one of them in his arms, if not for the fact that his world has just gone to pieces, collapsed in a heap of splinters and shards he doubted could ever be fitted back together again. He found that his voice had deserted him. His knees seemed about to deny him their service as well, and his cheeks were wet with tears. But all of that was nothing compared to what was going on inside him.

He remembered.

Gods, but he remembered now.

*   *   *

Breanne was restless.

She was anxious for Graeme, and for Pers and Finn as well. In her heart she'd adopted the two as something of an uncle and cousin, born on the wrong side of the road, perhaps, but truer and more valiant than all of Longvale's nobility put together.

But that wasn't all. It was more than just worry that had her pacing and fretting like an accused woman awaiting the verdict. Ever since she'd used the Key against the Slayer, it had been calling her, constantly, insistently, no matter she was awake or asleep. Time and again, she caught her hands nestling at the ties of her shirt, following a will of their own, or the Key's, but in any case not hers. Last night she'd woken to find herself clutching the bag, her fingers fumbling with the drawstring.

It was frightening, like a slow poison subverting her mind. So far, she'd resisted. But she was beginning to see that it was just a question of time before the Key gained the upper hand and bent and twisted her until she became its willing instrument. By now, she understood all too well why Torgrim had refused to even touch it. If she'd known in the beginning what she knew now, she'd never have accepted it either.

And to think that her father had given it to her, had picked *it* of all things when there'd been a whole box full of jewelry to choose from. An unwitting contribution to Marillin's salvation? Some deep, dark instinct to take revenge on his daughter, to punish her for the disappointment she'd caused him?

Neither, she thought. Already then, the Key had been pulling the strings, his and hers. But the notion of what her father would have done with it if he'd known of its powers, and what it would have done to him... unthinkable.

She was relieved from her brooding by a soft whistle from Finn, who appeared out of the dark a moment later.

'Graeme? Pers?' she asked anxiously.

'They're fine,' Finn said. 'We had a tussle with the guards, but everything's taken care of.'

Breanne preferred not to ask what that meant. 'Why aren't they here, then?'

'Because Graeme thinks we should go in and finish it tonight. Element of surprise, and all that. He sent me to fetch the two of you.'

'What do you think?' she asked Torgrim. All this time he'd been sitting on a rock, silent and unmoving as if he were trying to become one himself.

'I think now is as good a time as any,' he said. 'Though I doubt we'll come as much of a surprise to Keon. No matter. We might as well get it over with.' He rose with a groan. 'Damn, but they could make these rocks a little bit softer. You ready for this, lass?'

Breanne nodded, swallowing hard. This was it, then. What they'd come here for. The end of the road.

'All right, then,' Torgrim said, giving them one of his boyish grins, his teeth shining white in the dark. 'Fortune favors fools, they say. So let's go do something foolish.'

Once they reached Salt, Finn led them past low, darkened houses to an inn, light shining from its windows and door.

The street outside was crowded with ragged, underfed people, all of them standing perfectly still and staring at the building as if something momentous were happening inside. Blessedly, from what she could see none of them were Bitten. But it still grieved her deeply to see how worn and haggard they were, and she wished she could use the Key to conjure up a wagonload of fine food for them. When they recognized Finn they quickly made way, gazing at the three of them with a mixture of curiosity and awe.

They found Graeme and Pers in the common room. It looked as if it had been hastily cleaned up after a wild free-for-all. There were broken chairs, a pile of shards swept into a corner, and dark stains on the floorboards that would take many a scrubbing to come out.

292

Towards the back, where a door led out to the kitchen, Breanne saw trails of congealing blood. Drag marks, she thought, and shuddered, trying not to imagine what she'd find if she went out there. Not that it was important.

Graeme was. Sitting at a table with Pers, a young woman, and an ancient, white-haired man, he suddenly seemed a stranger to her, as if she were seeing him for the first time. Perhaps it was due to his expression. He looked dazed, puzzled, like a man who'd been struck a blow on the head and was bemusedly wondering what had become of the better half of his wits. He also looked sad, and happy, and totally lost in between. But he saw her immediately, and smiled, standing to offer her a seat.

'My lady,' he said. 'This is Emelin, a brave young woman, and Corbin Oakes, the late king Oswin's Master of Horse. Master Corbin was just telling us of the day when all this began.'

'Aye,' Corbin said. 'I figured there might be some odds and ends in the story that could prove helpful to you when you go over there.' He gave a nod in the direction of the sea. Breanne supposed it was meant to indicate the island, Haunt. 'As I was saying, when your father rode up to the gates – '

'Please, a moment,' Breanne interrupted, jolted by the old man's words. She looked at Graeme. 'He said "your father." Does that mean your father was here when…'

'Yes,' Graeme said, taking her hand.

'And he rode with the king? But that means you're not from a farm up north at all. It means…'

'I'm from here,' Graeme said. 'Or rather from Arventon. Incredible as it sounds, Corbin here recognized me, even after all these years. And I remembered him as well. I… But that has to wait. I'll tell you all of it later. Right now, time's a-wasting, and we don't want Banesheart to receive more of a warning than he's already had. Though I wonder if we'll find him over there. Corbin says they saw all three of his ships leave yesterday. Still, we should go.'

Pressing Graeme's hand, Breanne leaned over and whispered in his ear. 'I'm so very glad for you. It doesn't change who you are, Graeme Banehunter, my love, but at least now you know where you came from. And I'll be very curious to hear the rest of the story.' Then she rose, before she could change her mind and run all the way back to the Vales.

'All right,' she said. 'Let's get this done.' For a wonder, she sounded brave and determined even to herself, though she'd never felt nearly as helpless and scared in her life.

*   *   *

Listening to Oakes' story, Graeme hadn't been sure he believed the part about the bridge. Connecting Haunt with the mainland, it had been built by magic, Oakes said, and in a single night to boot. But once they'd turned east at the harbor and were past the last of Salt's houses, there it was, a series of massive arches spanning the channel between the mainland and Haunt, a many-legged beast of stone crouched up to its knees in water black as ink.

Wary of an ambush, he drew his sword and went ahead to check the bridgehead but found no enemies lurking in its shadows. There was no one on the bridge either, though it would have made for a perfect choke point where a single Shifter could have caused untold mayhem. He even looked over the sides, thinking a Shifter might

294

cling to the stones there, wait until they were past, and then climb onto the bridge to attack them from behind.

There was nothing, not on the bridge, and not on the far side, where six steep, cobbled switchbacks led up to the castle, the open gate between the squat gatehouse towers a dark, yawning hole, the portcullis raised. The small hairs on the back of Graeme's neck stirred as he entered the barbican, but no arrows or quarrels came flying out of the murder holes in the barrel-vaulted ceiling.

They reached the outer ward unchallenged.

All around them, dark walls loomed high, throwing the courtyard into impenetrable shadow.

Looking up, for a moment he saw a huge, black shape clinging to one of the towers. He blinked, and the dark blob resolved itself into a turret.

Don't start imagining things, he cautioned himself, *or you'll end up overlooking the real dangers.*

'Which way?' he asked Torgrim, the only one among them with a knowledge of Gates.

'It could be anywhere,' Torgrim answered. 'And so could Keon, if he hasn't scarpered. Which seems more and more likely the longer I think about it. He's a sneaky bastard, and he prefers to have others do his dirty work. If he really did leave with the ships, then we can safely assume he's left behind some nasty surprises for us. It's exactly his style. All I can say is, we'll just have to follow our noses and be prepared for the worst. Sorry I can't be more precise.'

'I can,' Breanne said. 'At least I think so. It's the Key. It seems to know where it wants to go. I can feel it pulling... that way.' She pointed to an iron-banded door across the courtyard, the entrance to the main keep, it appeared.

'All right,' Graeme said. 'Finn, Pers, I want you to cover our flanks and rear. There's no way we can clear every room in this place as we go, so keep your eyes peeled. Torgrim and I will go first. Breanne, you stay in the middle where all four of us can look out for you. Right, let's go.'

The door was unlocked and opened soundlessly on well-oiled hinges. There was a short corridor beyond, lit by smoking torches, and then a great hall, hollow and cold as a midwinter night, their footsteps echoing and multiplying in the empty space until they sounded like a multitude of small, pattering paws.

Everything Graeme saw was made from Haunt's native stone, dark as charcoal: the walls, the flagstones, the vaulted ceiling, the huge, unlit fireplace opposite the entrance, and the wide stairs leading to the upper floors.

He halted, waiting for Breanne to determine which way they should go.

'There.' She pointed left, and he saw light flickering through a half-open door. Behind it, a narrow staircase spiraled downward, every second turn lit by a candle in a wall sconce. The candles looked to be fresh, and just recently lit. They'd gone down only a few turns when Pers gave a hiss.

'Someone behind us.'

'Aye,' Torgrim murmured. 'That was to be expected. They've been so kind as to light the way for us, and now they're making sure we don't turn around and get lost. Obliging hosts, I'd say, if I didn't have a feeling they're not planning to let us leave here alive. A trap forsooth, Keon, you dirty little prick.'

The stairs went down for a very long way.

At the bottom they found another corridor, this one hewn from the bedrock. It led to another open door. Behind it was a cave, several times the size of the hall upstairs and far too large for a half dozen torches to light more than a small area near the center.

There, seeming to waver and sway in the uncertain flicker of shadows and light, stood an object made from three huge slabs of dark stone and resembling nothing so much as a very large door-frame. To Graeme it looked somehow misplaced, standing there in isolation without the attendant reference of a wall.

'Damn! Bloody thing's stuck fast!' It was Pers. He was straining to close door they'd come through and keep whoever was following them from attacking their rear. But even with Finn pitching in it wouldn't budge.

Then, just when they'd given up and stepped back, it suddenly slammed shut with a bang, and Graeme saw movement in the shadowed recesses on either side. The next moment a dozen men in mail and plate stepped into the light, bared steel flashing in their gauntleted hands, hard, avid eyes glinting behind the slits of their helms.

*   *   *

19

Briefly, Breanne stood and watched her companions meet the oncoming men-at-arms. Graeme closed with the first of them, his blade ready to bite. Pers and Finn each loosed an arrow. One found its mark, the other glaned off a breastplate and went skidding across the cavern floor. She couldn't figure out what Torgrim was doing. Nothing at all, it seemed, just standing there staring at the ceiling like a man in a trance. She was about to rouse him with a shout when there was a sudden, sharp crack like the snap of a whip and several large chunks of rock broke off overhead, dropping onto the attackers and felling two of them.

Three of them were down, but the rest kept coming, and then it was hand-to-hand, swords, knives and hatchets dipping and whirling, steel clashing on steel, the attackers' armor glinting orange and red in the flickering torchlight.

Drawing the Key out of its pouch, Breanne headed straight for the standing stones. The sooner she managed to lock down the Gate, the sooner they could start looking for a way out.

Only she had no idea how she was supposed to accomplish the task. There was nothing that even vaguely resembled a keyhole, no depression that looked like any part of the circlet might fit into it, and the Key wasn't giving her any hints either.

On the contrary: it surprised her by pulling away from the stones as if, now that it had found the Gate, it had completely lost interest in it or discovered some other, more worthwhile destination instead.

With the fight ringing loud in her ears, she touched the circlet first to one, then to the other of the upright stones. Nothing happened. Desperate, she tried jabbing it at the empty space between. Still nothing – except for the Key's insistent drag to the right, away from the Gate. Behind her, more rocks came crashing down from the ceiling. Someone cried out in pain, the sound cut short by a thud and a grunt. She didn't dare look to see who had been hit, just prayed it wasn't one of her friends.

Concentrating on the Gate, she noticed for the first time that the stones looked oddly pristine, as if they'd been hewn into shape just recently. Then she spied a few chips lying close to their bases, mostly hidden in shadow, and a terrifying possibility occurred to her. Giving herself no time to consider the danger of what she was doing, she stepped through between the pillars.

And was still in the cave under Stormhold.

The Gate was a decoy. A dud.

Suddenly she saw movement in the dark depths beyond: three, four, five vague shapes like blacker holes in the night-deep shadows of the cavern's far end. Seeming to grow larger as she watched. Coming closer.

Something snake-like flicked out from one of the shapes, its black, shiny surface momentarily reflecting the light of a torch.

'Torgrim!' she yelled, just as a wave of fear worse than anything she'd experienced until now came rolling out of the darkness. 'Slayers! And the Gate is a fake! We've got to get out of here!'

She saw Torgrim look towards the door they'd come in through.

'No!' she shouted. 'Not that way! Over here!'

They heeded her call immediately, joining her at the false Gate. All four of them were unharmed, gods be thanked. The attackers still standing seemed content to let them go, likely in no hurry to get anywhere near the Slayers, the sweeping sensation of utter panic emanating from the terrifying things so strong Breanne had to summon up all her strength not to collapse on the floor in a shaking, gibbering heap.

As if that wasn't enough, the Key started calling to her more forcefully than ever, wanting to be used. It was all she could do to resist it. Holding it out in front of her, she ran in the direction it was pulling, desperately praying it would lead them to something other than a blank wall. She heard Graeme and the others behind her, hard on her heels.

Racing head-on into absolute darkness, she was sure she'd smack face-first into the side of the cavern any moment. But the space was apparently much larger than she'd thought. What slowed her down wasn't a wall of hard, unforgiving rock but a breath of cold air that carried a hint of the sea.

'There must be an opening here somewhere,' she said, groping blindly in the dark with her free hand. Somewhere behind them, she heard a dragging sound like dry snakeskin sliding over bare rock. The Slayers coming after them, unhurried, stalkers sure of their kill.

'Just a moment,' she heard Torgrim say, and then a tiny, pearly-white light sprang into being, a softly glowing firefly stuck to the tip of his staff. Small as it was, it sufficed to strike glittering reflections like miniature stars from specks of mica enclosed in the wall before them – a wall riven by a dark, triangular crack, large enough for even a tall man to pass through if he kept his head down.

'Go,' Torgrim said urgently. 'I'll bring up the rear.'

Graeme went first, then Finn, then Pers, then Breanne, stowing the circlet under her shirt. Just as she entered the crack in the wall she heard another sound from behind, a deep, slow growl that set the floor under her feet vibrating. She shivered as if an ice-cold hand had brushed over her back. Whatever had made that sound must be monstrous, and it scared her near witless, worse even than the Slay-ers.

A few yards in, the crack widened into a tunnel, high enough for even Graeme to walk without having to duck. With Torgrim bring-ing up the rear, there wasn't much light to see by up front, and the going was slow, much too slow for Breanne's liking. Then the ceil-ing began to slant downward, farther and farther, until they had to walk bent almost double and were finally forced to crawl on all fours. The walls on both sides moved in as well, and at some stage there came a passage so narrow, Breanne was sure they'd all get stuck and never see the light of day again. It felt as if the rock of Haunt were constricting around them like a giant fist of stone intent on squeezing them slowly to death. She would have had a fit then, screamed or fainted or simply gone stark raving mad, if not for the steady, cool breeze in her face, beckoning her onward and promising air and space somewhere up ahead if only she could reach it.

Just when she thought it couldn't get any worse, the tunnel became so tight she had to crawl on her belly, her shoulders scraping against the rough rock on either side, the back of her head bumping against the ceiling no matter her face was so close to the floor she could have licked it with the tip of her tongue. How Graeme had made it through was a mystery to her – but he had, and so could she.

Then the top of her head banged painfully against a wall of stone blocking her way forward, and she couldn't go on.

She was one, tiny step short of utter panic.

Graeme's voice came from somewhere above her, calm and soothing. 'You have to wriggle around onto your back,' he told her. 'Then you'll be able to stand up.'

Doing as he said, she squirmed and fought until she was facing upward, lying with her upper body in a narrow, vertical shaft, the rest of her still in the tunnel. And there were Graeme, Pers and Finn, kneeling on the lip of the shaft and looking down at her, Pers holding up a candle he must have grabbed from a sconce on the stairs and just now relit with flint and tinder, Graeme reaching out a strong, steady hand to help her wriggle all the way out of the tunnel. Once she was clear, he pulled her onto her feet and lifted her out of the hole, easy as a feather. They were in another cave, she saw, open on the far side. The air was heavy with brine, and she could hear the faint sound of waves breaking. Weak with relief, she allowed herself a moment to lean into the comfort of Graeme's arms.

'That was very, very scary,' she told him, her words muffled against his chest.

303

'It was,' he agreed. 'For a moment there, I thought I was good and stuck. If Finn hadn't helped me along by bracing my feet and giving me something to push on, I'd probably still be in there, blocking the way for the rest of you. But where's Torgrim? He should be here by now.'

'I don't know. I thought he was right behind me. Do you think…'

A faint rumbling sound came from the hole in the cavern floor.

'That sounded like the tunnel just collapsed a ways back,' Pers said. He and Finn were still kneeling by the shaft, waiting to help Torgrim out. But there was no Torgrim. Instead, a puff of dust blew out of the tunnel mouth. After that there was silence, broken only by the sough and hiss of the sea outside.

For the longest time, nothing happened.

Eventually Breanne heard a dragging, scraping noise, very similar to the sound the Slayers had made when they moved towards her across the larger cavern's floor. Releasing her, Graeme drew his sword. Finn and Pers moved back from the lip of the hole, readying their bows. Futile gestures, she knew, gripping the circlet tightly and preparing to don it the moment she saw the first, black tentacle snake out of the tunnel.

Another, smaller cloud of dust issued forth, followed by the sound of someone coughing. And then Torgrim's head appeared, his unruly hair gone all grey with dust.

'Phew!' he said when they'd heaved him out of the hole. 'That was close. Nasty buggers were practically chomping on the soles of my boots.'

'Are you all right?' Breanne asked, casting a worried look down to see whether his feet were still whole.

'I'm fine, lass, thanks for the concern. Lucky thing I found a nice, long fault line in the tunnel roof. Just a nudge was all it took to bring down a good thirty yards of it. I doubt it'll hold them up for long, though. We should be on our way.'

With a shudder, Breanne imagined the Slayers' black, smoky substance seeping through the smallest cracks in the rubble, pictured them flowing back into their man-like shapes as soon as they were past the blockage and then resuming the chase.

Graeme was the first to step out of the cave, wary of what might await them outside, and she was right behind him, the skin on her back tingling as if slick, black tentacles were already reaching for her from the mouth of the tunnel.

*   *   *

Graeme stepped out onto a narrow ledge.

They were halfway up a sheer cliff, he saw. The walls curved around on both sides, completely enclosing a large, canyon-like space. Far below, two hundred feet or more, he heard the slosh and slap of turbulent waters, recognized a patch of frothing white where the sea entered the rocky cauldron through a narrow gap on the opposite side, maybe a hundred yards from where they were standing.

Halfway across, a spire of black rock jutted out of the restlessly heaving sea. Looking up, he reckoned it rose to a level with the rim of the cauldron, easily another two hundred feet above their heads.

He glimpsed a few stars, and a dark shape perched on the rim that might have been a large boulder – though he thought he saw it stir half an eye-blink before a fast-moving bank of cloud blotted out what little light there was, making it impossible to see farther than the strip of rock they were standing on. His heart sank when he saw that the ledge broke off on both sides after just a few yards. It looked as if they'd reached the end of the road. There was no way out of this place. And neither was there a way back. Even if Torgrim hadn't brought down the tunnel roof, they'd never have gotten past the Slayers.

Pers' candle was abruptly extinguished as he stepped out behind Graeme and Breanne. The wind had picked up since they'd entered Stormhold. Now it thrummed through the canyon as if the Wind God himself were playing the vast round of rock like a gigantic pipe. The sea seemed to have become more agitated as well, even during the few moments they'd been standing there on the ledge.

'Graeme.' It was Breanne, clinging to his arm for dear life.

'What is it?'

'The Key. It's pulling so strongly now, I'm afraid it might drag me over the edge. And I can't swim.'

As if anyone could survive the fall, or stay afloat in those madly roiling waters even if they did. He laid an arm around her shoulders, hugging her tight. 'Where do you think it wants to go?'

'There.' She pointed to the spire, her outstretched hand traveling all the way up to the top.

Just then, there was a break in the clouds, allowing the first rays of the waning moon to steal over the rim of the canyon, and Graeme noticed something he'd missed earlier: there was a thin strip of darkness connecting the rim with the spire. A bridge, if he wasn't mistaken, though not the kind any sane person would want to set foot on. There was no railing, and the thing looked barely wide enough to accommodate two feet placed side by side. But the question whether it could be crossed was mute, since the moonlight still failed to reveal a way up the canyon wall.

His eyes were drawn back to the spire. Something about its shape...

He waited for another row of clouds to pass over the moon. When the light returned, he realized what it was that had caught his attention. There were regular, offset indentations on both sides of the spire: on the right, then farther down on the left, and again on the right, still farther down, and so on, from top to bottom. Then, with the moon rising higher and shedding more light, it all came together: he was looking at what must have been the world's most hair-raising staircase, winding around the needle-like rock in insane, dizzying spirals.

'There's no way up from here,' Torgrim said from the left-hand end of the ledge. 'But there's a way down. And, if my eyes aren't playing tricks on me, there's some sort of causeway down there, leading out to that pillar over there. Which some barking lunatic seems to have fitted with a staircase.'

Torgrim was right: there was a way down.
Beginning at the end of the ledge, steps had been cut into the cliff. Cleverly making use of irregularities in the rock, they zigzagged down from ledge to ledge, some comfortably large, others barely wide enough for a single person to make a careful, shuffling turn towards the next leg of the stairs.

The steps were ancient, worn and slick, some of them so weathered they crumbled under Graeme's feet. Taking the lead, he tested every single one of them before he trusted it with his full weight, warning the others whenever he hit one that was unsafe. The fickle light didn't help either; time and again, the moon was obscured by passing clouds, dipping them in near total darkness and forcing them to stop and wait until they could see again. Twice the treacherous stairs nearly cast him off, leaving him weak-kneed and breathless with the jolting shock of having escaped certain death by a hair.

But by far his greatest fear was for Breanne, who had not only the uncertain footing and changing light to contend with but also the Key's insistent pull threatening to drag her over the edge and down into the deep with each shaky step she took. Together with Torgrim he devised a railing of sorts for her, each of them holding on to one end of the mage's staff with Breanne walking between them. It wasn't much, and she still had to manage the turns largely unprotected, but it was better than nothing.

The last forty feet or so were the worst, with water and algae turning the stone slick as ice and making each step forward a reckless gamble against gravity. When they finally reached the bottom, every muscle in Graeme's legs was on fire. Breanne, still clutching Torgrim's staff, seemed past ready to collapse. Graeme looked back the way they'd come, searching the rock face for the Slayers, but saw no sign of them – yet.

'We'll rest for a moment,' he told the others, and helped Breanne to a seat on a rock close to the foot of the cliff where the icy spray from the waves slapping against the stones wasn't quite so bad. Ignoring the pain in his own legs, he squatted in front of her and tried to work the cramps out of her trembling calves.

They could have easily done with an hour's rest.

But after what seemed like no time at all they stirred and rose as if by some silent agreement. There was still no sign of the Slayers, but no doubt that could change any moment. Graeme suspected they would be able to manage the descent much faster than humans.

There was one thing that gave him a sliver of hope, though: the causeway.

The waves in the cauldron weren't all that high, maybe a couple of feet, but in the canyon's confines the water sloshed around wildly every which way, meaning that at any given moment three quarters of the causeway's surface lay under water. Somewhere between ankle and knee-deep, as far as Graeme could tell. He knew next to nothing about the Slayers, but if they were anything like the rest of the Bane, the crossing should at least give them pause. It was a long jump across the water to the base of the spire – too far for a Shifter, in any case.

Maybe the Slayers were better jumpers; maybe they would overcome the Bane's aversion to water and decide to get their feet wet; and maybe, just maybe, they'd take a short while to make up their minds, giving Graeme and the others a little more time to attempt the impossible climb up the spire.

The causeway's surface was slippery, the waves washing over it dragging at their legs and threatening to send them sliding over the edge into deep water. But compared to the stairs they'd just come down, the crossing was a casual stroll.

Then, standing drenched and chilled on a narrow strip of wet rock at the foot of the spire, Graeme got his first good look at the stairs spiraling upwards, and what little hope he'd held on to was shattered in an instant.

*   *   *

Seeing what awaited them, Breanne for the first time was ready to give up. Beside her, Pers heaved a groan. 'I think I'll just stay here and wait for the Slayers,' he said.

Breanne knew he was only trying for a half-hearted joke. But even if he'd been serious, she couldn't have faulted him. If anything, she felt like sitting down with him in this place that had to be the most depressing spot on earth, there to await the inevitable end with whatever composure she could muster instead of continuing a hopeless struggle for which she didn't have the strength left in any case.

The first dozen or so steps leading upward looked normal enough, but from there on the stairs were something only a sadistic madman could have created. No two steps were alike. Some of them were waist-high, others too narrow to fit a foot on sideways, and all of them sloped away at crazy angles, some downwards, some outwards, some slanted in both directions at once. It was an insane, screaming nightmare, an open invitation to suicide.

She'd just hit upon the alternative of simply jumping into the sea and drowning herself when she felt Graeme's arms envelop her from behind.

'I love you,' he said, kissing the top of her head. 'And just so you know: I'm not leaving here without you, and I'm not staying either. So there's your choice.'

'Not much of a choice,' she said, smiling despite everything as

310

she felt strength and warmth flow from Graeme into her, a gift freely given and gratefully received. 'But since I love you too, I guess I'll graciously fall for your clever trick. But just this once, mind you. We can't have you making a habit of it.'

He actually chuckled. 'That's my girl. No quarter to the enemy, even if it turns out to be a set of stairs.'

Desperate humor, she thought, snuggling into Graeme's arms. *We're spitting death in the eye when it's already got us by the scruff of the neck. Oh well – I suppose a long dive from that infernal tower of rock is still a sight better than losing our souls to the Slayers.*

Behind her, Pers cleared his throat. 'Not to interrupt, but I just wanted to say I've changed my mind about staying here. Meaning I'm good to go as soon as you two love-birds are done cooing.'

'Better listen to the man,' Torgrim said. 'Looks like at least one of the shady buggers has made it through.'

Jolted out of the comfort of Graeme's embrace, Breanne shot a glance at the cliff behind them. There, just below the mouth of the cave, a blob of darkness was flowing down the stairs like a quickly spreading stain.

The stairs up the spire were the most terrifying thing Breanne had ever encountered. No nightmare could have scared her half as much. Nightmares ended. Nightmares weren't real.

This *was* real, and there appeared to be no end to it. Graeme made her go first, so he'd have a chance to steady her from behind and catch her if she fell. But after the first few yards they were all on their hands and knees, and she knew it was all he could do to keep from sliding off himself. There was nothing to trust, nothing to grip and hold on to. Every time she placed a hand or a knee on a step, she immediately began to slowly slip away on the smooth, sloping surface. The only way to keep from falling was to desperately grope for the next step – and the next, and the next, quickly, before the one she was on threw her off.

There was no letting up, no crack or edge she could wedge her fingers behind and cling to and pause at least for a moment. She was forever slipping and sliding, always a hair's breadth from falling, her arms and legs on fire, her muscles shaking with uncontrollable spasms, screaming for a break she couldn't allow them.

There was the odd, back-cut step where she might have gotten at least a semblance of rest, had she been alone. As it was, she knew that if she gave in to her need and clung to that saving step, in the time she lingered the others would inevitably slip and plunge to their deaths.

At least the Key, tucked back into its pouch and resting against her belly under her shirt, wasn't pulling sideways anymore but up. It made her feel a little bit lighter – which wasn't really any help at all. With only friction to hold her in place, heavier would have been better, she figured.

She had no idea how far they'd come when she reached a point where the stairs in front of her flattened out and became a feature-less chute. The only thing marking one step from the next were shallow, horizontal grooves cut into the rock at irregular intervals. She was sure then that they'd reached the end of their journey. There was no way back, no way to turn around, and no staying in place. All she could do was crawl on until gravity did its job and ended it for her.

But, to her surprise and relief, she found that what looked like the worst stretch of the climb was actually the part where she felt safest. Jamming her fingertips into the first groove, she felt them catch on a tiny, rough edge, and for once her hands didn't immediately begin to slip. Then she was far enough along so she could wedge the tips of her boots into a groove, and she almost felt stable enough to rest for a moment. But she couldn't leave the others hanging on the slippery steps below. Only when she judged she'd climbed far enough up the chute for those behind her to have reached it as well did she stop and rest, bleeding fingers and cramping toes wedged into grooves, her cheek pressed against the smooth, cold stone for the extra bit of traction it might give her.

Lying there, she noticed for the first time that her face was wet. She'd been silently crying, not from fear or pain but from sheer exhaustion. Her body was so far past the limit, it was a wonder it hadn't simply given up and quit on her. Even her soul felt raw and worn to a nub.

But there was no time to feel sorry for herself.

Not long, and she felt Graeme behind her getting restless. Considerate as ever, he didn't say anything, but she knew all the same that he was waiting for her to move on. And he was right to worry. With all her senses focused solely on surviving the immediate peril of the stairs, she'd completely forgotten about the Slayers. With an involuntary groan she pried stiff, aching fingers from the groove she was holding on to, reaching for the next one up.

And bruised her knuckles on vertical stone. Her muddled mind slowly working its way through the problem, she concluded that the easy part was over. There were more of those insane steps ahead. Nearly paralyzed with dread, she forced herself to lift her head and look.

What she saw made no sense. Perhaps she was so far gone she'd begun to hallucinate. Yes, that must be it. No one in their right mind would carve such a freakish monster of a staircase out of the rock only to start making normal, regular steps three quarters of the way up. Then she remembered that whoever had created this abomination must have been barking mad to begin with – so what she was seeing did make sense in a very sick and twisted way.

Which meant that perhaps she wasn't hallucinating after all. Maybe she was looking at the ultimate mockery: drive anyone who attempted the ascent to mortal agony, and place the saving steps so far up they'd likely never reach them, wouldn't even know that redemption had been waiting somewhere farther up, perhaps as close as the next bend. No one but the creator of the stairs would be aware of this private, infinitely cruel joke, and he'd forever laugh over it alone.

But she had made it this far, had only to reach out and be safe – unless the jest wasn't over, and there was worse to come. Right this moment, she didn't care. She dragged herself up until there was room for the others below. Then she sat down, determined not to move until she'd stopped trembling like a leaf in a gale – and to hell with the Slayers.

*   *   *

20

Wil couldn't sleep.

His poor head was throbbing as if Sulcen the Smith had set up his divine anvil in there and was hammering away to his heart's content. Unfortunately, the pain didn't keep Wil's mind from worrying at questions such as what might await them back at Deepwall and how to handle the various options – though in truth he suspected there weren't all that many.

Fray must have made it back to the Vales by now and was surely doing his best to poison the minds of Longvale's nobles against Wil and the Watch, if only to distract from his own crimes. No doubt he'd present them as traitors, as mutineers and murderers, and Wil as the ringleader. Knowing the nobles, they'd readily accept Wil for a scapegoat rather than question the motives and sanity of one of their own.

Which left Wil with the choice of either sacrificing himself in hopes of buying a pardon for his comrades, or leading them into open conflict with Longvale's lords – a bloody and uncertain prospect even if those men of the Watch who'd stayed behind decided to join him, instead of playing it safe and sticking with the powers that be.

Neither option appealed to him. But, try as he might, he couldn't see a third way. Someone clever like Graeme or Arden surely would have found a solution by now, he reckoned. He simply didn't have a mind for politics, and at the moment he felt like he didn't have a mind for anything at all. Having his head smashed in clearly hadn't made him any smarter. He'd have to talk the whole thing through with Quillan and Gael the next day, their second on the road back to Deepwall. They'd reach Oldwall tomorrow evening, and Deepwall the day after. It would be nice to have some sort of plan by then.

Sleep continued to elude him.

The tent he'd inherited from Thorley felt more and more stifling the longer he lay there doing nothing, so he decided to go out for a breath of fresh air, maybe do a round and check on the sentries. Not that he felt any danger – they'd seen nothing more of the Bane since the attack on the hill. Even the lurkers were gone. For whatever unfathomable reason, the whole lot of them had left and gone south, he was fairly sure of it by now. He hoped their departure was a sign that things with Graeme, Breanne and Arden were going well.

But, Bane or no, you didn't go in one day from living in constant fear for your life to relaxing so far you forewent setting Wards and posted no watch. Besides, the men needed the comfort of routine tasks to keep up their morale, now more than ever. And letting them see he was up to doing the rounds couldn't hurt either.

Announcing himself with a soft whistle to each sentry in a timely fashion so as not to be taken for an intruder, Wil made the round of the camp. Except for the men holding watch, everyone was busy catching up on the sleep they'd missed during the past days and weeks. Good. They needed it, and he needed them rested and in fighting form the day after tomorrow at the latest, in case their welcome at Deepwall was even less warm than he expected.

Exchanging a few whispered words with the men on watch and noting in passing that the horses were quiet and content, he made his way around the perimeter. The first four sentries seemed alert enough, but the fifth gave no answering whistle to Wil's hail. Seeing how quiet things had been, he wasn't overly worried. Not right away.

Much as I understand how tired they all are, if the fellow's fallen asleep on guard duty he's in for a good telling-off. But no worse than that – though I'll make him sweat for a bit before I let him off the hook. We can't have discipline going to hell just because it looks as if we're no longer in immediate danger.

Twice more Wil whistled softly as he approached, and still he got no answer. Then, in the uncertain light of the waning moon, he saw the shape of a man sprawled facedown on the ground. There was something untidy about the way one arm was flung out to the side and the other wedged under the body, and the sight filled Wil with an immediate sense of foreboding.

*   *   *

'Breanne.' Someone was shaking her softly.

She came to with a start. And found herself staring into the chasm, the deep dragging at her with a force that was nearly equal to that of the Key pulling the other way. Graeme was sitting beside her, holding her with an arm around her waist, else she'd surely have fallen during her exhausted fugue. Pers, Finn and Torgrim were perched a few steps farther down, all of them looking the worse for wear but not half as bad as she felt.

Wanting to rub her tired eyes, she found that both her hands had somehow worked their way under her jerkin and were gripping the circlet in its pouch with the force of a vise. And the Key itself was shouting at her, louder than ever: *Use me! Use me! Use me!*

She made herself let go of it, tried to block out the insistent voice as best she could. She'd stopped trembling at least, though her whole body felt sore and stiff.

'I don't know if I can manage another step,' she said, resting her head against Graeme's shoulder for a moment. 'My legs feel like milk pudding – the kind that turns all runny if you just think the word "walk."'

'It's all right,' he said. 'It can't be that much longer to the top, and the stairs look good from here on. We're going to make it. I'll carry you if I have to.'

Looking up, she could see only to where the stairs curved out of sight, with no way to tell how far it still was to the spire's summit. But then she recalled looking down just a moment ago, remembering how very long the drop had appeared, and she supposed Graeme was right. It couldn't be that much farther.

'If you'll just help me up, I think I can make it,' she told him, and found that she could, once she had her legs under her.

The top was closer than she'd dared imagine.

Another half turn around the spire and the stairs entered a short tunnel, a man-made hole that cut through the rock and came out near

318

the edge of a perfectly flat piece of grassy ground the size of Thorhold's main courtyard and surrounded by a waist-high wall.

Close by was another doorway made of standing stones like the one in the cavern under Stormhold, only these were ancient and weathered, covered with pale lichen that must have taken centuries to grow from a few tiny, odd spores into patches that spread over most of the huge stones' surfaces. And she saw a faint but unmistakable shimmering in the space between them. She'd have known this was the real Gate even if the Key hadn't been pulling so hard it was threatening to drag her off her feet.

Taking in the rest of her surroundings, she saw they weren't alone. Across from where they stood, there was a break in the wall. Beyond it, a narrow, railing-less bridge led to the rim of the chasm – and to safety. But the way was blocked. Four Slayers stood just inside the gap, their black tentacles writhing in an almost lazy fashion, as if they saw no need to hurry anymore now that they had their prey securely cornered. And though they surely didn't need it, they'd brought backup.

Dreadful as the Slayers were, the thing crouching at the far end of the bridge was infinitely more terrifying, a huge blob of darkness that took on shape as she looked, becoming a gigantic, slavering bloodhound, its body a mass of writhing snakes that tested the air with darting, forked tongues, venom dripping from bared fangs longer than her fingers.

It was a revolting sight, but what scared and sickened her most of all was when the hound's features suddenly slipped and melted into a perfect likeness of a human face, one she knew all too well: her father, looking at her with eyes that were as hard and cold and as angry as ever. For long moments, that hateful gaze bored into her, burrowing down to her most secret, intimate places. Then he opened his mouth and let out a low, rumbling growl that shook the whole spire. But instead of frightening her further, the incongruous sound broke the spell, and she turned her attention back to the Slayers. For now, they were the more immediate danger.

She heard Graeme gasp at the sight of the thing.
Pers groaned, and Finn made a choking sound. They all had their weapons out and were surrounding her protectively.

But it doesn't make sense for them to protect me, she thought. *There's nothing they can do against the Slayers. I should be protecting them. That's what I have the Key for.*

She was interrupted by Torgrim. 'Leave the Slayers to me,' he said. 'I'll hold them off while you close the Gate. Just do me a favor and be quick about it.'

'How should I do it?' she asked him.

'I've no idea, lass,' he said. 'But I suspect the Key knows. Just do what it wants.' Then he raised his staff and advanced on the monsters.

What to do first? Breanne thought, her hands flying for the pouch under her shirt. *Close the Gate and risk all their lives? Or try to save her companions and endanger the whole mission?*

Before she could make up her mind, all four Slayers closed with Torgrim, as if eliminating him was first and foremost among their tasks. In a trice, they'd driven him back towards the Gate, no matter he was dealing them massive blows, his staff whirling faster than the eye could follow and striking showers of sparks each time it met with one of their tentacles.

Fumbling with the drawstrings of the pouch while the Key screamed in her head and the Slayers drove Torgrim ever farther back, Breanne didn't notice the tentacle snaking out of the tunnel behind her – not until it gripped her ankle and yanked her away and down into the dark hole.

Falling, she caught a last glimpse of Graeme's face, contorted in unspeakable anguish and horror, then she felt her very essence begin to fray and scatter as she was sucked into a lightless, bottomless maw from which she knew there would be no escape until time itself came to an end, and perhaps not even then.

*   *   *

Kneeling beside the fallen man, Wil felt for a pulse.
There wasn't one – he was dead. Rolling him over onto his back, Wil saw it was Dice, staring back at him with unseeing eyes, the mouth that to his comrades had been such an entertaining source of innumerable tall tales and filthy jokes wide open now in a silent scream. Running his hand over the dead man's body, Wil found no wound, nothing to tell him how Dice had died. But he wasn't ready to assume it had been of a natural cause. Not here, and not now. It wasn't until he thought to check Dice's neck that he found it: a darker stripe encircling the throat, hard to see in the feeble light but definitely there. Dice had been strangled.

Wil was just opening his mouth to sound the alarm when he felt the tiniest brush of air pass over his face, and then the noose that had killed Dice was tightening around his own neck with brutal force, cutting off his air and choking off the warning cry he'd been about

321

to utter.

Though a part of him knew it was useless, his fingers flew to his throat, frantically scrabbling at the thin, tightly braided leather cord cutting into his flesh. His head threatening to explode, he forced himself to reach back and try to grab his assailant, but his hands came up empty. Whoever it was had a hard knee firmly planted in the middle of Wil's back and was otherwise keeping his distance.

As his vision darkened and his senses began to slip, Wil made a last, violent effort and tried to stand. He was big, he was strong, and maybe he'd be able to shake the blighter off if he only managed to get his feet under him. But the man behind him was big and strong as well, and clearly no beginner at this kind of thing.

Fray! Wil thought, groping for his last reserves. *How stupid of me to assume he'd be gone. I should have known the treacherous vermin would try something like this.*

Strain and heave as he might, he couldn't get up off his knees, and struggling merely caused the cord to dig deeper and deeper.

The end came swiftly. The last thing he perceived was a sudden inrush of darkness that spun him around and away, tumbling him head over heels like a piece of flotsam seized by a violent breaker, and then it was over.

*   *   *

Torgrim was dealing the Slayers massive blows, his staff whirling faster than the eye could follow and striking showers of sparks each time it met with one of their tentacles. They'd driven him almost to the Gate, but now the tide seemed to be turning. One of the monsters was down and another was crippled, its tentacles shrunken to black worms that whipped about in a useless frenzy.

Then everything seemed to happen at once.

With a violent jolt, the ground beneath Graeme's feet suddenly shifted, as if a giant fist had struck the spire a glancing blow. Regaining his balance, he noticed a questing tentacle snake out of the tunnel and reach for Breanne. Gripping her hand, he yanked her out of the way just in time. Brought his sword down hard, even though he knew it wouldn't harm the thing. Then, in the instant before the blade bit, he felt a sudden pulse of power race into his left hand, still locked with Breanne's, and for the space of half a heartbeat he was connected through her to the Key.

The force shot through him and straight into the sword, the blade momentarily flashing a brilliant blue as it bit deep into the Slayer's alien flesh and took a good three feet off the tentacle. The shock of the encounter was so great, it shattered Graeme's blade, racing up his sword arm like a bolt of lightning and numbing it to the elbow.

The effect on the Slayer was stunning. With a high-pitched, ear-splitting screech it tumbled backwards through the tunnel and plunged into the deep, and Graeme knew without knowing that, somehow, he'd killed it – or the Key had.

Then he heard Breanne cry out.

He turned just in time to see the thing that had been lurking at the other end of the footbridge come flying through the air, headed straight for her. Seeing his dead sister Adelle riding the hound's monstrous body, a hurtling mass of necrotic flesh covered in mangy, lice-ridden pelt and huge, pus-weeping sores, nearly froze him with horror.

Nonetheless, he managed to pull Breanne out of the path of destruction a second time, if just barely. Only then did he notice that she was shouting at him to let her go. She was struggling with the circlet, trying to lift it to her head with her free hand.

The hound landed right on the spot where she'd been standing a moment ago, but for a wonder it didn't attack her. Without missing a beat, it launched into another jump, this time towards Torgrim..

'Torgrim! Beware!' Graeme yelled, but it was too late.

The attack took all of them completely by surprise. Before the Slayers could get out of the way or Torgrim could bring around his staff, the hound bowled into them and they all went tumbling through the Gate, leaving behind a sudden, eerie silence and a space that was empty save for the Slayer Torgrim had killed.

'No!' Breanne half snarled, half sobbed, holding the circlet in both hands now, poised to set it on her brow. 'You can't have him!'

She was about to don it when the Key was suddenly ripped out of her hands by some infinitely greater force and went flying straight as an arrow for the Gate.

With a CLANG! that nearly split Graeme's eardrums, it hit the faintly shimmering space between the stones and remained there, suspended in mid-air and shining with a blinding blue light. Though he knew it was madness, Graeme made to go after Torgrim. But the moment he tried to approach the Gate he was repulsed by a wall of blistering heat. His leathers smoldering and the jagged tip of his broken sword glowing red hot, he had no choice but to retreat. There was nothing he could do.

Torgrim was gone.

Meanwhile, an ominous hum had started up somewhere deep in the island's bedrock. Now it was quickly rising to a deafening rumble. The spire began to vibrate under their feet, then to shake. Graeme heard rocks fall.

'The bridge!' he shouted over the rising din. 'We have to get out of here!'

'But, what about Torgrim?' Breanne shouted, tears in her eyes.

'There's nothing we can do for him,' he told her, taking her hand. 'Except save ourselves, so his sacrifice wasn't in vain. Come, before the bridge collapses.'

Pers and Finn were already at the bridgehead. 'You youngsters go first,' Pers said. 'Just in case. You've got a lot more years ahead of you than I do.'

Graeme didn't argue. No time. Haunt's evil spirit clearly hadn't given up yet. After all the horrors they'd been through, it still had one more nasty surprise in store for them.

Gripping Breanne's hand, he set foot on the bridge. As he'd thought when he'd first seen it from below, it was barely wide enough to place two feet side by side. Only now it was shaking and swaying as if it wasn't made of solid stone at all but of something much more pliable and untrustworthy.

Step by trembling step, refusing to look down, they made their way onto the ridiculously narrow walkway, while all around huge chunks of rock shook loose from the canyon walls, tumbling away through the void until they plunged into the angry waters far, far below.

Halfway across, the bridge gave a sudden, violent lurch that nearly threw them off. Graeme barely managed to keep his balance and Breanne from falling. She was white as a sheet, her eyes wide with terror. So close to safety, the fear she'd so bravely conquered until now looked to be catching up with her. Hardly surprising, he thought, and was about to put another foot forward when he saw that a wide crack had appeared in the bridge right in front of them.

'Pers! Finn!' he shouted. 'Better not wait until we're across! The bridge isn't going to hold much longer!'

By a hair, they all made it over to the other side – though Pers, who came last, nearly went down when the bridge finally gave way and crumbled into the deep. If Finn hadn't grabbed the front of his jerkin and hauled him off the last few feet of the collapsing arch in the barest nick of time, he would have unfailingly fallen to his death.

'Thanks, lad.' For once, even unflappable Pers looked properly shaken. 'We'll empty a keg together on that one, I promise, as soon as we're out of here and somewhere they're civilized enough not to rip the ground out from under a man's feet.'

And still it wasn't over.

By now, the whole island was in the throes of a violent earthquake, bucking and shaking, the ground seeming to fall away under their feet in jerks and stutters, forcing them onto their hands and knees. Before them loomed Stormhold, its dark outlines frayed as if rats had been gnawing at the edges. Graeme saw half a wall's worth of merlons silhouetted against the moonlit sky wobble and break away like a row of rotten teeth. Next, a turret fell off the main keep and crashed into the bailey, the impact drowned in the general din of rumbling, grinding, groaning bedrock.

'The island is a death trap!' he shouted. 'We have to get to the

326

bridge!'

'You think it's still standing?' Pers shouted back.

'I don't know. Doesn't matter. If it's up, we walk; if not, we swim.'

It was a nightmarish trip, the heaving earth reducing them to toddlers crossing a particularly nasty stretch of hell. Now and then they were able to walk upright for a few steps, until another violent convulsion swept them off their feet and forced them to crawl on all fours again. Graeme led them over the least rugged terrain he could find, giving the castle the widest possible berth, and still they were in constant danger of being hit by falling stones or swallowed by one of the many cracks opening up in the ground as gigantic forces tore at the island and threatened to rip it apart.

When they'd finally rounded the castle, by now pretty much reduced to a few ragged walls rising out of a large pile of rubble, they found the bridge gone and the sea risen up the access road to the top of the second switchback, the water bubbling and roiling as if someone had lit a fire under a giant pot. It took Graeme a moment to grasp the import of what he was seeing: the whole cursed island was sinking into the sea. Haunt was going under, and it was taking everything on it down into the deep.

And then he saw something that seemed like a miraculous gift from the gods after what they'd been through during the last few hours. Down where the road dipped into the sea, at least a dozen small fishing boats were milling about in the troubled waters: the people of Salt, come out in force to rescue them.

*   *   *

327

Part IV – Three Kings

21

On *Nightshade,* Keon the Traitor remained wedged into his scrying device long after he'd shut it down, too stunned to move. What had looked like a clear path to victory had suddenly and unexpectedly turned into a total, unmitigated catastrophe. Moments ago, he'd been congratulating himself, jubilating over the removal of Torgrim, the only one he'd reckoned might still shove a spoke in his wheel – and now this.

All along I was convinced it was me they were after, seeking revenge for Simbalan. All this time, I thought Torgrim was the main danger, the one I needed to eliminate. And all the while the cunning whoreson was leading me a merry dance, distracting me from the real threat. Well, he's gotten his due, the deceitful bastard – for what little good it does me. And who would have ever suspected they'd go for the Gate? Who would have thought they'd even know about it?

They should never have gotten that far. They were supposed to die in the cavern under Stormhold, buried along with his most miserable failure to date, his aborted attempt to create a Gate of his own during the time the original had remained closed for so long. A hopeless endeavor, but he'd been desperate enough to try it anyway. As was to be expected, he'd never gotten any farther than setting up the stones, and those weren't even part of the Gate, just something to mark the spot where it was supposed to be. And now the real one was sinking into the sea, would soon be lost forever, and there was absolutely nothing he could do about it.

Damn Torgrim, and damn that blasted woman! Damn her to the bottom of the Void! He'd lost every one of the Darklings, never mind the Hellhound, and no way to get them back. He very much doubted he'd be able to control the rest of the Bane without them. His whole strategy ruined in the blink of an eye, the work of twenty years come to nothing, and his dream of becoming the next Vessel shattered. All because of an overblown, meddling bitch who happened to stumble across a Key and had the cheek to use it against him – against *him,* the Dark God's proxy on Vereld.

Thinking of Amut, he suddenly felt violently sick.

The God would not be pleased. No, not pleased at all. You didn't promise Amut the world and then fail to deliver. And if you did fail, you didn't expect to walk away in one piece. In fact, you didn't expect to go anywhere for the rest of eternity. Even the sickest, most twisted of human minds couldn't begin to imagine the kind of punishment the god meted out to subjects who fell short of his expectations.

Shuddering, he realized where he was, still wedged into the scrying device, and suddenly he felt an overwhelming need to get out – out of the machine, out of the cabin, out on deck where there was air to breathe and space to move about. If only he could get out of his contract with the god as well!

But that was impossible. The only way out of this mess was to come up with an alternative plan, something new and convincing enough to buy him a second chance – and he had to do it quickly. Once Amut had judged him, it would be too late. There'd be no reconsidering, no reprieve.

For hours he roamed the deck, restless and driven as a man on the brink of madness – which most likely he was – racking his brain for a solution to the dreadful predicament he'd managed to maneuver himself into.

The off-duty sailors and soldiers had long since melted away, driven below decks by a hard-earned sense for detecting their master's darker moods and the dangers they entailed for life and limb. When the wind picked up, driving squalls of icy rain across the deck, he retreated to the forward hold.

Ignoring the infernal stink wafting over from the main hold, crammed to capacity with a hundred sacrifices he'd now need more than ever, he grabbed a lantern from the companionway and continued his agitated pacing among sacks and barrels and boxes. Most of it was spoils from the *Nightshade's* most recent foray – back when the world was still in order and turning in the direction he desired. A sudden, black rage overcame him at the thought of what he'd lost – of what had been *stolen* from him – but it didn't last, soon giving way to a despair that seemed to have no bottom.

Weak, sick, desperate, he hung the lantern from a peg and lowered himself onto a box, staring at a pile of crates and wishing he could change places with one of them, needs be even with a sack of turnips. For the longest time he sat there, looking but not seeing, until ever so slowly his eyes focused on a detail, the marks on several of the boxes, and his mind began to make sense of what he'd been staring at for gods knew how long.

Each box carried three marks: one was that of a weaponsmith in Enemathea, where they made the finest and most highly prized blades in all of Vereld; the second belonged to the merchant who'd brokered the deal; and the third, the one that had caught his attention and now sent a thrill of recognition tingling up his spine, was the mark indicating the shipment's recipient. The Great Temple of Amut in Orr, capital of the Orrian Empire and the largest, richest city in the known world. Finding that mark here in the belly of one of a thousand ships that sailed the oceans could mean one thing only. It was a sign from the god.

His pulse racing, he found an abandoned cargo hook and pried open the topmost crate, not caring that he bent the tool and splintered the lid in the process. Inside were blades, some long and slender, some broad and short like the ones used for sacrificial knives, each one stamped with the sigil of the Brotherhood, the Black Priests of Amut. The black rats had been lucky to come through the fiasco at Similan unscathed, reneging on their promise to join Malamut at the last moment when they saw where things were headed. In the aftermath, they'd kept a low profile for years, anxious not to draw attention to the fact that a good many of them dabbled in sorcery and some of them did more than just dabble.

There were a few hundred of the blades, perhaps meant to replace the old ones made of obsidian. If so, together the crates held

enough of them to supply every temple in Aldara for the next thous-
and years or so.

Now they'd never arrive there, because undoubtedly the Dark
God himself had taken a hand in redirecting them towards a new
purpose, one that made even the mighty Keon quail with a fear so
profound it threatened to loosen his bowels.

For he understood now, understood perfectly what the god was asking of him, what the last chance he was being offered entailed. If he
could have escaped Amut's clutches by killing himself, he'd have
done it then. But that option had died a quiet death a long time ago.
Ever since, he'd belonged to the god, hide, hair, soul and all.

How well the god knew him! Knew that, strong as he was in the
Talent, he simply didn't have what it took to attempt the highest of
all paths known to sorcery, the one Malamut had successfully pur-
sued. The Six Steps, a long, painful, and incredibly demanding rit-
ual, a torturous ordeal that, had Keon attempted and survived it,
would have made him an Adept of the first order and brought him so
close to immortality as made practically no difference.

There was one other way to redeem himself and still have a hope
of making good on his promise, but the mere thought of it terrified
him like nothing else ever had. It was an obscure rite that to his
knowledge hadn't been practiced in centuries. That he knew of it at
all was a mere fluke, knowledge gleaned in passing from a book
he'd never really meant to read – but then, it might well have been
the god directing him already then, long before he'd ever even con-
templated joining the Dark Side. Called the Way of a Thousand
Cuts, it scared him witless for good reason. It was, in plain words,

the ultimate sacrifice.

The smallest mistake, and there'd be no need for Amut to punish him. Because the smallest mistake would automatically make him his own judge, jury, and executioner – or rather torturer. For there was no quick death in this game, only endless, unbearable pain.

Dreadful as they were, the god had given him the tools he needed. Now he just had to come up with a way to use them. And then finish what he'd begun.

*   *   *

Wil was remembering the rest of his dream.

Or finishing it, or dreaming it anew – impossible to say which. With gods in the picture, it seemed, time was a very loose concept. Whatever, of a sudden he understood what they wanted from him.

'You want me to die for them. Graeme, Breanne, Arden. So they can go on and finish the job.'

Moricanna nodded. She looked pained, and infinitely sad.

'Three times,' Wil said.

'Yes. Four, actually. There will still be your own death waiting for you. But now that I've heard myself put it into words, I hesitate more than ever to ask this of you. It's so very, very much, and so utterly unfair.'

'All right,' Wil blurted, though the prospect scared him witless.

Contrary to what Donal had said, there was something in this deal for Wil. To a god it might seem incidental, but to Wil it was something immensely precious: the lives of his friends.

'I'll do it. But if you ask me, I think you should have just gone ahead with it and not told me anything. It would be a damned sight

336

easier not having to know beforehand how many times I'll have to die.'

'You won't,' Verelda said. 'You won't, dear boy. We've thought of that. We're not monsters, you know. But we had to ask. Anything else would have been a terrible, terrible crime against you, and a betrayal of all we stand for. Now go, wake up, and forget. Your comrades are starving. They need you.'

For a moment, Wil was sure he was lying in his bedroll, three days out from Oldwall and hungrier than he'd ever been his life. *I need to go and talk to Dicken*. Captain *Dicken, it is now. We can't go on like this. The men are starving. Somebody has to make Thorley see reason.*

Then, without transition, he was in a place by the sea, if only as an incorporeal ghost. His body was somewhere far to the north, he realized, his connection to it so tenuous he wasn't sure there still was one at all – but yes, there was. Briefly he could feel himself jiggling and bumping around on the back of a horse, tied over the saddle like a sack of meal and for all intents and purposes still dead as mutton. Then the moment was past and he was hovering over a large crowd gathered on the beach east of a village he reckoned must be Salt. They seemed to be celebrating a Rite of Parting, although he saw neither a body nor a pyre.

He could have shouted for joy when he recognized Graeme and Breanne, standing in front of what looked to be the focus of everyone's attention: a large, smooth stone, set upright in the sand and bearing a few lines of crudely chiseled writing. Fearing it might be Arden who had died, Wil drifted closer until he was able to make out the words. *Torgrim of Eldinga,* it said there, and, *Never a truer companion in adversity.*

Not Arden, then. Graeme and Breanne both seemed very sad, as did the two men standing on either side of them, one young, the other old. All four of them looked as if they'd seen some rough times lately, which came as no big surprise.

Wil would have loved to clasp hands with Graeme and maybe take a knee and kiss Breanne's hand or, even better, take them both in a fierce bear hug – though he'd have to be careful with Breanne, wispy thing that she was. Despite the fact that she was obviously grieving for a friend she looked vigorous, full of life, as if in answer to the hardships she'd undoubtedly been through she'd... blossomed. Yes, that was the word for it. Shifting again, he smiled when he saw that she and Graeme were holding hands.

Good for them! It's past time someone was happy again for a change. I just hope Arden –

He never finished the thought.

Suddenly and seemingly out of nowhere, he felt a strong premonition of danger. He could have sworn there was someone standing right behind him, someone who could see him even though he was just a ghost. And the eyes on his back were anything but friendly. They felt threatening, malignant, *evil.*

Turning, he saw nothing. But in this strange in-between state he had an uncanny ability to sense and move over great distances in the blink of an eye, and so the next moment he found himself far out to sea, suspended over one of three black-hulled, black-sailed ships that somehow reeked of cruelty and suffering.

He hardly had time to take in the rough-looking men on deck and in the rigging before a lightning-swift line of darkness uncoiled from somewhere aft on the ship and lunged at him like a clawed hand reaching out to catch him.

But being a ghost had its advantages. Quicker than thought he was gone, racing back towards Salt.

I have to warn them! he thought, desperately trying to think of some way a bodiless specter might make itself felt or heard, or whatever. *They think they've done it. They believe it's over. But it's not. I have to –*

Then he was falling.

A violent jolt yanked him back into his body, and with a huge, labored THUMP! his heart started beating again.

'Dammit! Watch what you're doing!' That sounded like Gael.
'Sorry. But it's not like he's going to feel anything.' And that was Buck, good old Buck with the rabbit teeth and the two left hands.

'It's not about what he does or doesn't feel, you clumsy bumpkins. It's about respect. He's our captain, for the gods' sake, dead or alive makes no difference. Now see that you get him up into the tower without dropping him again, or I'll have you hand-picking horse shit for the rest of your miserable, worthless lives.'

'Hey! His eyes are open. Do you think that means anything?'

'What… wait. Here, put him down and let me see if he's got a pulse.'

'Reckon I do,' Wil said, giving Gael a weak smile. 'Don't be too hard on Buck. I think it was him dropping me that did the trick. Is there anything to eat? I'm starved.'

'Gods be good!' Gael said. 'Here the man comes back from the dead for the third bloody time in a row, and all he can think of is food. Welcome back, captain. And we're glad to see you too.'

'So am I, Gael, so am I. But dying's a hungry business, and I'd be really grateful for a bite of something. I feel like I haven't eaten in a week.'

'Alright, already. Just let's get you inside, and then I'll find you something. And you haven't, by the way.'

'Haven't what?'

'Eaten in a week. That's how long you were gone this time. And I'm sort of hoping it was the last, else next time we might end up having to lug your dead body around for months. You're one heavy bastard, you know. Ask Buck here if you don't believe me.'

'Get me inside where? Where are we?' Wil's brain definitely wasn't up to speed yet, lagging two thoughts behind like a lame nag at the races.

'The tower. We're at Oldwall.'

'You mean, it took you a whole week to get to Oldwall?' Wil was incredulous. They should have reached it in a day, easily.

'No. It took us a week to get here and then to Deepwall, where we hung around for a while before we came back here again. But that's a long story. Let's get you bedded down and fed. And then, if you're still up to it, I'll tell you what's been going on while you were busy holding your beauty sleep.'

Curious as he was, Wil had to give in, not least because of a sudden he felt tremendously tired.

'Beauty sleep, my arse,' he mumbled, his eyes closing before he'd given them permission. 'Didn't you know there's no rest for the dead?'

He was already asleep when they picked him up.

*   *   *

Graeme and Breanne were hard put to catch a moment alone.

There were a hundred and one things to see to, foremost of which was getting the people fed. With Keon gone and his guards and ships' crews no longer hogging most of the food, there was enough to go around. But taking stock of what there was and seeing that it was fairly distributed was just one of several full-time jobs Breanne had taken on.

On that front at least, things were looking up. During Keon's reign of terror, after two failed escape attempts only a very few fishermen had been allowed to cast their nets under strict surveillance and in sight of land, and the takings had been meager. But many had kept their boats and nets in working order as best they could, and now fish was again plentiful.

Another task she'd chosen for herself was visiting the old and the sick who had no families left and organizing proper care for them. At first she was received with awe and something close to reverence. But as she continued to go out among the people and became a familiar sight on the streets of Salt, one by one they slowly began to venture forth from their state of shocked silence and open up to her, these bitterly tested souls, cowed, oppressed and abused for so many years, some of them for as long as they could remember.

The stories they told – at first haltingly and then in a rush as if all of it needed to come out at once, unbearable foulness vomited out in a single, liberating stream – those stories were the stuff of nightmares. More than once, she found herself in tears, full of empathy for those who had suffered so horrifically, and sharing their helpless anger at the inconceivably cruel and heartless men who'd made their lives such a living hell.

Everyone had lost friends and relatives to Keon's insatiable hunger for human sacrifices, and nobody had escaped the abuse and torment dealt out by his minions. The guards' contempt for the imprisoned Salters had been limitless, she discovered. Among the many shocking incidents she heard of, there was one she found particularly vile: once, when Keon temporarily thought it expedient to mark out future sacrifices ahead of time, the guards decided to make recognizing and retrieving the designated victims later on easier by cutting off their noses – and they did it laughing, as if it were all an amusing joke.

A couple of those poor souls had somehow survived, but she had yet to see one of them. Apparently they felt so shamed by their disfigurement, they ventured forth only at night.

During the first days she saw little of Graeme.

He was busy organizing their defenses. Keon the Traitor was still out there, and no doubt it was just a question of time before he returned to take his revenge on the people who had caused him so much trouble. With Torgrim gone and the Key lost, there wasn't much to confront him with except Graeme, Pers, Finn, and the few more or less able-bodied men Graeme had found who knew a sword from a fishing rod. At least they had the dead guards' horses, weapons and armor, plus what they'd discovered in an arms cache down in the inn's cellar.

All told, the situation was dire bordering on hopeless. Keon had magic, and he had three ships' worth of fighting men. And Graeme was already thinking further. Even if by some miracle they managed to fend off Keon's forces, once word traveled north that the Bane was faltering the Barbary King might well see his chance to bring all of Baintry under his dominion. If dealing with Keon already looked like a desperate proposition, the notion of somehow stopping thousands of fierce, bloodthirsty Barbarian warriors from flooding over Haster's Pass and down into Marillin seemed entirely ludicrous.

But Graeme wasn't a man who gave up, ever, and he said that if worst came to worst there was a way to stop King Leith and his hordes, though he had yet to explain to her what it was.

It was only late at night that they found some privacy in the rooms they shared at the inn, now rid of the previous occupants' last traces, and it was here that Graeme finally told her his story – the real one, not the story he'd been living with for the better part of his life in the firm belief that it was true.

'Adelle,' he said. 'She was the only thing that was real. Everything else was borrowed. I've been able to piece together most of what really happened back then from what Corbin told me, and from the memories that have been coming back to me ever since the night I met him and he recognized me.

'It started here in Salt. Apparently there were all sorts of signs and portents, or so everyone's agreed nearly twenty years after the fact. But back then, no one recognized them for what they were.'

Spellbound, Breanne listened to the story as Graeme had been told it by Oakes. Oakes, who said that her Graeme was of royal blood, heir to the throne of Marillin. She was still chewing on that one. More so than Graeme, probably, who seemed set on ignoring the fact as best he could.

The first sign that things weren't as they should be in Salt was the fish disappearing from the waters around Haunt, usually the Salters' best fishing grounds and a convenient hundred yards from their doorstep. For the first time in living memory, their nets came up empty. But the fishermen of Salt – who five centuries after Redhands' demise still mistrusted the barren rock on their doorstep and wouldn't have set foot on it even if promised a boatload of gold – found fish aplenty elsewhere, and soon wasted no more thought than usual on the island, which is to say as little as possible.

Nor did they dwell for long on the fact that, soon after the fish had disappeared, the birds began to avoid the island as well. Seabirds ate fish, after all, and it was only natural for them to do as the Salters did and go where their food went.

Some time later, a man named Olf Fourfingers claimed he'd seen eldritch lights floating among the ruins across the water late at night. Since by anyone's reckoning Olf hadn't been sober of an evening since the reign of the current king's grandfather, his alleged sighting was dismissed as a drunkard's cross-eyed fantasy.

But when other, more reliable witnesses reported seeing the strange, darting lights on Haunt, long-drowned memories floated closer to the surface and a sense of unease began to spread among the people of Salt. There was even talk of sending a message to the king in Arventon, but nothing came of it.

What was there to report, after all? Weird lights in the dark?

King Oswin would laugh them off as the superstitious delusions of simple-minded peasants. Besides, come to think of it, nothing bad had actually happened.

'Yet,' Olf said. 'Just you wait and see: something's in the wind. Whatever it is, it's not over. Not by a long shot.'

But that was Olf for you: always seeing the worst in everything, tolling the bells of doom with the stubborn persistence of someone vindicated more often than not by the simple fact that, left to themselves and given half a chance, things tended to go wrong all on their own.

Likewise, no one in Salt was overly worried when the tremors started up. Small shivers and rumblings of the earth were a given in these parts. They might be absent for months or even years on end and then go on for days and weeks, but there hadn't been a Big One in living memory, so why worry? The people of Salt were practically born with sea legs, and a slight wobble in the ground wasn't about to make them lose their step.

That didn't happen until the ruins of Stormhold began to rise up from the ground as if rebuilding themselves through some residual, wild magic left over from Uthric's time. Every night, lights could be seen flitting to and fro among the stones, and every morning the Salters rose to see dark walls and towers grown by another foot or two.

Now they weren't just uneasy, they were frightened, and this time they didn't hesitate to send a messenger to the king. Unfortunately, Oswin was off in the mountains far to the north, inspecting the great wall built in Josrin's time to keep the forces of Barbary from invading Marillian territory. By the time the messenger had found the king and returned to Salt, the rebuilding of Stormhold looked to be complete, its dark mass of towers, turrets and battlements thrust high into the sky and hanging over Salt with the culminant threat of a raised warhammer.

It didn't take Olf to tell the Salters that, sooner or later, that hammer was bound to fall. Nor was anyone unaware of the fact that Salt lay foremost under its downward arc. Suddenly they were living under a shadow, and not liking it one bit. But there wasn't much they could do except hunker down and wait for the king to return from the north.

Several weeks passed, and nothing more happened.

Then one morning the Salters woke to an impossible sight: where the evening before there had been nothing but the usual, empty expanse of dark water separating Haunt from the mainland, a bridge now spanned the narrows, many-arched and wide enough for two wagons to travel abreast.

Salt was in an uproar – but in a very muted one, as if they all shared an unstated belief that someone or something over there was watching and listening, and that anything louder than a whisper might be overheard and lead to unforeseen consequences.

After hours of fruitless speculation, a few brave lads went down to cast rocks at the thing and see if it was real. Their first volley bounced off solid stone with ringing cracks, setting off an echo that seemed to race along the bridge from arc to arc and travel all the way to the island. In answer to their daring act there came a deep, tortured groan from Haunt, a sound as if the very bedrock were grinding upon itself, sending shivers across the channel's surface and causing the lads to drop what pebbles they still held and retreat with some haste. They did bring home the knowledge that, however it had gotten there, the bridge was by no means an illusion.

Now there were definitely the makings of a panic in the air.

A few impressionable souls wasted no time, loaded their most prized possessions onto carts and headed off to somewhere they deemed safer. But most stayed on, unwilling to abandon their homes and livelihoods and – as Olf observed not altogether mistakenly – spellbound by the unfolding events, caught in the invisible grip of whatever was brewing on Haunt like snapper lured by the treacherous light of a night-fishing lantern.

Yet another messenger was sent, duly inculcated with a sense of utmost urgency. Then, again and for weeks on end, nothing happened. There was no traffic on the bridge, not from Haunt to the mainland and most certainly not in the opposite direction. Finally, when hope was already beginning to wear thin, there was word from Oswin. He was coming. He was on his way back from the border, traveling with all due speed and scheduled only for a short stop in Arventon to exchange travel-worn troops for fresh ones. In the meantime, no one was to make any threatening moves against the occupants of Stormhold.

As if, the people of Salt said, shaking their heads in wonderment that anyone should give them credit for so much bravery or foolishness and settling down yet again to wait for their king to come and pull their bacon out of the fire. What none of them realized – the king included – was that the bridge constituted an invitation. Whoever had appropriated the island was waiting for Oswin to accept, which was why nothing continued to happen and the bridge remained deserted.

One afternoon a few weeks later, three war-cogs flying the royal colors came sailing down the coast. By the time they made fast in Salt's small harbor, cramming it to the limits of its capacity, everyone who wasn't actually moribund was down on the docks, craning their necks and jostling their neighbors to get a good look at their savior.

When the gangplank was lowered and Oswin came walking down it, the onlookers in the first row took a knee, the others being too tightly packed to do more than doff their caps and bow their heads. Oswin didn't seem to mind. Young, strong, handsome, he met everybody's expectation of what a proper king should look like. At the sight of him, the Salters immediately took heart. Here was the man who would set to rights whatever was amiss on yonder island, no doubt about it. Even Olf grudgingly agreed.

The king didn't leave the Salters much time to stand and goggle, however. While he repaired to the *Full Hold* to hear the mayor's report over a cup of watered wine, his lieutenants had the docks cleared and oversaw the offloading of the king's forces: two hundred men-at-arms, twenty knights, and a score of hulking destriers, skittish after the lengthy voyage over water.

Oswin wasn't one to waste time.

Less than an hour after the ships had made fast, the mysterious bridge rang under the iron-shod hooves of twenty-one horses as the king and his knights went to seek parley with whoever occupied

Stormhold.

Watching from afar, the Salters saw the keep's huge gates swing open at the party's approach and a lone, dark-robed figure step out and greet the king with a low, respectful bow. There was a short exchange, then Oswin and his men rode into the keep.

It took some time for the muffled boom of the gates closing behind them to reach the mainland, just as it took the Salters a moment or two to grasp what they had just witnessed. *Folly,* they would have said, had anyone dared speak the thought aloud. *Madness.* Then there was silence, disturbed only by small waves slapping the hulls of the ships and fishing boats and swirling around the pilings.

Hours passed, with no sign or word from the king.

The hours stretched on and turned into days. Time and again, messengers were sent across the bridge. But they received no answer to their hails, and the gates remained closed. Finally the king's lieutenants – against their monarch's orders and exceeding their authority by a measure that could cost them dearly if they were mistaken and things went wrong – gathered the remaining forces and marched them to the bridgehead. Equipped with scaling hooks and ladders as well as a couple of jury-rigged and hopelessly underdimensioned catapults, they were resolved to free King Oswin by any means necessary. Behind them marched nearly a hundred Salters armed with pitchforks, boathooks, fishing spears and the odd, rusty sword. They were still very much afraid of what awaited them at the other end of the bridge, but they were also quite angry: they were attached to their king, and not about to see him snatched away without putting up a fight.

Just as the vanguard was about to set foot on the accursed stones the low, throbbing moan of a war horn sounded from the island. Startled, the men paused to watch as the dark keep's mighty gates swung open and the king and his knights rode out.

The cheers and shouts of joy quickly died on the men's lips. Something was very wrong.

Gone were the knights' fluttering pennants and the gaudy colors of their tabards, gone was the sparkle on their armor and the sheen on their horses' flanks. The royal banner hung in stains and tatters, and the king himself...

It was a sight too terrible to contemplate.
None of them, neither the Salters nor the soldiers, would have forgotten it for the rest of their lives, had they had any meaningful stretch of time left to live.

As it was, all they could do was stand and stare at the once so splendid figures approaching: ghosts in rusted armor, missing limbs and swinging pitted swords in skeletal hands. Their open visors revealed eyeless faces, some of them wholly devoid of flesh, gnawed to the bone – by what, none dared imagine – and baring gumless teeth in fatal, grinning ricti.

The watchers still had time to notice that the riders and their horses were covered in spreading patches of greenish fuzz, some sort of fungal or algal growth, and that the twenty-one were not alone. The gates of Stormhold remained open, and from them there poured forth a host of horrors too terrifying to have been spawned even in the darkest depths of any earthly cave or sea. Then, preceded by an overpowering stench of rotten flesh, the king and his knights were upon them.

Overcome by a sudden, strange lassitude, the men at the bridge-head went to their deaths almost willingly. Hardly a one of them put up much of a fight, and the king and his knights were nearly done with their bloody work by the time the first of the Others, the ones that would eventually come to be named the Bane, came slithering and oozing across the bridge, spilling onto the mainland like a slow but deadly tide. Some few Salters managed to flee inland, running as far as their feet would carry them. But, as it turned out, far was never far enough.

All day long, the killing continued, spreading out from Salt to the neighboring counties. And still the gates stood open, and still the armies of perdition issued forth, as if their master were determined to inundate the entire world with death and final darkness.

Marillin would fall and the fate of the rest of Baintry hang by a fragile thread before the Bane came to a stop at a crumbling wall that had once been built to defend in the opposite direction. But the halt was only temporary, no more than a hiccup in the plans and ma-chinations of the mind that controlled the creatures of the Bane.

Once the wall was breached – and sooner or later it *would* be breached – it would take a miracle to do more than fend off the monstrous creatures for a little while longer, until the inevitable end came anyway.

'Once Keon had infected my father and his knights with the Bane sickness,' Graeme took up the story, 'he must have let them loose on the rest of Marillin, fully intending the horrific consequences that followed.

'I don't know whether he somehow compelled them to return to

Arventon, or whether it was perhaps some residual memory of what they'd been before the Change that drove what was left of my father and his men back to Arvend Castle. If it was in fact a memory that brought him there, it wasn't enough to keep my father from killing everyone he chanced upon, including his family.

'The day it happened, I was playing hide and seek with Adelle in the Great Hall. She was fifteen then, too old for those kinds of games, but she loved me, and indulged me to a point where even our generous mother was concerned that my sister might be spoiling me beyond redemption.

'We had no idea yet of what had occurred in Salt, no inkling of what was coming our way. So when father stepped into the hall, his armor rusted, a terrible wound disfiguring his face and his left hand stripped of flesh to the bone, everyone who was nearby rushed to his aid, shocked and concerned, foremost of all my mother. He killed them all. Slaughtered them, and not just with his sword. It was... not human.'

His voice faltering, Graeme pressed the bridge of his nose with white-knuckled fingers. Though she felt for him with all her heart, Breanne knew to say nothing. Finally, he took a deep breath and continued.

'Amid the screaming and the blood, Adelle somehow kept her head. She grabbed me by the hand, and together we ran to her room. As soon as we were there she locked the door and told me to hide under the bed. I remember thinking how dusty it was under there, and that my mother would give the maids a proper scolding if she knew what a sloppy job they'd been doing. Then suddenly there was a loud crash and the sound of splintering wood, and I heard Adelle say "Please father, no. It's me, Adelle, don't you see?"

'He didn't. I heard her gasp once, felt something heavy fall onto the bed, heard dull, thudding sounds as the mattress bulged and the whole bed shook under the weight of heavy blows. Many blows. After that there was a spell of silence, and then the scrape and jingle of my father's spurs as he walked away, looking for more people to kill.

'I lay there for what felt like hours, hardly daring to breathe, sure he'd come back any moment, find me, drag me out from under the bed and do the same thing to me he'd done to Adelle. But he must have run out of victims eventually, for he left the castle and took his rampage elsewhere.

'A few people survived his mad fury. One of them was Owain, the Lord Chamberlain, and it was he who finally found me and took me away. He was a man of great loyalty and honor, a man who never gave a thought to his own safety nor considered his duty to House Arvend done as long as there was a member of the royal family left alive. "I'm taking you to the Vales," he told me. "You'll be safe there." I didn't answer, not then, and not later. I'd stopped talking.'

He fell silent, lost somewhere between then and now, Breanne assumed.

'You shut down,' she said after a lengthy silence, gently rousing from his fugue. 'Because what had happened was simply too terrible for a boy of ten to deal with.'

'What? Oh. Yes. Though I didn't consciously decide anything – it simply happened. Owain did his best not to let me see my sister's body when he pulled me out from under the bed, but I did. I suppose that, after having watched my father kill my mother, seeing what he'd done to Adelle was more than my mind could still accommodate.

'That was when I forgot, lost all memory of that day as if it had never happened. And not just of that day but of my whole life until then, as if I'd never existed before the moment I saw my sister lying there. The only thing I took with me out of that room was Adelle's dead face. I became a boy without a story, a nobody. And because nobodies don't have words, I couldn't answer Owain, though the good, faithful man tried everything he could think of to get me to start talking again.

'I remember hardly anything of the following weeks and the long trek north, only that we somehow managed to get ahead of the Bane and made it through most of Marillin unscathed, until one day I caught my first glimpse of the snow-covered Tallamors, and Owain told me that behind those high mountains we'd be safe.'

'And then you met Tobin.'

'And then we met Tobin. It was late in the day and I was exhausted. We never stopped for the night before it was fully dark. Owain had taken my hand a while back, after I'd stumbled and fallen twice. He would have carried me, old as he was, but that was more than my sense of dignity would allow. And then I saw a young boy sitting by the side of the road a short ways up ahead. You know how it is with these rare encounters where you meet someone and right away there's a connection, almost as if you'd already known each other before.'

Breanne thought of all the people she'd met, all the way back to

Carlyn and Aidith, her childhood playmates, and she found that, no, she hadn't known how it was to meet someone in such a way – not until she'd stood at Graeme's door on the night she'd come from Vereldal and for the first time bothered to really look at him.

'Anyway, we were friends from the moment our eyes first met, and Owain seemed to feel something too, for without saying anything he stopped, held out his free hand and waited until Tobin got up and took it. From then on, there were three of us.'

'It turned out Tobin was as mute as I was,' Graeme continued.
'At least around Owain he was, though I'm sure he liked the old man and trusted him completely. But, strange as it may seem, we boys could talk to each other, and we did, holding secret, whispered conversations at night when Owain was asleep. My own past remained a complete blank, but Tobin remembered his well enough, and eventually he told me the story of how the Shifters had killed his two brothers, his parents and his grandma. The only thing missing was a sister. He didn't have one.

'Four days after Tobin joined us, the Bane caught up with us. It was around nightfall. We must have all felt them behind us, for we turned as one. Two Shifters were following us, apparently in no great hurry, seeing as they could catch us any time they wanted. Their attitude changed the moment they realized we'd seen them. I was sure we were as good as dead then.

'But Owain kept his nerve. He told us to run and not to stop until we were the other side of Oldwall, said he'd catch up with us later. So we ran, all through the night, while he died buying us precious time to get away. Only we didn't really get away – at least Tobin didn't.

'They got him early in the morning, just before first light. He was dead before we even knew they were there. I would have died too, if it hadn't been for a family of refugees bedded down for the night by the side of the road just a short stone's throw away. Our screams must have woken them up, and their women started screaming in turn when they saw the Shifters ripping what was left of Tobin apart, fighting over his body like crows over carrion.

'With all the noise the women were making, they caught the Shifters' attention. With such bountiful prey right in front of them, the beasts forgot about me for the moment, and I seized the opportunity and ran. Not until afterwards did it occur to me that perhaps I should have stayed and tried to help those poor people, but by then it was too late and I was far away.'

Graeme fell silent again.

'Oh, my dear Graeme, what could you have done?' Breanne understood all too well what was tormenting him. Even after so many years, some part of him still felt responsible for the deaths of everyone he'd lost.

'You would have died with them, and how would that have helped anyone? Who would have stood against the Bane, who would have ousted Keon and closed the Gate and freed Marillin if a ten-year-old boy had tried to play the hero back then? No. You did the only thing you could, the only *sane* thing. And it was the right thing, too.'

'I suppose,' Graeme said with a sigh. 'At least in a way I kept Tobin alive. Because, somewhere between there and Oldwall, I became him in all but name. I guess after everyone I'd lost, Tobin was just one too many, and I couldn't let him be dead as well.'

'You'd lost even yourself,' Breanne said wonderingly, suddenly seeing with absolute clarity why and how it had all happened. 'You were an empty vessel waiting to be filled.'

'Almost empty,' Graeme said. 'There was still Adelle. Her I kept, and fitted her into Tobin's story as best I could.'

'You loved her very much, didn't you?'

'Yes. She was my favorite person in the world. You would have loved her too, if you'd ever gotten to know her.'

'I do love her. How could I not? She brought you to me, after all. Because it seems to me that all those years her memory was like a compass guiding you, keeping you sane and safe. Who knows, but you might have gotten lost without her, and nothing of what we've accomplished together might have ever happened.'

'And now I have you,' he said with a smile. 'Another wise and loving woman to keep me on course. And luckily you're neither dead nor my sister.' He drew her closer, snuggling his face into her hair. 'Tell me, wise woman: are you very tired?'

'Let me see,' she said, a welcoming warmth already spreading through her body. 'Yes, I'm very tired. And no, I'm not *that* tired – provided we both have the same thing in mind.'

'I'm guessing we do,' Graeme still managed to say before her lips found his and sealed them with a kiss that turned into something long, and intense, and very fulfilling.

*   *   *

22

Six weeks had gone by since the fall of Stormhold and the sinking of Haunt, and so far Graeme hadn't dared leave Salt, fearing that Keon might return while he was gone.

'He's out there somewhere,' he told Breanne. 'And he's up to no good, that much is for sure. I just wish I knew what it is he's planning, and what's taking him so long.'

But finally the need to know what had become of the Bane did drive him out into the forestlands beyond the Blood Runes, though he left behind every man he had under arms to guard Salt, and took only Pers and Finn with him.

What they found went far beyond his wildest hopes – although as far as the Rooters were concerned it was more a question of what they didn't find. Hard as they looked, they didn't see a single one of the things sheltering from daylight in the forest's denser and more deeply shadowed reaches or waiting for nightfall in the cool, dark ravines they usually haunted, nor laid up in any of the abandoned farms that would have made perfect hiding places for creatures that feared and hated the sun. Where they'd gotten to was a mystery. But they were gone, no doubt about it.

What they did find were dead Lurkers, rotting, stinking like nothing on earth, spread in large, roundish patches of moldy sludge over the forest floor or oozing down the trunks of trees they'd inhabited. But it wasn't until a sheer overpowering stench guided them to a grey-green puddle of decay just barely recognizable as the remains of a Shifter that Graeme was finally prepared to believe what his eyes and nose were telling him.

The Bane was finished, or at least coming to an end.

Riding on, they found three more Shifters, all of them in the final stages of decay, all of them turning into fuzzy green mold, and even that looked to be dying.

'I wonder what did for the Lurkers,' Pers said when they'd reached breathable air again. 'And for the Grey Men. Damn things used to be hard as hell to kill, and now we seem to be stumbling over dead ones every time we turn around.'

'I don't know,' Graeme said. 'But, keeping in mind that they came from a different world, I'd venture a guess that all the creatures of the Bane were somehow connected, like the many individual parts of a single, greater organism – though I'll admit that's stretching the imagination a ways. But looking at what's left of them now, I have a feeling the green stuff might have actually been at the center of the Bane. Perhaps it *was* the Bane. And maybe closing the Gate and cutting it off from the source is what's killing it.'

'Might well have been the only way of killing it,' Finn offered.

Graeme nodded.

'Sounds outlandish,' Pers mused. 'But no more outlandish than the rest of what's happened – sorcerers, mages, magical circlets, sinking islands and all that. So yes, I'll buy it, seeing as it's probably the best explanation anyone's ever going to come up with.'

'Right,' Graeme decided. 'I think we've seen enough. Time to head back to Salt.'

He didn't have to explain why he set such a brisk pace on the way back. Keon was never far from any of their minds.

They needn't have worried.

The Traitor hadn't shown up while they were gone. But there were other visitors, as they found when they stepped into the inn's common room after seeing to the horses.

Breanne was there, and Corbin, and the girl Emelin, who'd become something of an aide-de-camp to Breanne. There were also four strangers, hard and weather-beaten fellows, sailors by the looks of them, or fishermen, but not from Salt. They looked far too healthy and well fed for that.

'Graeme,' Breanne said, rising to greet him. 'These are Egard, Darin, Ern, and Brion, from the Farney Islands.'

The Farneys. Graeme had completely forgotten about the group of a dozen or so islands west of Arventon – another piece of information left behind along with his prior life twenty years ago.

'M'lord,' Egard said, all four of them taking a knee. 'It's an honor, and a great joy, finding you here.'

'Come,' Graeme said, still very uncomfortable with people kneeling before him. 'Sit, and tell me what brings you here.'

'Well, m'lord,' Egard said once they were all seated. 'It's like this: ever since the Bane began, we've been pretty much stuck out there on our islands. And though the Farneys are the fairest bunch of isles you can ever hope to find, you can't help but feel sort of pent up after a time if there's nowhere else you can go, seeing as there was only the Bane or Barbary to choose from.

'We did go over to the mainland once in a while for wood to build and burn, so as not to end up sitting on bare rocks. In fact, Ern and Brion here went a week ago, and that's how we knew that things had begun to change for the better. So the four of us decided to go for a jaunt along the coast and see what we would find. We were of half a mind to turn around at Arventon, but thank the gods we didn't, and here we are.'

It turned out there were close to three thousand people living on the islands, many of them refugees from the mainland. Unlike Windward, the Farneys had welcomed everyone fleeing from the Bane. It was heartening news.

'Do you know of any other place where people might have survived?' Graeme asked.

'Well, there's Pine Island north of the Farneys, and Bow Island north of that. I know there's people on Pine, and they say they've seen smoke over the Coon Mountains on the mainland many a time and always in the same two places, and that they thought it was too contained and regular to be forest fires.'

Graeme was thrilled. There might well be far more survivors out there then anyone had dared to hope.

'We should be in Arventon,' he told Breanne. 'If others decide to come looking, that's where they'll go.'

'We can't abandon Salt,' she said. 'Not as long as Keon is still out there.'

'I know. I'll send someone, then. I think it's safe enough to go

362

there now. We found nothing of the Bane except dead Lurkers and Shifters. It looks to be the same around the Farneys, and we can hope it's happening elsewhere as well.'

'And you, my friends,' he addressed the men from the islands. 'You're welcome to stay as long as you like. But I'd ask that on your way back you to spread the word that the Bane is weakening and may soon be over, provided our luck holds. And I'd also ask you to make it known that Marillin needs a fighting force. The man who brought the Bane upon us is still out there, and he remains a clear and present danger. And it may well be that Barbary decides we're easy pickings, once they find out it's safe again to set foot south of the walls. Will you do this for me?'

'Aye, m'lord, we will.' To Graeme's surprise, Egard looked as if he'd just been handed a precious gift, or a medal of honor. So did his companions. 'It's what we've been waiting for all these years, a chance to fight back. We're with you, m'lord, whatever you need.'

Over the following weeks, others came.

A few keeps had held out here and there, the people hunting and gathering during the days and fighting off the Bane at night. In the Coons they'd closed off a whole valley and managed to keep the Bane out for twenty years. The same had happened in the Bluebacks. And in the western Tallamors.

Incredible feats of valor, inventiveness and sheer, stubborn refusal to give in and die had seen a surprising number of people through the darkest days the land had ever known. And with them, Marillin had survived.

First to arrive, ten days after the Farneymen, were Gamel and

Brother Ulric, together with two dozen men from Archer's Rock and Deer Island. It was a happy reunion for all of them, especially for Pers and Finn, and Breanne embraced Ulric like a long-lost favorite uncle.

'What of the Bane between here and Mirror Lake?' Graeme asked Ulric after the first excitement was over and things had quieted down. 'What did you see of it?'

'Only dead things,' Ulric said, looking as if he were actually saddened by the dreadful creatures' fate. But he immediately cheered up again. 'And we saw many hundreds of Stricken. Thousands, maybe. Don't worry. They've all settled down. Put down roots for good, it would seem. They're not going anywhere. They've become part of the forest.'

'Arden,' Breanne said, a hand going to her heart. 'That's his doing. It must be.'

'We thought as much,' Ulric said.

'Did you see him? Is he well? And Wulfwyn?'

'No.' Ulric shook his head. 'We didn't. But I'm sure he's out there. Perhaps his job isn't finished yet. Marillin is a big place, and he has a lot of ground to cover.'

Breanne looked disappointed, and sad. Graeme pressed her hand.

'I'm sure he'll come find us once he's done. And if not we'll go and look for him as soon as we can.'

He didn't add that it might be a very long time still before they could get away and go looking for Arden. She knew the stakes as well as he did.

Breanne enlisted Ulric and his extensive knowledge of healing in

364

her efforts to better the Salters' lot, and Graeme didn't see much of either of them during the next couple of weeks. Besides, he had more than enough to keep him busy as it was.

What Egard had said about the fires in the Coons had given him an idea. He soon had everyone who was willing and able collecting wood and building a bonfire on the hill they'd used as a lookout when they'd first come to Salt. He asked that it be kept burning day and night, with green stuff added during the daytime to make a column of smoke that would be visible from a long way off. He also made the two-day ride to Arventon with Pers and two men who'd volunteered to stay and tend a fire there as well.

It was a curious sensation to see the place of his birth and childhood again after so many years and under such strange and tragic circumstances. Like most every other town he'd seen during the long journey south, Arventon was deserted by all but the ghosts of the past, and he wasn't tempted to linger. He and Pers inspected Arvend Keep's armory, finding it still well stocked and in surprisingly good condition, but that was as far as they ventured into his childhood home. They made a quick inventory, and Graeme chose a few things he would need: a light hauberk, a breastplate, vambraces and a helm with nose and cheekguards, all of it as good as new under a protective layer of time-hardened grease.

Looking for a sword to replace the one he'd broken on the Slayer, he found something totally unexpected: his grandfather's sword *Barensverd,* an exceptionally fine Enemathean blade he'd always admired as a boy, wishing that one day he'd have one like it. He remembered it hanging on the wall in the Great Hall, one in a long row of ancestral weapons. How it had ended up in the armory was a mystery, but one he didn't question.

The last item he chose was a shield, the kind a knight would have carried in his father's time, bearing the arms of House Arvend: three stars on a dark blue field, one red, one silver, and one gold. Thinking back to what Torgrim had said about the red comet, he wondered if whoever had come up with the device had been guided by foresight, and hoped that the silver and gold stars might be a favorable omen.

Pers chose light mail shirts and helms for himself and Finn. 'It's all we need,' he said. 'We're used to fighting light. Anything more would just slow us down. Though it seems a shame to leave all this stuff behind.'

'We won't,' Graeme told him. 'We'll send a couple of wagons to fetch the rest, once we're back in Salt. Speaking of which – we should be heading back.'

'You're not still worried about Keon showing up, are you?'

'Not in Salt, no.'

'So then it's your heartstrings pulling you back, eh?' Pers gave him a sly grin. 'Though maybe mentioning that kind of stuff is sort of overstepping the line, now that you're a king and all.'

'I'm not a king, Pers, not by a long shot. And even if I was, I'd still want to hang on to my friends, no matter they tend to run at the mouth once in a while.'

'Fine,' Pers said. 'Then I suppose I can continue to put up with you even when you are a king. Provided you let me teach you how to handle a bow properly.'

Graeme smiled. There was no having the last word with the old wisecracker.

The day after they got back, a ship from Windward came sailing along the coast and made fast in Salt. It was the *Goldspray.* Graeme, come down to the harbor with Breanne, Pers and Finn to meet her, couldn't have wished for a more welcome sight than Captain Goderun Spray walking down the gangplank with a piratey swagger.

'Captain,' he greeted her. 'Good to see you still afloat.'

'Ach,' she said. 'That'll be the day, when a bloody, lumbering cog manages to catch *Goldspray,* no matter how many of those scary blighters they've got on board. And you don't seem to have done half bad yourselves. So where's that sweet-talking rascal Torgrim? And what happened to the blasted island my charts keep insisting should be here? I nearly sailed right on by, thought I'd come to the wrong place.'

'Why don't we all go up to the *Full Hold?*' Breanne said. 'I'm sure Mistress Goderun could do with a drink and a meal after the long voyage.'

'Now you're talking.' Goderun gave Breanne a wink and a smile. 'Lead on, luv. I'm right behind you.'

Goderun was clearly shocked and saddened when Graeme told her about Torgrim's death. But she didn't seem surprised to hear that Keon was still at large.

'That arsehole's the reason I came here,' she said, though a sideways glance at Finn suggested it wasn't the only one. 'I heard some news I reckoned you might find interesting. Nearly three weeks ago, people out on Windward's eastern shore saw three black ships headed north.'

'What the … ' Graeme couldn't make sense of it.

'Hang on, dear,' Goderun said. 'I'm not done yet. I had a run up to Eastvale scheduled in any case, so I thought I'd go see if maybe those ships put in at Cumbre. Turns out they did – well, not quite. They anchored offshore, and a single man rowed over in a skiff and came ashore. Apparently he made the rounds of Cumbre's taverns, hitting it off with the Barbarians. Bought them a lot of drinks and asked all sorts of questions about Barbary. Said he was an Orrian merchant looking to expand into new territories, though he seemed more interested in certain customs and traditions than in actual business opportunities.

'It appears he made it in to see the Barbarian chieftain in command of Cumbre, and departed with a mark of recommendation in his pocket. It's rumored the chief was left with a bit of something in his pocket as well. A large bit of something. The man rowed back out to his ships that same evening, and they sailed north on the morning tide. Funny thing is, nobody could remember what the bugger looked like, only that he wore gloves and a deep hood he never let down.'

'Keon,' Graeme said. 'So now we know where he's gotten to.'

*   *   *

Wil's first thought when he awoke in the third-floor room of Oldwall's eastern tower was that he had to warn Graeme and Breanne of the terrible danger they were in. Then the impossibility of it hit him: hundreds of miles lay between Oldwall and Salt, and though the Bane had withdrawn from the north, there was no telling how things stood farther south. Maybe the damned critters had left because they were all going after Graeme.

But no, it doesn't feel that way. It feels as if... as if the Bane is somehow lessening, going to ground, giving up and quietly passing away – though that's probably just me indulging in some wishful thinking.

No matter. It would take weeks to get to Salt, if the journey was feasible at all. There was no way he could reach them in time. As he lay there fretting, images of what he'd seen in that strange in-between began to appear unbidden before his inner eye, one after the other and so insistently that he had no choice but to pay attention. Once he did, he became aware of certain details he hadn't really noticed before. Repeating in his mind the transition from the beach to the black ships, but this time much more slowly, he realized two important things: the ships had been far from Salt, a hundred miles or more, he reckoned; and they'd been heading north, away from, not towards his friends. He found himself breathing easier. So the danger wasn't as imminent as he'd thought. On the contrary, it was retreating from Salt. Coming north. Which meant... his way.

So maybe he was right where he needed to be. Just like Arden had said when he'd refused to let Wil come with him and Wulfwyn into the Bane.

All right then, Wil. Let's think this through some more, try to find out what exactly it is we're supposed to be doing here. Which re-minds me. I still don't know what happened at Deepwall. I should get up and go talk to Gael or Quillan. Just a moment to gather my wits, and then I'll...

That was as far as he got before he fell asleep again, his maltreated body resolutely asserting its right to heal in peace and quiet.

When next he woke, he was feeling much better, well enough to rise and brave the stairs, though his legs felt about as solid as a couple of wet rags and he had to sit down and rest twice on the way down. But it was worth the trouble, he decided when he tottered down the last steps and found the world outside marvelously bright and clean under a clear, blue sky.

Someone had collected a few rocks and built a small bench right by the door, the perfect place to sit with one's back against the tower's sun-warmed stones and catch one's breath.

There seemed to be no one about – though he could hear voices farther along the wall, and the faint sound of axes chopping wood carried over from the stand of pines two hundred yards south – so he reckoned he'd just sit there for a while, enjoy the sun, listen to the birds and the mild breeze rustling through the grass and whispering around the tower until someone showed up and told him where he might find some food. He vaguely remembered having eaten something last night, but his stomach was telling him it hadn't been nearly enough.

There was something else amiss, though, a dearth that went way deeper than mere hunger. He felt... thin. Translucent almost. Like something a middling breeze would blow right through. As if part of him hadn't quite made it back from wherever he'd been while he wasn't... here. Leaving an empty place inside him that he suspected no amount of food could fill. Perhaps nothing ever would. He had an uncomfortable feeling it would stay with him for the rest of his days, like living with one foot already in the grave.

But then – isn't that how we all go through life, only some of us are better at not thinking about it? Which isn't really all that stupid. There's nothing tires a man out like thinking too much.

'Well, look who's back from the dead.'

Wil started. He'd drifted off again. Quillan was there, grinning from ear to ear. 'And about time, too. How are we lowly sergeants supposed to maintain order and discipline when all our captain's doing is loafing in bed and making mighty inroads on the food stores between snoozes?'

'Quillan,' Wil said. 'Sounds to me like you've been keeping the men busy enough. And speaking of rations…'

'Don't worry. There's still some leftovers from breakfast. Just give me a moment, and I'll see what I can rustle up.'

Wil couldn't believe his eyes when Quillan came back with half a loaf of fresh bread, a bowl of stew with carrots and potatoes in it, and even a cup of kaf. 'You should have told me this is just a dream,' he said accusingly. 'Then I'd have ordered roast pig and dumplings, and a mug of ale to wash it all down.'

The sergeant laughed. 'Sorry. No dream, and no dumplings. This is the best we can do, and that's only thanks to Raulin.'

'Raulin? What's *he* doing here?'

'Best start from the beginning,' Quillan said, hunkering down beside Wil. 'You might remember I told you last night that we'd been to Deepwall.'

Wil nodded, his mouth too full to answer.

'Right. Well, they wouldn't let us in. Made us wait until they'd gone and fetched the new Lord Commander and his newly appoint-

371

ed captain. Didn't take them long to appear on the gatehouse wall, almost as if they'd been expecting us. Care to guess who it was?'

Wil shook his head. 'Tell me,' he mumbled around a mouthful of stew and bread.

'Rothger Paxton. And Fray. Paxton said we were all traitors and cursed by the Bane. But he might consider setting up a quarantine station outside the wall and see who survived, provided we handed you over to him to be judged for your evil deeds. Heinous, is what he actually called them.'

'You should have agreed,' Wil said. 'You'd all be safe behind Deepwall by now.'

Quillan gave him an incredulous look. 'You really believe that? You reckon Fray's going to let anyone in alive who can refute the lies he's surely been telling about what happened out there? Lad, if that's what you think, that noggin of yours must have taken more damage than I thought. Any road. I said to Paxton I'd tell him to stick it where the sun don't shine except his head was already so far up Fray's arse that if he wanted to see daylight again, he should just ask Fray to open his mouth.'

'You said that to Paxton?' Wil goggled. '*Lord* Paxton?'

'Yup.' Quillan actually looked quite pleased with himself. 'And I'd have come up with more of the same if they hadn't started shooting at us. So I just gave him the finger, and then we cleared out.'

'Well,' Wil said. 'Well, well. And now what? We're stuck out here? Outlaws? What do the men say? Most of them have family down there, you know.'

'I do. As you can imagine, they're not exactly thrilled how things turned out. But there's not a one of them would have done

372

any different. They're very clear about who saved all their lives back on yonder hill. They'd die before they gave you up to Paxton.'

'So, what? We're staying here?'

'That's up to you. You're the captain. But I've got them started fixing the wall and building a shelter, and half of them are out hunting so we can lay in some stores.'

'Stores,' Wil said. 'That reminds me. What's this business with Raulin?'

'Well, after what Thorley did to him, old Raulin was mightily pissed off at the whole setup down there, and seeing Fray return and spread his lies made him even angrier. Paxton not letting us in was the last straw. Raulin's never going to walk straight again, but he can still drive a wagon. So that same night, he loaded one up and snuck out the gate. I'm thinking he must have had help, but he won't say one way or another. Whatever – he's here, he brought us a wagonload of food and, all told, we're better off than we've been in a long while.'

'I'm going to thank the man personally,' Wil said, leaning back with a satisfied belch. Then a chilling thought abruptly displaced his feeling of wellbeing. 'We're good for now. But what do we do when winter comes? How are we going to survive then?'

Quillan grinned. 'That's what we've got you for, isn't it? We're relying on you to come up with one of your brilliant ideas. Meaning, everyone's hoping and praying for our captain's brains to start working again before we all get stuck in a snowdrift.'

'Very funny,' Wil said. 'All right. Let's start with the obvious. As long as we're here, we're going to be a thorn in Paxton's side. Sooner or later, he might just feel uncomfortable enough to do

373

something stupid, like mounting an expedition and coming out here to finish us off.'

Quillan nodded, his grin fading as he listened to Wil.

'So here's what I want: I want the wall fixed. And I don't mean a makeshift job, I mean fixed so it's good as new. Better even. I want a first-rate gate that can withstand some serious battering. I want at least four sets of reliable stairs up to the walkways. I want catapults on the battlements. Trey should know how to build them. And he's to get every man who knows how busy making arrows.

'Besides food stores, we'll need to put in hay for the horses, just in case. And we'll need shelter for them as well. We should also start making better use of the game we hunt. We'll be needing pelts, leather, sinew for backing bows, bone for arrowheads in case we run out of be broadheads. Speaking of which, we should have some men comb those ruined farms down south for every scrap of iron they can find. Bone will do fine for hunting, but we'll need bodkins in case Paxton does show up.'

'Is that it?' Despite the length of Wil's list, Quillan looked happy, as if a weight had been lifted off his shoulders.

'Probably not the half of it,' Wil said. 'Don't worry. I'll think of the rest as we go along. Needs be, I'll make something up, just so you fellows don't get bored.'

'Right, captain.' Quillan rose. 'I'll get to it, then.'

'Oh, and, Quillan.'

'Sir?'

'You might find this strange, and I couldn't say why, but I have a feeling we're right where we're supposed to be. There's a reason for all this.'

'Funny you should say that.' Quillan scratched the graying stubble on his head. 'I've been thinking the same thing. Can't explain it either, though.'

Watching the sergeant walk away, Wil wished he had at least some idea of what was coming their way.

So much to think of, so much to prepare. Easier if I knew what exactly I was preparing for.

He sighed. They'd just do the best they could, hope it was enough. And maybe it was better not to know what awaited them. It might be worse than anything any of them could imagine.

*   *   *

23

Breanne found Graeme at the training grounds on the northern edge of town. Walking up to where he was explaining swordplay to a group of Salters, she wordlessly held out her hand to him. He understood immediately, handed the length of wood he'd been using as a training sword to one of the men, and let her lead him away down a cart track running towards distant farms between meadows and hedgerows.

It was one of the many things she loved about him: it didn't take a lot of words to let him know what she needed. There were even times when he knew before she did. The thought made her stop for a moment and hug him tight. It wasn't enough. Standing on tiptoes, she took his face in her hands and gave him a lingering kiss.

'Boy,' he said when she was done. 'I must have done something right.'

'No, you're luckier than that. You don't have to do anything except be who you are.'

'Good thing I found out who that is, then.' He looked so different when he smiled, she thought. Younger, innocent.

She turned serious. 'Keon,' she said. 'Tell me. All of it.'

He sighed. 'All right. Here's what I think. He's going to try and take control of Barbary, levy an army, and come at us from the north.'

'And how is he going to accomplish all that?'

'There are ways. He has ways, I'd guess. It's what I'd do in his place. It's the only logical move.'

'So what are we going to do about it?'

'Try and stop him. And the one place we have a hope of doing it is Oldwall. There's only the one pass over the Tallamors, and he's not going to lead an army through those mountains using footpaths and game trails.'

'What if he doesn't come over land at all but by sea?'

'He might. But I'm pretty sure he won't. For one, as far as I can gauge him he's a methodical person. He'll want to make a clean sweep, not land, split up his forces and fight in twenty different places at once. Remember, he's not about conquering. He's about killing and destroying, hard as it is to grasp. And for another, he won't want to leave his back open to the Vales. So they'll be first on his list. The rest follows logically, and brings us back to Oldwall.'

'You're going there.' An icy hand gripped Breanne's heart.

'Yes. It's our only chance. Warn the Vales, hopefully in time so they can join us, or at least try to get out of the way. Man Oldwall, and put a spoke in Keon's wheel.'

'All right,' she said, though it wasn't. 'But I'm coming with you. No, don't argue. I won't be a whit safer here than at Oldwall. And I want to be with you. We want to be with you.' She gave him her sweetest smile.

'What's that supposed to... don't tell me... are you... ?'

'Yes, love. I'm with child. I do realize it's a terribly inconvenient time to…'

She didn't get any further, because he was suddenly hugging her so hard she could feel her spine cracking. Then, remembering himself, he loosened the embrace and left her space to breathe again.

'Sleeping Wood,' he said. 'Now I get it.'

'Get what?'

'Don't you see? Aside from Arden, you're the last one on the Thorley family tree. A branch that looked to remain fruitless. But the wood was only sleeping. Now it's budding.'

'You're right,' she said, marveling at how, one after another, the riddles of her vision were revealing their true meaning. Only she wasn't sure she wanted the child to grow up a Thorley.

'Would you agree that it's best for a child to be born in wed-lock?' he asked, nuzzling her hair, reading her thoughts again.

'No,' she said. 'I think it's best for a child if his parents truly love each other, and him – or her. But I'll marry you anyway, if that's what you're getting at. Provided a lowly noblewoman – and from a foreign country to boot – will do for the king of Marillin.'

'I'm not a king. In fact, just a few weeks ago I was a simple sol-dier and an outlaw on the run, and still good enough for a high-and-mighty lady from the Vales. So yes, I think you'll do quite nicely.'

'Good, that's settled then. We could ask Ulric to perform the ceremony before we leave for Oldwall. Speaking of which. How do you plan to get us there?'

'I'm hoping Goderun will give us a lift down the coast and drop us off somewhere south of the Tallamors. From there, we'll walk.

Or ride, if she'll take horses. With the men from Archer's Rock and Deer Island, we've got sixty men under arms. And I've already sent messengers to the Farneys and everyone else we can hope to reach, asking them to send as many men as they can straight to Oldwall. If Goderun agrees to take us, I was thinking of leaving as soon as we're ready, maybe the day after tomorrow.'

'All right. I'll go talk to Ulric, then. And find someone who knows how to iron.'

The dress she'd had made in Old Harbor was still resting at the bottom of her pack, rumpled beyond redemption. It would take an ironing genius to straighten it out. But she'd be damned if she got married in boots and leathers. That needed to be taken care of, and then Ulric. Anything to keep her busy and her mind from straying beyond tomorrow and into territory that looked dauntingly dark and frightening.

*   *   *

Though it took some patience and he was forced to go through several intermediaries, Keon eventually made it into the presence of the Barbary King, Leith of Culmorran.

The king's hall in Colasar, built of massive logs, windowless and smoky and littered with leftover food, mangy dogs, pregnant wives, snot-nosed children and drunken clansmen, was a middling shack compared to Stormhold's Great Hall, which could have accommodated this Barbarian pigsty three times over.

I should have started on this end, Keon thought. *This bunch of drunken layabouts would have made for easy pickings. But it's never too late to change tactics.*

Checking his collar and cuffs to make sure no green was showing, he stepped forward.

Leith, a large, thickset man in his fifties with rings of copper, silver and gold braided into his hair and beard, was lounging in a crudely carved and gaudily painted monstrosity of a chair placed on a raised dais at the upper end of the hall. He was listening to a dispute between two men who seemed to be accusing each other of one and the same crime, while a dozen or so clan chiefs sitting three steps down at a long table were dividing their attention between the arguing parties and large, wooden tankards no doubt filled with some unspeakably vile Barbarian brew.

Keon waited patiently until the argument had been settled.

Then he stepped up to the dais. Leith studied him with unfriendly eyes that were reddened by drink. The two burly warriors standing on either side of his throne looked as if it would take no more than a nod from the king and they'd kill Keon out of hand.

'Who's this?' Leith asked of no one in particular. 'What does he want?'

'I am Keon Ormagh, son of Kendric, son of Kell. The Kell of Ormagh who left his house and land in Glarmoch to travel and see the world nigh on a hundred years ago, and made his fortune in the Empire. My mother was a Malley, stolen from the Landsend clan by my late father. Any road, I'm Kell's grandson, returned to the land of my ancestors.'

It was a complete fabrication. But Keon had done his homework and knew that no one would be able to refute his claim. There had been a Kell of Ormag, and he had left Barbary on a ship bound for

381

Orr – though both Kell and the ship had been resting at the bottom of the Middle Sea for nearly a century. And stealing women was a Barbarian national sport, meaning it was a pretty sure bet that some Malley or other had gone missing around the time in question. What was important was that Keon be accepted as having Barbarian roots, otherwise his plan wouldn't work.

'Glarmoch, eh?' Leith said. 'Well, you'll not find anything there but a pile of rotting logs. If you still want it back, you'll have to talk to Regan there.' Leith gestured vaguely towards one of the chiefs.

'Oh, I want more than that,' Keon said. 'Leith of Culmorran, I hereby challenge you to trial by battle. The object of contention being the throne of Barbary.'

There was a stunned silence. Leith gave a chuckle. And another. Then he began to laugh uproariously, joined by everyone else in the hall. Keon waited patiently for things to quiet down, though he was sorely tempted to do something drastic right there and then. But that wouldn't do. This had to be handled the traditional way, else he'd never have the Barbarians behind him. Showing his hand by employing sorcery at this stage would ruin everything.

'Good joke,' Leith said, still chuckling and wiping a tear of mirth from the corner of his eye. 'Now go get yourself a drink and have it out with Regan.'

'It's not a joke,' Keon said easily. 'So I'd like to know whether you intend to fight yourself or name a champion.'

Leith stared at him for a moment with narrowed eyes, as if squinting might help figure out this gaunt, aging, grey-faced scarecrow of a man who had the cheek to appear out of nowhere and challenge him in his own hall.

Reaching a decision, he gave one of his guards a low-voiced command, sending him off to fetch someone or something. Then he leaned back in his chair to wait for whoever it was to arrive, drumming his fingers on the ugly throne's grease-blackened armrests and studying Keon curiously, his expression one of anticipation, a cat planning the demise of a mouse.

Not long, and the guard returned, followed by the person Leith had sent for.

Had he been standing in anyone else's shoes, Keon would have been impressed. Terrified. If Leith was big, this man was a giant. He had to stoop coming through the doorway. Standing straight, his head nearly brushed the crossbeams. Keon saw bare arms thick as an ordinary man's thighs, hands like shovels, blunt, coarse features, flat, expressionless eyes. A man perfectly suited to violence – born to it, one might have said.

The king was still staring at Keon, looking for a reaction. Keon didn't give him one. If Leith was expecting him to buckle at the sight of his half-tamed monster, he was sorely mistaken.

'All right, then,' Keon said. 'Here's the deal. If I win, your life is forfeit, and the throne is mine.'

Leith grinned. 'And if you don't, you'll be dead anyway. But I'll take your ships.'

So he knew about the ships. Not as clueless as he pretended, the good king. No matter. Leith's champion didn't stand a chance. The man was as good as dead.

'In seven days,' Keon said, observing custom to the dot.

Leith nodded. 'Seven days. If I were you I'd enjoy them, because they'll be your last.'

Not bothering with a riposte, Keon left, heading back for the harbor. He'd be spending the next days at sea, and they were going to be anything but enjoyable. What awaited him back on board *Nightshade* were a hundred sacrifices, a thousand blades, and pain beyond anyone's wildest imagining.

*   *   *

24

Goderun wasn't happy with the idea of horses on her ship, mumbling something about the bloody beasts fouling up her deck. In the end, she agreed to take one each for Breanne and Graeme, and had stalls built for them on deck. Which Breanne thought was fine, seeing as none of the forty-odd men accompanying them had ever sat a horse. Graeme of course wished he had a whole company of horse, or better yet, ten, and a few thousand foot besides. Perhaps he'd see at least part of his wish fulfilled at Oldwall, which the message he'd sent out had designated as rallying point where the men of Marillin who were fit to bear arms should gather with all haste. Gods give there were many of those, and that all of them would answer the call.

Much to everyone's relief, the voyage north went smoothly, though Graeme spent most of it worrying. Would the Marillians answer his call? How many would come? Would they be enough to hold Oldwall against gods knew how many Barbarians? And Wil, what had happened to him? Was he alive, or had Breanne's vision come true? Not least, Graeme fretted over Breanne and their unborn child. He didn't say as much, but she knew all the same, and loved him all the more for it.

Much too soon, Goderun dropped them off in sight of the Tallamors' eastern foothills, wishing them all the luck in the world and saying she'd hang about these waters for spell, just in case things didn't go as planned and they needed to get out of there in a hurry. It was the first time Breanne saw the captain close to tears. The sight moved her to embrace Goderun, who, much to Breanne's surprise, answered with a fierce hug before sending her off with a hearty slap on the back.

'You take care now, you hear?' she said. 'I want to see that bairn of yours back here safe and sound. How else am I going to decide which of you two pretties it favors?'

When the horses and gear were unloaded, they set off, Graeme looking back one last time and smiling when he saw that Goderun had raised the Marillian colors high on *Goldspray's* main mast. Breanne didn't see him smile again until they reached Oldwall a week later and found a wonderful surprise awaiting them.

*   *   *

They were all set for battle.

Standing with Wil on the walkway over the gatehouse, Graeme went over their preparations one last time – though it was more for something to occupy his mind than because he thought they might have forgotten anything.

Wil had done a superb job with the resources he had. The wall and towers were in fine shape. They had provisions to last them a month, three thousand arrows and counting, missiles for the four ballistae Trey had built, and the master armorer had outdone himself

386

by constructing a giant mangonel that could fire off either huge, single rocks or a deadly scattershot of smaller stones. He'd even put it on wheels so it could be rolled along behind the wall to the best firing position. Should Keon bring catapults of his own, moving the mangonel every so often would also make it much harder for the enemy to score a hit and destroy it.

One thing that did have Graeme worried was the gate. Wil had found seasoned wood, beams and boards from abandoned farmsteads that were still usable and several large trees felled by storms in years past, but most of that had gone into Trey's engines and the additional stairs leading up to the walkways. Of the gate's three plies, two were green wood, not what Graeme would have wished for but the best anyone could have done under the circumstances.

His other, greater worry was that they still had only a hundred and forty men to defend nearly three hundred yards of wall against gods knew how many thousands of attackers. None of the Marillians he'd sent messages to had shown up yet, and he was slowly beginning to lose hope that they'd arrive in time. Scouting down the north side of Haster's Pass two days ago, he'd seen several columns of dark smoke rising from the land beyond Deepwall.

It had been his second trip there. On the first, seeing as none of them were welcome in Longvale and would likely be greeted with a bolt or the noose, he'd tied a carefully worded message to an arrow and planted it in the middle of the gate under the wary eyes of the gate guards on duty. They didn't recognize him from afar in his armor and helm, and answered his lone arrow with a halfhearted volley that fell short by fifty yards. That had been nearly two weeks ago, and there'd been no reaction since. His warning had gone unheeded, it seemed, as had his invitation to join forces and take shelter behind Oldwall.

Now Longvale was burning. Keon was on the move. It wouldn't be long.

Finding Wil alive and hale had been a joyous moment.
They greeted each other like old friends, and Graeme felt something akin to paternal pride when he saw how Wil had grown and matured.

No wonder the men chose him as their captain. He fills the post in every respect. And still he looks for my approval, thinks he needs it. That need is the one thing he's still got to lose to become a truly great leader of men. And he will, eventually. I tend to forget how young he still is.

Despite how poorly Thorley had treated her, Breanne was saddened by the news of his death, especially by the dreadful manner of it.

'He didn't deserve such an end,' she told Graeme. 'He wasn't a bad man, only someone who completely lost his way.'

Graeme accompanied her on the two-day ride to Watch Hill, as Wil and his men had begun calling it with something approaching fond remembrance, a place where they'd faced certain death and been miraculously redeemed. In Wil's case, it appeared, in more than just a figurative sense.

Breanne picked a spray of wildflowers and laid them on Thorley's cairn, wishing him a safe journey to wherever it was he needed to go. Upon their return to Oldwall she asked Wil to gather his men, and explained to them that she held no grudge against any of them for how things had gone between the Watch and her father. Quite the opposite, she said: they'd done the right thing, and saved him from burdening his soul with worse than he already had. The men didn't cheer her – the occasion was too solemn for that – but there was no mistaking she'd found her way into their hearts with her little speech.

She's shown them she cares, Graeme thought, *and they love her for it. It's as simple as that – if you have the makings of a true queen. And she does. Who would have thought it, seeing her back in Thorhold before all this began? Who would have guessed what a strong, beautiful woman was hiding inside that mouse in the shadows? I certainly didn't, but I'll forever thank the gods for giving me the chance to find out.*

As for himself – he was still struggling with the idea that of a sudden he was supposed to be so much more than a simple soldier. Granted, men tended to heed his advice, even came to him and asked for it, and he could have seen himself as, say, a captain like Wil. But a king?

Suddenly he heard shouts. For a moment he thought someone with sharper eyes than Wil and himself had spotted the Barbarian vanguard coming over the rise at the northern end of Haster's Pass. Then he realized the men were all pointing south. Turning to look, he saw three, no, four riders coming up the pass, followed by two wagons and an orderly column of men on foot, maybe forty of them. Forty – not the hundreds he'd been hoping for.

And still his heart soared. Decimated and beaten down as they were, the Marillians were rallying to his call. Gods give they were

389

lucky and this was just the beginning.

'They're well organized,' Wil said. 'Almost like real soldiers. And it looks like they've thought to bring their own provisions.'

'Lords,' Graeme said. All four riders carried full-size shields slung over their left shoulders, not the common soldier's small, round bucklers. 'Lords and their bannermen. Gods, but that's a welcome sight. Those are real soldiers, Wil. Come, let's go down and meet them.'

He'd been right, he saw, once the new arrivals had reached the wall where Breanne, Ulric, Gamel and Pers had come to join him and Wil, alerted by the calls. He was surprised when the riders, an older man and three youths, father and sons by the looks of them, dismounted and without hesitating took a knee before him.

They seem well informed, he thought. *Someone must have given them a very good description of me.*

'Your grace.' The older man was white-haired, stocky, in his late fifties or early sixties. 'Bois of Coldlake, at your service. I've come to pledge you my sword, my sons, and forty-six men. Would that I could have brought you more, but times have been hard.'

'Rise, Sir Bois, and welcome. Welcome to you all. In times such as these, fifty brave men are a gift from the gods.'

The old man rose, a bit stiff in the joints, and made his obeisance to Breanne. Well informed, indeed. But the three sons continued to kneel, baring their swords and laying them at Graeme's feet with the hilts pointing towards him.

'Your grace,' one of them said. 'Keir of Coldlake. These are my brothers, Conn and Clellan. We would ask a boon of you. We would join your Kingsguard, if it please your grace and there are positions

390

left to fill.'

A Kingsguard! Dear gods, these nobles and their high-flying standards. 'I'm not – '

He caught himself just in time, realizing that the moment had suddenly turned into a watershed, and that he'd barely avoided making a grave mistake. Like it or not, he wasn't Graeme Banehunter anymore. Nor was he dealing with the likes of Asher Thorley. These were good men come to offer their aid and allegiance and looking to him for leadership. He couldn't deny them, not if he didn't want to rob Marillin of its only chance for a future, slim as it might look right now.

'I'll grant your wish, young sirs, and gladly. Providing you accept whomever else I may appoint to the Guard as equals and brothers in arms.'

There, that wasn't so hard.

Out of the corner of his eye he noticed Breanne give an approving nod.

'And you, my lord,' he addressed Sir Bois. 'I most cordially invite you to join the other members of my council: her grace, the Lady Breanne, Chief Gamel of Archer's Rock, and Sir Wil of Watch Hill.'

Wil gave a jerk as if he'd been stung by a wasp, shooting Graeme a disbelieving look. Breanne on the other hand smiled, looking pleased.

Might have gotten a bit carried away there, Graeme thought. *But what the hell! The job comes with certain privileges, if I'm not mistaken, and I'll be damned if I won't make use of them once in a while. So young Wil's just been raised to knighthood. Tough. He'll thank me yet, once he sees what it means to be a captain and deal with lords.* He smiled to himself. *Me, I think just seeing the look on his face was worth it. Still, I'd better make it official when we get a moment in private, do the bit with the sword on the shoulder and all that.*

Leading the newcomers off to inspect the living quarters and defensive works, he gave Wil a wide, unrepentant grin, and the lad finally caught on, his mien suddenly lightening as he answered in kind.

That same afternoon, Graeme, Breanne, and Wil convened in Asher Thorley's gaudily striped tent for Wil's knighting. Graeme kept the ceremony short and sweet, and still it stirred up far more emotion in him than he'd expected. Maybe it was the look on Wil's face, a glow of pride and happiness warring with apprehension and awe. Maybe it was Breanne, her eyes gone all teary even though she was wearing a smile radiant enough to eclipse the sun. Most likely, though, it was because Graeme was just so damned proud of the lad.

He'd just wound things up when there was a scratch on the tent flap and Pers came in, carrying a sack over his shoulder. He threw Breanne and Wil a sketchy salute, and gave Graeme a cocky grin.

'Your grace – '

'Call me that one more time in private,' Graeme threatened good-naturedly, 'and I'll promote you to something really odious, like the quartermaster's first clerk's assistant pen sharpener.'

'You might want to *have* a first clerk before you go making promises you can't keep,' Pers said airily. 'And anyhow, I was only practicing my courtly moves, seeing as I didn't get fed all that high-

and-mighty stuff on my mother's teat like certain other people I could name. Actually I was going to give you something. But if you don't want it, just say the word and I'll keep it for myself.'

Graeme smiled. 'All right, I'll bite. What's in the sack?'

'Something I picked up in Arventon. Thought it might come in handy.' Pers reached into the sack and pulled out a helm, which he proudly presented to Graeme.

'But I've already… ' Graeme started to say. Then he realized this wasn't just any old helm. It was a beautifully wrought piece, chased in silver and encircled with a band of gold set with three star-shaped stones above the eye-guard: one red, one white, one yellow. The Arvend battle crown. The crown of Marillin.

'It's for you to wear in battle,' Pers explained. 'I was thinking it might make it easier for us simple grunts to tell you apart from the enemy once things start to get confusing. Wouldn't want to shoot you by mistake now, would I?'

Graeme was touched. 'Thank you, my friend. I'll wear it when the time comes. And now, since you're so eager to perfect your courtly ways, why don't you take young Wil here for a walk and practice calling him "my lord?"'

'That'll be the day.' Pers chuckled. 'But I'll take him off your hands anyway. I can see you two young lovebirds could use – '

He never finished his sentence, his last words lost in the moan of war horns and the urgent shouts and rushing footsteps of men running for the wall. The enemy had arrived.

*   *   *

393

Ever since Malamut's downfall, Keon had nurtured hopes of succeeding him, of being chosen as the God's living Vessel on Vereld. The loss of the Gate and the destruction of his army of alien creatures had dashed those hopes, at least for the nonce. No matter how many times he told himself it wasn't his fault, that only the low cunning and improbable luck of his enemies were to blame, Amut wouldn't have cared a whit for his protestations – had he been foolish enough to voice them aloud.

Instead, he'd become the God's weapon, Amut's champion, a role that required some radical adjustments. For one, he was used to wielding others as his weapons. Finding himself in their place, even if it was the God's own hand that now wielded him, was a hateful and humiliating experience. For another, there was the Pain.

Where he'd believed his battle against the Bane sickness a severe hardship, the Way of a Thousand Cuts had taught him different. The combined agony of a thousand blades fusing with his living flesh – while every muscle, bone and tendon in his body stretched and grew to accommodate the magic as he gorged himself on a hundred life forces – went far beyond anything mere words could hope to capture. During the three days it took him to perform the rite, there had been many a time – a thousand times, to be precise – when he'd been a breath away from abandoning the whole undertaking and delivering himself up to whatever punishment Amut might see fit to inflict upon him. What kept him going was the absolute certainty that the God's retribution would be far worse and last much, much longer. So he went on, only to be left with the bitter realization that the pain didn't end with the ceremony.

Driven by the rite's dark magic, the steel of the tangs had melded with his flesh. Now his whole body save his head and the palms of his hands was covered with an impregnable, scaled armor made of a thousand knives – sharp, unforgiving blades that rested cold against his unprotected skin and were wont to cut him at the slightest careless move.

In the beginning he'd suffered scores of cuts and left a trail of blood wherever he went, until he'd been sure the cursed armor would bleed him out and kill him long before he faced an enemy. Things had gotten to a point where he remained on his feet for days on end, not daring to sit or lie down for fear of receiving more injuries than his body could sustain. So he stood, his legs slowly trembling their way into screaming cramps, the weight of so much steel threatening to sink him into the ground.

But, over time, his flesh and the blades reached an understanding of sorts and the cuts became less frequent, though a blind man could have still tracked him by the scent of his bloody footsteps alone.

In a way, it was like acquiring some new and basic skill. His muscles learned new tricks – or perhaps he sprouted a whole new set of them – until he was able to control each individual blade and wear his armor like a fearsome plumage, feathers made of cutting steel.

That was when he began to see that not everything the rite had brought him was bad, that there were indeed advantages. With a sturdy helm added to his armor he was practically invulnerable. And once his body had adjusted to the change, the life forces he'd incorporated flooded him with a physical strength no ordinary mortal could match. Which meant he was also as good as unstoppable.

Wielding a huge, spiked mace, chosen from the weapons cache on board the Nightshade with an eye to his ineptitude with all but sorcerous weapons, he was determined to make short work of Leith Cullamor's champion and shorter work of the king himself.

The sight of him entering the king's hall in his new armor gave them pause. Leith hadn't bothered to have much of a space cleared for the fight, no more than a few tables and benches pushed haphazardly aside, secure in his belief that Keon stood no chance at all against his giant champion.

Now, sitting there surrounded by his chiefs, he looked decidedly more worried, pale and sweating, gripping the arms of his throne with whitening knuckles. If he noticed that Keon was head and shoulders taller than when they'd last met, almost of a height with the champion, he was too rattled or scared to mention it.

Keon didn't bother with protocol or small talk. He was done with niceties. 'Come, then,' he told Leith's hulking stand-in. 'Let's get this over with.'

The man spared Keon's mace a dismissive glance – a sneer, actually. Then, with a look of utter confidence on his bovine features he raised his giant two-hander, hefting it one-handed. Still sneering, he made a small feint in Keon's direction, an insulting, offhand move that said, 'You're too pathetic to be worth fighting, so I'll just play with you for a while before I kill you.'

If he'd expected Keon to cringe and run, he was disappointed. What he got was a level stare that clearly communicated a wealth of revulsion and contempt, which was all this inferior lump of brainless muscle deserved as a farewell message.

Keon raised his mace, easy as lifting a feather.

With a mighty roar, the champion swung at Keon's arm.

Keon didn't sidestep, left his arm where it was, tightened muscles reinforced by a trickle of power from the vast reservoir of life forces stored inside his body, coursing through his veins like sweet poison, raging in every cell like a perfect storm.

The force of the blow jarred the champion's arm up to the shoulder.

Keon's arm didn't budge. Not an inch. Not a fraction of an inch.

The two-hander gave an ugly crack as a good foot of the tip broke off and went spinning away, burying itself in an upright beam next to the head of one of the chiefs.

The champion had lost the sneer. To him, it must have felt like hitting a rock. A very big rock.

Keon brought down the mace. Once. Twice. After that, he stopped counting. It wasn't that he took any pleasure in what he was doing, but he had a lesson to impart. One he wanted to get through and stick the first time around. Although, to be entirely honest, seeing what he was capable of accomplishing with his newly gained powers *was* more than a little gratifying.

When it was over, not even the champion's own mother would have recognized her son in the bloody mess smeared across the floor. Stepping over the remains, Keon strode up onto the dais and smashed Leith's skull with a single blow, scattering blood, bone, and brains over the throne and leaving a deep gash in the carved and painted wood of the backrest. No matter. He wasn't planning to spend much time sitting on the ugly thing.

The chiefs in their low-slung chairs were mute with shock.

As they slowly began to digest what had just taken place, he saw anger rise in them, and fear. That was good: he'd use both to twist them to his purpose. Then one of the chiefs rose, an older man with outrage written all over his plain, weathered features.

'There is no honor in this,' he said. 'It is no way for a king to die.'

A sudden rage boiled up in Keon, taking him completely by surprise – him, who'd always seen himself as a coldly calculating hatcher of long-term plans and strategies, unimpaired by useless emotions, that fatal weakness of ordinary men. He would have struck the man down, would have smashed the whole lot of them to a bloody pulp if not for the fact that he needed them. So he reined in the sheer overwhelming hatred and contempt he felt for these lesser creatures, though it cost him.

'I assume it's not the way you want to die, either,' he said coldly. 'Which is why I'd counsel you to hold your tongue and listen to what I have to say before you do something you'll regret.'

The man wavered for a moment, clearly torn between his absurd notion of honor and the wish to go on living. Finally he sat down heavily.

'Good,' Keon said. 'I see we've reached an understanding.' Then he commenced to remind them of the days of old, the glory days, when Barbarians had been feared and fearless warriors and the mere sight of their longboats had struck terror and despair in the hearts of men on every coast around the Middle Sea.

'Leith may have been a warrior once, a man of honor. But that was long ago. He lost that honor when he refused to meet the Bane.

Instead he chose to hide behind three walls and let a bunch of farmers defend his borders for him.'

The chiefs were paying attention now. His words had struck a nerve. As he'd known they would.

'Leith lost his honor, and, perhaps without your even noticing, you allowed him to drag you down with him. Barbary became a nation of old, toothless women, with the oldest and most toothless of them all sitting on this very throne for nigh on twenty years, not doing a thing worth mentioning, much less worth turning into a song. If you ask me, he died exactly as he deserved.'

He saw heads begin to nod in agreement. He had them now.

'So now the Bane is defeated, no thanks to Leith.'

This was news to them, he saw, and it had them sitting up. 'Yes, the Bane is defeated, and a whole kingdom lies fallow, ripe for the taking. Should we wait until someone else thinks to go and collect Marillin's unclaimed treasures?'

They were shaking their heads in unison, a gleam of excited greed in all their eyes.

'Should we leave the pitiful few who have survived over there time enough to get back on their feet, to regain their strength and deny us what by rights is ours now?'

'No!' one of the chiefs growled. 'No!' others chimed in.

'And then there are the Vales,' Keon went on. 'Do we still need them? I think not. Far too long we've hidden behind their apron strings, allowing them to feel superior, as if *they* were the warriors, and we the feckless dirt-eaters. Shame, I say! It's time to teach them a lesson, show them who their masters are. Just think of all the beddable young women over there who've had to make do with blunt plowshares, when surely they've been dreaming all these years of keen Barbarian swords.'

That got him a few chuckles and replaced the last of the tension with a collective air of eager anticipation.

'So, my friends,' he said. *Friends!* How he hated that word and its deceiving implications. As if there existed a single man who would hesitate to stick the knife in a 'friend's' back, if only the price was right. He had to force himself not to spit it out like something rotten.

'Like it or not, you have a new king, and one who's not going to sit idle on this throne until all of you are too old to lift a blade. If anyone feels they need to challenge me, they should do it now. Otherwise we go to war, and no man who can hold a sword shall stay behind. I have great plans for you. Marillin and the Vales are just the beginning.'

There was no more resistance. Even the man who'd spoken against him in the outset had come around, he could see. Greed and lust, always a sure bet when one wanted to steer men to what would ultimately be their doom. So easy. Bloody animal instincts. Bloody emotions.

'Hail Keon!' they roared, standing and raising bared blades. 'Hail the king!'

'Mead! Meat! Wenches!' he shouted, once they were done hailing. 'Barbary has woken, and it feels a mighty hunger!'

Keon didn't waste any time putting his plans into action.

Crossing through the Vales was a breeze, most of the Valers having put self-preservation before valor and disappeared into the dividing mountains like rats down a hole. He hated having them at his back but was loath to spend weeks or even months rooting them out of their hiding places, scattering his forces and losing the momentum he'd so painstakingly built. But then, they weren't really all that much of a threat. Time enough to mop them up on the way back.

What female flesh the Barbarians did ferret out wasn't nearly enough to go around, meaning that in order to keep them happy he had to let them loot and burn and have their bit of fun, a bunch of overgrown infants blowing off excess energy. He didn't mind the destruction, but he did rue every hour wasted.

And now, here he was – stuck in Haster's Pass.
Two massive walls running across the whole of Baintry from coast to coast, and all he'd had to do was open the gates and walk through – only to be stopped dead by a handful of obstinate troublemakers and two hundred yards of flimsy, crumbling wall. Well, not all that flimsy. The thing was over twenty feet high, and they'd obviously spent some time repairing it.

He didn't have to guess who was responsible for this unexpected holdup. Though his scrying device had stayed aboard *Nightshade,* he could feel them there behind the wall, could practically taste the flavor of the renitent, meddling, thrice-cursed vermin that had caused him so much trouble down south.

If only he'd stayed on Haunt to oversee their entrapment himself, they'd be securely dead by now. At least Torgrim had been eliminated. But the woman was there, and even without the Key she was a force to be reckoned with – provided she knew how to handle the power he felt coming off her like an annoying odor. Which he rather

401

doubted. If she did, she'd have shown up in his sights much earlier.

And then there was the 'Warrior', as Keon had dubbed him. Initially he hadn't paid the fellow much attention, seeing as he had no power to speak of. But the events on Haunt had forced to him reassess the man and his role in recent events. Though he had no Talent, he did have... something. Keon couldn't put his finger on what it was, only that it continued to pose a serious threat to his plans. As did the woman.

Fortunately, they'd put themselves right in his way, in a place where he could reach them easily enough once the damned wall was breached. If they thought a few piled-up stones would hold him up for long, they were badly mistaken. Thinking of them, he felt that strange, unaccustomed rage raise its ugly head again and quickly stamped down on it. It was of no use to him, and though he refused to acknowledge the fact it also frightened him: a creeping, coiled thing that had nested inside him and was slowly, insidiously trying to usurp control over his decisions.

Turning away from studying his enemies' defenses, he sent runners to fetch the chiefs to his tent for a war council. Not that he wanted their advice. What he wanted was to see that blasted wall come down as soon as possible, and for that he needed them to build him the appropriate tools. A few catapults, a couple of siege towers, a ram. Yes, those should do the trick. The rest was a question of manpower. Oh, he'd give the chiefs their moment of glory, let them go through with their Barbarian-style attack plans and try to swarm the wall with ladders. If they succeeded, so much the better. But somehow he doubted they would.

From what he'd seen so far, they were hopelessly few over there, far too few to hold out against five thousand bloodthirsty Barbarians panting after hoards of gold and gems that continued to grow ever larger and more desirable as their greedy little imaginations examined the notion time and again – and thank the god for those weak, corruptible minds.

Few or no, he sensed a grim determination in the wall's defenders, the kind that could turn ordinary soldiers into fearsome warriors, men who would fight to the death rather than cede an inch of ground.

He could have reduced the gate to splinters himself, provided it wasn't heavily Warded. But he was reluctant to waste power on such a mundane task, and felt no inclination at all to join the actual fighting in any case. Besides, his Barbarian army wasn't anywhere near ready for the revelation that their new king was in truth a sorcerer. That was knowledge they needed to be fed in digestible bits and increments. Corrupting men properly required time and patience. More so if your aim was to twist them beyond any hope of redemption.

For the nonce, he pretended that his strange armor was removable like any other panoply. Secretly, he fought an increasing urge to strut through camp and splay his blades like a preening peacock. Like the sudden rages, the alien impulse left him deeply disturbed.

*   *   *

25

Standing on the gatehouse wall with Breanne, Pers, and Sir Bois, Graeme watched the Barbarian army appear over the rise at the northern end of Haster's Pass, blackening the road and the meadows to either side like a swarm of locusts. Their vanguard – if that was what you cared to call an undisciplined band of savage fighters who looked more than half animal in their furs, antlered helms and painted faces – reached the wall an hour later.

Yelling taunts and insults that promised the Marillians and their wives, mothers, and daughters all manner of gruesome torture and death, they strutted in front of the gate just out of bowshot range.

'I've a mind to waste an arrow or three on those foul-mouthed louts,' Pers said. 'Talking like that in front of a lady.'

Breanne smiled, though in truth Graeme had seen her wince at the Barbarians' uncouth language.

'Considering the range,' Sir Bois said, fingering his grizzled beard, 'and even granting a lucky shot, your arrows would likely just get snagged in those stinking pelts. Though I'll concede you might stand a chance of killing several score lice.'

'Ha!' Pers snorted. 'Lucky shot! We'll see about that. I'll bet you – '

'Leave it, Pers,' Graeme said. 'I have a better idea.'

The men on the mangonel could do with a bit of practice. He waved a signal to the catapult's crew, and with a mighty WHANG! the big machine, already positioned with the help of a lookout on the wall, released a round of scattershot. Their aim was slightly off, or perhaps the stiff westerly breeze was to blame, but a few of the fist-sized rocks did find targets with meaty smacks and the crunch of buckling plate and breaking bones that could be heard all the way up on the wall. Yelling threats and curses, the Barbarians backed off, dragging away two wounded and leaving behind three dead.

Later, when the rest of the Barbarian army arrived, they took care to set up camp well out of the catapult's range.

Since then, three days had passed, and nothing much had happened. The Barbarians felled a large number of trees, many more than they could possibly need for cooking fires even if the wood hadn't been green – seeing as every scrap of seasoned wood in Haster's Pass had long since gone into Trey's engines – but it took no great leap of the imagination to figure out what they were using it for: scaling ladders, a ram, engines of their own perhaps, if they had anyone over there capable of building them.

Their usual style of warfare had always been to land their long-boats on some deserted shore from where they could sneak in quietly and take some unsuspecting village by surprise, preferably in the wee hours before dawn, when it was easy work to slaughter bleary-eyed, sleep-drugged men as they came stumbling out of their homes, most often barefoot and in nothing but their smallclothes.

Laying a siege against a wall defended by seasoned soldiers was a different proposition, and one of the few things about the impending fight that gave Graeme a measure of hope, if only a small one. They were still less than two hundred against several thousand, impossible odds even by the most favorable reckoning.

This morning, sleep having eluded him since the wee hours, he stood in his usual place on the wall, surveying the field for what felt like the thousandth time. As the first light of dawn crept into the sky, it revealed dense fog filling the valley north Oldwall from end to end like a sea of dirty cotton. Only the Tallamors' highest peaks showed above of the mist, their snow-covered flanks aglow with a faint, rosy hue, forerunner of the sun that was still far in the east and hours away from rising over the pass. For all Graeme could see, the world could have ended thirty yards from the wall. There could have been ten enemy camps out there, or none at all.

Wrapped in his cloak against the early morning chill, he stared out into the mist as if it were hiding all the answers from him while he battled with a decision his heart had already made. Nonetheless, his mind was still searching for another way, hoping that a miracle would occur, that any moment now the horns would sound and a thousand men come marching out of the south to help defend the wall and save Marillin from Keon and the Barbarians. He was fooling himself, and knew it. Amazing, how under pressure the mind could turn from a useful tool into a floundering deceiver, leading a man down a path of certain ruin if he followed it too trustingly.

Back on *Goldspray,* sailing north from Salt, there'd been a moment when he was hard put not to ask Goderun to change course and take them all away from this seemingly endless nightmare, somewhere across the sea to a place where there was no Bane and no Keon, where he and Breanne could raise their child and live out their lives in peace.

He'd quickly recognized the notion for the illusion it was. Running away would solve nothing. They'd merely be betraying their own purpose, setting themselves up for a measure of suffering, grief and regret far worse than anything that could come out of holding to a just cause and fighting to an honorable end.

Besides, he knew in his bones that if Keon wasn't stopped here and now, he would simply keep on coming, gathering force and momentum, and no place on Vereld would be safe from the senseless, brutal destruction the man carried and spread like pure evil become a rabidly cankerous disease.

His train of thought was interrupted by footfalls on the tower stairs. Wil and Pers, come to join him in his vigil. Seeing them, he reached a final decision. Here were two good men he could save. He could spare them, and the others, and Breanne and their child, a premature death. At least he could try.

He'd have to tell them what he intended to do, though. He'd need someone to guard his back – for all the good it would do if things went badly. Who better than them, though? But first, the sun had to come out and burn off this cursed fog, else they'd only get themselves killed by the first Barbarian outpost they ran into.

'There's something I... ' he started to say, but never finished.

Too late! He'd left it too late, damn his stupid tendency to overthink.

The fog, up until a moment ago a uniform grey, seemed to have suddenly developed a rash of darker spots. Moving spots that darkened further as they strove for definitive shape. Coming closer.

'Sound the alarm!' he shouted, just as the first Barbarians broke free of the mist, abandoning stealth the moment they heard his cry. In a heartbeat, scaling ladders were being raised along the wall for as far as he could see in both directions.

Blessedly, Wil had been keeping half the men on watch at all times, and now they were ready to repulse the first wave while the other half scrambled for the wall and up the stairs in a mad but controlled rush, Graeme sending silent thanks to Gael and Quillan, who'd made them practice for exactly this situation until they could do it backwards in their sleep if necessary.

Pers was already shooting, as were most of the other men on the wall. They knew to make every shot count, and Graeme was pleased to see that hardly an arrow went astray.

As if the gods had heard his prayers, the Barbarians spaced their attack evenly along the entire wall, meaning three or four defenders could work together picking them off and repulsing the ladders before their hooks could lock onto the parapet. Had the attackers chosen to concentrate their assault on a shorter stretch of wall and raised a score of ladders side by side, they'd have been up and over in no time at all.

No doubt that was what they'd do next time. They may have been a rash, impulsive lot, but they weren't stupid.

Loosing arrow after arrow, Graeme easily fell into the disjointed madness of battle, where time seemed to alternately pass in a blur and slow down to a near standstill. More and more roaring, battle-crazed Barbarians poured out of the fog, only to find themselves stuck in the killing zone with no ladders up and no way forward. It was unmitigated slaughter, a turkey shoot. Scores of them went down and stayed down. But there were thousands more where those had come from.

Then a ladder went up and latched onto the wall. Immediately, attackers were swarming up it like ants on a rampage. Suddenly there were a dozen or more Barbarians on the walkway, threatening to overwhelm the few defenders.

Pers shifted his aim to the spot, maybe thirty yards down from the western tower. Seeing that it would take more than arrows to contain the enemy, Graeme shouldered his bow. Drawing his sword, he ran through the tower and along the walkway.

He was met by a huge Barbarian with a horned skull for a helm, his face and beard caked with cracking blue and green paint, swinging a war-hammer that an ordinary man would have had trouble lifting. Graeme saw three of his own men sprawled dead on the ground below, their helms and skulls staved in. Then the hammer came whistling, and all else became unimportant.

Dodging and ducking, the giant hammer striking sparks and flying chips from the merlons as it missed him by a hair's breadth, Graeme somehow managed to survive the first, mad onslaught. Eventually the Barbarian got careless, swinging too hard and giving Graeme an opening. Quick as lightning his sword darted in, found unprotected flesh.

The giant didn't even seem to notice he'd been cut. Bleeding

410

from a deep gash in his thigh – and soon after from another across his chest, and a third on his left arm – he just kept on coming.

Step by step, Graeme was forced to fall back. He was just about backed up against the tower when his opponent suddenly stopped dead in his tracks. Let the head of his hammer drop to the stones. Stood slightly swaying, a surprised look on his painted face. Then he spit a gob of bright red blood. Not because of anything Graeme had done, though. There was an arrow sprouting from the man's throat, he saw. One of Pers', he'd bet. Not many could shoot along a walkway filled with fighting men and hit the one they were aiming for.

Slowly, the giant slumped over the crenels like a wet rag hung out to dry. There was no respite, though. The next Barbarian was already coming up behind him, and another, and another. Then Wil was there beside Graeme, his big axe helping to clear the rest of the way. And there were Gael and Buck, come from the other side, Gael lifting a rock that must have weighed at least twice as much as the man himself and dropping it onto the head of the next Barbarian com-ing up. It swept the ladder clean of attackers, reducing most of the rungs to splinters in the process, and the wall was safe again, or as safe as it could be with Barbarian arrows flying thick, now that they'd realized their mistaken strategy.

But the volleys weren't the precursors of a new attack, Graeme saw. He'd hardly noticed the sun come out, but here it was, fast burning off the fog and leaving the enemy without cover. The cata-pults, useless until now, had cranked up and loosed the first rounds, to devastating effect. The Barbarians were retreating, making for safer ground with some haste.

More than a hundred of them were left lying dead at the foot of the wall – as compared to four dead and seven wounded among the defenders, making for a ratio of ten to one.

Not bad. But with the difference in numbers, at this rate there would still be a few thousand Barbarians left when the last man died on the wall.

Graeme's mind was made up.

'Come,' he said to Wil. 'Let's go find Pers. I need to talk to the two of you. There's something I have to do. And I could use your help.'

An hour later Graeme, Wil and Pers rode out under a flag of parley, followed by the three lads of Graeme's 'Kingsguard', who'd refused to be left behind when their sovereign rode into danger.

They were met by a trio of chiefs. Graeme made it clear to them that he would speak to their king, and only to him. One of them went to fetch Keon, who made a point of letting Graeme wait.

When he finally showed up, he brought the rest of the chiefs with him. Like them, he was on foot, probably because there existed no horse in all of Baintry strong enough to carry his weight.

The sight of the man made Graeme shiver, no matter the dazzling, high-altitude sun was beginning to slowly cook him inside his armor. Suppressing an urge to turn around and gallop back through the gate, he dismounted and handed the reins to Pers. He would meet this monster of a man on equal terms, and not give the ugly brute the slightest reason to think he was afraid, even though he could practically smell the stink of sorcery coming off Keon, especially off that strange armor of his.

412

Just then, as if to confirm Graeme's suspicion, one of the blades on Keon's right forearm twitched, briefly rising up and falling back into place like the scale of a living beast moving to the involuntary jerk of some minor muscle.

'Keon the Traitor,' Graeme said. 'I imagined you a smaller man.' He looked around with as insouciant an air as he could manage. 'And are these men meant to become your new Bane? Will you put a spell on them and turn them into monsters?'

'Have a care how you speak to the King of Barbary,' Keon snarled, clearly not eager to be connected with the Bane in front of his men. 'Say what you want, cur, and then begone. Unless it's unconditional surrender you have to offer. That I might consider.'

'Well, now. "Cur" is certainly no way to address the King of Marillin. Not if you're expecting civility in return.'

Keon gave a snort of disbelief, but Graeme saw realization dawn in the man's eyes. And something that might have been a glimmer of alarm.

'And no,' he went on, 'I'm not offering surrender, unconditional or otherwise. Quite the contrary: I've come to challenge you for the crown of Barbary.'

Keon's guffaw sounded half amused at best. 'You can't challenge me, kingling. As you should know if you're really who you say you are. Only a man of Barbarian blood can fight for the throne. So you'd better – '

'I have Barbarian blood,' Graeme interrupted him. 'Though I have to say it pains me to share the honor with someone like you. Brithwen Edarren, king Kenric's daughter, was my grandmother.'

'Mother's blood,' one of the chiefs said. 'He has the right.' The

413

others nodded. According to tradition, it was a man's maternal lineage that decided whether he had the right to claim Barbarian blood or not.

'Prove it,' Keon said, grasping at straws now, caught in a trap of his own making.

'I'll prove it with this,' Graeme said, laying a hand on the hilt of his grandfather's sword. 'As is the way.'

'As is the way,' several of the chiefs murmured, and Graeme thought he saw interest in their eyes rather than worry over Keon's wellbeing. That might have been because they held their new king to be invincible. Another possibility was that it would by no means break their hearts to be parted from him.

'Since we all seem to be agreed,' Graeme said, 'I suggest we dispense with the seven-day reprieve and settle this right here and now. Unless you'd prefer to name a champion, that is. From what I've heard, you're not usually inclined to fight your own fights.'

'Worm!' Keon spat, showing Graeme that the barb had struck home. 'You'll not leave this field alive.'

'Maybe not.' Graeme shrugged. 'But then, neither will you.'

*   *   *

Numb with fear and worry, Breanne stood on the gatehouse walkway. Without knowing it, she'd chosen the exact same spot Graeme had occupied a few hours earlier.

When he'd come to tell her what he planned to do, she hadn't tried to talk him out of it, even though her heart was silently screaming in protest. This was no time to listen to her private feelings. Though on the face of it what he proposed seemed a terrible risk, she knew it was their only chance to survive this madness. She'd seen the wounded, treated them with her own hands, and was well aware of how narrowly they'd all escaped death in this morning's skirmish. Somehow, she decided, she'd brave it out, and continue to firmly believe that Graeme would come back to her alive and hale.

But when she saw the giant, hulking figure that came to meet him on the field, she nearly fainted. Only Quillan's discreet hand on her elbow kept her from sinking to her knees. With a thankful nod to him, she rallied. And then, between one anxious heartbeat and the next, of a sudden and without forewarning something twisted free in her.

Something that, though she didn't know it, had been loosened by all the times she'd used the Key. Now, though the artifact was lost to her, the extreme emotional pressure she was under had nudged that something into life. Her Talent, the innate power she'd come into this world with, was finally beginning to awaken.

She had no idea what was happening to her, only that she could suddenly see and hear what was going on out there between Graeme and Keon as if she were just a few feet away from them, suspended in the air like an invisible specter.

Graeme was oblivious to her presence, but Keon must have felt something, for he turned his head this way and that, searching, a wild, disturbed look in his eye. Eventually, he found her. Staring right at her, he grinned, his gaunt, cadaverous face twisting in an evil grimace that promised he'd do his very worst to destroy every last thing she loved and cherished.

Back on the walkway, she felt her hand go to her throat. Vaguely, she registered Quillan and Bois standing either side of her, the strangeness of being here and at the same time there unsettling to the point of making her nauseous.

The next moment she was with Graeme again. Keon seemed to have blotted her presence from his mind entirely. He'd donned his helm with the spiked golden circlet representing the seven-antlered crown of Barbary, and raised the head of his monstrous mace off the ground.

'Come, then, kingling,' he said to Graeme, who looked small as a child beside him. 'Let's get this over with. You've wasted enough of my time as it is.'

He'd hardly finished speaking, and already the mace was swinging down in a deadly arc. Graeme stepped aside, the wickedly spiked head missing him by a hair and burying itself deep in the ground. His blade flashed once, darting in and leaving a deep cut on the base of Keon's thumb.

Breanne briefly wondered why Graeme would go for the sorcerer's hands, but then she realized they were the only place Graeme could hurt him, except for the eye-slits of his helm. But to reach those, Graeme would have to risk the mace, one strike of which would probably end it for him then and there. And, barring the helm, even without Keon's magic the armor would have been virtually impenetrable. As it was, she could see scores of life forces squirming inside him like lost souls writhing in the pits of hell, his body so saturated with dark power it was bleeding from his every orifice like a poisonous fug.

All Graeme could do was lead Keon a merry dance, doing damage to the sorcerer's hands whenever he could and hoping to wear

416

down his opponent without taking a direct hit. There was no chance of that happening, she knew: with his immense reserves of power stolen from all the people he'd murdered, Keon could keep going long after Graeme dropped dead from sheer exhaustion.

With an angry roar, Keon yanked his mace free of the turf and swung again. Again he missed, and again Graeme managed to cut his hand.

Realizing his mistake, Keon changed tactics, swinging sideways now instead of downward, and this time Graeme wasn't fast enough. Splinters flew as the mace crashed into his shield and split it down the middle, sending a sizeable part of it spinning off along the ground.

Wincing, Graeme shook off what remained of his broken, useless shield. From the way he favored his left arm, Breanne feared it had been damaged as well. If so, he didn't let it slow him down – not until Keon managed to hit him again, this time a glancing blow across the chest so forceful it ripped off Graeme's breastplate, tearing through the chainmail and gambeson he wore underneath and leaving a deep, ugly gash that immediately began to bleed profusely.

It was an ugly wound.

Seeing her worst fears about to come true, Breanne wished the men with him would intervene and drag him out of death's reach before it was too late.

They didn't. And Graeme persevered, retaliating with a fast lunge. Turning it into a twisting cut at the last moment and taking off most of Keon's right thumb. Forcing the sorcerer to switch the mace to his weaker hand – a switch he never completed because

Graeme's blade was there again, getting in the way of the exchange and slapping the ugly weapon out of Keon's blood-slicked grip.

Before he could bend down to pick it up, Graeme was on him. Injured arm or no, there was a dagger in his left hand now, raised high and aimed straight for Keon's right eye.

But Keon wasn't out of tricks yet. Suddenly splaying his scales, he made himself a thicket of blades, an iron maiden turned inside out, some of the knives on his chest and stomach over a foot long. And instead of fending off Graeme's attack, he welcomed it with open arms.

Grabbing the smaller man by the shoulders, Keon lifted Graeme off his feet and embraced him in a tremendous, deadly bear hug. With Graeme's breastplate gone, Keon's knives went through him easily, a few of the longer points coming out of his back. Gasping, still not giving up, Graeme drove his dagger deep into Keon's eye-slit.

There was a silent explosion of pent-up power, enveloping the adversaries in a shroud of darkness that remained impenetrable even to Breanne's heightened senses.

Then, as a hundred trapped souls found release and streamed away into the ether, the space around them cleared, and she could see Graeme again, still impaled on Keon's armor. Near senseless with shock, she heard him breathe her name. Then his head lolled to the side, and she knew he was gone.

Locked in death's embrace, the two combatants fell as one.

The sound of someone screaming brought her back to herself.

For a moment she was completely disoriented – until she realized that she was the one who was screaming. Quillan and Bois were holding her up with gentle hands, their miens etched deep with sorrow and compassion. She forced herself to quiet, and drew a breath.

'It's all right,' she lied. 'I'm all right. We need to see to our defenses. The enemy will leave us no time to grieve.'

She spoke in a sort of lucid daze, feeling as if she were drowning, floundering in the waters of the overwhelmingly impossible. Shaking off the debilitating sensation as well as the men's supporting hands, she stepped up to the parapet and looked down.

There were Wil and Pers, and the three lads right behind them, riding hell for leather towards the gate, arrows falling all around them. They'd somehow managed to extricate Graeme from Keon's death grip. Wil was holding him in his arms protectively, as if keeping him safe still mattered...

Suddenly it all caught up with her, swamping her with a grief so absolute it threatened to grind her down into nothingness. But she felt anger as well, at the senselessness, at the utter unfairness, at the immensity of Keon's crime, and at the men out there who had helped him perpetrate it. She would have lashed out at them, struck them dead, but it was all she could do to stand there and keep her knees from buckling.

When the horns sounded, she didn't understand at first what it might mean. The Barbarians were making no move to attack. Instead, they simply stood there, rooted in place, openmouthed with disbelief, staring up at... what? At her? But why...

Again she heard the horns, and then it dawned on her, and she turned to see the men of Marillin arrive, scores upon hundreds of

419

them marching towards her in a line that stretched south for as far as she could see.

The sight should have gladdened her, and it would have, half an hour earlier. Now, she found no solace in their arrival, the irony of it almost more than she could bear.

Her anger flaring, she turned back to face the Barbarians.

Please gods, let them attack now. This time I will crush them, and not a one of them shall live to see his home again.

But the gods weren't listening, it seemed. The field was fast emptying, the Barbarians fleeing head over heels.

How very strange, she thought. *I'd have thought them braver men, and not so easily frightened off by a few war-horns blowing out of turn.*

*   *   *

Wil had seen the same thing the Barbarians had, so he knew why they had run. Galloping for the gate with Graeme's body in his arms, he looked up for a moment to see a terrifying apparition standing on the gatehouse wall, a tall and fearsome goddess wreathed in light and shadow, rapt in boundless grief and wrath that seemed to flow out from her like rapidly streaming water, gathering force and descending on the Barbarians in a tidal wave.

Meeting with the edge of it, he felt it like a powerful physical blow that left him breathless and scared near out of his wits even though it wasn't directed at him.

What it must have felt like to the Barbarians, he could only imagine. Worse, no doubt. Much, much worse. He reckoned that, in their place, he'd have done the same, and run as far and fast as his

420

feet could carry him.

By the time he laid Graeme's body at Breanne's feet she'd become an ordinary woman again, small and frail, her slight frame straining under the weight of the blow she'd just been dealt.

With a wail fit to break the heart of every man who heard it, she threw herself on Graeme's body, embracing his dead flesh as if the enormity of her grief could somehow bring him back to life, burying her face against his cooling neck, weeping as if there'd never be an end to her tears.

In truth, Wil was crying too, unashamedly, as were Pers, Finn, and Quillan, Gael, Buck, and most every other man of the Watch who stood nearby. The Marillians weren't doing any better, even those who'd never met Graeme while he was still alive. It wasn't just a slain king they mourned. It was their future lying dead before them. The only one whose eyes remained dry was Bois. It was perhaps some kind of noble thing, not shedding tears in public, but loss and honest sorrow had gouged a whole new set of furrows on his weathered face, crevasses you could have dropped a pebble into and never heard it hit the bottom.

Now, twelve hours into Graeme's death watch, standing beside Breanne's chair in the eastern tower's third-floor room – the very same room where they'd stayed when Graeme had first brought him and Arden out to Oldwall – Wil thought back to the Marillians' arrival.

Half an hour. Half an hour lost somewhere on their long march north, most likely because of some unimportant, stupid little thing. Half an hour that had cost Graeme's life. It could drive a man crazy, just thinking on it. The only one who seemed to be able to make some sense of it was Brother Ulric – him, and Aldric.

Aldric was an honest-to-gods bard, older than Baintry's bedrock but still sharp as you like and possessed of a singing voice an angel would envy. He'd journeyed north with the Marillian forces, saying that any bard who stayed at home during times such as these had clearly missed his calling and would be better employed plucking the tines of a pitchfork while singing to the cows and sheep.

The old man had composed a song on the way here, one that brought a measure of comfort to everyone's hearts, though it also made some of them cry all over again. It was called *The Treesinger King,* and it was about Arden. It spoke of how he'd sung to the Stricken and given them peace and a place to rest; how he'd lost Wulfwyn, his love, even her soul destroyed for all times when she'd thrown herself at the Slayer to save his life; how, mad with grief, he'd carried her dead body through the woods in his arms for days on end until he'd finally found a place where he could lay her to rest, a loamy spot with water nearby and a gentle breeze stirring the leaves overhead, with just the right mix of shade and sun, and, most important of all, close to the grandfather of all trees. For he'd chosen the great tree as his hall, his home, and as his way of completing the Planting.

Arden was already become legend, it appeared, the people believing that he lived on inside the tree, sitting on a throne of roots and leaves, grieving for his lost love and only coming out once every full moon to tend to the sapling he'd planted on Wulfwyn's grave.

It was a sad story and a heartbreaking song.
But it was also quite beautiful, Wil thought, though he was certainly

no judge of such things as music and poetry. He did like how Aldric had adopted the name the people of Archer's Rock had given Arden, calling him Treesinger and making him a king – or maybe the people had come up with that as well. In any case it was fitting, and worthy, and Arden surely deserved it.

Wil tried with all his might to suppress a yawn, but the need was stronger. It wasn't the first one, either. He'd already been through a sleepless night and a long day before the vigil started, and by now he was slowly but surely losing the battle against sleep.

He felt a gentle hand on his arm and opened his eyes. He'd been nodding off, he realized, falling asleep on his feet.

'Dear Wil,' Breanne said. 'You need to go find yourself a bed. I'm sure Graeme wouldn't begrudge you a few hours' sleep. Go. I'll be fine without you for a spell.'

Too tired for more than a mumbled, 'M'lady', Wil stumbled off to his quarters and was asleep the moment he lay down.

He dreamed he was walking over a high plain.

There was a thinness to the air and a blueness to the plain's far edge that told him he was somewhere very high up – closer to the sky than to the lowlands, he thought. It was a barren, desert-like land-scape, nothing but sharp-edged rocks and very fine sand that squeak-ed under his boots like snow did when the weather was very cold. The air was dry as bones, and his every step raised a puff of ochre dust.

There was a strange familiarity to the place that continued to nag at him as he trudged along for what seemed like hours, or days, or weeks. Suddenly it hit him, stopping him dead in his tracks. He'd been here before. And then the memory of his last visit, of whom he'd met and what had passed, came flooding back. All of it.

He'd made a deal, suffered one of three painful deaths in the belief that he was saving Graeme's life, but all he'd gotten out of it was a measly few months' respite for his friend and mentor. Now Graeme was dead anyway, and with him the hopes and future of a whole nation.

How could he have been so stupid? The gods were a fickle, unreliable bunch, anyone who'd ever dealt with them could tell you that. But, naively, he'd thought that at least the old gods would hold to their given word.

Instead, they'd used him for their own ends, whatever those were. They'd taken him for the trusting fool he was, a mere mortal on whom they could renege without a second thought. Well, not anymore. Even if it was too late to save Graeme, he was going to hold them accountable, give them a piece of his mind, and to hell with the consequences. Let them strike him dead, if they were that petty, but he would have his say.

Picking up his pace, he stomped on through the endless, dusty waste, filled with righteous anger, thinking of bitter, stinging words to hurl in their faces and wishing it wouldn't take so bloody long to get from one place to another in this blasted realm of choking dust and faithless, lying gods.

After only a few steps, he stopped again.

Someone was coming his way, wavering out of the overheated distance until the approaching figure was close enough for the uncertain image to solidify and connect to the ground, its feet throwing up

424

plumes of dust as it crossed the last fifty or so yards that separated it from Wil.

It was a man, Wil saw, and by all appearances a mortal like himself. His long, black hair and beard were unkempt, a curly riot shot through with silver, his robe a mess of tears and tatters. There was a nasty gash on his forehead, and he had fresh scabs on his knuckles as if he'd recently been in a fight. There was also a roguish twinkle in his eyes.

'Ah,' he said. 'You must be young Wil. Interesting that we should meet here, of all places. But not all that surprising, really.'

'And you are?' Wil asked, baffled that the stranger should know him.

'Oh. Sorry. I forget we haven't met. Torgrim's the name. Torgrim of Eldinga.'

'But... but they said you were dead,' Wil said, thoroughly confused now.

'Wouldn't be the first time.' The man – Torgrim – chuckled. 'Seems I'm a tough one to kill. No, I'm just passing through, like you are. Going to see the gods, then?'

'Am I ever,' Wil said, his momentarily forgotten anger boiling up again with a vengeance. 'I have a score to settle with that bunch of conniving, dishonest, two-bit tricksters.'

'No better time than now, then,' Torgrim said. 'Seeing as I just finished having a little talk with them that I suspect has left them somewhat rattled. But don't be too hard on them if you can help it. They've had a lot to deal with lately, and trying to contain an utterly evil freak like Amut can drive even them to distraction. And though you might not see it that way right now, they're still the good guys.

Any road, I'm sure you'll do just fine. And I should be going. Got a longish trip ahead of me yet.'

'Farewell, then, and smooth traveling,' was all Wil could think to say.

'I doubt it,' Torgrim said. 'But thanks, anyway.' With that, he left. Wil didn't see him walking away. He was simply there one moment, and gone the next.

It took Wil an eternity still to reach the gods, as if they were purposefully stretching out his journey, trying to avoid him for as long as they could. But he ploughed on, hell-bent on his mission. And then he stood before them, feeling none of the overwhelming awe they'd inspired in him the last time. Well, a little, maybe.

All four of them looked exhausted. Wasted, actually. Pale, hollow-eyed, rumpled, like people who hadn't slept in weeks. He almost felt sorry for them. But no – gods didn't sleep, and they might well be wearing those tired faces just to soften him up.

'You let Graeme die,' he said, not bothering to check the anger and reproach in his voice. 'Even though we had a deal.'

'I told you he wasn't going to let it slide,' Donal said, looking smug but not nearly managing his usual, flippant tone.

Verelda and Moricanna sighed almost in unison.

'That was Amut's doing,' Urufin rumbled. 'Go see him if you're looking for someone to complain to.'

'I don't give a quarter copper about Amut,' Wil said. 'We had a deal. You promised Graeme would live. Do you have any idea what his death means to Breanne, and the Watch, and Marillin? If your aim really was to make things right down there, then all I can say is, you've left the job half done. In my eyes, that's hardly better than not doing it at all. Worse, maybe.'

'We're sorry, Wil,' Verelda intervened. 'Truly we are. And we all wish it had gone differently. But the Bane is defeated. Keon is dead. And Graeme left Marillin with an heir. Breanne is pregnant, in case you didn't know. The boy is destined to play a significant role in Marillin's and Baintry's future. So, you see, Graeme's death wasn't in vain.'

'Maybe not,' Wil said. 'But it was gratuitous and entirely unnecessary. And it may yet turn out a greater loss than you think. That child is twenty years away from securing Marillin's throne. Do you honestly believe Barbary's going to hold still that long? And the Marillian nobles? I'll bet not all of them are as nice as Bois.

'The kid is going to be surrounded by enemies from day one. And even if he lives long enough to take the throne, he'll still grow up without a father. Do you realize what that means? Nothing against Breanne, she's a great lady, but a kid needs a father, too. And Graeme would have made the best father in the world. Just think of everything he could have taught...'

Wil faltered, a sudden image of Graeme showing him and Arden Wards popping into his mind and threatening to overwhelm him with a fresh wave of grief.

'I want him back,' he said when he could halfway trust his voice again.

'He's got a point there,' Donal said, much to Wil's surprise.

So at least one of them was actually listening to him.

'Come to think of it, that joker Torgrim is causing a rather sub-

427

stantial disturbance in the fabric of the Law with his antics,' Urufin mused. 'Ripped a hole that's big enough to sail a ship through. Shame not to put it to some use before it closes up again.'

'You do realize that Amut is going to throw a fit of unprecedented proportions if the only prize he's gotten out of this fiasco goes missing,' Moricanna said, wrapping a strand of long, red hair around a slender, white finger.'

She's cute, Wil thought. *Damned pretty, in fact. If she wasn't a goddess...*

'He's just lost his second potential avatar in a mere twenty years,' she went on, throwing Wil an amused, knowing look that caused his ears to redden. 'And he's already mad as a cut snake. And that's him still thinking he's at least eliminated Torgrim.'

'So he's already spitting mad,' Urufin said. 'How much worse can it get? Besides, since Torgrim's responsible for the breach we have full deniability. Nothing to do with us, should anyone come asking.'

'Except we'd still have to find Graeme and somehow sneak him out of Amut's realm before we could send him through,' Donal said. 'Not sure we can pull it off without the black bastard noticing.' He looked to Verelda. 'Grandmum? What's your take on this?'

Verelda heaved a sigh so deep, Wil felt the ground beneath his feet tremble in sympathy. Exhaustion and worry battling for control over the network of wrinkles that furrowed her ancient features, she pondered the question in silence.

'I fear it's too late,' she finally said. 'Nearly a whole day has passed since Graeme died. He's probably far beyond our reach by now.'

Wil's heart sank – and then did an about-face when Verelda added, 'But I suppose we can try. Though I have to say, any more of this and we'll be endangering the Law to a degree that will make Torgrim's hole look like a harmless pinprick in comparison.'

She looked at Wil, a gaze weighed down by aeons. 'No promises, young Wil. No guarantees. It's very unlikely that we'll succeed. So don't get your hopes up. And now, off with you. This place is not for mortals, and you've already spent too much time here as it is.'

At least Wil was spared the long walk back. He simply fell out of the picture and straight into a deep, dreamless sleep from which he awoke surprisingly refreshed and without the slightest recollection of where he'd been or what he'd done.

*   *   *

26

The first time Breanne visited the Great Tree, it felt very much like déjà vu. Arden was there, leaning against the tree just like in the vision she'd had of him. He looked changed: older, more mature. Strong. And sad. He smiled at her, though the sadness in his eyes remained. Then he reached up and broke off a small, dead branch.

In her vision the twig had turned into a lute, and Arden had played and sung a strange and beautiful tune. Now it was just a twig. Still, she thought there was music in the air, just beyond her range of hearing.

There were so many things she wanted to ask him, so much she wanted to tell him about. Instead, she burst into tears.

Wordlessly, he took her in his arms, big with child as she was, and let her weep against his chest, spill a river of pain, shed a rain of tears that fell upon the forest floor and was absorbed by the soft, green moss with a serene indifference she found oddly comforting, as if Nature herself were embracing her and the child, offering absolution. Finally, she was simply too tired to go on crying.

When she looked up, Arden was gone. Strangely, she wasn't disappointed, feeling instead that more had passed between them than any number of words could have possibly conveyed. And she found that she was holding a small branch in her hands, the same one he'd broken off the tree. Only it wasn't dead anymore. At its very tip a single, fat bud had formed. As she stood looking at it in wonder, it burst open into a blossom that was the exact color of a clear, early morning sky promising a glorious day.

Since then, she'd pilgrimaged to the Great Tree once every spring. Four years had passed, and Arden hadn't shown himself again. But she could feel his presence in the tree, and knew he felt hers, and that was all she could ask for, a rare gift from the gods, who weren't often inclined to make such presents.

Her son Arn's hand in hers felt small and soft – still. He'd be turning four soon. Two more years and he'd be starting weapons training, his young hands hardening to the sword. She abhorred the thought of him raising a blade against another man and putting himself in danger but knew there was no way around it. A king who couldn't lead his men in battle wasn't apt to reign for long. That was how it was. That was how the world spun.

Gripping Arn's hand tighter, she thought of the people she'd lost, one way or another. Arden, Torgrim, Griselde, Wulfwyn, her father; Pers, taken by a sudden fever last year; Finn, gone off to sail the seven seas with Goderun and hopefully pursuing a career of honest commerce rather than piracy; Roana, who'd proved herself a friend among enemies, killed by Barbarian deserters along with the rest of Vereldal's Sisters.

Suddenly the ground beneath her feet gave a slight hitch, as if the world had slipped a fraction of an inch, and she was swept by a wave of cutting, rending grief so overwhelmingly intense it seemed to have little or no bearing on the people she'd been thinking of, much as she missed them.

For a moment, she felt displaced, as if she'd taken a wrong turn somewhere along the way and ended up in a place where things could have gone differently, where Graeme might have succeeded in ridding himself of his broken shield, as he'd tried to, and not still had it to bring between himself and Keon's blades at the very last moment before they pierced him through and through. He'd been grievously injured all the same, but he'd survived, and healed over time, scarred but whole.

Right there on the battlefield, hurt and bleeding from a dozen wounds, he'd stood unaided to receive the chieftains when they came to offer him the crown of Barbary. He refused it, and asked instead that they swear in the name of their children and their children's children to keep the peace with Marillin and the Vales. It was a tense moment, waiting to see how they'd react. They could have ended it then and there, with Graeme undefended save for Pers and Wil and the three young men of his guard standing by his side.

But the Barbarians weren't bad men at heart, she found out that day. Leastwise they were no worse than other men. They swore an oath of peace, and then, gripped by awe and admiration, or a big-hearted impulse, or their Barbarian sense of honor, they knelt, offering Graeme their swords, and swore fealty as well, even though he hadn't asked it of them. Whether their oaths would outlast their gratitude towards Graeme for ridding them of Keon remained to be seen, but swear they did.

If Graeme hadn't already achieved hero status before, he did then. It was the stuff out of which songs were made, and songs there were, indeed.

Aldric's *Treesinger King* had become an instant classic that would likely still be sung centuries from now. There were half a dozen songs about Graeme and herself, and not a bard who didn't insist on performing at least one of them when putting in an appearance at Arventon.

Graeme found it embarrassing to be celebrated thus but bore the 'fuss', as he called it, with resigned good grace and patience. Breanne minded less, and actually liked the one called *Banehunter's Bounty,* a tune sprung from some nameless tavern poet's wine-fueled wit, emphasizing the parts of the story that had to do with fated love and secret passion. It was slightly ribald, good-natured and funny, and it made her laugh, something she felt she couldn't do too often these days.

Another of her favorites was *Wil of the Three Lives*. Someone with a very lively imagination must have come up with that one, to make believe the gods would ever involve themselves with human matters in such a direct fashion. In fact, it should have been Wil of the four lives, seeing as he was still alive and kicking. But that was poetic license for you: anything for a smooth rhyme, even if it meant bending the facts.

Still, it was eerie. Wil swore he'd died three times, though he had no idea why, or why he'd come back to life each time. And Graeme had been saved from a death that had looked almost certain.

So why did she feel as if she'd lost him, the very center of her life, the most precious thing besides her son, who she realized was staring up at her with a worried question in his eyes?

Then, just as suddenly, the world slipped again, back into its familiar groove, and she breathed easier as the weight that had descended on her soul lifted and blew away like chaff on the wind. She gave Arn's hand a reassuring squeeze.

Feeling an irresistible need to reassure herself as well, she picked him up, holding him on her left arm while with her right she reached out and sought the comfort and security of Graeme's embrace, his strong arms easily encircling her and Arn both.

'What?' Graeme said. He knew her so well, she thought, well enough to have noticed her discomfort of a moment ago.

'Nothing,' she said. 'We should go soon. It's getting chilly with the sun gone.'

She put Arn down. Rid of the chore of visiting an uncle he couldn't see, he ran towards the one he could, already crowing happily.

Wil, done with his own private communion with Arden, was waiting by the horses. Acting the fearsome monster, he growled and wrestled Arn into a bear hug that had the boy squealing with delight.

Breanne, following more slowly with Graeme, stopped him with a hand on his arm and then leaned into him for a long, lingering kiss.

'Boy,' he said when she let him up for air, his words carrying an echo of another moment. 'I must have done something right.'

'You're here,' she said, taking his face between her hands and smiling up at him. 'What more can I ask for?'

Around the same time as Breanne, Graeme, Arn and Wil were mounting up to ride home to Arventon, something exceedingly strange took place some eighty miles farther east and roughly four hundred feet over the spot where Haunt had disappeared some years ago – though the only living witness was a lone seagull, circling the evening sky in search of a bedtime snack.

Seemingly out of nowhere, a human head appeared in mid-air, long black hair and beard an unruly tangle streaked with silver, sharp eyes studying the sea below with a purposeful look.

A hand followed the head. A finger was wetted and held up as if testing the wind.

Next, both head and hand retreated.

Then the whole man came flying out of a patch of empty air that seemed to faintly shimmer for a moment, dragging behind him a bunch of long, slender ropes attached to a very large and more or less round piece of fabric, obviously woven by hand from what must have been millions of extremely fine strands of some nearly trans-lucent, alien-looking material.

As gravity took hold of him, he began to plummet towards the sea below. Then the fabric caught an updraft, billowing and spread-ing out into a great umbrella that wafted down in the evening breeze and set the man down on the water's gently undulating surface with hardly a splash.

The seagull, a curious bird by nature, risked an overflight to see if what had just landed in the water might be edible. Regrettably, the thing turned out to be pretty big, and alive, and was already swim-ming for the shore with long, easy strokes.

Reaching land, the man climbed out of the water, dripping wet and looking quite pleased with himself.

Nobody except the seagull saw any of this happen. Which was probably just as well, because nobody would have believed it in any case.

*   *   *

www.vereldan.com

greg@vereldan.com

www.ingramcontent.com/pod-product-compliance
Lightning Source LLC
Chambersburg PA
CBHW071637260626
47170CB00001B/134